THE BRIGHTEST STAR IN THE SKY

THE BRIGHTEST STAR
IN THE SKY

MARIAN KEYES

THORNDIKE
WINDSOR
PARAGON

This Large Print edition is published by Thorndike Press, Waterville, Maine, USA and by BBC Audiobooks Ltd, Bath, England.

Thorndike Press, a part of Gale, Cengage Learning.

The text of this Large Print edition is unabridged.

Other aspects of the book may vary from the original edition.

Set in 16 pt. Plantin.

Printed on permanent paper.

LIBRARY OF CONGRESS CATALOGING-IN-PUBLICATION DATA

Keyes, Marian.
    The brightest star in the sky / by Marian Keyes.
       p. cm. — (Thorndike Press large print core)
    ISBN-13: 978-1-4104-2403-7 (alk. paper)
    ISBN-10: 1-4104-2403-0 (alk. paper)
    1. Apartment houses—Fiction. 2. Dublin (Ireland)—Fiction.
    3. Chick lit. 4. Large type books. I. Title.
    PR6061.E88B75 2010b
    823'.914—dc22   2009048464

BRITISH LIBRARY CATALOGUING-IN-PUBLICATION DATA AVAILABLE

Published in 2010 in the U.S. by arrangement with Viking, a member of Penguin Group (USA) Inc.

Published in 2010 in the U.K. by arrangement with Penguin Books Ltd.

U.K. Hardcover: 978 1 408 48609 2 (Windsor Large Print)
U.K. Softcover: 978 1 408 48610 8 (Paragon Large Print)

Printed in the United States of America
1 2 3 4 5 6 7 14 13 12 11 10

For Dylan Martin

Once upon a time
I was you
Keeping secret
Being True

What happened child
Of golden hair
What happened then
I wasn't there

Running wild
Laughing free
Bursting sun
You reached for me

But another won your heart
That day
A smiling lie
Danced your way

You followed him
Into a wood

No one saw
The wolf in hood

And now you stand
And stare at me
Your frock is stained
Your knees are green

How do I hold your hand and stay
How do I heal
That death
In May

This day
This night
This hour
Long due

This ink
This page
This prayer
For you . . .

"Little Red Riding Hood"
by Christina Reihill
From *Diving for a White Rose*

There is a crack, a crack in everything.
It's how the light gets in.

Leonard Cohen

DAY 61

June the first, a bright summer's evening, a Monday. I've been flying over the streets and houses of Dublin and now, finally, I'm here. I enter through the roof. Via a skylight I slide into a living room and right away I know it's a woman who lives here. There's a femininity to the furnishings — pastel-colored throws on the sofa, that sort of thing. Two plants. Both alive. A television of modest size.

I appear to have arrived in the middle of some event. Several people are standing in an awkward circle, sipping from glasses of champagne and pretending to laugh at what the others are saying. A variety of ages and sexes suggests that this is a family occasion.

Birthday cards abound. Discarded wrapping paper. Presents. Talk of leaving for the restaurant. Hungry for information I read the cards. They're addressed to someone called Katie and she appears to be celebrating her fortieth birthday. I wouldn't have thought that that called for much celebration but it takes all sorts, I'm told.

I locate Katie. She looks a good deal younger than forty, but forty is the new twenty, according to my information. She's tallish and dark-haired and bosomy and gamely doing her best to stay upright in a pair of spike-heeled knee-boots. Her force field is a pleasant one; she vibrates with level-headed warmth, like a slightly sexy primary-school teacher. (Although that's not actually her job. I know this because I know an awful lot.)

The man next to Katie, glowing with dark pride — the pride is in large part to do with the new platinum watch on Katie's wrist — is her boyfriend, partner, loved one, whatever you want to call it.

An interesting man, with a compelling life force, his vibrations are so powerful they're almost visible. I'll be honest: I'm intrigued.

Conall, they're calling this man. The more polite members of the group, at least. A few other names are hovering in the ether — Show-off; Flash bastard — but remain unuttered. *Fascinating.* The men don't like him *at all.* I've identified Katie's father, brother and brother-in-law and not one of them is keen. However, the women — Katie's mother, sister and best friend — don't seem to mind him as much.

I'll tell you something else: this Conall doesn't live here. A man on a frequency as potent as his wouldn't stand for a television of such modest size. Or plant-watering.

I waft past Katie and she puts a hand up to the nape of her neck and shivers.

"What?" Conall looks ready to do battle.

"Nothing. Someone just walked over my grave."

Oh come now! Hardly!

"Hey!" Naomi — older sister of Katie — is pointing at a mirror that's propped on the floor against a cupboard. "Is your new mirror not up yet?"

"Not yet," Katie says, sudden tension leaking from between her teeth.

"But you've had it for ages! I thought Conall was going to do it for you."

"Conall *is* going to do it," Katie says very firmly. "Tomorrow morning, before he goes to Helsinki. Aren't you, Conall?"

Friction! Zinging around the room, rebounding off the walls. Conall, Katie and Naomi volleying waves of tension against each other in a fast-moving taut triangle, the repercussions expanding ever outwards to include everyone else there. *Entre nous,* I'm *dying* to find out what's going on but, to my alarm, I'm being overtaken by some sort of force. Something bigger or better than me is moving me downwards. Through the 100 percent wool rug, past some dodgy joists, which are frankly *riddled* with woodworm — someone should be told — and into another place: the flat below Katie's. I'm in a kitchen. An astonishingly dirty kitchen. Pots and pans and plates are piled higgledy-piggledy in the sink, soaking in stagnant water, the linoleum floor hasn't been washed in an age, and the stove top sports many elaborate splashes of old food as if a gang of action painters has recently paid a visit. Two muscular young men are leaning on the kitchen table, talking in Polish. Their faces are close together and the conversation is urgent, almost panicked. They're both pulsing with angst, so much so that their vibrations have become entangled and I can't get a handle on either of them. Luckily, I discover I am fluent in Polish, and here's a rude translation of what they're saying:

"Jan, you tell her."

"No, Andrei, you tell her."

"I tried the last time."

"Andrei, she respects you more."

"No, Jan. Hard as it is for me, a Polish man, to understand, she doesn't respect either of us. Irish women are beyond me."

"Andrei, you tell her and I'll give you three stuffed cabbages."

"Four and you're on."

(I'm afraid I made up those last two sentences.)

Into the kitchen comes the object of their

14

earnest discussion and I can't see what they're so afraid of, two fine big lads like them, with their tattoos and slightly menacing buzz cuts. This little creature — Irish, unlike the two boys — is *lovely.* A pretty little minx with mischievous eyes and spiky eyelashes and a head of charming jack-in-the-box curls that spring all the way down past her shoulders. Mid-twenties, by the look of her, and exuding vibrations so zesty they zigzag through the air.

In her hand she's carrying a pre-prepared dinner. A wretched-looking repast. (Grayish roast beef, in case you're interested.)

"Go on," Jan hisses at Andrei.

"Lydia." Andrei gestures at the, quite frankly, filthy kitchen. Speaking English, he says, "You clean sometime."

"Sometime," she agrees, scooping up a fork from the draining board. "But sadly not in this lifetime. Now move."

With alacrity Andrei clears a path for her to access the microwave. Viciously, she jabs her fork into the cellophane covering her dinner. Four times, each puncture making a noise like a small explosion, loud enough to make Jan's left eye twitch, then she slams the carton into the microwave. I take this opportunity to drift up behind her to introduce myself, but to my surprise she swats me away as though I were a pesky fly.

15

Me!
Don't you know who I am?

Andrei is giving it another go. "Lydia, pliz . . . Jan and I, we clean menny, menny times."

"Good for you." Breezy delivery from Lydia as she locates the least dirty-looking knife in the murk of the sink and runs it under the tap for half a second.

"We hev made schedule." Feebly Andrei waves a piece of paper at her.

"Good for you *again.*" Oh how white her teeth are, how dazzling her smile!

"You are livingk here three weeks. You hev not cleaned. You must clean."

An unexpected pulse of emotion radiates from Lydia, black and bitter. Apparently, she *does* clean. But not here? Where, then?

"Andrei, my little Polish cabbage, and you too, Jan, my other little Polish cabbage, let's imagine things were the other way round." She waves her (still soiled) knife to emphasize her point. In fact, I know that there are 273 different bacteria thriving and flourishing on that knife. However, I also know by now that it would take the bravest and most heroic of bacteria to get the better of this Lydia.

"The other way round?" Andrei asks anxiously.

"Say it was two women and one man living in this flat. The man would never do anything.

16

The women would do it all. Wouldn't they?"

The microwave beeps. She whisks her unappetizing dinner from it and, with a charming smile, leaves the room to look up something on the internet.

What a peppy little madam! A most fascinating little firebrand!

"She called us cabbages," Jan said stonily. "I hate when she calls us cabbages."

But, eager as I am to see what transpires next — tears from Jan, perhaps? — I'm being moved again. Onwards, downwards, through the health-hazard linoleum, through more porous timber-work, and I find myself in yet another flat. This one is darker. Full of heavy furniture too big and brown for the room. It features several rugs of conflicting patterns, and net curtains so dense they appear to be crocheted. Seated on a sturdy armchair is a dour-looking elderly woman. Knees apart, slippered feet planted firmly on the floor. She must be at least a hundred and sixteen. She's watching a gardening program and, from the furrow-browed expression on her face, you'd swear she's never heard such outrageous idiocy in her life. Hardy perennials? No such thing, you stupid, stupid man! Everything dies!

I float past her and into a small gloomy bedroom, then into a slightly bigger but just as gloomy, second bedroom, where I'm surprised to meet a large, long-eared dog so big and gray that momentarily I think he's a donkey. He's slumped in a corner, his head on his paws, sulking — then he senses my presence and instantly he's alert. You can't get away with it, with animals. Different frequencies, see. It's all about the frequencies.

Frozen with awe and fear, his long donkey-ears cocked, he growls softly, then changes his mind, poor confused fool. Am I friend or foe? He hasn't a notion.

And the name of this creature? Well, oddly enough it would appear to be "Grudge." But that can't be right, that's not a name. The problem is, there's too much *stuff* in this flat and it's slowing the vibrations down, messing with their patterns.

Leaving the donkey dog behind, I flit back into the sitting room, where there's a mahogany roll-top desk as dense and weighty as a fully grown elephant. A modest pile of opened mail tells me that the crone's name is Jemima.

Beside the mail is a silver-framed photo of a young man, and with a flash of insight I know his name is Fionn. It means "Fair One." So who is he? Jemima's betrothed who was killed in the Boer War? Or was he carried off in the flu epidemic of 1918? But the photostyle is wrong for a First World War type. Those men, in their narrow-cut uniforms, are always so rigid and four-square to the camera

18

you could believe their own rifle had been shoved up their back passage. Invariably, they wear a scrubbing brush on their upper lip and, from the lifeless, glassy-eyed way they face the viewer, they look as if they've died and been stuffed. Fionn, by contrast, looks like a prince from a child's storybook. It's all in the hair — which is fairish and longish and wavyish — and the jaw, which is square. He's wearing a leather jacket and faded jeans and is crouching down in what appears to be a flower bed, and he has a handful of soil, which he's proffering to me with a cheeky smile, *saucy* almost, like he's offering a lot more than — ! God Almighty! He's just winked at me! Yes, he winked! His photograph winked! And a silver star pinged from his smile! I can scarcely believe it.

"I can feel your presence!" Jemima suddenly barks, scaring the living daylights out of me. I'd forgotten about her, I was so engrossed in Fionn the Prince and his winking and twinkling.

"I know you're here," she says. "And you don't frighten me!"

She's on to me! And I haven't gone near her. More sensitive than she looks.

"Show yourself," she commands.

I will, missus, oh I will. But not just yet. Your time will have to be bided. Anyway, I appear to be off again, being pulled and stretched ever downwards. I'm in the ground-floor flat now. I can see the street through the living-room window. I'm sensing a lot of love here. And something else . . .

On a sofa, washed by the flickering light of the television (32 inch) is . . . is . . . well, it's a man and a woman, but they're clinging so tightly to each other that for a moment I think they are one and the same, some strange mythological, two-headed, three-legged thing, which is all I need right now. (The fourth leg is there, simply hidden beneath their bodies.)

On the floor are two plates, on which the remains of a hearty dinner can be discerned: potatoes, red meat, gravy, carrots — a mite heavy for June, I would have thought, but what do I know?

The woman — Maeve — now that I can make her out, is blond and rosy-cheeked, like an angel from a painting. There's a chubby, cheruby freshness about her because she was once a farm girl. She might be living in Dublin now, but the sweet clean air of the countryside still clings to her. This woman has no fear of mud. Or cow's udders. Or hens going into labor. (Somehow I sense that I've got that slightly wrong.) But this woman fears other things . . .

It's hard to get a look at the man — Matt — because they're interwoven so tightly; his face is almost entirely hidden. Funnily enough, they're watching the same gardening program as Jemima one floor above them. But unlike Jemima, they appear to think it's a marvelous piece of televisual entertainment.

Unexpectedly, I sense the presence of another man here. It's faint but it's enough to send me scooting round the place to check it out. Like the other three flats in the building, there are two bedrooms, but here only one functions as an actual bedroom. The other, the smaller of the two rooms, has been turned into a home-office-cum-skip — a desk and a computer and abandoned sporting goods (walking poles, badminton racquets, riding boots, that type of thing), but nothing on which a person could sleep.

I sniff around a bit more. Two matching Podge and Rodge cups in the kitchen, two matching Tigger cereal bowls, two matching everythings. Whatever this extra male presence is, he doesn't live here. And from the wild, overgrown state of the back garden that you can see from the bedroom window, he doesn't cut the grass either. Back in the living room, I move up close to the angelic Maeve, to introduce myself — being *friendly* — but she starts flapping her arms, like someone swimming on dry land, disentangling herself from Matt. She breaks free of him and sits bolt upright. The blood has drained from her face and her mouth has opened into a big silent O.

Matt, struggling from the couch's saggy

embrace to a seated position, is equally distressed. "Maeve! Maeve. It's only about gardening! Did they say something?" Alarm is written all over him. Now that I get a better look, I see he's got a young, likable, confident face, and I suspect that, when he isn't so concerned, he's one of life's smilers.

"No, nothing . . ." Maeve says. "Sorry, Matt, I just felt . . . no, it's okay, I'm okay."

They settle — a little uneasily — back into their clinging positions. But I've upset her. I've upset them both and I don't want to do that. I've taken a liking to them; I'm touched by the uncommon tenderness they share.

"All right," I said (although of course they couldn't hear me), "I'm going."

I sit outside on the front step, a little disconsolate. One more time I check the address: 66 Star Street, Dublin 8. A red-bricked Georgian house with a blue front door and a knocker in the shape of a banana. (One of the previous occupants was a fun-loving metal-worker. Everyone hated him.) Yes, the house is definitely red-bricked. Yes, Georgian. Yes, a blue front door. Yes, a knocker in the shape of a banana. I'm in the right place. But I hadn't been warned that so many people live here.

Expect the unexpected, I'd been advised. But this isn't the type of unexpected I'd expected. This is the *wrong* unexpected.

And there's no one I can ask. I've been cut

loose, like an agent in deep cover. I'll just have to work it out for myself.

DAY 61 . . .

I spent my first evening in 66 Star Street rattling from flat to flat, wondering anxiously which one was mine. Katie's flat was empty. Shortly after my arrival her crew had departed, in a cloud of tension, to some expensive restaurant. In the flat below, while Andrei and Jan cleaned the kitchen, Lydia parked herself at the little desk wedged into a corner of their living room and spent long intense minutes surfing the net. When she went to her bedroom for a snooze and Jan and Andrei retired to their twin-bedded room to study their business management books — such good boys — I descended yet another floor, to Jemima's. I took care to keep myself well clear of her; I didn't want her shouting abuse at me again. But I must admit that I got great entertainment out of toying with the dog, Grudge — if that really is the creature's name. I shimmered before him and he stared in rapt, paralyzed amazement. On the spur of the moment I decided to do a little dance and — all credit to him — his big gray head moved in perfect time with me. I undulated faster and faster and twirled above his head, and he did his best to keep up, poor eejit, until he'd mesmerized himself so much

23

he collapsed in a giddy heap, snickering and dog-laughing away to himself. At that point, regretfully, I stopped. It wouldn't do if he vomited.

Then, finally, I returned to Matt and Maeve. It's where I'd wanted to be all along but, professional that I was, I'd thought I'd better explore every avenue. Well, they were explored for the moment at least so, with a clear conscience, I could rejoin the loved-up pair on their sofa.

Whatever show they'd been watching had just ended and Maeve automatically opened her arms to free Matt from her embrace. He rolled off the couch and on to the floor, then sprang to his feet, like a Secret Service person entering an enemy embassy. A smooth, slick routine, obviously a frequent one, and luckily the dinner plates that had been there earlier had been removed or else Matt's nice T-shirt would have been stained with gravy.

"Tea?" Matt asked.

"Tea," Maeve confirmed.

In the little kitchen, Matt put the kettle on and opened a cupboard and was almost brained by the avalanche of cookies and buns that poured out. He selected two packets — chocolate mini-rolls and chocolate ginger nuts, the mini-rolls were Maeve's favorites, the ginger nuts were his — then he used both his hands to cram the remaining packets back into the cupboard and slammed the door

24

shut very quickly before they could fall out again.

While he was waiting for the kettle to boil, he tore open the ginger nuts and absent-mindedly ate two, barely tasting them. Such a casual attitude to trans-fat and refined sugar led me to suspect that he consumed a fair amount of them, and on closer inspection I noted that he had a hint, the merest . . . oh . . . *whiff* of a suggestion of a tinge of tubbiness. His entire body was padded with a surplus of — honestly — no more than a millimeter of fat. I must insist that this is not a cowardly attempt to break the news that he was a fatso. His stomach was not bursting its way out of his T-shirt, and he only had the one chin and a nice strong one it was too. Yes, perhaps he could have lost a little weight, but it suited him, the way he was. If he were half a stone lighter, he might shrink into someone a little less charming; he might seem too ambitious, too efficacious, his haircut a tad too sharp.

Two spoons of sugar each in their tea and back in to Maeve. A new program had begun, another favorite of theirs from what I could gather. A cookery one this time, presented by a personable young man called Neven Maguire. They curled up next to each other and watched scallops being sautéed and drank their tea and made serious inroads into the cookies. In a spirit of inclusivity, Maeve ate one of Matt's ginger nuts even though they were dark chocolate ones, which she didn't like, and Matt ate one of Maeve's mini-rolls even though they were so sweet they made the hinges of his jaws hurt. They were very, very kind to each other and, in my discombobulated state, this was soothing.

A cynical type might suggest that it was all a little too perfect. But a cynical type would be wrong. Matt and Maeve weren't just acting the part of people who are Very Much In Love. It was the real thing because their heart vibrations were in perfect harmony.

Not everyone knows this but each human heart gives off an electric current that extends outwards from the body to a distance of ten feet. People wonder why they take instant likes or dislikes to people. They assume it's to do with associations: if they meet a short, mono-browed woman, they remember the time that another short, mono-browed woman had helped them get their car out of a ditch and cannot help but feel warmly to this new, entirely unconnected, short, mono-browed woman. Or the first man who short-changed them was called Carl and from that day forth all Carls were regarded as suspect. But instant likes or dislikes are also the result of the harmony (or disharmony) of heart currents and Matt's and Maeve's hearts Beat As One.

■ ■ ■ ■

The moment that Matt fell in love with Maeve . . .

That moment had been coming for quite a while, to be honest, and it finally arrived on a bone-cold March morning, roughly four and a quarter years ago, when Maeve was twenty-six and Matt was twenty-eight. They were on the Dart train, and they weren't alone — they were with three others, two girls and a young man, all of them on their way to a one-day training course. The five of them worked at Goliath, a software multinational, where Matt headed up one of the sales teams. Matt was actually Maeve's boss (in fact, he was also the boss of the other three people present), although he never behaved in a particularly bossy way — his style of management was to encourage and praise and he got the best out of his team because they were all — male and female — half in love with him.

The thing was that Matt wasn't even meant to be there. He had a company car so he usually drove to his appointments (he always offered lifts to those less fortunate than him), but on this particular day his car had refused to start, so he had to bundle himself up against the elements and go on the Dart with the rest of them. Often, in the agonizing times that followed, he wondered whether, if his car hadn't broken down, he would have crossed the line from being fond of Maeve to actually being in love with her. But the answer was, of course, yes. He and Maeve were destined for each other, *something* would have happened.

Matt was a city boy, born and bred in Dublin. He'd never been within a hundred yards of a cow. But Maeve had lived on a farm in Galway for the first eighteen years of her life — in fact, her nickname among her co-workers was Farmgirl. She'd recently been "down home" to help out with the calving and she was full of a life-and-death saga of a calf called Bessie who was born prematurely, then rejected by her mother. Although Matt had less than zero interest in farm stuff, he was drawn in by the story of Bessie's struggle for survival. When Maeve got to the end of the tale and confirmed that Bessie was now "thriving," he was surprised by how relieved he felt.

"It's a mistake to get too attached to any of the animals?" he asked.

"A mistake is right." Maeve sighed. "I'd a pet pig for a while. Poor Winifred. They took her away to make rashers of her. I won't make that mistake again. Now I've a drake and at least the only thing he'll die of is natural causes."

"A drake?" Matt asked.

"A male duck."

"I knew that." At least, now that she'd said it, he did.

She laughed at his bluster. "Oh! You're *such* a blagger."

The three other team members stiffened slightly. Easy-going as he was, Matt was still their boss. Was it okay to call him a blagger? But Maeve's laughter was full of affection for Matt and Matt certainly didn't seem offended. He and Maeve were twinkling and smiling at each other. In fact, they twinkled and smiled at each other a lot . . .

"Here, I've a photo of him in my wallet," Maeve said. "Roger. He's a beauty."

"A photo of a duck?" Matt didn't know what to make of this; he thought it was very odd but also very funny. "This gets better and better. And he's called Roger? Like, why *Roger?*"

"He looks like a Roger. No, he really does. I'll show you." Maeve pulled her wallet from her satchel, looking for the photo. But, in her enthusiasm, she accidentally opened her purse and, with an ominous flash of metal, a waterfall of change roared toward the floor of the Dart, coins cracking and bouncing and rolling the full length of the carriage.

All the other passengers tried to pretend that nothing had happened. Those that were hit on the foot by a coin kicked it away or flicked a quick look down just to check that it wasn't a mouse chewing their shoe, then returned to their texting or their magazine or their grumpy introspection.

"Oh cripes!" Maeve stood up and laughed helplessly. "There goes my change for the laundrette." As if she had a magnetic draw, all thirteen passengers raised their heads, and suddenly Matt saw the power she possessed. Not a swaggery, arrogant power, not the power granted by expensive clothes or glossy makeup — because Maeve's jeans and Uggs and tangled curls would hardly have bouncers in nightclubs rushing to remove the red rope and usher her forward. What made Maeve so potent was that she expected the best from other people.

She never considered that the strangers around her wouldn't want to help — and her faith was repaid. Matt watched, transfixed, as nearly everyone in the carriage dropped automatically to their knees, as if they were in the presence of an awe-inspiring deity, scrambling for any coins that they could see. Matt and the others were in there, helping, but so were Lithuanian naturopaths and Syrian kitchen porters and Filipino nurses and Irish schoolboys. They were all on the floor gathering and walking in a low crouch, like slow-motion Cossacks. "Thank you," Maeve said, over and over, receiving the returned coins. "Thank you, oh thank you, you're so decent, more power to you, fair play, outstanding, God bless, thanks."

This is the person I want to be with, Matt found himself thinking. Then he revised it. No, he thought, this is the person I want to *be.*

Two stops later, when Matt and his team got off, Maeve called out, "Thanks again, you were very decent," and you could have roasted potatoes in the warmth that she left in her slipstream. Matt knew that everyone would go home that evening and relate the story. "A two-euro coin hit me on the foot and I thought, feck it, missus, you dropped the money, you get to pick it up, I mean, I've had a hard week, but she seemed like a nice person so I *did* help to pick up the money, and you know what, I'm happy that I did, I feel good about myself —"

My trip down Matt and Maeve's memory lane is interrupted by sudden activity from two floors above and I scoot up to check it out.

DAY 61 . . .

Andrei and Jan had put their textbooks away neatly and were emerging into the hall, casting fearful looks for Lydia. I was still finding it hard to tell them apart — they existed in such a fug of Lydia-fear that their vibrations were quite corrupted. I noted this much: Andrei had astonishing blue eyes which burned with the intensity of a religious zealot's, but

31

he was *not* a religious zealot. Jan also had blue eyes, but his did not burn with the intensity of a religious zealot's. However . . . yes, however . . . he had a prayer book which he read frequently with some — yes! — *zeal.*

So true what they say: one really cannot judge on appearances.

They equipped themselves with beer and Pringles and took their seats in the living room for *Entourage.* They were mad for *Entourage.* It was their favorite show, one of the high points of their week. They longed to go to America and live an *Entourage* life, with sunshine and cars and, of course, beautiful women, but, above all else, the unbreachable walls of male solidarity.

Silent and worshipful before the television, they didn't hear Lydia enter the room. They only knew she was there when she broke the *Entourage* spell by saying, "Boys, boys, why so glum?"

"What is glum?" Jan asked anxiously. Instantly, he was sorry he had spoken. Andrei's constant advice was: Do not engage with her.

"What is glum?" Lydia considered. "Glum is unhappy, sad, downcast, low, gloomy, of little cheer." She gazed at them with an expression that was intended to seem fond. "Homesick, that's what Dr. Lydia has diagnosed." In a voice dripping with insincere sympathy she asked gently, "My little dumplings, are you missing Minsk?"

Neither boy spoke. Over the past three miserable weeks, they had become familiar with this routine in which Lydia threw about city names ending in "sk."

"Minnn*sssskkk!*" Lydia savored the sound. "*Sssskkk?* Missing it?"

When she got no response, she said in fake surprise, "Not missing it? But how unpatriotic you are."

This was too much for Jan, who, every waking moment he was in Ireland, yearned with desperate passion to be back home. "Irishgirl, we are not from Minsk! We are from Gdansk! Poles, not Belarussians!"

As soon as the words were uttered, Jan wanted to cut out his tongue. Lydia had broken him! Once again he had betrayed the resistance!

Deeply ashamed, he looked at Andrei. *I'm sorry. I'm not as strong as you.*

It's okay, Andrei replied silently. *You must not blame yourself. She could destroy even the bravest man.*

(Okay, their separate identities are coming into focus for me now. Andrei — older, smarter, stronger. Jan — younger, sweeter, dafter.)

Lydia left, and after a lengthy silence Jan admitted, "I am glum."

Several seconds elapsed before Andrei

spoke. "I too am glum."

DAY 61 . . .

Back on the ground floor, it seemed that
Matt and Maeve were planning to pop out
for a late-night jog. In their bedroom — an
Ikean wonderland, the bedside cabinets
slightly off-kilter because the assembly instructions in the boxes had been in Czech
and Matt said that if he had to go back to
Ikea to get the English ones, he'd drive
himself at high speed into a wall — they
undressed, Maeve turning away from Matt as
she removed her bra. Immediately, they
proceeded to get dressed again, seeming to
put on even more clothes than they had
already been wearing. Maeve was now covered neck to ankle in gray sweats and Matt
was kitted out in jocks, baggy jogging pants
and a long-sleeved T-shirt. Then . . . bafflingly! . . . they got into bed! Why so
swaddled? It was a warm night out there.

It suddenly occurred to me that perhaps
they were about to play a sexy undressing
game. But what was wrong with removing
the clothes they'd already been wearing?

I was far from happy at the thought of
witnessing whatever strange jiggery-pokery
they were about to unleash but I forced
myself to linger. I had no choice! It was
important to get the lay of the land. Propped

up on his pillow, Matt flicked his way through a car magazine, snapping the pages, hungry to see what the next contained, meanwhile on her side of the bed, Maeve read *Pride and Prejudice* . . . and that's all that happened. I lingered some more, noting the hefty little pile of other Jane Austens on Maeve's night-stand — clearly a fan. And I lingered still more, until it became clear that no sexy undressing game was about to kick off.

I must admit to a little relief.

The only problem with Matt falling in love with Maeve four and a quarter years ago was that Matt already had a girlfriend . . .

Yes, the lovely Natalie. And she really was lovely. Of all the beautiful, brainy girls at Goliath — and there were more than two hundred youthful employees so there were many to choose from — Natalie was the most beautiful, the most brainy of all: smooth brown skin; long, lean thighs; a defiant question mark in her eye; a great facility for her job. (A Belgian national, she was a wonderful advertisement for her famously dull country.)

Matt — smiling, lovable Matt, with the widely acknowledged conviction that he would Go Far — was a partner worthy of the lovely Natalie.

Matt and Nat each headed up a sales team and, lovers though they were, they were also rivals. They competed against each other, gloating (with great good humor, of course) every time they closed a sale of one of Goliath's software packages. "One less for you, bud."

So when Maeve joined as a trainee, it was no surprise that Matt, with his glossy girlfriend and his demanding job, barely noticed her. Mind you, Goliath being what it was (a company enjoying exponential growth), new people were appearing round the clock — on the same day that Maeve had started, so had Tarik from Pakistan and Yen-way from Taiwan — so there were always fresh faces enjoying a brainstorming game of ping-pong in the chill room or queueing to partake of the free breakfast granola. It was hard to keep up.

Maeve, friendly and positive, with a musical, rounded accent, was popular among her colleagues, but she still hadn't registered as a meaningful presence on Matt's radar until one night when Matt and Nat were leaving work. They clicked quickly down the shiny marble hallway, black leather footwear flashing, serious tailoring flying, the storm troopers of Sales. Moving in harmony, they powered through Goliath's massive double doors — taking a door each — passing Maeve who was crouched low, unlocking her bike.

"Goodnight, lads," she said.

With perfect synchronicity, Matt and Nat swung their smooth, perfectly shaped heads to see who had spoken and — as one —

exploded into uncontrollable laughter.

"What?" Maeve asked. Realization dawned and a smile spread across her face. "Is it my hat?"

"Yes!"

Maeve's hat was an orange and pink Inca-patterned knitted helmet. A triangle of yarn covered each ear, woolen plaits fell to her chest and the top came to a sharp point, on which an orange pompom was perched.

"Is it very bad?" Maeve was still smiling.

"Very bad," Nat said.

"But it's all the rage on the Machu Picchu trail and it keeps my ears warm." This made all three of them laugh even harder. Then, with a rough rush of metal, Maeve liberated her bike from its chain, hopped on to the saddle and, moving fluidly, freewheeled out into the traffic.

"She's so sweet." Nat sighed. "What do you think about her and David? Is it the real thing?"

Matt hadn't a clue. He'd barely noticed Maeve until five minutes ago, much less known that she was going out with David.

"So much in common." Nat smiled fondly. "Seeing as they're both Galwegians."

(David was actually from Manchester — it wasn't necessary to come from Galway to qualify for Galwegian status. It was an umbrella term that implied fondness for falafels, frizzy sweaters and festivals — music, obviously, but comedy, poetry, beer . . . anything would do. If it involved mud and pints, it was perfect. If the festival could be combined with a protest march, then so much the better. Indeed, the ideal weekend, a veritable *utopia* for a Galwegian, was to get caught up in an anti-globalism riot, cracked on the skull with a truncheon and thrown into a police cell for twenty-four hours with a trio of hard-core protesters from Genoa. Galwegians were hardy; they slept like babies on their friends' cold hard floors. Galwegians were proud of being Irish — even when they weren't actually Irish — and they dropped many Irish words into conversation. Much of Goliath's multicultural staff spoke basic Galwegian. A popular phrase was "Egg choct egg oal?" It meant "Coming for a drink?')

The funny thing was that at the time, Matt coveted David far more than he coveted Maeve.

"I'd love to get David on my team," he said wistfully.

"You and me both," Natalie replied.

David was on Godric's team and was Godric's most valuable asset. He was super-brainy, a mathematics whiz, and he could disentangle the knottiest implementation problems. He just kept plugging away, trying things this way, trying things that way, until he'd unlocked and ordered things into a way that worked.

"David could be a team leader himself if he wanted to," Matt said.

David was probably older than almost everyone else in Goliath, only by a few years, but enough to make him a natural leader. Nevertheless, he resisted all attempts to be steered in the direction of management.

"What do you think the story is?" Matt asked Nat.

"Doesn't want to be pigeon-holed, he said."

David had packed an awful lot already into his thirty years. He'd traveled all over and done an impressive variety of jobs from teaching physics in Guyana to being a nanny for three children in a progressive-thinking family in Vancouver.

"Doesn't want a 'career path,' he told me." Nat shook her head and laughed. She couldn't understand people who didn't have the same ambition that she did.

"Very noble of him."

"Maybe he's a little too noble?"

"Mmmm."

They were both remembering the incident the previous week when David — always passionate about injustice — became so enraged by pro-Russian coverage of the ongoing war in Chechnya that he printed out the offending article from the Reuters site and gathered several acolytes around his desk while he ceremoniously burned the page. It had set off all the smoke alarms.

"And lucky the sprinklers didn't start," Matt said.

"He could have destroyed all our machines," Nat said.

"And he didn't care. Said the principle was more important."

"Principle." Nat rolled her eyes. "For God's sake."

After the laughing-at-the-hat incident, Matt knew who Maeve was and a week or so later, when he was driving to work and saw an orange pompom bobbing above the traffic, he was able to say to himself: It's that Maeve girl, the one with the hat.

On her bike, she wove in and out of lanes until she disappeared from view, then the lights changed and Matt took off and caught up with her. While he was once again stalled in a sea of cars, she was diligently working her way away from him and into the distance, then the lights changed and he lurched forward, closing the gap. It became a pattern. She'd get ahead of him, he'd chase after her, searching for the jaunty orange pompom, then she'd put some distance between them while he clenched his hands on the steering wheel, waiting for the chance to move.

Although she knew nothing about it, he felt they were in a race. His journey to work had never been more fun.

As he approached the busy intersection of

Hanlon's Corner he was in the lead. The lights were green, but anxiety that he'd get too far ahead of Maeve made him slow down and the lights obliged by changing to yellow. Just as the lights turned red, Maeve whizzed up the inside lane to the head of the traffic and stopped for the briefest moment while making a series of high-speed calculations. Matt could actually feel her judging her speed, the length of time available to her and the distance of the drivers who were gunning their engines, ready for their green light, now that the opposite lights had gone red. Then she shot out into the empty space, looking small and astonishingly brave, like a student squaring up to an army tank. All eyes were on the orange pompom as she raced through the danger zone, and when she reached the safety of the other side Matt was buoyed up with relief and admiration.

The episode made such an impression that when he got in to work he made a special visit to the crowded cube she shared with the other trainees.

"Morning, Miss Maeve. Has anyone ever told you you're an excellent breaker of red lights? So calm, so daring?"

She looked up from her screen, her eyes dancing with amusement. "Has anyone ever told you you're full of guff?"

"Guff?"

"You know, chat, blather, blarney."

41

"Right." Some Galwegian word, obviously. "I saw you on the way to work. Crossing Hanlon's Corner when the lights were against you. Nerves of steel."

"I believe in taking my chances."

"You're lucky you weren't killed."

"Fortune favors the bold."

"You wouldn't catch me cycling in this city."

"You should try it. It ennobles the soul."

"My soul is noble enough."

"Is it now?" she asked, looking at him, her expression amused.

"Stop it!"

"What?"

"Looking at me like you know something about me that I don't."

"Me?" She laughed. "I know nothing."

Matt didn't tell Natalie about the morning he'd raced Maeve to work. There was no need, it was no biggie. The funny thing was that Natalie was just as fond of Maeve as he was and together they'd claimed a sort of ownership of her the way you would an adorable, harmless puppy. At Friday-night drinks in the pub, they made sure they were sitting near her, listening to her melodic accent and the strange words she used. "Ganzey" when she meant sweater — that type of thing.

One Friday evening, Nat swung by Matt's desk. "You ready?"

"Ten minutes."

"See you in the pub. Make sure Maeve's there." And she was gone.

Matt knew better than to ask Nat to wait for him. Nat never wasted time.

When he'd finished, he made his way to Maeve's cube. "Coming for a drink?"

"A drink?" Maeve gazed at nothing as she considered. She seemed to disappear inside her head. After a short pause she smiled and said, "No, not tonight, Matt."

"Why not, Farmgirl?" He felt, well, he felt quite . . . *rejected.* "Off out with your boyfriend?"

"And what if I am?" Her tone was lighthearted.

"Nothing." Matt was assailed by a sudden stab of intense dislike for David. He was so right-on and decent, always supporting causes and organizing charity things and being so *caring.*

"I'm on the bike," Maeve said.

Matt looked blank.

"I can't have more than one drink if I'm on the bike," she explained. "I'd rather have none than one."

Instantly, Matt shifted his dislike from David to Maeve's bike, like it was a chaperone keeping him from her.

"Well, *I'm* going for a drink," Matt said, with defiance that he didn't really understand.

"More power to you."

"*Yes,* more power to me."

In the pub, Nat asked, "Where's Maeve?"

"Not coming."

"She's not?" Nat seemed disproportionately disappointed.

Matt looked at her warily. "What's up?"

"Maeve's finishing her training next week."

"Already?"

"Two weeks early. It's a secret. She's done really well. I want her on my team."

But I want her.

"And she wants to be on Team Nat?"

"I haven't asked her. I was going to float it tonight."

"So she doesn't know anything about it yet?"

"No."

I'll get to her first.

When Matt persuaded Pong from Thailand to leave his team for Nat's and took Maeve for himself, Nat seemed a little shaken by Matt's treachery. Nevertheless, she raised a glass and declared him "a worthy adversary."

In the following weeks, Matt started saying "guff" and "more power to you" and sometimes "more power to your elbow."

"More power to my elbow?" Nat laughed. "My little Galwegian boy."

It was her joke. As if she, the lovely Natalie, would ever go out with a Galwegian.

By 11:30 p.m. Star Street had fallen silent. I'd been waiting for Katie to come home and I realized she wasn't going to. I located her across the city, entering a large Victorian house, about to receive a birthday pleasuring from potent Conall.

She was very chatty. The result of large quantities of champagne. Conall was trying, with admirable good humor, to unlock his front door and simultaneously keep Katie upright.

"Who'd beat who in a fight?" Katie was asking. "Hedge-fund manager or you?"

"Me." Conall's tone of voice gave me to understand that this line of questioning had been going on for some time.

His fingers circled her arm, as he led them into the house and disabled the alarm.

Katie leaned against a light switch and exclaimed in drunken delight as half the house lit up. "I do that? Let there be light! No need to hold on to me, I won't fall over."

"Fall over if you like. It's your birthday."

"I drank a lot of champagne." She nodded her head seriously. "Bit pissed. Could happen."

Conall steered her to the staircase and together, very slowly, they ascended, Katie having to take frequent pauses to laugh for no reason.

On step four she refused to budge. "This is a good one! Conall, who'd beat who in a fight? President of the World Bank or you?"

"Me."

"It's nice to just lean back, you know? Like this." She allowed all her weight to fall against the arm Conall had around her waist. "You won't let me fall. Used to do it at school, see how much we trusted someone."

"Ups-a-daisy. We'll keep moving."

On the ninth step she stopped again. "Who'd beat who in a fight? The CEO of Jasmine Foods or you?"

"Me. With both hands tied behind my back."

That made her laugh long and wheezily, and all progress halted. "Can't walk and laugh at same time."

Finally, they reached the landing and he opened the bedroom door. Katie toppled in, made it as far as the bed, lay on her back and stuck one leg up in the air. "Take off my boots."

"No, leave them on."

"Oh? Ooh. Okay. Who'd beat who in a —"

He covered her mouth with his and, after a moment, she ceased her questioning. She would never know who would beat who in a fight, the head of the International Monetary Fund or Conall, but suddenly it no longer seemed important. The birthday pleasuring had begun.

■ ■ ■ ■

In her wardrobe in Star Street, I compressed myself into a red-soled, peep-toe shoe and accessed some of her memories.

How Katie met Conall . . .

Well, just like Matt and Maeve's story, this too happened at work. Katie was head publicist at Apex Entertainment Ireland. They called themselves Apex *Entertainment,* because they wanted to seem twenty-first-century and multimedia, but basically they were a record company, the Irish outpost of a much bigger multinational. Katie had been there for five years, welcoming visiting rock stars to Ireland, organizing their interviews, hanging around backstage wearing a laminated pass, then — the most important part of her job as far as she could see — taking them drinking. It was harder than it sounded, because she was the one who had to remain sober and coherent enough to sign for all the bottles of Cristal, get the artistes home to bed, then show up at her desk at ten o'clock the following morning after four hours' sleep.

If you met her at a christening, you'd probably never guess she worked for a record company. Admittedly, she always wore high heels and sometimes tight jeans but she didn't take cocaine and her thighs were wider than her knees. Despite these impediments, Katie was popular with the visiting rock stars, who referred to her as "Auntie Katie," which she didn't mind too much. Or "Mum," which she did. Artistes returning to Ireland greeted her like an old friend and sometimes, late at night, they tried to wrestle her and her thighs into bed, but she knew their heart was never really in it, it was just an instinctive reaction, something they'd been programmed to do in the presence of any woman. She almost always turned them down.

So yes, Katie was working away, not exactly happy but not exactly unhappy either, when a rumor started doing the rounds that the European arm of Apex was going to be cut free from their U.S. owners and sold to the highest bidder, who would promptly sack everyone. But that particular rumor regularly did the rounds, so Katie decided not to bother worrying. She didn't have the same energy she used to have and over the years she'd wasted too much adrenaline and anxiety on disasters that had never had the decency to occur.

Then it really happened. A press release announced that they'd been bought by Sony, who planned to keep Apex as a separate label. The relief engendered by this was short-lived because the next sentence said that Apex would be "rationalized" by Morehampton Green.

"Who are they?" Tamsin asked. (Low-grade frequency. Not too bright. Wore white lipstick. Long legs, large breasts. Popular with visiting artistes.)

"Who cares?" Katie said. Her frequency had gone haywire, quivering with fear. It wasn't as though she loved her job but now that there was a chance she might lose it . . .

"Vultures," Danno said, with contempt. (Danno, aged twenty-three. Shrill, fast-vibrating frequency. Needed very little sleep. Always wore black. Could consume copious amounts of cocaine without any apparent ill effects. Also popular with visiting artistes.)

"Morehampton Green descend on companies that are underperforming," Danno explained. "Strip them of their assets, sack most of the staff and leave nothing in their wake but shock and awe."

"And what good's that?" Katie asked.

"They make it much more efficient, save loads of money, *the usual.* Normally, Morehampton Green ply their nasty business in Southeast Asia, but they're prepared to make an exception for us."

"Decent of them."

"What's going to happen to us, Katie?" Tamsin asked.

"I don't know."

In a strange hierarchical glitch, Katie didn't really have a boss. Officially, her manager was Howard Cookman, president of European publicity, but he was based in London and had no interest at all in the Irish end of things, which usually suited Katie just fine because he had a tendency to bore on in an atrocious accent, part LA, part *EastEnders,* about the times he'd met a) Mark Knopfler, b) Simon Le Bon and c) Debbie Gibson.

Katie had made it a point to protect her little slice of autonomy, but all of a sudden she was sorry. It wasn't nice being the only grown-up and she yearned for someone with more power than her to come along and promise that everything was going to be okay.

Alerted by a swishing noise, everyone present (all six of the Public Relations staff and all fourteen of Marketing) turned to the *Star Trek*-style automatic glass doors. It was Graham from Human Resources. Under normal circumstances he exuded smug confident vibrations but today his life force was much reduced.

Silently, he gave a memo to everyone in the room: two brief lines that said a Mr. Conall Hathaway would be making contact "shortly."

"Who's he?" Katie asked.

"The axman sent by our new owners," Graham said. "He *is* Morehampton Green."

"What do you mean, he *is* Morehampton Green?" Danno asked, irate that someone knew more than him.

"I mean Morehampton Green is pretty much a one-man band. He's bound to have a

50

busload of number-crunchers with him but Conall Hathaway makes all the decisions."

"Control freak," Danno said, with great contempt.

"Why will he be contacting me?" Tamsin cried.

Graham bowed his head and said nothing.

"To let you know whether you still have a job or not," Katie deduced. "Am I right, Graham?"

Graham nodded, with resignation.

"Conall Hathaway? Surely you mean Conall the Barbarian?" said Danno. Danno enjoyed nicknames. (Those on his frequency usually do.)

For two days nothing happened. Everyone continued working as normal, because until something occurred there was always a chance that it mightn't. But on the afternoon of the third day, Danno was in possession of such an important tidbit of news to share with his colleagues that the glass doors didn't swish open quickly enough and Danno crashed into them, catching an unpleasant blow to his right temple. "Open, you useless pieces of —" he yelped, stamping around on the floor, trying to activate whatever needed to be activated. At this point he had the attention of everyone within. Finally, the doors juddered apart and Danno burst into the office, like he'd been spat from a machine.

"He has the cold dead eyes of a killer!"

Danno declared. "He got into the lift with me just now and, I swear, I nearly shat myself."

"Who?"

"Slasher Hathaway. Conall the Barbarian. He's come to sack us all!"

"So soon?" Katie was alarmed. "It's almost indecent."

"He's got several orcs with him, pimply younglings learning his dirty trade, but he's a hands-on merchant. He'll be on the prowl," Danno warned. "Keep an eye out. We'll be toast before this day is out."

Katie eyed him with uncertainty. Danno was a catastrophist; he seemed to thrive on disaster. More than once she'd wondered if he was perhaps addicted to adrenaline, the poor man's cocaine.

She summoned Audrey. (A vibration that was so muted it was almost apologetic. Reliable, trustworthy, meticulous. Not as popular with visiting artistes as Tamsin or Danno.) "Go and check on this Conall character. Be discreet."

Within minutes, Audrey had reappeared, wearing her hangman's face. "It's true. He's in with Graham. They're going through personnel contracts."

Katie bit her knuckle. "What does he look like?"

After consideration, Audrey said, "Cruel."

"Christ!"

"Lean and hungry."

"That's not so bad."

"Lean and hungry *and* cruel." Then she added, "He's eating chocolate."

"What?"

"There's a huge bar of Mint Crisp on the desk and he's eating it while he's talking to Graham. Entire rows in one go. Not breaking it into squares or anything."

"How huge? A hundred grams? Two hundred grams?"

"One of those massive ones you can only get in the duty-free. Five hundred grams, I think. You know what, Katie? He's actually really good-looking. I think I fancy him. I always fancy men who have power over me."

"Don't fancy him," Katie said. "You think that all a cruel-looking man needs is the love of a good woman and then he won't be cruel any more. But he stays cruel and you eat your heart out." It made her feel old, giving this sort of advice.

"You might fancy him too," Audrey suggested.

"I won't fancy him."

"Say what you like, but we have no control over these things," Audrey warned darkly.

The phone rang: the cars had arrived.

Katie had a moment, a delicious little pin-prick of a moment, when she considered just walking away from it all and sparing herself tonight's ordeal with Knight Ryders and their

53

grumpiness. If she was going to be made redundant anyway . . .

But what if she was one of the ones who got to keep her job?

"Okay," Katie called. "Danno, Audrey, saddle up, the cars are here."

They were off to the Four Seasons to pick up Knight Ryders for tonight's gig. Knight Ryders were a metal band, a quartet of hoary old rockers who'd survived addiction, divorces, bankruptcy, near-death heart failure, motorbike crashes, internal strife, kiss-n-tells from their adopted children and much, much more. Many of their audience, who paid the high ticket prices, came along not in order to hear their hits from the early seventies, but simply to marvel that all four of them were still alive.

The boys were on their eighth month of a nine-month world tour and they'd been in Ireland for two very long days. Katie's greatest worry was Elijah Knight, lead singer, living legend and proud owner of a secondhand liver (one careful previous owner). He'd been clean and sober for almost a year but whispers had reached Katie's ears that he was wearying of it all. Certainly it was true that every word out of his mouth to Katie was a complaint: the Irish hotel was too chintzy; the Irish press were too fawning; the Irish AA meetings had too little whooping.

Katie or one of her team made it their business to be with him at all times — Tamsin was over there right now — and a "body-guard" (i.e., guard) kept watch at night outside his bedroom.

As Katie slid into the back seat of a blacked-out limo, she got a call from Tamsin. "It's Elijah."

"What's up?"

"It's time for him to start backcombing his hair, but he's just sitting there with his arms folded, like a child."

"I'm on my way." Katie crossed her fingers and said a silent prayer that tonight would not be the night that Elijah Knight went back on the sauce. Not on her watch. If he could just wait until tomorrow, when he and his three big-haired, craggy-faced, liver-damaged compadres left for Germany, she'd be very grateful.

The problem, however, was that everything went off fine. With Katie's kindly inveigling, Elijah obediently backcombed his hair until it stood a full eleven inches above his head; the Knight Ryders played an entire set and none of them had a stroke; they even bowed out of a gratis trip to Dublin's finest brothel.

This meant that when Katie got home at the unexpectedly early hour of 2 a.m. there was room in her head for the reality of her job situation to hit her. She was done for, she abruptly realized. She might as well face it:

getting Elijah Knight safely home to bed might have been her last act as Senior PR of Apex Entertainment.

It made sense to get rid of her — of the six PR staff, she was paid the most. Also, a more painful acknowledgment, she was the oldest, and the music business was a young woman's game. I'm thirty-nine, she said to herself, in wonder. Thirty-nine! It's a miracle I've survived this long.

She had to go to sleep now. But how could she? Tomorrow she was going to be sacked and she'd have no money, and in these recessionary days she'd never get another job because she was qualified for nothing except bringing rock stars to nightclubs.

I'm ruined, she thought.

She would lose her flat and her car and her highlights and her personal trainer, even though she had only one session a week, but her time with the behemoth that was Florence was *vital* — without it she mightn't be able to get herself to do any exercise at all.

And, oh, her lovely flat. There wasn't a chance she could keep it. Her mortgage payments were gulp-inducing, even on her current salary. She'd bought at the height of the boom, when cardboard boxes were changing hands for a million euro. She'd paid dearly for every square foot of her home. But how she loved it. It was only small — being an attic conversion, most of her rooms had been short-changed of their corners — but it was cozy and got loads of light and was walking distance from town. Not that she'd ever tested it, not in her shoes.

The killer was that she'd never meant to work in the music business. Oh why had she, *why?* Because she'd been wildly flattered when they offered her the job, that was why, so flattered that she'd turned a blind eye to the fact that the money wasn't as good as you might have thought. All she'd cared about was that they must have thought she was cool if they wanted to employ her. But she should have taken the job in the government press office instead. Old people weren't mocked in that industry; they were valued, revered for their wisdom. No one cared if you had big thighs. No one cared if you had facial hair (and you were a woman) (not that she had). In fact, they positively *liked* fat ugly spokespeople in politics because they had more credibility.

Ruined, she thought. Yes, *ruined.*

As the night ticked away, her head buzzed with calibrations and calculations: if she let out her flat would she earn enough to cover her mortgage and hairdressing bills? If she got a job in Blockbuster, how would she manage for food? She'd read a thing in the paper about people on the minimum wage: even if they ate the gone-off half-price things in Tesco, they were still perpetually hungry. Coexisting with her appetite was tricky enough on a healthy salary, when even as she had her first bite of something she was worried about the last. How would she cope with genuine hunger?

She wouldn't even be able to afford to kill herself. For the last couple of years, probably since Jason, she'd had a whimsical contingency plan in case life ever became truly unbearable, like the cyanide pills spies used to carry in their teeth in case they were captured. Her cunning notion was that she'd eat herself to death — it happened, people really did it, doctors were forever warning the obese that if they continued with their bad habits they'd snuff it. She'd always thought it be a joyous way to go, gorged to the gills on chocolate cheesecake. But chocolate cheesecake cost money and she'd need an awful lot of it to administer a fatal dose. Gripped by middle-of-the-night terror she saw what a wasteful fool she'd been all these years. She should have started stockpiling baked goods long before now. But she wasn't a stockpiler. If it was in her flat she ate it. Fact. Nothing lasted more than a day.

All of a sudden her thoughts veered off in an unexpected direction and she began to blame Jason. (Between the ages of thirty-one and thirty-seven, Jason had been her boyfriend. In their sixth year, just as they'd started trying for a baby, they had the tremendous shock of discovering that they were no longer in love. They faked it for almost a year, hoping to rekindle the flame, but they were kaput. Kiboshed. All washed up.)

If she and Jason had got married and had a baby, and if Jason wasn't marrying Donanda the Portuguese stunner instead, she wouldn't have these worries.

But oh no! He had to decide to stop loving Katie and then they had to split up and she had to buy a flat on her own. Well, in fairness, she'd stopped loving him too, but that was *also* Jason's fault because if only he hadn't become unlovable everything would be different.

Her anger filled her stomach, then her chest, until she began having difficulty breathing, and even though it was five past six in the morning and far too late to take a sleeping tablet — Curses! She hadn't had an ounce of sleep! — she had to sit up and turn on the light and get her de-bittering books off the shelf, to stop herself from drowning in her own bile.

Gasping, she read a few lines of *My Happiness, My Responsibility,* but it did nothing. She cast it aside and hungrily scanned *The Spiritual Laws of Success:* nonsense, *rubbish!* She was starting to think she'd have to ring for an ambulance when she opened the next book and a line jumped out at her: "The

Chinese word for "crisis" also means "opportunity."

That's what did it.

She felt as if she'd been hacking through dense jungle and suddenly found herself on top of a mountain where the light was clear and the air was thin. A load fell away from her. Yes, her life was over! *Yes*, she was a goner. Unemployed — indeed, possibly unemployable — but her crisis could become her opportunity. Surely she could do something else with her life? Live in Thailand and learn scuba diving? Or, better still, go to India and become enlightened, and when she came back — *if* she came back, hoho — she wouldn't mind being homeless and carless and having to wear terrible shoes and having to do her own motivation to go for a run.

It would all be okay.

DAY 60

Sixty-six Star Street remained silent until 5:30 a.m., when Lydia got up. She lurched into the bathroom where she showered — there's only one word for it — resentfully. She disliked getting wet. She feared the water. (She wasn't to know this but in a previous life she'd been a meerkat, a creature of the desert and a stranger to moisture. Some traits linger into subsequent lives.)

She reached behind her for her conditioner and her elbow dislodged Andrei's shower gel from the shelf. No! There was a slippery scramble as she tried to catch it but it leaped from her sudsy grasp and landed on the floor of the shower with an echoey three-bounce clatter. Irkutsk! She didn't want to wake Andrei or Jan. They were bad enough when they got a full night's sleep, the miserable bloody pair; they'd be even more stony-faced and grumpy if they were woken prematurely.

God, they were hard work. Not once in three weeks had she seen them laugh. And no one could say she hadn't made an effort, trying to jolly them along with good-humored bad mouthing, the kind she employed with all men. But instead of rising to the challenge and giving as good as they got, they were baffled.

And she was stuck with them: it was their lease. In fact, she wondered why they didn't just tell her to hop it, because it was so obvious that they hated her.

Perhaps it was because her room was laughably small, barely more than a cupboard. (Apparently, it used to be the kitchen — a cramped, walk-in galley — before some mysterious previous owner had decided to convert the second bedroom into a bigger kitchen, spacious enough to house a table. All well and good, but it meant that the remaining space was barely deserving of the title "room.")

Lydia suspected — correctly — that the ex-kitchen had been turned down by many viewers before she had shown up. The bed was narrow and short, there was no dressing-table mirror (because there was no dressing table) to drape her string of orange flower-shaped lights around, and there was no wardrobe so most of Lydia's clothes were kept in boxes under her bed. She also suspected — again correctly; Lydia didn't get much wrong — that Andrei and Jan had expected she'd bring a woman's touch to the flat. They were, of course, mistaken. It hadn't been easy to resist Andrei and his schedules, because he was a determined type, and it had taken every ounce of her considerable resolve, but it was important to establish from the get-go who was boss. As soon as she was certain that the lads didn't *expect* her to clean, then she would fall into line.

Perhaps . . .

In the meantime, the rent was astonishingly reasonable, a massive one hundred euro a week cheaper than her previous billet, and the house was conveniently close to the city center. And when she'd discovered that the lads hailed from Gdansk, she had been alerted — inadvertently on their part — to the excellence of words ending in "sk." Gdansk! She'd enjoyed saying it so much that she'd hit the net, looking for similar city names. And there were loads of them! Tomsk and Omsk, Minsk and Murmansk. She used them a lot. She couldn't exactly say why, she just liked them. Gdansk was a positive word, because it sort of sounded like "thanks," but all the others, especially Minsk and Irkutsk, sounded like swear words, only far hissier and snakier than the ones she usually called upon. Minsk! How pissed-off that sounded! It was great. You could scare the bejayzus out of someone if you said it right. Irkutsk! How riled you could seem if you put a bit of effort into the delivery. These were quality swear words that had cost precisely nothing and, in her current cash-strapped circumstances, she was grateful for free pleasures.

All the same, despite the gratis gift of new swear words, she badly missed Sissy and the lovely, large airy flat they'd shared. Hard to believe such luxury now, but she and Sissy *had had a cleaning lady.* In fairness, she'd only come once a week but it had been enough. Even when the kitchen was very bad, filthy enough for mice to be dancing jigs on the draining board, Lydia had been able to literally blind herself to it because she knew it would be fixed in a day or so.

And Sissy was exactly the same. Sissy didn't care. She would *never* have hit Lydia up with a cleaning schedule. Days off were for staying in your pajamas and huddling under a blanket, watching telly and eating twelve bowls of Coco Pops; they were not for rolling up your sleeves and pulling on rubber gloves and running the hot tap.

But the days of cleaners and wardrobes and a normal flatmate were in Lydia's past . . . She stood before the bathroom mirror and poured large quantities of a serum designed to combat frizz on to her head. For no matter how impoverished her circumstances, she would never give up her hair. She would go hungry before she did without her serum. She and her wild springy curls were engaged in an ongoing battle of wills. Just because she was short of money was no excuse to simply give in and surrender, like many a lesser woman would have done. Lydia's hair was not her master. No, she was the boss of *it.*

Into the kitchen, where she heaped eight spoonfuls of instant coffee into a massive mug, which was called Lydia's Mug, and filled it halfway with boiling water, then the rest with tap water. She swallowed it like medicine, gagging slightly on the last mouthful, abandoned the mug on the table, dressed quickly in jeans, trainers and a hoodie, then left.

Down in the street, the morning was sunny but chilly and Lydia made her way to a taxi. A taxi? What kind of flashy minx spurns public transport?

Well, what a surprise when she climbed into the driver's seat! One could be forgiven for thinking she was proposing to hot-wire the vehicle, but when she shoved a key in the ignition it became clear that she owned it and that she was a taxi driver by trade!

It was some sort of generic Toyota, not a good car. Not a bad one either, just one of those unexciting ones that taxi drivers seem to favor. But interestingly, given Lydia's attitude to hygiene in the home, her car was clean and fragrant. She took evident pride in her charabanc.

Amid much static noise, she got on her radio and received word of a fare: picking a man up from the Shelbourne and driving him to the airport.

She did a screechy U-turn and headed toward town, the traffic lights changing to green just as she neared them. "Gdansk," she said, with satisfaction, almost smacking her lips with the pleasure of saying it.

The next lights were also green. "Gdansk." She nodded her thanks at them.

But when she pulled up outside the Shelbourne and the fare climbed into the back of her car, she saw him do a double-take. *Irkutsk!* she thought.

"You're a girl!" he declared.

"Last time I checked," she said stonily. *Irkutsk! Irkutsk! Irkutsk!*

Why a chatty one? Why? When it was so early and she'd had only eight spoonfuls of coffee?

"What's it like?" the fare asked eagerly. "Being a female taxi driver?"

Her mouth tightened. What did he think it was like? It was exactly like being a male taxi driver, only with gobshites like him asking unanswerable questions at some ungodly hour in the morning.

"How do you deal with trouble?" he asked. The question they all asked. "If someone won't pay?"

"Can I ask *you* a question?" she asked.

"By all means!" He was delighted by the interplay with this springy-haired little stunner, still damp and fragrant from her early-morning shower.

"Have you accepted Christ Jesus into your life as your lord and savior?"

That shut him up. They drove the rest of the way in silence.

DAY 60 . . .

Back at 66 Star Street, people were stirring. Andrei had been awake since 5:35 when Lydia had deliberately dropped something on the bathroom floor, with clattery force. Since she had moved in, he and Jan had been in a state of shock. They had never met a girl like her and the only good thing about her was that she was small. Small enough to fit into the tiny bed in the tiny room.

Andrei stared wistfully into space, remembering the halcyon days with their previous tenant, a Ukrainian electrician-cum-accordion player named Oleksander. Life with him had been so harmonious — because he was never there. He'd spent every night at the much swankier digs of his girlfriend, Viktoriya, and his room at 66 Star Street functioned mostly as his wardrobe. Until Viktoriya had fallen for the charms of an Irishman, a civil servant who held a high-ranking post in the Department of Agriculture, and Oleksander was thrown back on his own resources. He'd endured a succession of sleepless nights with his legs extending six inches over the end of his narrow single bed. When he'd tried to remedy the shortfall by putting a chair there, to rest his heels on, the wooden footboard had cut into his calves, marking him with two livid purple weals which linger to this day. He successfully managed to remove said wooden footboard and the only downside was that the frame of the bed collapsed entirely. His next solution was to sleep with the mattress directly on the floor, but the lumbar region of his back set up a clamor of objections and after thirty-four days of excruciating pain, he told Andrei he could take no more.

Lots of people, most of them Polish men, had come to view the room but without exception declared themselves too big to fit into the bed. They also enjoyed much mirth at the thought of Oleksander Shevchenko (who was a well-known figure; his busking outside Trinity had become almost a tourist landmark) trying to get some shut-eye in such doll-like quarters. So when Irish Lydia arrived, Andrei and Jan had been so dazzled by her suitably miniature proportions they entirely neglected to notice that she was an evil little pixie.

Now they were paying the price.

They had endless discussions, when they asked each other: *Why?* Why was she so unpleasant? So lazy? So cruel?

Andrei warned Jan that they might never get answers. It would probably be best, he advised, if they accepted that her sour nature was a fact of life, as inevitable as the rain, like everything else in this damp unpleasant country.

After washing and dressing, the boys descended to the street, where they extended the palms of their hands outwards and expressed lengthy and sarcastic surprise that it wasn't pissing rain, before walking ten minutes to the Luas stop. There they went in different directions, Andrei east to an industrial estate and Jan north to a shopping mall.

Jan liked to say he worked in IT, which in a way he did. He was employed in an enormous supermarket, filling the online orders. His days were spent toiling in the aisles, pushing a massive super-trolley device off which branched twelve baskets, representing twelve different customers, each with a separate grocery list. When he'd located every item on all twelve lists and put them into the correct baskets, he'd deposit the merchandise in the loading area, for the truck to spirit throughout Dublin, then he'd trudge to the printer to pick up another twelve lists, hook twelve new empty baskets to his super-trolley and commence the whole procedure again. He lost track of how many times a day he repeated this exercise.

Andrei also worked in IT. Except that he really did. He drove around the city in a white van, fixing broken computers for office workers. The van itself took up a lot of his thoughts. He was a pragmatic man and it irked him terribly that he was obliged to return it to base every evening, where it idled for fourteen useless hours in a parking lot, when it could be used for his own purposes — specifically, picking up Rosie. He fantasized about parking outside the house she shared with four other nurses, honking the horn and seeing her skipping down the steps, van-shaped admiration on her heart-shaped face. He had been dating Rosie (an Irish girl, but in all other respects entirely different from evil pixie Lydia) for two months and eight days and thus far she had refused from surrender her virginity to him. Andrei, with his muscles and astonishing blue-eyed good looks, was accustomed to getting his way with the girls but he was genuinely impressed by Rosie's old-fashioned virtue and his initial lust had blossomed into something far more complex.

DAY 60 . . .

On the ground floor of 66 Star Street, Matt and Maeve were roused gently from their slumber and welcomed into the day by a Zen alarm clock, a plinky-plonky affair, which sounded like Tibetan goat bells. It started off with isolated peaceful plinks, like an occasional tap on a xylophone, then over ten minutes it built up into a cacophony of delightful chimes. Not very Matt. He seemed more like a man who'd prefer an alarm that behaved like a defibrillator, issuing a cruel discordant BRRRING to make every nerve in his body stand on end and oust him instantly from the bed, to beat his chest in a Tarzan roar. "Yaaaar! Watch out world, I'm coming to get you!"

But Maeve wanted the chimes, so Maeve got the chimes. She also got a leisurely breakfast. Matt, I suspect, would have been happy to mindlessly scarf down a Snickers bar while rushing to work, but instead he made tea for Maeve, Maeve made porridge for him, then they sat at their kitchen counter, mirroring each other's actions, checking that the other had honey, orange juice and other breakfast paraphernalia.

On their kitchen windowsill, in a curlicued silver frame, was a photo of them on their wedding day. They glammed up well, the pair of them, I must say. Maeve, in particular. Judging from the picture, they'd gone for a traditional wedding, the full white monty. Maeve's dress was one of those deceptively simple numbers: a slender unadorned fall of heavy satin, from an empire-line bodice. An off-the-shoulder neckline revealed a pair of pretty creamy-skinned shoulders, and a pearl headdress gathered her thick fair hair into a bun from which slinky ringlets escaped, framing her face. She looked like a girl from one of those Jane Austen novels she seemed so fond of reading. Matt, clutching onto Maeve and gazing at the camera with the expression of a man who has just won the lottery but is trying not to gloat about it, was kitted out in a dark, serious-looking suit. The kind of suit that people wear to sign peace treaties. Evidently, he had tracked down the most impressive rig-out he could find, to convey just how momentous his marriage was to him. (Without wishing to be unkind, there was considerably less of them three years ago, when this photo was taken. Both of them were a lot, well, *narrower.* Clearly, the trans-fat didn't play so *large* — forgive the pun — a part in their lives back then.)

Maeve swallowed the last of her orange juice, Matt clattered his spoon into his empty bowl, they each took their vitamin tablet, knocking it back with a shared glass of water, and — finally — left the flat and prepared to go to work. Matt had a car, polished shoes, a sharp suit and a sharp haircut. Maeve had a bicycle, flavorless chapstick and a pair of cords so unattractive (too big for her and a most unappealing shade of olive-green) that it seemed as if they had been chosen specially for their ugliness.

They kissed and said goodbye. "Be careful," Matt said.

Of what? I wondered. Anyone foolhardy enough to negotiate a bicycle through rush-hour traffic could expect admonitions from their nearest and dearest, but, all the same, I knew that coming a cropper at the hand of a careless car was not what Maeve feared. Oh she was definitely scared, don't get me wrong, but I didn't know what of; she was blocking me. All I could tell from looking at her was that she had no fear of being mocked for her crap clothes. *Fascinating.*

Matt stared after Maeve until she was absorbed by the gridlock, then he thought about his car. It was parked so far away that he wondered if he should get a bus to it.

DAY 60 . . .

In Jemima's flat, the dog was suffering no ill effects from the dizzying he'd received the previous night. Jemima was trying to tempt him to the kitchen but he was playing hard to get. "Grudge, Grudge, my lovely Grudge." So it seemed the beast really was called Grudge! How . . . well, how *peculiar.*

Jemima had been washed and dressed since 6:15 a.m. She couldn't abide slugabed behavior. She hunkered down, her knees cracking like pistol shots, until her face was level with Grudge's sulky one. "Just because Fionn is coming doesn't mean I'll love you any less," she said.

All became clear: Grudge was sulking because he'd discovered that "The Fair One" was due to visit.

"Come and be fed."

Within moments Grudge was dancing the Dance of Breakfast. A thin-skinned creature, slow to forgive, except when food was involved.

I kept my distance from Jemima. I didn't want to frighten her. Not unless I had to. Nonetheless, her thoughts reached me. She was pulsing on a strong, steady, strident vibration, which fought its way through the clutter of the flat and insisted on attention.

She was thinking with great fondness about the word *grudge.* Such a splendid noun, she thought. So suitable for purpose: you couldn't possibly utter it without your face contorting itself into a sour prune of grudgingness. *Krompir* was another word she savored; it was Serbian for potato and had a most satisfying chomping sound. Or *bizarre,* possibly her most favorite word of all, a festive, joyous sound, which always brought to mind the jangling of tambourines.

Grudge was regarded by many as a strange name for a dog, but when people were crass enough to mention this, Jemima's answer was that he had chosen it himself. They'd told her at the pound that his name was Declan but he was no more a Declan than she was. She believed that he should be trusted to make the best choice for himself, so when she got him home — where he wedged himself tightly into a corner and sat, low and mournful, on his paws — Jemima reeled out a long list of high-esteem dog names. Champion? Hero? Rebel? Prince? She watched carefully for a positive reaction but, after each suggestion, Declan growled, "GGGGrrrrr," followed by a short little bark which sounded like "Udge." Eventually, she heard him: Grudge it was.

They'd warned her in the pound that he was a very damaged dog. There was a lot he couldn't tolerate. Men in wigs. Folk singers. The color yellow. The smell of hairspray.

But he could be soothed by the rustling of Crunchie wrappers. Girls with red hair. Yorkshire accents. The music of George Michael, though only the earlier stuff (and not Wham! — he abhorred Wham!).

He was a highly strung, mercurial creature, who would require careful handling, but Jemima wasn't daunted. Her philosophy, which she related to the man at the pound, was that a well-balanced dog would always get a home, but it was the poor damaged ones who really needed it.

Entre nous, I'm wondering if I was too quick with my initial judgment of Jemima as a prickly old crone.

His breakfast consumed, Grudge stared at Jemima with melting Malteser eyes, then flicked a few anxious sideways glances around the room. He was a wonderful dog, Jemima thought with pride. More intuitive than most humans. Which wouldn't be difficult, seeing as the vast majority were walking about with their heads stuck up their own fundaments.

"Yes, I feel it too," Jemima told Grudge. "But we won't be bowed!" She whirled around one-hundred-and-eighty degrees and planted her legs wide, like a warrior woman. "You hear me?" she said — nay, *demanded* — glaring hard (but into the wrong corner of the room, God love her). In ringing tones, she repeated, "We won't be bowed!"

Keep your pants on, Jemima. It's not all about you.

DAY 60 . . .

Matt liked to get his daily Act of Kindness out of the way early. As he drove to work, he scanned the streets looking for a chance to do good. At the upcoming bus stop a lone woman was waiting. It was clear that she'd just missed a bus because at this time of day usually dozens of people were gathered, watching each other like hawks, careful not to be left at the back of the melee when the bus eventually did show up.

He opened the passenger window and called out, "Where are you going?"

Startled, the woman looked up from her texting. A well-upholstered type, bundled into an orange jacket, she was aged roughly between thirty-seven and sixty-six. "What's it to you?"

"Would you like a lift?"

"With *you?* I can't get into a car with a strange man! Don't you read the papers, son?"

Ouff!

"I'm not a strange man, I'm a nice man."

"Well, you're hardly going to admit you're an ax murderer."

"I'm married. I love my wife. I don't own an ax."

"Kids?"

"Not yet."

"I've four."

"Hop in, you can tell me about them."

"Yeah and you can show me your ax."

"I sell software for a living."

"So did Jack the Ripper."

"He didn't!"

"Look." She sighed. "You might be a lovely lad, in fairness you look like a lovely lad, but I can't take the chance. My kids wouldn't even be able to remember what I was wearing to tell the police. And all the recent photographs of me are bad, very jowly. I couldn't have them stuck to the lamp posts around the city. On your way, son."

Feck.

Dispirited, Matt drove off. His daily Act of Kindness was like a millstone around his neck. It needled him all day long, like an eyelash trapped in his eye. And the days came round so fast, it felt like as soon he'd achieved one AOK, a brand-new day had dawned and it was time to do another. And woe betide him if he got home in the evening without having Acted Kindly At Least Once During The Day. He was unable to lie to Maeve, and guilt would bounce him back out into the world, forbidding him to return until the needful had been carried out.

It was harder than you'd think to be kind. There were all these bloody rules (Maeve's). Buying copies of *The Big Issue*s didn't count: it was too easy. Giving money to a busker didn't count either — not unless you engaged them in chat, praised their playing, made a request and stood and listened to it while displaying bodily appreciation (foot-tapping or head-nodding was acceptable; if you forced yourself to dance, you'd actually have over-done it, although none of the excess could be carried over as credit toward the following day).

The AOK had to cost emotionally. It had to be something he really didn't want to do.

However, going to work didn't count. Funnily enough, Matt usually enjoyed his job at Edios (Easy Does It Office Systems). (He'd moved on from Goliath some time ago.) But this Bank of British Columbia thing was doing his head in. You could say it was his own fault, he acknowledged. The bank had been perfectly happy with their old software system. *Perfectly* happy, until Matt had started stalking them, trying to persuade them to change over to Edios. But what was he to do? It was his job to drum up new business. He'd cold-called the bank's Irish office and when they told him to sling it, he dusted himself down and called again, then again, and eventually their procurement people had caved and wearily agreed to a meeting. Matt had been triumphant. A face-to-facer might look like merely the start of a process but, as far as he was concerned, it meant the deal was as good as done. That's not to say it was ever easy. The effort of will required from Matt was always enormous, like single-handedly turning around a huge cruise ship. The amount of charm he'd expended selling software over the years would have brought peace to the Middle East. Nevertheless, he was accustomed to getting results.

Except that the Bank of British Columbia was leading him a merry dance. Over the course of the last eight months, they'd flirted and teased and enjoyed innumerable outings at Edios's expense — a seven-hour dinner in one of Dublin's most expensive restaurants, a movie premier, a day at the races. Now they were making noises about Wimbledon tickets — Wimbledon tickets were like gold dust! — and they still had given no indication whether or not they were going to buy the system. Matt knew the names of everyone's wives, girlfriends, children and dogs but, unusually for him, he had no instinct on which way they'd jump.

The bank had requested a meeting, yet another one, for this morning and Matt couldn't think why. He and his team had done five dazzling presentations; every query and question had been answered satisfactorily; he had personally fielded calls at all hours of the day and night during which he'd promised the earth in terms of modifications, backup and speedy implementation. What more could they want?

Center Court tickets, probably.

He brooded resentfully for four seconds until his attention was caught by the radio and he snapped out of it. (Resentful brooding wasn't natural to him and he couldn't ever sustain it for long.) Boulders of ice had started to fall mysteriously out of the sky across Europe. One, the size of an armchair, had crashed through the windscreen of a parked car in Madrid. A week later, another, just as big, had burst through the roof of a house in Amsterdam, and only a day later, yet another had shot to earth in Berlin, toppling a statue of some military bloke off its plinth and into the street. Experts had been brought in to examine the phenomenon but, to date, no one could say definitively what was causing the lumps of ice. Or where the next one might land.

Matt listened with enjoyment. He liked this sort of thing. It was in the same vein as alien landings.

He was so caught up in the story that he didn't notice that he'd got through two green lights in a row. Then three. It was only when the fourth light was in his favor that he saw what had happened. Four green lights in a row! During rush hour! Could that count as one of today's Trio of Blessings? He didn't think Maeve would buy it; she wouldn't accept a parking space right outside their flat as a blessing, so she was hardly going to approve four green lights in a row. But it felt like a blessing to *him.*

For a moment he mused on how unexpectedly his life had turned out, with Acts of Kindness and Trios of Blessings and suchlike. All down to Maeve, to the fact that she'd spilled her money around the floor of the Dart four and a quarter years ago and he'd realized: Christ, I'm in love. And it's not with my girlfriend.

He tried to pretend it wasn't happening. He couldn't be in love with Maeve because he and Natalie were perfect. Natalie with her elegant neck and her beautiful brown eyes and her quick wit. He'd been going out with Natalie for almost a year, but Maeve kept taking up space in his head. She was his first thought every morning, and all day, every day, he was tormented by malign ghostly whispers: *You're living in the wrong life.*

He was so frightened that he completely lost his appetite. He'd never had to make such a grown-up decision before and it was obvious that he'd have to hurt Natalie, he'd have to cause upheaval and distress.

And he suddenly woke up to the Maeve and David love story. Beady-eyed surveillance revealed that they were very much an item. Did Maeve love David? Matt concluded that she probably did because she wasn't the type to toy with people's affections. But even if she didn't, surely there wasn't a man alive who wouldn't want her for himself? He'd have to do battle with each and every one of them. Which he was willing to do. But a girl as worthy as Maeve probably despised him and his suit-wearing, car-driving, non-Galwegian lifestyle. He'd never even been tear-gassed!

What if he failed to win her heart? How could he live?

Then his essential optimism reasserted itself. He had as much chance with Maeve as the next man, surely? He was a decent bloke, he'd never knowingly done anyone any harm and while he'd never been passionate about any causes, that was probably because he just hadn't found the right one yet. Dolphins! He liked dolphins! Maybe he should get a Save the Dolphins T-shirt and wear it to work. Unless . . . could he be wrong . . . maybe dolphins weren't endangered? Well, *something* was. It could be turtles . . . but this was the sort of problem you ran into when you tried to be someone you weren't. He was Matt Geary, decent bloke. Maybe that would be enough for Maeve. And, of course, he could always change a little, meet Maeve halfway, as it were. Like . . . look at Brad Pitt, one minute he's a shallow pretty-boy, doing mad diets with Jennifer Aniston, the next he's a worthy man, adopting children left, right and center with the lovely Angelina on his arm.

As subtly as possible, Matt set about gathering information on Maeve. She was an only child, he learned, a beloved daughter who was born late in life to parents who had thought they would never be blessed. She had an honors degree in economics from Galway university. After she'd left university, she'd gone to Australia — *with a boyfriend* — and lived in Melbourne for two years, until her visa ran out. Then she spent a year traveling through Asia and South America — *not with the boyfriend; they'd obviously split up* — before washing back up in Ireland and starting at Goliath.

Matt hoarded these little gems of knowledge about Maeve, always hungry for more — then he'd come to his senses. What the hell was he at?

He tried to talk himself into being the person he'd been before that fateful Dart journey. He was in agony, so haunted and conflicted he was surprised that no one had noticed.

There were moments when he knew with certainty that he and Natalie were done for and other times when he was just as sure that they were still rock solid and that it was only a matter of time before they moved in together.

In an attempt to make it less difficult to extricate himself, Matt tried to find fault with Natalie, but all he could come up with was that she plucked her eyebrows too much. Sometimes there were little beads of blood on her socket bone. Sore-looking. What kind of woman would do that to herself? What kind of woman would *mutilate* her own body?

Ten days after Matt's first inkling, he was lying on Natalie's bed, watching her getting ready to go out.

She tried on a pair of jeans and considered herself in the mirror, but whatever she saw she didn't like because she tore the jeans off and pulled on another pair. Those didn't meet with her approval either, so she put on another pair. Soon they too were lying on the floor and eventually Matt asked, "How many pairs of jeans do you own?"

"I don't know."

If she didn't know, that was already too many! "Guess," he urged. "Five?"

"More."

"Ten?"

"More."

"More?"

She paused to add things up in her head. "About sixteen," she concluded. "But, *obviously,* I don't wear them all."

"Obviously?"

"Because boot-cut is over. I'll never wear them again. I should just give them to Ox-fam."

"I thought boot-cut was back."

"Different kind of boot-cut."

"How many pairs of jeans do you think Maeve owns?" Matt asked. This was a daring question. Would Natalie wonder why he was talking about Maeve?

But Nat had also fallen for Maeve, she thought she was the cutest thing ever, and Matt had a wild moment when he wondered if perhaps the three of them could set up home together.

"Maeve? I don't know. Two?"

Two. Yes, the correct number of jeans for one human being. You wear one pair while the other is in the wash. Any number over two was grotesque, consumption gone mad. Then Matt remembered that he owned at least six pairs himself. But all that would change, he vowed silently, all that would change when . . . No! No, he couldn't think about it. It wasn't going to happen. Nothing was going to change. He and Natalie would be together forever.

Natalie was ready. She stood before him, slender-limbed and smooth-throated, in one of her sixteen pairs of jeans.

"You look beautiful," he said.

But with a plunge of fear, he knew it wasn't enough.

DAY 60 . . .

At 5:35 a.m., in Conall's obscenely comfortable bed, Katie had been woken by Conall leaning over her to kiss her goodbye. He was shaved and suited and fragranced with something sharp and citrusy. "I'll ring," he said.

" 'Kay," she mumbled, tumbling back down into sleep. She'd taken the day off work. Not a fake sickie, when she rang and put on a deep groany voice and said, "I think it's food poisoning," but a genuine day of her annual leave, which she'd booked in advance because she'd wanted to be able to drink as much as she liked at her birthday dinner without having to worry about going to work today, exhausted and fighting the desire to vomit. Of course, in a perfect world, no one would celebrate their birthday on a Monday night — and in fact it wasn't her actual birthday until Friday — but it had to be Monday night because Conall had to go to Helsinki this morning, to slash jobs and plant terror in the hearts of some misfortunate Finns, just like he'd done to everyone in Apex Entertainment Ireland ten months ago . . .

The morning after Katie's epiphany about her crisis being her opportunity to go to India, Danno greeted her by saying, "The night of the long knives. Half of Sales have been sacked. I hear Slasher Hathaway sold their desks on eBay overnight."

"How much of that is true?" Katie asked. She was more focused on getting Knight Ryders out of Ireland. Once they passed into German airspace they were no longer her responsibility.

"He's sacked five of Sales," Danno said, a little sulkily.

Katie checked her emails: the plane to take the entourage to Germany had landed at Dublin airport . . .

"Out of how many?"

"Thirty-seven."

. . . Lila-May was at the Four Seasons, picking up Elijah and the boys . . .

"Not exactly half, is it?" Nonetheless, a thrill of fear ran through her. People were being sacked. It was happening. "Did he really sell their desks?"

"Indeed he did." Danno believed that when caught out in a lie, one should never lose face. "He got fifteen euro for the lot. They've been bought by a Spanish company who make wooden trains. Toy ones. And doll's houses. And —"

Katie's phone rang and she had a moment of prescience: she should not answer this call. It would ruin her life.

It was Lila-May. "Elijah Knight's gone AWOL."

Katie's first thought was: Will I be blamed? And then she thought: I'm going to be sacked anyway, who cares?

Elijah might have gone out to buy socks, but it was unlikely. Especially when Lila-May said, "He hit the guard on the head with the heel of his cowboy boot and ran away. Your man will need stitches."

Katie pressed her hand over her eyes. Living legends were such hard bloody work.

"Okay, get them to search the hotel. Check all the bars." She hung up and called out, "Everyone, stop whatever you're doing. Elijah's run off."

Appalled yelps rose into the air, some even from members of Marketing, which was decent of them because this was PR's problem.

Danno grabbed a thick black marker and began inhaling it as discreetly as possible, to ready himself for the drama ahead.

"George!" Katie said. "Ring every journalist you know, every contact you have on gossip desks, in case people have rung in with sightings."

(George's vibration was frothy and insubstantial; only a cold steely seam of bitchiness kept him from dissolving into absolute nothingness. He enjoyed great popularity with journalists, who regarded him as a true gossip hound.)

"We shouldn't try to contain this?" Audrey asked anxiously.

"No, we've no time." In the midst of her panic, Katie noticed that a man — he had to be the lean and hungry Barbarian — had appeared in the office. "Splash it everywhere, we'll find him quicker."

He was at her desk now. "I'm Conall Hathaway," he said. "And you are?"

"Katie Richmond."

He nodded, as if he was filing away the knowledge for when he needed to sack her, she couldn't help but think.

"What's going on?" He gestured around

the room, at the panic that was almost visible.

"We've lost a lead singer. Elijah Knight." With a sarcasm that was uncharacteristic, she added, "He's with Knight Ryders, a metal band who are signed to Apex —"

"I know who they are."

Her phone rang, interrupting their exchange. It was the tour manager, who wanted to know how long he should hold the plane. Katie clutched the front of her head and squeezed hard, seeking the right decision. Stay or go? Go or stay? The crew needed at least five hours to assemble the set. But what use was a stage without a singer? Then again, what use was a singer without a stage?

"Katie . . . ?"

"Go now." Her digestive system clenched with fear that she'd called it wrong. "Get the crew to Berlin — they need the time to get set up for tonight. If I can't get Elijah on a scheduled flight later, I'll sort out a private charter."

I'm the one who gave the order for Elijah's plane to fly off without him. What if I can't get him on another flight? It'll be embarrassing enough to make the newspapers.

Conall Hathaway was still there, his eyes like gravel. He was looking speculatively at her mug, planning to sell it on eBay, no doubt. She put a protective arm around it.

I hate my job. I hate this anxiety. I hate that

*the consequences of my decisions affect so
many people.*

"If you're here to sack me," she said to
Conall, too fearful to be careful, "it'll have to
wait." She whistled to Danno like she would
to a faithful hound. "You. Here. With me.
And you too, Audrey." To Conall Hathaway
she said, "Because I'm going out to look for
Elijah."

"What happens if he can't be found?"

"He must be found. They're playing to
eighty thousand people tonight in Berlin."
The thought of it!

"Where will you look?"

"We'll start in pubs."

"And if you can't find him there?"

"There are some ladies of the night . . ."

"And what if he's not with them?"

"I suppose . . . ah . . . I suppose —" Katie
stared into the middle distance and began to
feel the full weight of her sleepless night, her
adrenal burnout, her crisis/opportunity co-
nundrum, and heard herself say — "I suppose it'll have to be an instrumental version
tonight in Berlin. The fans will probably riot,
eighty thousand dreams will be dashed, millions of euro will be lost and . . ."

"And?"

"And . . ." She shrugged her shoulders and
smiled with relief because, for a moment,
everything was clear. "And I suppose one day
we'll all be dead and none of this will matter."

91

■ ■ ■ ■

As it happened, it all worked out. Following a tip-off from a helpful member of the public, Elijah had been discovered, completely soused and sentimental, in a snug in Neary's. Katie and Danno had bundled him onto a plane, flown with him to Berlin, deposited him with the German publicist, then flown straight back to Dublin. Elijah went on to sing as usual and no harm was done. But aftershocks from the debacle were still plaguing Katie a day later: what if they hadn't found Elijah? Or what if he'd been too drunk to perform? Of course, if she was going to be made redundant anyway, what did it matter? At lunchtime, looking for comfort, she decided to go to the local stationery shop. She liked to browse through the pens and notebooks, finding their colorful beauty had a healing effect on her bruised soul. She came across a journal which had dried pansies pressed into the paper. Beautiful. Admittedly, the pages were probably too lumpy to be of any practical use, but she didn't care, she liked it and she was going to buy it for herself and . . . Curses! Brooding by the colored Post-its and unenthusiastically feeding square after square of Cadbury Fruit & Nut bar into his mouth was none other than Slasher Hathaway.

Why did he have to be here in her sanctuary?

Instantly, she began to retreat. She'd go to a drugstore instead; she enjoyed them just as much as stationery shops. She could lose hours browsing among the blister plasters, homeopathic remedies and hair bobbles. A drugstore was a cornucopia of delight, a force for good, a beacon of light in a world that was frequently dark . . . Too late! Conall Hathaway had spotted her! Their eyes connected, he crushed the chocolate paper into a small ball and quickly wiped his mouth with the back of his hand.

"Katie. Hello." His Adam's apple leaped as the last piece of chocolate was forced down his esophagus. "How are you?"

"Fine." A silence opened up and with the reflex politeness of someone who worked in PR she asked, "How's things?"

Conall shrugged helplessly. "I'm not exactly flavor of the month in Apex."

The nerve of the man! So very . . . what was the word? Yes, she had it! *Disingenuous.*

She turned a bland face to him and thought to herself: *You are disingenuous. I am behind my face here, thinking you're disingenuous and you don't know it. You're probably going to slash my job but I can still think you're disingenuous and there's nothing, oho nothing, you can do about it.*

It was very enjoyable. So enjoyable that she said, "Maybe you should have gone into a different line of work." Then she elaborated, "If it's love you're looking for." *Did I really say that?* To her further astonishment she added, "The priesthood, maybe?"

India, she thought, looking into his startled face. India. Nothing he could do could hurt her. The worst travail he could visit upon her was to make her redundant and then she'd be off to India. Where she would be enlightened. Also, hopefully, where she would contract a water-borne digestive-tract infection and lose tons of weight. It didn't have to be *tons.* Not even a stone. A ten-pound loss would be gratefully received, and would make all the difference really. The problem was food; if only she wasn't so very fond of it. But India would take care of all of that. India, she thought. *India.*

"The priesthood?" Conall asked.

"Or perhaps a doctor who cures blindness?" she suggested. "They probably get a lot of love."

Conall stared wistfully after Katie as she strode from the shop maintaining admirable, straight-backed posture in her four-inch heels. Impressive girl. Not that she was really a girl, he acknowledged. She was older than his usual type — he'd read all about Katie in her personnel file so he knew her salary, her

94

address, her *age:* thirty-nine. But he was forty-two and perhaps it was time he had a girlfriend who wasn't a decade younger than him, someone who shared the same cultural references as him, who remembered David Bowie from the first time round. And the second time round.

Conall Hathaway was badly smitten. It was that comment Katie had made yesterday: "One day we'll all be dead and none of this will matter." For a moment it had opened up a sliver of insight into an entirely different way of thinking. He was always so caught up in the extreme focus of his work, of the brutal choices he had to make, but suddenly all that anxiety had diminished and he saw his life as a small, unimportant thing, his decisions as essentially meaningless, and he was astonished by how free he felt. He was intrigued by Katie's originality, her courage and, most of all, her wisdom. Even more impressive was that she had laughed at him, at his manifest shock.

If only he had known that the truth was far, oh yes far more complex. First and foremost, Conall's and Katie's heart vibrations were in harmony. In addition, the shape of Katie's face — the wide-spacing of her eyes and the sweet tapering of her chin — stirred a murky memory in Conall's subconscious of the teacher he'd had a tearful crush on at the tender age of five.

Into this incendiary mix came a compelling petroleum smell — from Danno's thick black marker — which cast Conall back into his illicit yet thrilling teenage years. And, of course, Conall had noticed Katie's generous bosom, buttoned up in a clinging cashmere cardigan which, in a delicious, delirious conflict, made her seem both maternal and very, very unmaternal.

What was he to do, he wondered, staring balefully at a container of colored thumbtacks as if they had just farted. He could hardly ask her out, then sack her. Or sack her and then ask her out. Another option, of course, was to not sack her, but he wasn't sure if that could be justified.

It was a hellishly awkward position he found himself in. Usually, when he wanted something, it was his. I'm Conall Hathaway, he thought, and I always get what I want.

Disconsolately, he picked up a slab of red heart-shaped Post-its and made his way to the checkout.

DAY 60 . . .

In the park, Grudge dreamed of being a steeplechaser. He sprang high and long, clearing invisible obstacles, while Jemima sat on a bench and inhaled the oxygen-rich, life-giving morning air. Grudge bounded and soared,

96

his long donkey-like ears flattened against his head, his crimped gray hair flying in the wind. A man sat down beside her and watched Grudge's athletics with an interest bordering on the fascination. "Look at that dog," he said.

"He's mine," Jemima said briskly. "And much beloved." She said this in order to save the man from embarrassing them both by saying, "Isn't he the maddest-looking article you've ever seen?"

"He's full of vim, that's for sure . . . Ah . . . what kind is he?"

"They told me in the pound that he was a cocker spaniel —"

"A *spaniel?* Not a bit tall for a spaniel?"

"— crossed with collie —"

"Collies, lovely creatures, very even temperament."

"— with a smattering of box terrier —"

"Box terrier? Actually, yes —" the man squinted doubtfully — "maybe I can see that . . ."

"— and I'm told one of his great-grandparents was an Irish Wolfhound."

"Nice patriotic dogs."

Jemima got to her feet and whistled for Grudge. "Must get on," she told the man. "My son Fionn is coming to stay. Want to get the place in shape."

She didn't really have to go home, she just wanted an excuse to say those delicious

97

words: *My son Fionn is coming.*

Of course he wasn't really her son, he was her foster son, but no need to tell the man that.

"He's a gardener." She couldn't stop herself, the pride was simply too great. "And he's just been given his own television show. For six weeks. Initially. But if it flies . . ." Yes, she checked with herself, *flies* was almost certainly the word Fionn had used. "If it flies, they might recommission it."

"Very good."

"He lives in Monaghan, but he'll be staying with me for the filming. They offered to put him up in a hotel but he said he'd prefer to be with me."

"Very good." The man shifted a little.

"There's a gap in the market — indeed, one could call it an echoing void — for a good gardening program. I've been doing a survey and their paucity beggars belief. Last night I had the misfortune to watch something hosted by one Monty Don and, really, such balderdash . . ."

"But Monty Don is marvelous!"

"Hardly *relevant,* though, is he?"

"He's a gardener who does gardening programs about gardens. How much more relevant does he need to be?"

"My son's show will offer much more. 'An entire support system for our twenty-first-century lifestyle.' " She was quoting directly from the pitch Fionn had sent her. " 'Our lives are moving ever faster, but we have a need to get back to the land. The buzzwords are *Fresh! Organic! Grow your own!* "

"Fair play." The man got to his feet.

"It's called *Your Own Private Eden,*" Jemima called after him, as he hurried away. "Watch out for it. Channel 8, coming soon."

DAY 60 . . .

Maeve's journey to work was such a high-risk performance you could have sold tickets to it. She was even more daring and audacious than she'd been four and a half years ago when Matt had first noticed her orange bobbled–hat moving through the traffic. Now, she zipped like a streak of light through narrow canyons formed by buses and trucks, she zigzagged complicated patterns between nose-to-tail lines of cars and — most breathtaking of all — she hurtled through red lights and wove miraculous paths between the startled drivers who poured at her from both the left and the right. An adrenaline-riddled exercise that seemed quite at odds with her gentle, nerve-soothing alarm clock.

She no longer worked in a software company but was employed in the reservations department of Emerald, a smallish hotel chain. Emerald's administrative staff were housed in the basement of their flagship hotel, the Isle. Maeve passed through the long office, nodding and smiling, and arrived at her desk, which was right down at the end.

She switched on her monitor, reached into her in tray and began work immediately. All around her, her many colleagues were discussing what they'd each had for their dinner the previous evening but Maeve kept her eyes on her screen and tapped away diligently.

It seemed that Maeve not only worked in the reservations department, but that she *was* the reservations department. Just her. Her twenty or so co-workers were payroll people, or procurements, or goods inward or outward, which meant that Maeve had little need to stop by anyone's desk and say something like, "See this reservation, can you sort out the four weasels they're asking for?" However, she didn't indulge much in banter and chat with her colleagues either. Everything perfectly civil, don't get me wrong, but Maeve kept herself to herself, which was surprising. As was the uncomplicated, unchallenging nature of her work — frankly, a well-trained monkey could have done it and it wasn't at all what you'd expect from a woman of her charm and ability. Who knew what had happened since the glory days in Goliath when she'd shown such promise that her training period had finished two weeks early? Perhaps, after Matt had spurned the lovely Natalie in favor of Maeve, things had become awkward and they had found it preferable to work elsewhere, and in the current economic climate this was all she'd been able to find?

All morning Maeve carried out her duties, allocating non-smoking suites and twin-bedded rooms according to request. She experienced a certain pride in her endeavors: people visited strange cities and found beds awaiting them because Maeve made it happen.

At one o'clock sharp, she left her cubicle and went to a nearby sandwich bar, where she was greeted with warmth by the mumsy woman behind the counter.

"Hi, Maeve. What'll it be?"

"Hi, Doreen. Ham salad —"

"— sandwich, brown bread, no mustard? Bag of plain crisps and one can of Fanta? Don't know why I bother asking."

"One day I might surprise you," she said.

"Don't. I couldn't take the shock. There's too much uncertainty in life as it is, I like it like this."

Armed with her lunch, Maeve sat in the sunshine on the flight of steps outside the Central Bank, scanning the swarms of tourists and shoppers, looking for a chance to do her daily Act of Kindness. Was she right in thinking that it was easier in the colder months, she wondered. She'd started this back in March, a month when people were still trailing highly droppable items like gloves, scarves, hats, and all Maeve had to do was pick up the abandoned garment and race after the person then bask in the glow of their gratitude. Then again, the summer had brought tourists, poor foreigners who were perplexed by Dublin's illogical street systems, and in the last few weeks Maeve's daily duty had often landed right in her lap, when some baffled Italian or American asked for directions. She always made a big effort to ensure the visitors knew exactly where they were going, sometimes even accompanying them part of the way. But today was a slow one. No one was consulting a map in bewilderment, nobody needed help carrying a pram up the steps, no one needed to urgently borrow a phone. It was ten to two, almost time to go back to work, and she still hadn't found a person to be kind to when — aha! — she saw her prospects. A young couple, obviously tourists. The girl was standing next to a very Irishy-looking green letter box and the boy was taking a photo of her.

Maeve pushed herself to her feet. She didn't want to do this, she never *wanted* to, but she'd feel better afterward. She walked into their line of sight and forced herself to smile. "Would you like me to take a picture of both of you together? Next to the letter box?"

They stared at her as if they'd been turned

to stone. Maybe they didn't understand English?

"French?" she asked. *"Voulez-vous —"*

"We're American," the girl said.

"So would you like a shot of the two of you together? Next to the, um, mailbox?"

"Er . . ." the boy said, cradling his camera protectively.

Then Maeve understood. "Look, I'm not going to steal your camera. Here —" she offered the girl her satchel — "have this as security." The girl resisted. "Please," Maeve said. "I only want to help."

"Is it like a random act of kindness thing?" the girl asked.

"Exactly!" Maeve's face lit up.

"It's okay," the girl said to the boy. "I get it. Give her the camera."

Maeve took several shots and the pair were lovely and grateful and said that she was "pretty solid" and "If you're ever in Seattle . . ."

"You'll take a photo of me and my husband?"

"Yeah!"

All in all, she felt considerably better. The thing was that the book that had recommended this daily practice — some self-help yoke — hadn't taken account of the fact that recipients of Maeve's kindness weren't always grateful. Often they were confused or mistrustful or downright blasé. Only last week she'd spent twenty minutes of her lunch hour carrying a Brabantia kitchen trash can — not that heavy, but very awkward — through the crowds, all the way from Abbey Street to Tara Street Dart station, and the woman, the random stranger who owned it, had seemed quite put out that Maeve wasn't going to get the Dart with her and help her carry the trash can at the other end.

But today was a good one. She wondered how Matt was getting on with his AOK. Bound to be something to do with his car, letting another driver out of a side road, that sort of thing. It always was. In many ways she and Matt were so different that it was mad they'd ended up together. But she'd always had a tenderness for him and she could still pinpoint the exact moment when she'd started to fall in love . . .

It was four and a bit years ago, a Saturday evening in April. Maeve was curled up in David's bed, half-in-half-out of a dreamy doze, when suddenly she jolted back into alertness. She grabbed his wrist to look at his watch.

"Cripes, David, it's half-eight. Get up! Who wants to go in the shower first?"

"Wait." He dismissed her agitation. "Slow down a minute."

"But the others will be waiting! If we don't get going, we might even miss the band."

"Easy," he soothed. He stared into her eyes,

and she felt herself eddy back down into calmness. "Easy," he repeated. "Five or ten minutes won't make any difference."

"Okay," she said, releasing all her anxiety in one long breath.

"Okay."

David and Maeve. Maeve and David. In a way, Goliath was like one big dating agency. There were over two hundred employees, the vast majority of them under the age of thirty and they tended to travel in large packs, doing communal Galwegian-style things like going to gigs and festivals and benefits. If you fancied someone you made sure you ended up in the same gang as them. Proper dates, like one-on-one dinners, were scorned, at least among the worker bees. Of course it was different for management — team leaders like Matt and Nat were another breed, into country hotel mini-breaks, couples massages, room service, all that caper. But no judgment was made; it was horses for courses, each to their own.

Soon after Maeve had started her training at Goliath, she realized that her colleagues were great believers in "giving back." Almost before she knew where the coffee machine was, she'd found herself roped onto a committee to organize a comedy benefit in aid of the homeless. David was the driving force behind it. He and the other volunteers persuaded several well-known comedians to do a gig — waiving their fees, of course — for Goliath's staff, with all the proceeds going to the charity. During the following month, when Maeve gave up many of her evenings to help pull the event together, she became aware of David's focus on her, which became more and more intense as the event got nearer. She also noticed that some of the other girls on the committee were jealous of David's interest in her — and she couldn't help feeling a bit flattered. David was well traveled and brainy and passionate about injustice and he was a little bit older than the rest of them, yet she was the one he liked. Her previous boyfriend, Harry, whom she'd met in college in Galway and with whom she'd gone to Australia, had been nice and all that, but not impressive the way David was.

The night of the gig finally arrived and it went great, thanks to the very efficient organization. Thousands of euro were raised and afterward, when the committee had finished their celebratory drinks, Maeve did what she knew for weeks she'd be doing on this night: she went home with David.

And that was that, they were together. They had plenty in common. Bicycles. Pints. Touareg bands. Boogie-boarding in Clare. Hummus in the fridge. Barbara Kingsolver novels. Altruistic tendencies. David was the most principled, the most truly *good* person Maeve had ever met.

"Right, I'm getting in the shower," Maeve said.

But David pulled her tightly to him and twirled one of her curls around his finger. "Let's not go."

"What? Where?"

"Let's not go out tonight."

She was taken aback. "What would we do instead?"

"I can think of plenty."

But they'd spent the afternoon in bed. She'd had enough of it for the moment.

"I've never seen Fanfare Ciocrlia," she said. "I want to go."

"And I want to stay in with you."

"We've paid for the tickets." That would work, she thought. He didn't like waste of any kind.

"It's only money."

"Yeah, but . . ."

"Okay." He sighed. "You'd prefer to be with the people you work with than with me."

"David —" But he'd slid from the bed and was on his way to the bathroom.

Then at the gig — a group of gypsy musicians frenetically playing James Bond themes on tubas — who should she bump in to, only Matt! He was dancing along madly with everyone else! It was a surprise because, other than Friday-night drinks, team leaders didn't tend to socialize with their staff. But it was a nice surprise because everyone loved Matt. His was the best team to be on. Right enough, it was work and it was often frustrating, anxious work, but because of the way Matt was always cheery and upbeat, you had a laugh. "Matt!" Maeve yelled over the music. "I didn't know you liked this sort of thing,"

"Neither did I, but it's fecking mighty!"

Fecking mighty?

"Where's Nat?" she shouted.

"Not here. Not for her."

Fair play to him for coming without her, and what made him even more endearing was that he was so . . . he was . . . well, he was such a bad dancer. Flinging himself around like a puppy and no fear of being laughed at. It was cute. With a heart softened by his sweetness, Maeve thought, *Matt . . .*

This popping in and out of their memory pools — I'm able to do it but it's not clean. I can't just jump into their pasts, find what I want and hop out again, leaving everything as it was. I'm already causing ripples, disquiet, upsets. I'm weaving my way into their lives, showing up in their dreams, haunting the edges of their thoughts. In the days and weeks afterward, everyone will admit they'd felt this was on its way. That they knew.

DAY 60 . . .

Fionn was about a hundred miles away in the stony gray soil of County Monaghan but there was such a strong cord of connection between Jemima and him that all you'd have to do was hook onto it, like a cable car on a wire, and whiz through the ether. He was to be found in a low white house, on a small rocky plot of land, two miles outside a medium-sized town called Pokey. A place of heartbreaking, back-breaking beauty. A mist had snaked around his house, but the sun was also in evidence, shining furiously, trying to counteract the mist, so his home looked like it was wearing a halo.

And my word, the vibrations coming off the man himself! So powerful, they were colored: golden notes of charm, chocolate-brown earthiness — and something else . . . a silver-gray mercurial strand, only visible when it wasn't being looked at directly.

I admit it. I couldn't get a proper read on him. Not yet anyway.

But I could tell you this much: his hair could probably have done with a wash. So could his jeans. So could his kitchen counters. Not filthy, no, not that bad, just a little less than *pristine.* Fionn, it seemed, distrusted hygiene. Subconsciously, he suspected it was an artificial concept, the invention of Proctor & Gamble, to scare people into buying unnecessary chemicals like Shake'n Vac. A few germs wouldn't kill you, he often said. (Except, of course, for those that would.)

He was cramming spoonfuls of muesilix into his mouth at the same time as pulling on his socks at the same time as slurping tea from a mug. Five past two and he was late for work. Fionn had more customers than he could handle; most of them were women, dotted around the townland of Pokey like little red lights pulsing on a map.

Fionn lived alone — you only had to look at the place. His sheets were a polyester mix, his pillows were so old they were almost flat and his couch lacked bounce. Everything was functional, bare, almost sad.

He gulped down the last spoonful of muesilix then he held the bowl above his face and tipped the dregs of the milk into his mouth. Signaling the grand finale of his breakfast, he wiped milk off his chin with his sleeve, then slung on his jacket and a pair of Chelsea boots — a very impractical choice for a gardener — and headed outside.

In his garden he tramped down a muddy ditch, grabbed a handful of long green fronds and hoicked five fat, orange carrots from the ground. All the land around his house had been given over to growing food. There were tomatoes under glass, raspberries growing up stakes and a large potato patch. He shook the worst of the dirt from the carrots, dropped them on the passenger seat of his very old (thirteen years) car and headed toward the town.

DAY 60 . . .

Katie had slept until midday and woke alone in Conall's magnificent bed in Conall's beautiful bedroom in Conall's enormous house. The magic duvet, which felt stuffed with the softest marshmallows, wrapped itself around her with profound love. *All is well,* it whispered, *all is well.* The facing wall, in a delicate washed-out shade called Dusty Plum, smiled at her. The lofty ceiling gazed benignly down, telling her, *It is my honor to act as your ceiling.* The heavy fall of silk curtains rustled and swished, asking if she was ready to have shiny daylight admitted. This bedroom was divine. When she and Conall came to an end — as everyone confidently predicted they would — it was one of the things she would miss most.

That and the "pleasuring."

All the women she knew (with the exception of her mother) hungered for detailed descriptions of how Conall performed between his delightfully textured sheets.

"Good," Katie always said. "Nice."

"Good? Nice? Not out-of-this-world?"

"Good, nice."

"But he's so good-looking, so powerful, so moody . . . I thought it would be amazing."

"At the end of the day —" Katie had mastered a wonderfully carefree shrug to accompany this sentence — "he's just a man."

No one enjoyed hearing this. But, as Katie thought, if every person in her life gave well-meant advice that she should hold a certain amount of herself back from Conall, they couldn't very well object when she did. (Or at least pretended she did. Yes, she was careful not to be overwhelmed by Conall's forceful personality and supersized mattress but the pleasuring was the one area where she surrendered completely. She was thirty-nine — well, okay, nearly forty now — she was a woman in her sexual prime!)

Out on the landing, the naked floorboards felt splintery and rough against her bare feet, and the dusty walls looked like open wounds. Bored one weekend, Conall had decided to strip the wallpaper, but quickly abandoned the job when he discovered about seven or eight different layers of paper beneath the one he was tearing off. On the floor of the hall, paintings were carelessly stacked up against each other and several packing crates were still unopened. Apart from the bedroom and bathroom, the whole house was exactly as it was when Conall had moved in, nearly three years earlier. The beautiful bedroom was courtesy of Katie's predecessor, a girl called Saffron, who clearly had wonderful taste; but, sadly, Conall had broken up with her before she'd brought her skill to bear on any of the other rooms. (The bathroom was thanks to Kym, the girl before Saffron, but in Katie's opinion Kym didn't have Saffron's gifts.)

The kitchen was the worst room, a riot of geometric-patterned orange and yellow linoleum and mustard-colored cabinets that were falling to bits. Scattered over the never-used table were brochures from German companies, makers of sleek, gorgeous kitchens, and samples of marble, stone and different woods that Conall had ordered but never got around to making a decision on. Sometimes Katie's gaze snagged on these — especially the wide-planked limed oak — and she almost jack-knifed with longing and frustration. She could make this place so lovely! Well, in fairness, anyone with access to Conall's money could.

She turned away from the beautiful wood because she was on the hunt for food. There wouldn't be anything proper to eat in any of Conall's cupboards, but there was always chocolate, bars and bars of it, and bag after bag of jelly sweets, and she could absolutely depend on finding a dazzling choice of ice cream in the freezer. Her usual ritual was to

wrench open the freezer door and gaze ador-
ingly at the selection — pint tubs of Ben &
Jerry's, perhaps two or even three of them, all
in different flavors, and an imaginative selection of six or seven individual bars: Galaxy
Swirls and Icebergers and Maltesers and Cornettos and, the ultimate prize, Green &
Black's Double Chocolate. All full-sized, of
course. None of this fun-sized stuff for Conall Hathaway. Katie agreed: an ice-cream that
was gone after two bites — where was the
fun in that?

But the next time she'd be in his kitchen —
and it mightn't be long afterward, perhaps
less than a week — all that ice cream would
have disappeared, and been replaced with an
entirely different, but equally impressive, selection.

Sugar, Conall seemed to live on the stuff.
He was the only man she knew who ate des-
sert. But thanks to his man metabolism, sugar
didn't extract the same price from him as it
did from her. His thighs were hard and
muscled, not a bit of wobbliness anywhere,
unlike her own wretched pair. God, she
envied him.

But today she didn't get as far as the
freezer. Laid out on the ugly, knife-scored
counter was a series of gifts for her. A bottle
of champagne with a Post-it saying "Drink
me," a kilo box of Godiva chocolates saying
"Eat me," a huge bunch of roses saying

"Smell me," and a pink beribboned box of wispy underwear saying "Wear me."

She gathered them in her arms and took them back to bed, sad that Conall wasn't there to share them with her. She wondered how the Finns were getting on, whether Conall had slashed loads of them already.

She still remembered when the slashings in Apex had begun in earnest . . .

Conall had started on the ground floor, eventually wiping out a fifth of Sales, and steadily worked his way up the building. On the first floor, a quarter of Accounts were cast into the outer darkness. Next would be Legal on the second floor. Meanwhile, on the third floor, at the top of the house, Publicity and Marketing crouched, anxious and white-faced, waiting for the fall of the executioner's ax.

The building had been overrun with what Danno called orcs — underlings provided by Sony — who grabbed a desk wherever they could, poring over contracts, making feasibility assessments to Conall Hathaway, with whom the buck stopped ultimately.

"He is Shiva, destroyer of worlds," Danno said and, for once, Katie didn't think he was exaggerating. It wasn't just employees who were being axed; the plug was being pulled on many of the label's less successful acts. Countless lives were being destroyed because of one man's decisions.

"What must that job do to a person's soul?" Katie wondered.

"Soul?" Danno scoffed. "Conall Hathaway has no soul."

"He sold his soul to the devil," Lila-May said.

"Kih!" Danno said. "You mean, the devil sold his soul to *him.* Then Conall streamlined the bejayzus out of it and sold it on for a filthy profit. Anyway, Katie Richmond, what are you worried about? You're the one person who'll still have a job when this is all over."

Bizarre as it was, Conall seemed to be fascinated by Katie. Nobody believed it at first, then people believed it but didn't understand it. Why Katie, when there were so many younger, sexier girls on site?

But Conall evinced no interest in them. Although he was meant to be rationalizing Apex's entire European operations, he was spending a disproportionate time on the Dublin office and kept appearing on unscheduled, unsettling roams before homing in on Katie with some spurious question that one of the orcs could just as easily have asked. By acting as a draw to Conall, Katie was deeply resented by her colleagues.

"I was on the phone to my mate in Calgary," Lila-May said, "when I looked up and saw Slasher Hathaway standing right next to me. He was supposed to be in Amsterdam.

My heart nearly stopped! Just because he wanted his hourly look at Katie's knockers."

Lila-May, a vixen-like little beauty, wasn't comfortable being overshadowed by Katie. Neither was Tamsin. Audrey, however, didn't mind.

"I'm Conall Hathaway and I always get what I want!" Danno leaped to his feet and began swaggering about the office. He grabbed Katie, tipped her backward into his left arm, placed his lips close to hers and risked putting his free hand on her left breast. "I must have you," he growled. "I *will* have you."

"Stop it, Danno!" Katie fought her way out of his grip. "For God's sake, stop doing that."

"Why you?" Lila-May mused, assessing Katie with a gaze like an X-ray. "I mean . . . why you?"

Katie was as baffled as everyone else. Men like Conall, with their obvious suits and their obvious watches and their obvious air of power, would have obvious girlfriends. She was too old, too bruised by life, too *thigh-y,* for the likes of him.

"I don't know but when you live long enough, nothing surprises," she said.

"You're not that old," Danno said.

"So why are you all acting like I am?"

"Will you sleep with him to save our jobs?" George asked.

"That won't save our jobs."

"Aha! So you *are* thinking of sleeping with him!"

Well, of course she was. Did they think she was stupid as well as ancient?

But Conall Hathaway was going round sacking people in droves — her colleagues, probably even Katie herself in a couple of days. It would be tantamount to collaboration.

"She is! She is!" Danno crowed. "But you despise him."

Yes, she did despise him and his job, but, interestingly, since he'd made it so clear how attractive he found her, she despised him less. Not because she was a blank canvas, one of those women who automatically fancied a man just because he fancied her, but because he'd surprised her. As her colleagues were so fond of pointing out, Conall could have hit on young, lush Lila-May, or young, almost-as-lush Tamsin, or young, not-really-lush-at-all-but-still-more-lush-than-Katie Audrey. But he'd spurned all of them and gravitated straight for the older woman. How could anyone fail to be impressed by that?

And no matter what Danno said, Conall Hathaway didn't have the cold dead eyes of a killer. Certainly not all of the time. There were times when his eyes made her —

"You'd better be careful," Danno warned. "You're a parched forest floor that hasn't seen a drop of rain for a year. If you let Conall

Hathaway light your fire it could ignite an inferno big enough to destroy us all."

Annoying though Danno was, he spoke the truth. It was a year since she'd had sex. (Zerogamy, her friend Sinead called it.) It was important, nay *vital,* that she didn't behave like a middle-aged spinster desperate for the touch of a man.

Because she wasn't.

DAY 60 . . .

Fionn drove one-handed and too fast. Within ten minutes, he'd pulled into the driveway of a large, ranch-style house — a hideous Southfork-type residence — and sauntered around to the rear, casually swinging his bunch of carrots.

"Jill," he called, rapping on the glass of the back door. "It's Fionn."

(Jill, a fraught woman with energies so given over to others — her four children, her husband, her elderly mother — that there was almost none left for herself. Apart from a thin line of pulsing fear, her life force was so depleted that for a short time I thought she was dead.)

At the sound of Fionn's voice, she flared with an infusion of energy. Fionn was her gift to herself, part of a secret internal deal she'd made so that she wouldn't go round the bend. Her one pleasure used to be a nightly sleeping tablet, which delivered seven hours of merciful nothingness, until Tandy, her fifteen-year-old daughter, stole the prescription and took an overdose. Tandy immediately told everyone what she'd done so there was plenty of time for stomach-pumping, but it marked the end of the sleeping tablets for Jill. You could have *nothing* with a teenage daughter in the house, not mascara, not ankle boots, not breadknives, not sedatives; they took everything, selfish little bitches! As soon as Tandy came home from hospital, she ferried the breadknife off to her bedroom and tried a couple of experimental grazes on her forearm — she'd read about self-harm in *Take a Break* and it appealed to her — but to her astonishment it was horribly painful. The girl in the magazine had said she'd felt nothing, that she was totally numb. While Tandy cast around, looking for another dramatic way to get attention, thinking that maybe she should get pregnant, Jill had to soldier on with a life devoid of sleeping tablets, of that promise of oblivion at the end of every day.

But then she met Fionn and no one could take him away from her. Except perhaps Fionn himself. He was so much in demand that he could abandon her for another whenever the humor took him.

He was forty minutes late today — he was never on time and she'd been thinking that this might be the day that he wouldn't come at all — but in the rush of his presence, her terror faded to nothing.

"Come in." She closed her eyes to the clods of mud he distributed across her clean wooden floor.

Fionn slung the carrots onto the kitchen table. "Out of the ground not ten minutes ago."

"Carrots!" Jill received the gift with the same wonder and delight as if they were diamonds. "With pieces of your garden still attached!"

"Lovely and sweet," he said, with a twinkly smile. "Not unlike yourself. Now, I've a bit of news. I'm away to Dublin for a while."

"Is it . . . that TV thing?" Jill held her breath.

Everyone in Pokey had heard what had happened when Carmine Butcher's sister Grainne, the one who "worked in television," had come for Carmine junior's christening; how she'd met Fionn and decided that he might have enough star quality to have his own gardening show; how a silver BMW had appeared a few days later outside Fionn's small white house and ferried him away to Dublin, where he was subjected to screen tests, autocue skills, interviews with the production company and no end of other things.

"It's the TV thing," Fionn confirmed. "Bad time of year to go, the most growthy time of year for the gardens, but might as well give it a stab and see what happens."

"Oh . . ." Jill was bereft, but there was undeniable kudos in your gardener having his own television show. "You'll be brilliant, everyone thinks."

"Would you stop." He twisted awkwardly.

"You'd better remember me when you're the big star."

"I won't be a big star. It's just a gardening show. And I'll only be gone a month or so."

"They'll have to put you up in a hotel."

"Ah no. I'll stay with Jemima."

"Would they not fork out for it?" Already Jill's awe was receding.

"They would. But I'd prefer to be with Jemima."

"You would?" Jill was disappointed. Nothing against Jemima, she was nice enough for a do-goodery Protestant, but Jill was obsessed with hotels. Her favorite fantasy was that her Southfork house had fallen into a hole, it was the builder's fault so there was insurance money, and while it was being straightened up she had to live in a hotel. She adored hotels. You could make shit of the place, absolute shit — abandon towels on the floor, get make-up on the sheets, spill ketchup on the carpet, even break wine glasses — and it was all someone else's problem. (Sometimes, on bad days, the fantasy included the subplot that her four children, her husband and her mother were trapped in the up-ended house. She entertained no ill will toward them, she simply didn't want them in the hotel with her, so they were alive and well, playing lots of Monopoly and subsisting on canned foods.)

"I'll get on." Fionn gestured at the garden through the window. "The whole place has done a lot of growing since I was last here."

"Don't be gone too long. The garden will miss you," Jill said. "And so will I," she added, daringly.

"I'll miss you too," said Fionn, treating her to a second go of the twinkly smile. Flirty, very, very flirty.

For a breathless moment Jill wondered if Fionn ever would . . .

But he wouldn't.

Fionn flirted with everyone — even his photograph flirted — but he didn't get involved with married women. It wasn't right. Or worth it. He didn't want irate husbands showing up at his house and making shite of his garden. (It had happened once, a misunderstanding. Francy Higgins's wife had been enjoying afternoon trysts with Carmine Butcher but Francy decided that Fionn must be the lover — on the basis that Fionn was moviestar handsome and Carmine a bit of a horror-show. Fionn managed to defuse Francy but not before Francy had put his boot through the glass of the tomato house and thrown several of Fionn's potatoes at Fionn's car. No real harm had been done, but the incident had distressed the plants and Fionn couldn't be doing with that. A potato had never asked to be a potato; it had never asked to be wrenched prematurely from the ground and bounced off a car windshield.)

No wonder I was having such difficulty getting a read on Fionn: he was a man of great contradictions. He wanted the whole world to love him — but he was not a womanizer, at least not in the strict sense of the word. He believed in monogamy. Even if he couldn't always manage it.

Girls seemed to pitch up in Fionn's life and express an interest in being his significant other and, if they were pleasant and attractive enough, he was happy to oblige. However, there were times when a pleasant and attractive girl pitched up and expressed an interest in being his significant other but, on examination of the facts, it would transpire that Fionn already *had* a significant other. In those cases, he found it best to let the girls sort it out themselves. Sometimes they tried to involve him with tearful showdowns, ordering him to choose one of them, but he kept well out of it. If he picked one over the other, the rejected one would be angry with him and he didn't enjoy people being angry with him. The truth was that he felt that no matter what way the whole thing shook down, he'd be happy enough — the new girl, the old one, whatever the outcome was, whoever he ended up with, it was all fine.

But sometimes the winning girl took a notion that she and Fionn would get married and leave the polyester-sheeted bachelor pad and move into a cul-de-sac in Pokey where the couches had bounce and the houses had central heating. Invariably, the girl had a vision of turning Fionn into a proper, money-making enterprise with official invoices and a clean new van with his mobile number painted on the side. It was usually around then that they made the discovery that Fionn was easy-going only up to a point. When something mattered enough to him, Fionn would resist.

DAY 60 . . .

Up in the top-floor flat of 66 Star Street, I've noticed that Potent Conall never came this morning to hang Katie's mirror before he went to Helsinki. It's still sitting on the floor. This makes me unaccountably nervous. Trouble will ensue — of this I am confident — if the mirror is not smiling down from the wall when Katie comes home.

Oh God, and here she comes . . .

She dumped her bag and shucked off her boots, one landing safely on the floor but the other bouncing off the skirting board, then she went straight to the living room, looking for her mirror.

First — perhaps naively? — she looked on the wall, and when she couldn't see it there she turned her gaze to the floor. There it was, exactly as it had been the last time she'd seen it, propped against the cupboards looking, if this could be possible, apologetic for its lay-about status.

She stared at it for a long, long time, her mouth in a thin line as if she was sucking something unpleasant.

Katie didn't get angry often but she was angry now.

I didn't want a platinum watch, she was thinking. It had made everyone else's presents look like jokes (her mother had given her a bread-box). She hadn't wanted Conall to pay for last night's dinner for all ten of them, because every male member of her family had a chip on his shoulder about Conall being rich. (She'd heard her dad muttering about "flashy bastards," no matter how much he denied it.) All she'd wanted for her birthday present was for Conall to make good on his seventeen days of promises and put a thing in the wall so she could hang up her new mirror. She'd shown him where she wanted it, she'd marked the spot with a biro and he'd said with great believability that he'd nip over in the morning before he left for Helsinki and do the job. Five minutes, it would take, he promised her.

He'd made it sound so simple that she'd wondered if she should try it herself, but she didn't have a drill and she didn't want a drill and she wasn't going down that road with pink toolboxes and sparkly Rawlplugs and suchlike.

Conall could have organized a man to do it, a carpenter or a handyman of some sort — when she'd bought the mirror, that's what he'd offered — but she stuck to her guns. Her mirror was to be hoisted on to her wall by the efforts of Conall and Conall alone. She wanted a gesture from him, a gift of his time and energy, something that money couldn't buy.

She lunged at her phone and clicked off a rapid-fire text.

Mirror, mirror on the wall. Whoops, no. Mirror, mirror, still on the floor.

She was very incensed, oh very incensed indeed. Conall is a selfish liar, she was thinking, Conall is an unreliable bastard. Only she was thinking these thoughts a lot faster and hotter and with more color. All the promises Conall had broken were whizzing around like multicolored flying saucers and it was herself she was most angry with. She should never have agreed to go out with him in the first place.

Eight working days after Conall first arrived at Apex, he requested a meeting with Katie. She'd known what was going to happen and had plenty of time to prepare a refusal. But she hadn't.

He kicked things off by talking about work. "I have news," he said.

"You're going to sell me on eBay?"

"No. I have reports from the artists. They're fond of you. They say you mother them. You get to keep your job."

"How about my team?"

"They get to keep their jobs too."

"*All* of them?"

"All of them."

"Same salary packages?"

"Same salary packages."

She watched him suspiciously.

"There's no catch," he said. "It's all above board. New employment contacts are being drawn up and will be with you within the hour. Now, will you go out with me?"

She lowered her eyes and said nothing. This was the moment when her self-interest clashed with her loyalty to those of her colleagues he had sacked.

"Can I take you to the ballet?" she heard him ask.

She jerked her head up. "God, no. I find it so tedious I want to cry, and when they go up on their pointes I get an excruciating pain in my big toes in sympathy."

A smile touched his face, perhaps the first ever smile she'd seen from him. "Pains in your big toes?" He gazed at her as if she was both rare and fascinating. "I see. How about the opera? Would you like that?"

"No, no, no. I can't stand it. I have to listen to too much music for my job. I hate it all."

"All of it?" He seemed astounded. "Even Leonard Cohen?"

"Even Leonard Cohen."

"Christ, that's a shame. Like, for you . . . I love music."

"Because you're a man."

That made him laugh. Silently, but it was still a laugh.

"So what sort of music do you like?" she asked.

"Opera, obviously, but anything really. Except maybe power ballads."

"Well, I like silence."

"Silence?" He shook his head with wonder. She was in the highly unusual position where every word that came out of her mouth was being received as enthralling. Savor this, she told herself. The memory will keep you company in your old age.

"You don't like the ballet, you don't like

the opera, you don't like music. What do you like?"

She thought about it. "Eating. Sleeping. Drinking wine with my friends and discussing celebrity meltdowns." The days of lying to a man to make herself sound fascinating were far in the past.

"Eating . . . ?" he asked. "Sleeping . . . ?" Again his face was radiant with admiration.

She'd had no idea that she was so interesting.

"Especially eating," she said.

"You don't look like you love to eat."

If only he knew the battle she fought with her appetite. The bloody thing was like a Rottweiler, pulling and straining, trying to escape her hold and eat all in sight.

"I have a personal trainer," she admitted.

"So do I," he said.

"Mine's called Florence. She takes me out running in the rain and makes me do jumping jacks in Tesco's parking lot. I only see her once a week but she trusts me to do stuff on my own and I feel guilty if I don't."

"Mine's called Igor. We go to the gym."

"I never wanted to be the kind of person who had a personal trainer," she confided.

But she'd never wanted to be the kind of person who wore size 18 jeans either and, left to her own devices, that's exactly what she'd be.

"How about next Saturday?" he asked.

"Why do you want to go out with me? I can't be your usual type."

"You're not. But I'm . . ." He shook his head. "I'm, ah, you know, can't stop thinking about you."

She looked at him beseechingly. This was very difficult.

"Just one date," he said.

One date. It wasn't as if he was asking her to marry him. Not that Katie wanted to get married. Yes, once upon a time she'd wanted the ring and the dress and the babies — so shoot her. There were lots of things she had wanted once upon a time: to be size 8; to be fluent in Italian; to hear that Brad had got back with Jennifer. None of those things had come to pass but she'd survived.

Even if she wanted to get married, it was obvious it wouldn't happen with Conall. It was highly unusual for a man to reach the age of forty-two (as Conall had) without having accidentally got married. Even a commitment-dodger as nimble as George Clooney had a failed marriage lurking somewhere in his past.

"What were you doing in the stationery shop?" she asked, with sudden urgency. "Remember one day, I met you —"

"I remember. I was just . . . looking at stuff . . ."

"You mean, you didn't go in to buy something specific? You were just . . . browsing?"

"Browsing?" He tried out the word. "I suppose you could say that. I guess I . . . *like* . . . stationery shops."

Her heartbeat quickened: they had a common interest. "How do you feel about drugstores? Do you ever just browse in them?"

"I *like* them," he said cautiously.

"I love them. They're such a force for good. They can help you sleep better, take away indigestion, tan your skin . . ."

"I agree. But what I really enjoy is a good hardware shop. You?"

"Well, they're useful," she acknowledged with the same caution he had employed. She couldn't abide hardware stores, they were always so cold. But she was prepared to show willing.

"Saturday?" he said, sensing that she'd softened.

What about the people he had sacked? Then again, you only got one life and one shot at happiness . . .

"Do you have any chocolate?" she asked.

He looked surprised. "Yes."

"I mean on you, right now?"

He patted a pocket. "Yes."

"Do you always have chocolate with you?"

"Um . . . yeah."

A man who always had chocolate on him? It would mean the kiss of death for her battle with food. But how could she not be charmed — even a little — by a man who loved what

132

she loved?

"Okay," she said. "Saturday."

He sighed. "Bless you."

It caused consternation among Katie's friends and family. Everyone had an opinion.

Her friend Sinead was ecstatic. "Hope for us all!" Sinead and Katie had soldiered together in the single-girl trenches. "Promise me, Katie, that you'll have sex all the time. Do it for me, for the rest of us deprived singletons."

Her friend MaryRose, however, was more cautious. "Ride rings around yourself, by all means, but don't think that just because you're ancient you can't get up the pole." MaryRose, aged forty and a half, had recently become a first-time — and single — mother. "Let your mantra be: Precautions, precautions, precautions!"

Katie's mum, Penny, said, "I don't know why you're wasting your time with him. If he's forty-two and never been married, he's hardly likely to get married now."

And Katie's sister Naomi had the darkest prediction. "He'll make mincemeat of you."

"He won't," Katie protested. "I'm not going to fall for him."

"So why are you bothering at all?"

"Just killing time until I die."

Day 59

Things Lydia hates (in no particular order):

Buskers
Cyclists
Cabbage
People who say, "I know how you feel," when they don't
Her brother Murdy
People who say "Supper" when they mean "Dinner"
Bus drivers
Student drivers
Van drivers
Cavan accents
Valentine's Day
Her brother Ronnie
The aging process

Please note: this is not a complete list.

Day 59 . . .

Maeve had barely sat down at her desk when Matt rang her. "I've already done today's act of kindness!"

"It's not really about how fast you do it, Matt." But she was smiling.

"It is for me. Do you want to hear?"

"Course."

"I let someone out of a side turning on the way to work."

"Matt! They're always traffic-related!"

"But Maeve, it was hard! I had to hold up a queue of cars behind me! They went mad beeping me! I thought I was going to be lynched."

She had to laugh. He was so cute.

Four and a bit years ago . . .

David and Maeve were in bed reading the *Observer* when, in the middle of an article on aid to Africa, Maeve suddenly thought of something. "Hey, David, wasn't it funny Matt coming to the gig last night?"

"Matt Geary," David said thoughtfully. "A Young Man Going Places." He made it sound like a really shameful thing to be.

"Oh! I think he's really decent," Maeve said. "He's an outstanding boss."

"Yeah?"

"He keeps morale high. He's excellent at giving you confidence."

"So he can get more work out of you."

"He buys the pints on Friday nights, he never forgets a birthday . . ." He was always the first to lead the telling off of a difficult client, and if Maeve had had to sum Matt up in one word it would be *yummy*. Not that she and the rest of the team sat around giggling about Matt's yumminess. They were serious about their jobs; it wouldn't be cool.

And she certainly wasn't going to tell David.

"He's always laughing and joking," David said, contemptuously.

What's wrong with that, Maeve wondered.

"Anyway," David said. "I want to talk to you. Next Friday, you've got Mahmoud's leaving party. But Marta and Holly are going away for the weekend." Marta and Holly were his flatmates. "We've the place to ourselves. So how about you skip the drinks?"

She shook her head. "I can't."

"Yes, you can."

"No, I mean I can't do either thing. I've to go down home for the weekend. I've got my driving test tomorrow week and I can't afford any more lessons and I need some sort of vehicle to practice on."

"Right."

There was a funny pause, then David spoke. "Can I come?" he asked. "Down home with you?"

" 'Course you can." She didn't know why she hadn't thought of it. "It'd be nice." Maybe. "It's just that Mam and Dad are, like, you know, farmers. Country people. Not a smarty, like you. You won't laugh at them?"

"Laugh at them?" He was indignant. "Why would I laugh at them?"

How could she explain? David was so erudite and knew so much about everything, and Mam and Dad . . . well, their world was small and uncomplicated. Cows' udders played a large part in their day-to-day life and they'd probably never heard of Darfur so they wouldn't know what to say if David started going on about it.

"It's about time I met your mum and dad," David said. "I've been thinking . . ."

"Mmmm?"

"Why don't we move in together?" He fixed her with that intense look of his and she was lost for words.

". . . Ah . . . you mean, like, the two of us? Just the two of us?"

It wouldn't be the first time Maeve had lived with someone. Four years ago, when she'd gone to Australia with Harry, her boyfriend at the time, naturally they'd shared a flat. But that had been more for practical reasons than for romantic ones — they'd traveled there together from Galway, they were eking out their funds, they were slightly adrift in a strange new place and they needed each other for emotional back-up. More importantly, it wasn't real life. Their visas were for two years and Maeve knew that when they had to leave Australia, everything would change. The whole business had a limited life span built into it and sure enough, by the end of their time there, she and Harry were well and truly done with each other. Friends still, in a way — if they ever saw each other, which they didn't — but no hint of a romance remaining.

This, what David was suggesting, felt very different. Serious. Almost scary.

"Well?" He was still gazing at her, waiting for her answer, his pupils pinpricks of concentration.

". . . the thing is, I'd have to think about it, David."

"Think about it?" He looked confused, then hurt.

"It's a big thing," she protested.

"Hardly. We've been together for five months."

"It's only four."

"Four and a half."

"David, it just feels a bit . . . fast."

"Fast?"

"Yes. Fast."

He stared at her in silence. "Okay." He waved his hands in defeat. "Take whatever time you need. Let me know when it doesn't feel so . . . *fast.*"

DAY 59 . . .

"Did Slasher turn up?" Danno yelled at Katie as she came into the office.

138

"What?" God, she was barely in the door!

"I said," Danno repeated with elaborate patience. "Did Slasher turn up for your birthday dinner?"

"Yes."

"Really? Shite!"

Across the office, George crowed with delight. "Told you he would! Where's my tenner?"

Katie watched Danno open a strange-textured wallet — he claimed it was made from human skin — and pass a ten-euro note to George.

"You're taking bets?" On whether Conall would turn up or cancel?

"I was sure he wouldn't show," Danno said. He gestured at his screen. He kept a graph of all the times that Conall canceled on Katie. Initially, it had been an average of one in four, then one in three. "Extrapolating from the data that he canceled on you three times in succession, that your relationship was in essence *flatlining,* I calculated that he wouldn't come. Any mathematician would have done the same."

"But I'm an intuitor, I work from my gut," George said. "I feel the three-cancellations-in-a-row was a blip. Also it was your birthday, he couldn't let you down. Finally, because the dinner was to facilitate him, on account of him being away for your actual birthday, he had to be there."

"A fallacy." Danno raised a finger knowingly. "He could have rung the restaurant from Mogadishu or wherever he was slashing jobs, and given them his credit card number. Katie's family and friends could still have had their dinner and expensive wine without him actually having to be there. Everyone else would probably have preferred it, no? Katie?"

"Probably," she admitted.

"Lots of tension?" George asked, striving for sympathy.

"Yes," she said. "He showed up at my flat with champagne."

"Kih!" Danno scoffed. "That's so over! No one drinks champagne. It's all Prosecco, these days."

George gazed at his screen with exaggerated intensity; George *adored* champagne. If he overlapped all of his fantasies, he would spend his days drinking Veuve from a pair of black patent Christian Louboutin platforms that had once been worn by Nicole Kidman.

"Charlie —" Katie said.

"That's her brother," Danno told George.

"I *know.*"

"Charlie wouldn't accept a glass because champagne makes him fart."

George winced at such crassness.

"And Ralph —"

"That's her brother-in-law," Danno told George.

"I *know*."

"— wouldn't have any because only girls drink it."

"Honestly!" George rolled his eyes. "And did your mother ask Conall if he has any intention of marrying you?"

"Not out loud. But you could still hear it."

"And did Conall answer her?"

"Not out loud. But you could still hear it. I'd better do some work," Katie said, going to her desk, but then she seemed to change her mind. "Show me the graph," she said to Danno. "Print it out."

"Why torture yourself?" George said.

"Let her torture herself if she wants! Let her enjoy the few pleasures that are left to her. She's forty in two days' time."

Danno laid his graph before her and Katie looked at the pattern over the last couple of months. She had to admit it was a good graph, very easy to follow.

"See these black areas here," Danno said. "That's where he's let you down. As you can see, he missed MaryRose's baby's christening, your mother's seventieth birthday and the dinner to make up for missing your nine-month anniversary."

"Thank you, Danno," she murmured. "You've set this out very clearly."

"Working backward —" he tapped with his pen — "we're soon into another black area. That would be the night he missed the charity ball followed by the time you tried to surprise him with the Coco de Mer knickers."

That had been a particularly mortifying one, Katie admitted. She had let herself into his house, strewn the place with rose petals, climbed into the ridiculously uncomfortable underwear and waited for Conall to come home. And waited . . . and waited . . . and eventually discovered that he wasn't stuck in traffic but in Schipol airport, waiting for a connection to Singapore. An emergency, apparently.

"What are these gold bits?" George asked.

"Those areas correlate to the times Conall actually did turn up."

Katie studied the graph. There were sizable gold bits, but also sizable black parts. She thought about the mirror, still on the floor, the text that she'd fired off and still hadn't had a response to . . .

"Did Conall give you a birthday gift?" George interrupted her introspection.

She raised her hand in the air, so her sleeve fell to her elbow.

At the sight of the watch, George went pale. "Platinum? Diamonds? Tiffany? Oh *girl*friend. This man is in looooove."

"Not at all," Danno said briskly. "Slasher Hathaway marks his territory by spending money. He might as well have pissed on her. It means nothing."

Day 59 . . .

More things Lydia hates:

Golfers
Socks with holes in the big toe
People who say, "Thanking you."
Her brother Raymond
Mental illness
The smell of other people's urine
People who say, "Thank you kindly."
People who say, "Ta, love."
People who say, "Ta muchly."
People who say, *"Muchas gracias."* (Unless
 they're Spanish, but they never are.)
People who say, "*Merci* bow-coup." (Unless
 they're French, but they never are.)
Customers who ask for receipts
People who say, "Here's the thing."
People whose names are actually surnames
 (e.g., Mr. Buchanan Buchanan)
Schoolchildren, particularly the very young
Red lights
Pedestrian crossings
Her father

Please note: this is not a complete list.

Day 59 . . .

Jemima was on the afternoon shift. "Hello,
Celtic Psychic Line, Mystic Maureen speak-
ing, how may I help? Cards? Very well, dear.
And your name? Laurie. Now what appears

to be the problem?"

Jemima listened. And listened. When the tale of woe eventually ended, Jemima said briskly, "No, dear heart, he's not going to marry you."

"That's on the cards?" Laurie's voice yelped.

Jemima hadn't actually consulted the cards yet. Quickly, she cut the deck. The Knave of Hearts, a young bachelor devoted to enjoyment: that came as no surprise. She cut again. The ten of Swords: grief, sorrow, loss of freedom.

"Dear heart, permit me to be frank: one doesn't need to be psychic to know that this chap of yours is a wastrel and a scoundrel. A scut, if I may be so bold. Kick him to the curb!" She picked another card. The Queen of Diamonds. Oh my! "And don't be surprised if he subsequently makes overtures to your sister."

"But she's seven months pregnant."

"I'm seeing a fair-haired woman given to gossip and wanting in refinement. A spiteful flirt."

"That's my mum! He's hardly going to put the moves on my mum!"

"There are few limits to this young man's perfidy," Jemima said darkly. "Yes, he's a wrong 'un and no mistake."

"But I love him."

"You merely think you do. But there is

144

someone far better on his way to you." She felt there was no harm in saying this. There probably *was* someone on his way to Laurie, but she'd never meet him if she stuck with this ne'er-do-well. She picked another card. The Ace of Cups. "You will be calm and content."

"I don't want to be calm and content. I'm nineteen!"

"Quite right." She picked another card. The Ten of Clubs. "I see travel by sea."

"The Dublin Bay Sea Thrill." Laurie sounded downcast.

Jemima picked the final card. The Ace of Clubs. This was a very good one, even though you were supposed to pretend there was no such thing as "good" or "bad" cards and that it was all a matter of interpretation. "Aha. Pleasant tidings. Money is on its way to you."

"Okay, that's a bit better."

"I wish you well, my dear, and I urge you not to ring again. The cost-per-minute is dreadfully high — I'm afraid I have no influence over what they charge — and the answer isn't going to change. Spend your money on something better. Buy yourself a nice . . ." What did young people wear? ". . . a nice thong and go out . . ." What did young women do? ". . . go out binge-drinking with the money."

"Binge-drinking?"

"Not to the point of incapacity, but have a

few . . . what are those delightful-looking, ruby-hued drinks? Sea-breezes? Yes. Go dancing. Smile. Have fun. Forget this cad. Bye for now."

She hung up. She was supposed to keep them on the line for as long as possible, running up astronomical costs on their credit cards. It was a disgraceful racket, one of the many ways the modern world took advantage of the sad and lonely, and in her own small way Jemima was quite the subversive. Sooner or later the owners of this wretched Celtic Psychic Line would find out what she was up to but, in the meantime, so many people to help, so little time.

As she waited for the next call, and it wouldn't take long — there seemed to be an endless stream of lovelorn young women seeking psychic guidance — she looked around at her dark, crowded living room. It never failed to lift her spirits.

Jemima had lived in her little flat for five years and she adored it. Her now-deceased and much-missed husband, one Giles, had been an architect who had designed an award-winning example of "High Modernism," which was built (due to vocal objections from residents in almost every other part of Ireland) in County Monaghan. "High Modernism" meant glass, lots and lots of glass. Acres of the stuff. Jemima used to have nightmares that she'd been charged with the task of cleaning all the windows in the world and her only tools were a small bottle of Windowlene and an old newspaper. Then she would discover that she was not, in fact, asleep.

In addition to the constant daily round of window-cleaning, Jemima had never felt entirely comfortable in attending to her private needs. For example, if she was rereading *Madame Bovary* and was overtaken by an irresistible basic need — as can happen to all human beings, regardless of their moral rectitude or exalted position in life — such as to scratch her bottom, she was obliged to check first that three or four bored locals didn't have their sights trained on her. That was the main trouble with Pokey: there was absolutely nothing to do, and spying on the oddball Protestant in her ludicrous glass cube was accepted as a hobby by local employers on job applications, along with compulsive gambling and suicide ideation.

When Giles shuffled off his mortal coil, Jemima felt his loss with shocking impact but she wasted no time putting the Glass House on the market. To the almost-orgasmic pleasure of the agent, she said she was prepared to throw in all the lightweight titanium furniture, which had been specifically designed for the house. They were welcome to it, she thought. She was off to Dublin, armed with great plans to trawl auction rooms, seeking dark, heavy stuff, furniture of substance.

She'd had enough of Pokey. There weren't enough needy people to give her do-goodery tendencies their full rein. Also, if she were to be perfectly honest, she was sick to her craw of green fields. Yes, it was buzzy Dublin for her, as close to the city center as she could afford. She wanted to feel life going on all around her. Luckily, Dublin house prices having been what they were five years ago, her needs were modest. Two bedrooms, so that Fionn could stay whenever he wanted, but otherwise a small little place was perfect for her needs. She wanted minimal housework, no window cleaning and — most liberating of all — no wretched garden with its need for perpetual upkeep!

The move was not without its upheaval. Fionn was the issue. She would miss him terribly and, of course, he would miss her. But she wouldn't be alive for ever. Time to cut the apron strings.

DAY 59 . . .

Lydia was having a right old Irkutsky day of it. The city was riddled with summer tourists and a busker — a bloody busker, no less, some madman with an accordion — had attracted such a large crowd in Westmoreland Street that people had spilled into the street, *dancing,* causing her to swerve and almost

148

collide with a cyclist, who shrieked red-faced, moral-high-ground, no-carbon-emissions abuse at her. She hated buskers with their passive-aggressive pretense at providing a service. Even when they were atrocious you felt obliged to give them a couple of bob because they were making the effort. People who simply sat on the pavement begging for money, *that* she could deal with. It was a much more honest transaction because you knew what you were getting, which was precisely nothing.

And she hated cyclists — another sanctimonious bunch with their namby-pamby whining about doing their best for the environment so it was okay for them to navigate the roads like lunatics and it was up to taxi drivers, decent people such as herself, to be responsible for their safety. If she ruled the world, cyclists would be shot on sight.

Then she unwrapped her breakfast bagel to discover that the boy in the sandwich shop had, on his own, added chopped cabbage to her cream cheese. Even if she didn't abhor cabbage — which surely all non-madzers did — in what universe did he think that cream cheese and cabbage would go together?

Overwhelmed by the bagel atrocity, she began thinking about other atrocities until she had to pull into a parking space and ring her brother Murdy, who murmured, "I know how you feel," when clearly he didn't because, if he did, he'd do something.

"Come down at the weekend," he said. "We'll discuss it over supper. I've got to go now."

Tears of Murmansky frustration interfering with her vision, she pulled back out into the traffic and, in quick succession, almost drove into a bus, almost rear-ended a scaredy-cat student driver and almost took the side off a white van, the driver of which treated her to a stream of abuse in a strong Cavan accent. Abuse she could take, abuse she was used to, but abuse in a Cavan accent, now that was pushing it. Taxi drivers, she thought grimly, are the scapegoats of the driving world. We are everybody's whipping boy.

All the same, perhaps she should wait until she was a little bit calmer before continuing her day's work. As soon as she found another vacant spot, she parked and rang her brother Ronnie, then wished she hadn't. Novosibirsk!

DAY 59 . . .

Brutal and all as Danno's assessment was of Katie's relationship with Conall, Katie had to admit that he had a point. This is all my own fault, she acknowledged. Right from the very first time she'd gone out with Conall, the warning signs were there. After that shambles, she thought darkly, she should have killed the whole thing there and then.

It had been such a big deal, the first date. Conall had actually presented her with a travel folder. "Tomorrow a car will pick you up from home at twelve. You're flying to Heathrow at two."

"And then what?"

"Everything will unfold on a need-to-know."

"We couldn't do something small and normal, like going a round the corner for something to eat?"

He'd laughed; he'd thought she was joking.

"What am I meant to wear for this magical mystery tour? Because if it's sturdy boots and a hat with earflaps, I'm not coming."

He laughed again. He was still finding her every utterance absolutely enchanting. "A dress. Formalish."

A little desperately, she said, "I need more information than that."

"Really, you'll look great no matter what you wear."

"I'm serious. If you don't tell me more, I can't come."

"Oh . . . okay . . . A black dress. High heels. A small pointless bag."

She hurried home and emptied her wardrobe onto her bed. A black dress was no problem; she had dozens, almost impossible for anyone other than her to tell apart. And at least he hadn't told her to be fashion-forward (although would a straight man even know such a term?). She'd never done cutting-edge with conviction, not even when she'd been the right age (sixteen to twenty-two). Something to do with the size of her chest meant she looked uproariously funny in trend items: if she wore sparkly hairbands, for example, she looked like a simpleton daughter who was still living with her parents at the age of forty-nine.

With her wardrobe laid bare before her, she was alarmed by the amount of well-cut, classic stuff it featured. She was like a bloody French woman! Curses! She didn't want to be a French woman. She didn't *think* like a French woman. She'd rather be one of the those early-nineties Slaves of New York types with red and black striped tights, eighteen-hole Doc Martens and denim shorts, but you had to be skinny, skinny, skinny for that look.

Thank God for shoes and bags. Even if she had to play it safe with the basics, her shoes and bags were defiantly hip. And at least she could wear jeans again. At the height of things with Jason, when all they did was nestle in domestic bliss and eat apple tarts, she was far too lardy for jeans. Then it had ended and it was awful, but on the up side she'd lost three stone.

For the mystery date with Conall, she finally decided on a severely tailored (black, of course) dress, cut with hip-narrowing, stomach-flattening deftness. For the flight she covered it with a roomy jacket and a certain amount of resentment: it was embarrassing having to get on a plane — alone — in a sexy dress and sexy shoes in the middle of the day. People might think she was a delusional type, like those mad old duchesses who went to the dry-cleaners in their tiara and dressing gown.

When she exited the plane at Heathrow, a man was waiting with a whiteboard featuring her name. He took her away down some secret steps and her back was aflame with the accusing, jealous stares of all the others who'd been on the flight. "Where does she think she's going?" she heard someone say. "Snotty bitch."

The man put her into a big fat car and drove her a short distance to — what was this? — a helicopter. "What's going on?" she asked.

"You get on the helicopter."

"But where am I going?"

"I don't know. You could try asking the pilot, I suppose."

But the pilot was too caught up in making sure she put on her headphones and a safety harness.

"Where are we going?" she asked.

"Pull that a bit tighter."

"It's tight. Where are we going?"

"Glyndebourne."

And Katie was thinking, *Glyndebourne?*

What did she know about Glyndebourne? Opera, that's what she knew. But perhaps other things besides opera happened at Glyndebourne. Because she detested opera and Conall knew she detested opera, so he was hardly going to bring her on a date to something she detested.

When the chopper came in to land Conall was standing waiting, wearing a dark suit and looking like a handsome undertaker.

With her hand on her head, she ran across the asphalt and said, "What on earth —"

He smiled, appearing very happy, and said, "Just one favor. Don't ask questions yet. Trust me. You look beautiful, by the way."

Trust him. But they were at the opera place. Everyone was dressed up and walking around the beautiful gardens holding programs and talking about — yes! — opera. Conall ferried her off to a secluded little arbor, where they drank champagne and he refused to answer questions. Then he said, "Time to go." Everyone else was moving in the same direction and he led her into an auditorium and she was thinking: This *can't* be opera because I told him how much I hate it. She gave him a searching look and he stared into her eyes and repeated, "Trust me," and even though she was extremely unsure, she said, "Ooooookay." The lights dimmed, the curtain went up and the next thing was there was a load of fat people on the stage, singing their

154

fat pompous heads off. Yes, *opera*. She was so stunned, she didn't know what to think. She decided that she was very angry. Then she changed her mind and decided that she was very sad: why did nobody ever listen to her? For a thrilling instant she considered standing up and pushing her way to the exit, but she envisioned a sniper with night-vision goggles killing her with one shot to the head. Interruptions were frowned upon at the opera; you couldn't even cough.

After an epoch of screeching elapsed, an interval finally came.

"Well?" Conall said, as the lights went on.

"Are you having a laugh?" Katie asked, getting to her feet.

"What?" He looked stunned.

"An expensive, elaborate laugh?"

"What?" He hurried behind her, trying to keep up.

She turned to face him, as people streamed past them. "It's opera. Yes? I told you I couldn't abide opera. Didn't I?"

"But why don't you like it?"

Enraged, she spluttered, "I just don't. For one reason, not that I have to give you any, the men singers always sound like they're constipated."

"I thought if you heard good stuff you'd change your mind."

This, his apology, actually incensed her further. "What? You thought that I was so . . .

uncultured that I couldn't have an informed opinion?"

"No, I —"

"You didn't listen to me."

He looked pale and chastened. "I was wrong. I'm sorry. Because I love it, I wanted to share it with you. I wanted to surprise you."

"Oh you surprised me all right." Even though she worked in the music business and was exposed on a daily basis to gigantic egos, she'd never before met such a selfish, self-willed megalomaniac. "I couldn't have made myself clearer."

"I'm so sorry."

"I actually think —" she furrowed her brow and shook her head — "I actually think you're slightly insane. And I want to go home now."

"I'll ring the chopper."

But the chopper was two hours away.

"What do you want to do while you're waiting?" Conall asked.

"Sit in the bar, drink a bottle of red wine and send texts to my sister and my friend, telling them what a mad bastard you are."

He swallowed. "Would you like me to keep you company?"

"No."

DAY 59 . . .

Things Lydia loves (in no particular order):

Chips
City names ending in "sk" (e.g., Gdansk
 and Murmansk)
Her mum
Gilbert. Possibly.

Please note: this *is* a complete list.

Lydia's day hadn't got any better. Each fare was more annoying than the previous. In quick succession she'd had a "Thanking you," a "Thank you kindly," a "Ta, love," a *"Muchas gracias"* and a *"Merci* bow-coup" — all five of them receipt-seekers! Was there no end to her trials! But these pains-in-the-arse were as nothing compared to Buchanan, the American tourist who explained the U.S. electoral system to her, beginning each sentence with "Here's the thing." She'd tried to shut him up by asking her fail-safe "Christ Jesus" question (she'd noticed it scared people lots more when it was "Christ Jesus" rather than "Jesus Christ"), but he actually already *had* accepted Christ Jesus as his lord and savior and was happy to have a good chinwag about it. Hoist with her own Christ Jesus petard!

The traffic was appalling. She was caught by red lights, roadworks, pedestrian crossings and, worst of all, crossing guards. When she finally knocked it on the head for the day, she hoped the lads wouldn't be at home.

But the lads were at home. Jan too had had a bad day. A woman in Enniskerry had got tarragon vinegar when she had ordered white wine vinegar, while a woman in Terenure, whose entire life was dependent on the tarragon vinegar, had received the white wine vinegar. It was a disaster and it was all Jan's fault.

Jan was sorrowfully recounting the scolding he'd received when Lydia came in, cranky and exhausted. She saw them sitting in the living room and stopped dead.

"Love of God!" she declared. "A more miserable-looking pair I've never seen. What's up?"

"We are glum," Jan said, almost happily. What a useful word this *glum* was. Glum, glum, glum.

"Why?"

"I mix up order. I give wrong vinegars to womans. My boss, she go apeshit. I get bollocked."

Lydia looked at him in surprise. "My God, Jan, your English is really coming along."

"Thenks." He smiled with shy pride.

"So Andrei, why are *you* so glum?"

Andrei didn't tell her the truth, which was: I am glum because I have to live with you.

He shrugged. "I did not come to this

country to be happy. I came to earn money for my family. I do not expect to be happy."

"That's no way to live." Mind you, she was a fine one to talk. She'd left the beautiful flat she'd shared with Sissy for this poky hole. She was working seventy hours a week but was too afraid to buy new summer clothes — last week's splurge in Primark of a mingy seven euro on a three-pack of undershirts had made her feel so shitty she'd nearly taken them back.

"I am strong," Andrei said. "I will endure."

"Yeah, me too." She sighed extravagantly. Then, without warning, the itch was upon her: she had to go on the net. She had to check again. Maybe this time it would be different. She pulled the stool up to the little plastic desk wedged into the corner by the window and started bumping and battering the mouse.

Behind her Andrei asked, "You goingk out tonight?"

She clattered the keys and glared at the screen. *Come on, come on. What's taking you so long?*

"Lydia? Goingk out tonight?"

". . . You'll be happy to hear I am."

The boys were indeed happy. They had plans to plonk themselves in front of *The Apprentice* and take detailed notes. One day they too would be like Donald Trump. Without

159

the dodgy hair.

"You goingk out with Poor Fucker?"

When Lydia had first moved in and mentioned she had a boyfriend, Andrei hadn't been able to hide his disbelief. "You have boyfriend?"

"Of course I've a boyfriend!" The nerve of him.

Andrei thought his heart would burst, so great was his pity for this unknown man. There was no Polish phrase that adequately expressed the extent of his misfortune so Andrei was obliged to utilize English. "Poor Fucker."

"Yes, I'm going out with Poor Fucker. And don't call him that. His name is Gilbert."

Day 59 . . .

So! Gilbert! What kind of man was he? Surely he'd have to be someone fairly special to handle Lydia. (And was he the mystery person she cleaned for? The reason she refused to wash the pots in her own flat?)

Gilbert was to be found in a small, dark pub, almost an illicit bar, in a side street on the north side of the city, gathered around a table with four other men, going at it hot and heavy in Yoruba. Originally a native of Lagos, Nigeria, he had made Dublin his home for the past six years.

When Lydia came through the door, the

argument among the men was so angry and intent that they didn't see her. Lydia didn't speak Yoruba — apart from the few vulgar phrases Gilbert had taught her for wheeling out at Nigerian parties, to make people laugh in delight — but it sounded as though they were planning a coup.

"Forest Floor," she heard. Then, "Strawberry Delight." Hmmm.

Suddenly, they noticed Lydia and the conversation ceased abruptly and the four men melted away, leaving only Gilbert sitting at the table.

"Baby," he said. His voice was like Valrhona. He reached out to her with his long fingers (he had beautiful, elegant hands, the hands of a musician) (which he wasn't). He was, like Lydia, a taxi driver, which was how they'd met — at some café frequented only by taxi drivers and only in the middle of the night. It was a safe haven from the public where drivers could have a cup of tea and rant about the obnoxious behavior of their customers.

On the night in question Lydia slowly ate her rasher sandwich and checked out Gilbert's tightly cut hair, his beautifully shaped head, his long, long eyelashes and thought, yes, in*deed*. She knew she wasn't to every man's taste — something to do with her caustic tongue scared loads of them away, the spineless saps — but she reckoned Gilbert was man enough for her.

I, unlike lesser beings, am not swayed by appearance but by vibrations, and Gilbert's spiky life force alerts me to his tendency to secret-keeping. He's a little too fond of compartmentalizing his life, keeping certain areas of it from colliding with others. I don't entirely trust him, but I cannot help but like him.

A man evidently partial to fancy clothing, Gilbert. Tonight he sported a pair of midnight-blue boots that were — if one were to speak frankly — a little girly. More worrying still was his jacket. There was something *very odd* about the waist region: nipped-in, almost like a corset.

Lydia seemed like the kind of person who would make extravagant fun of those who took their look too seriously, but she snuggled into Gilbert like a cat and no mockery ensued.

"Hi, guys," she called to the four men who had got up at her arrival. She knew them well; they were all taxi drivers. "What's going on? What were you shouting about?"

They began to edge into her orbit, drawn back toward the seats they'd recently vacated.

"Be gone," Gilbert said.

"No, let them sit down. I want to know what's happening."

The four men resumed their seats.

"Well?" Lydia asked. "What was all the shouting about?"

Eventually, Abiola spoke. "It's Odenigbo." At this, Odenigbo exploded into heated Yoruba, then so did everyone else.

Lydia picked up the occasional English word — lemon meringue, rainstorm — and she held up a hand, silencing the men. Irritably, she said, "Little trees? Again? I'm sick of this conversation."

Unlike Lydia, who owned her own car, the Nigerians shared three taxis between seven drivers. One man's choice of little tree air freshener had consequences for everyone.

"I *like* Strawberry Delight," Odenigbo said, with a defiance that suggested he was alone.

A splutter of disagreement greeted his words. "Strawberry Delight is detestable," Gilbert said.

"Worse than the smell of smelliness," Modupe said.

"Worse than the smell of the passengers!"

"We've been through this a million times!" Lydia said. "Forest Floor is fine, so is Spice Market, the rest are gank! End of. Now, who wants to buy me a drink?"

It quickly became clear that Gilbert treated Lydia like a queen. After he'd bought her two drinks in the bar, he ferried her off to his home, a big, old, ramshackle house that he shared with six others. In a kitchen that

163

pulsed with music, he cooked dinner for her
— a humble pizza. Not due to his limitations
as a cook but out of respect for her cautious
Irish palate. Wafting in the air were the
hangovers of previous experiments in which
he had served up Nigerian delights for her
delectation: spicy oysters, goat soup, jollof
rice. They had not been a success. The words
rank and *gank* still lingered. It seemed that
Lydia's taste for the exotic was only in men.

She ate her pizza with silent concentration.
Gilbert tried to engage her in conversation
but she cut him off with a curt, "Shush." She
brooked no distractions while she was eating.
When she'd consumed all six triangles and
licked pizza grease off her fingers, she shoved
her empty plate across the table at Gilbert
and he then clattered it into the sink.

"Thanks," she remembered to say.

In accordance with house rules, Gilbert
made a desultory effort to clean up, using a
sopping cloth to wipe the table surface in
sweeping, lackluster arches, leaving visible
semicircles of droplets behind, then he
dashed the plates under a lukewarm running
tap.

Lydia sat and watched him. She didn't lift
a finger. Whoever it was that she — oh so
resentfully — housekept for, it was obviously
not Gilbert.

"Right," she said, getting to her feet as soon
as the plates had been deposited on the drain-

ing board. "Let's go."

They went to a party in a cavernous club, with very loud music and very little light. The other revelers were almost all Nigerians, many of whom interrupted Gilbert's and Lydia's kissing in order to respectfully fist-bump Gilbert. When Lydia tired of the incessant shoulder-tapping and of shouting above the music, "What am I? Invisible?" she insisted that they leave and they made their way back home to his bed.

There was a strong connection between them and they were well-attuned physically but — mark me here — their hearts did NOT beat as one. However, that didn't mean that they wouldn't at some stage. There were no obvious impediments . . . except for the large sums Gilbert shelled out on his fancy duds.

Not that Lydia seemed concerned. She lay on his bed, watching as he lovingly secreted his corset-like jacket inside a dust-cover. "You're a dandy," she said.

He liked this. "Say it again."

"Gilbert Okuma, you're a dandy."

"Dandy." He laughed, his teeth very white in his dark face. "Do you know any other words?"

She loved his accent, the deliberate drawl and the tiny little pause between each word.

"A peacock," she suggested. "A fashion

victim? A fop? A banty-cock? A gadfly?"
Indeed, the local youths, Dublin natives, were
happy to supply another description. *Spanner.* As in, "Look at that spanner! Look at the
shoes on him! And the coat!"

But Gilbert was unconcerned. Those boys
were uneducated peasants, hobbledehoys
who knew no better.

Gilbert, an interesting man, lived for the moment.
For the moment . . .
But all that might be about to change.

DAY 59 . . .

Matt and Maeve enjoyed a leisurely evening
during which they ate a large, meat-based
dinner followed by a variety of confectionery,
all the while entwined tightly on the couch,
watching home makeover shows. It was an
uplifting demonstration of two people very
much in love — and yet now and again there
was that faint whiff of a third party, the presence of some man curling his way, like
cigarette smoke, through the flat.

At 11 p.m., Matt and Maeve retired to their
bedroom and I was keen to see what would
happen this time. Just like the first night, they
got undressed *and then got dressed again,* as
if they were about to go jogging. But instead
they got into bed. They read for a while then

Maeve opened a bedside drawer and I braced myself for furry handcuffs, blindfolds and other sexy folderols. But instead of sex toys, Maeve produced two notebooks, one with a glossy photograph of a red Lamborghini on the cover, the other bearing a reproduction of a Chagall painting, a man holding hands with a woman who was flying over his head like a balloon.

With a certain amount of gloom, Matt accepted the Lamborghini notebook and a pen. At the top of a blank page, he wrote TODAY'S TRIO OF BLESSINGS. Then he seemed to run out of inspiration. He gazed at the empty page and sucked the top of his pen like he was sitting an exam and knew none of the answers.

He needed to locate three good things that had happened today. But nothing was coming. God, he hated this, so he did.

With a gold-colored pen, Maeve wrote, "I saw a green balloon by a green traffic light."

On the next line she put, "A little girl smiled at me for no reason."

And her third blessing? "Matt," she wrote, and shut the notebook, feeling peaceful and satisfied.

Matt was still sucking his pen; he hadn't produced a single word. Then! Struck by sudden inspiration, he scribbled:

A mysterious lump of ice didn't fall on my car.

A mysterious lump of ice didn't fall on my flat.

A mysterious lump of ice didn't fall on my

. . . on my . . .

Stumped, he looked around the room. What else was he glad that a mysterious lump of ice hadn't fallen on? What did he value? Well, Maeve, obviously. He picked up his pen again.

A mysterious lump of ice didn't fall on my car.

A mysterious lump of ice didn't fall on my flat.

A mysterious lump of ice didn't fall on my wife.

There! He scored a thick happy line across the page and, very pleased with himself, tossed the notebook back to Maeve. That was a good list. Sometimes Maeve inspected his list of blessings just to make sure he was doing it right, but he was entirely confident with what he'd written today.

DAY 58

Fionn didn't like Dublin. Even though he'd lived there until the age of twelve and it could be called home, there were too many unhappy memories. He waited until everyone else had climbed off the bus — the Monaghan Meteorite — before he stood up and descended into the chaos of the bus station.

He needed to find a taxi. Excellent Little Productions was expecting him for a meeting and he hadn't a clue how to get there. Searching for signs for the taxi stand, he jostled through clusters of people and for a shockingly vulnerable moment he thought he'd have to fight his way back on to the Meteorite and insist on being taken home to Pokey.

Only the thought of how disappointed Jemima would be kept him moving forward.

He straightened his back, squared his already square jaw, threw his bag over his shoulder and sauntered toward the taxi rank. He was twenty minutes late and counting.

Three miles away, in a converted mews house, Grainne Butcher paced in the double-height, light-flooded greeting area, watching for the taxi. Mobile in hand, she hit redial for the seventh time and once again got Fionn's voicemail.

"Who turns off their mobile?" she asked, incredulous. She turned to stare at Alina, who was cowering behind the curved blond-wood reception desk.

"Don't know," Alina mumbled. As the lowest of the low, she ultimately got all the flak. There were several chronically angry people in the company, from Mervyn Fossil, the owner and producer of the company, and Grainne, the director (who also happened to be Mervyn's wife), to the stylist, and a neat chain of blame operated in which Mervyn dumped on Grainne, who dumped on the editor, who dumped on the senior researcher, who dumped on the junior researcher, who dumped on the runner, who dumped on Alina. The only person who wasn't part of the chain of rage was the stylist and that was because she was freelance.

"And he hasn't rung?" Grainne Butcher asked again.

"I would have told you if he had."

"Don't be glib! Just yes or no answers."

"No," Alina whispered. "No, he hasn't rung."

Mervyn Fossil hurtled into the hallway.

"Where? The hell? *Is he?*"

"Coming," Grainne muttered. "Go on, go away, keep making calls, I'll tell you when he's here."

Mervyn, a short fake-tanned tyrant, stared at Grainne, his mouth curled into a sneer.

"Go *on,*" she said.

With a silent but deadly glare, he returned to his office. As soon as his door shut, Grainne started pacing again.

"Here he is! Thanks be to Christ!" A taxi had drawn up outside. Grainne strode out, thrust a tenner at the driver — "Keep the change!" — then hoicked Fionn from the car. She clicked open the boot and stared at the emptiness. "Where's your stuff?"

Fionn indicated the one medium-sized bag on his shoulder.

"That's all you have? For a whole month?"

"What do I need?"

Then Grainne remembered why she'd fallen under his spell in the first place.

Who would have thought that in the miserable shit-hole that was Pokey she'd have stumbled across the likes of Fionn? She didn't even know why she'd decided to go for Carmine junior's christening: she hated her brother, she hated his wife, she hated the very air of Pokey.

She'd been sitting at her sister-in-law's kitchen table, fighting for breath and counting down the minutes to her departure, when Fionn had shown up to do Loretta's garden. Grainne took one look at the hair, the jaw, the big spade-like hands, and got that tingly feeling — so rare and so cherished.

"What planet has he come from?" she asked Loretta.

"He's local."

"Since when?"

"Years and years."

"I don't remember meeting him when I lived here." If she had perhaps she wouldn't have been so quick to leave.

"You might have. Moved here with his mother when he was about twelve. She couldn't cope, poor woman. He ran a bit wild, teenage tear-away and all that, till he was taken in by the Churchills. Adopted. No, fostered."

"Who? Oh, the posh old pair in the big glass house in the valley."

"Yes, Giles passed on a few years back and the wife, Jemima, moved to Dublin."

Out of nowhere, Grainne was flooded with a memory of a beautiful, confused woman being unable to pay for her basket of food in the supermarket. Angeline, Fionn's mother. "God, yes, I remember the mother!" Then she remembered Fionn. His time in Pokey had overlapped with Grainne's for perhaps only a year before Grainne, aged seventeen, skipped for Dublin. Even then, at whatever age Fionn was — twelve or thirteen, probably — he'd been possessed of beauty but he'd been far too young and too wild for Grainne.

Who could have guessed he'd turn out like this?

Watched by Loretta, who was aghast at her brazenness, Grainne marched right into the garden shed and said to Fionn, "Any chance of a quick gardening lesson?"

He paused in the act of hoisting up a bag of soil. "And you are?"

"Grainne, Carmine's sister."

"And you want a gardening lesson?"

"That's right."

He didn't seem terribly surprised — probably used to women throwing themselves at him, she decided.

"I haven't time for lessons but you can come round with me," he said. "You can watch what I'm doing."

Easy-going, she thought. *Good.* She followed him out into the garden where a row of potted plants waited beside a patch of raw earth.

He crouched down and tenderly removed one from its pot. His hands! "You want to help me bed in these lilies?"

"Okay."

"On your knees," he added, slowing down his delivery. Deeply surprised, she narrowed her eyes, trying to gauge if he'd meant to sound suggestive. She had already written him off as physically devastating but dumb as a post, on the basis that God gave only a certain amount of good fortune to any one person. But was she wrong? "Not much you can do standing up there," he added, in a voice that was now entirely innocent.

The things she did for her job, she thought, reluctantly falling to her knees in a patch of moist soil and letting him put the plant into her cupped hands.

"Scoop out a hole," he said, once again sounding like he was talking about sex; she wasn't imagining it, she was certain of it. Almost certain . . .

"Are there gloves?" She didn't want pieces of nature stuck under her nails.

"No gloves," he said. "Get your hands right in. Don't be afraid of getting dirty."

This time there was no mistaking the saucy overtones. She looked at him and they maintained a long, steady gaze, reading the smirks in each other's eyes.

He was mocking himself. Mocking the persona that Loretta and the other Pokey housewives fancied, the persona that he knew Grainne could see through. She liked him all the better for it. Even though her admiration was purely professional, she was glad he wasn't stupid. At least he'd be able to remember his lines.

"So you love being a gardener, do you?"

she asked. He didn't know it but he was being interviewed for a job.

"Love it!"

"Seriously," she said. She got it that she'd underestimated him. They were both agreed on that. But now they really did need a significant talk.

"Seriously? You want me to be serious? Okay." He sighed. He could be serious too. He could be anything any woman wanted. For a short time, at least. "I couldn't imagine doing anything else."

"Why?"

"Flowers, plants . . . they're like miracles. You put a gnarly little bulb in the ground. All around it everything dies, then lo and behold, two or three or five months later, Lazarus flowers start poking up through the soil. Back from the dead."

"Go on . . ." The way his face lit up! She could just see how the camera would catch it. Televisual gold!

"And it's not just about making the world beautiful; you could grow your own food."

"*I* couldn't. My garden's the size of a matchbox."

"You don't need much land. This here," Fionn swept his hand around Carmine and Loretta's quarter acre, "this could be your personal garden of Eden."

Grainne almost doubled over with the painful perfection of it all: Your Personal Eden!

That's what they'd call the show! Or perhaps Your Secret Garden, which had delicious sexual overtones, so handy with Fionn being astonishingly handsome. Her head began firing with ideas and when she took them back to Excellent Little Productions they argued the toss for a long time: Your Private Eden? Your Secret Garden? Garden of Eden? Days were spent searching for the best title, but they weren't wasted days because, in television, once you had the name right, the rest was easy.

"Let's get going," Mervyn Fossil said, hooshing people toward the meeting room. "We've wasted enough time waiting on . . ." He caught a warning look from Grainne: don't openly insult the talent. Reluctantly, he swallowed back the words *this fool.* "Come on," he said instead. "Let's get to work."

But Fionn stayed where he was, put his hand into his jacket pocket and drew out a sprig of something. "What's this? Badly squashed but it looks like . . . valerian?" He proffered it to Mervyn Fossil. "Does it look like valerian to you?"

Mervyn Fossil recoiled. "I wouldn't know valerian if it jumped up and bit me on the bollocks."

Fionn looked slightly puzzled — clearly, he hadn't had much exposure to people as unpleasant as Mervyn Fossil. But it didn't seem to rattle him. Taking his own sweet time, he reached into another pocket and produced a little book, dog-eared and very soiled. It was a herb encyclopedia, which contained both illustrations and descriptions. Leisurely, he flicked through the flimsy pages until he found valerian and compared it with the sprig in his hand. "Yip, just like I thought, valerian. Brings soothing, calming, hope, freedom from grief . . ." He passed a speculative gaze along Grainne, Mervyn, the stylist and the others, but didn't find whatever he was looking for. Then he twirled on his heel to face the desk behind him, where Alina was sitting, utterly agog.

"You," he said. "What's your name?"

"Alina."

"Alina, you might need this."

After a startled silence, she accepted the sprig of valerian, then fat dramatic tears began to flow down her face.

"What?" Mervyn snapped.

"My cat died yesterday."

"Oh dear," Grainne — a cat person — murmured.

Her wet face radiant with gratitude, Alina asked Fionn, "How did you know?"

"I didn't," he said modestly.

"But you did."

Mervyn Fossil narrowed his eyes suspiciously at Fionn and said, "What's your game, son?"

"Shut up," Grainne said sharply, so he did.

DAY 58 . . .

Cycling to work, Maeve came within inches of having her back wheel clipped by a car, but the car swerved just in time and she was grand. It made her think of some line she vaguely remembered from *The Great Gatsby* about it being okay to be a reckless driver because everyone else would be careful. Not that she was actually driving, of course. Because she couldn't drive.

No, four years ago she'd failed her driving test, and she often wondered whether, if she had passed it instead, things would have turned out the way they did.

Four years ago . . .
"Well?" At least ten expectant people were waiting at Maeve's desk and she sensed a celebratory card, a cake, maybe even a bottle of something fizzy. All she had to do was say the magic word and they'd be whipped out from their hiding places.

Maeve dipped her chin. "I failed."

"Ohhhh!"

No one had expected that, not really. Of course, everyone had horror stories about driving tests, about all the unexpected things that could happen to even the best-prepared person, but in her soft, easy-going way,

Maeve was quite the achiever.

Quickly, David rallied. "Everyone fails the first time," he said. "It's a rite of passage. We'd have thought you were a weirdo if you'd passed."

"Absolutely!"

"We got you a cake," David said and Roja produced it from behind her back. The cake was iced with a big loopy "Congratulations."

"Obviously, that's 'Congratulations on not passing,' " David said. "Renzo, will you cut it into slices?"

"We also got you a bottle of fizz," Tarik said.

Humbled, Maeve shook her head. "I work with the nicest people in the world."

But she shared a little smile with David to tell him that she knew he'd been the force behind all this love.

"Drink it now or wait until finishing work?" David asked.

"Sure, what the hell, let's have it now!"

The cork was eased off and plastic cups were passed around. "To failure!"

Fatima, distributing slices of chocolate cake on napkins, asked, "Do you want to talk about it?"

"Sure, okay." Maeve was feeling better now. The first sting of humiliation had passed. "Well, the most important piece of advice I can give anyone hoping to pass their driving test is, do not do your practice on your dad's tractor! It was no preparation for the real

179

thing. I felt so low on the road, it was all wrong!"

She didn't need to explain how expensive driving lessons were, everyone knew.

"But you know what's really at me? My dad has a car."

"So why didn't he let you practice in it?" Franz asked. "Did he think you'd crash it?"

"No," Maeve said gloomily. "The opposite. He says that anyone can drive a car but it takes real skill to drive a tractor. He thinks I'm brilliant, he thinks I can do anything. It's a scourge."

"He's not going to be happy when he hears." David had seen, firsthand, how her parents doted on her.

"He already knows," Maeve said. "And he's in flitters. A miscarriage of justice, he's calling it. He wants to know the name of the examiner so he can make an official complaint."

Into the laughter, interrupting Maeve as she was saying, "At least I can plow a field, no problem, beautiful straight furrows —" came Matt's voice.

"I just heard!" he said. "I was in a meeting and I just heard!"

He moved with purpose toward Maeve and a clear path leading directly to her opened up as, instinctively, people moved out of the way.

"Driving test bastards! Two-bit tyrants." Matt took Maeve into his arms, in a comforting embrace, laying her head on the shoulder of his dark suit. Everyone was touched by his humanity. It was one thing for them, Maeve's peers, to care about her, but Matt, for all his accessibility, was her boss. And the embrace was no mealy-mouthed, in-and-out quickie either; it went on for longer than the obligatory half a second. Matt was clearly sincere in his sorrow for Maeve's humiliation. How kind he was, everyone thought. What a great guy he was. Several people were smiling, their eyes suspiciously bright. Then came the first prickles of alarm. The embrace should have broken up by now. It had lasted a second longer than was acceptable. It was time for it to stop. *End it. End it now!* But Matt and Maeve remained locked in each other's arms. To widespread confusion, Matt actually tightened his hold and Maeve pushed her face further into Matt's neck.

Break away now and no harm will have been done. Smiles were freezing and falling from the watchers' faces. They stood like statues around the two-becomes-one figure and exchanged fearful, questioning looks — although no one looked directly at David.

Emotion radiated like heat from Matt and Maeve, moving beyond the immediate circle and out into the furthest parts of the office, where it reached Natalie. *Something is wrong.* She got to her feet and made her way to the cluster around Maeve's desk.

Finally, to the giddy relief of the audience, there was movement. Maeve lifted her head. *Step away from each other,* the collective thoughts urged. *Matt, go back to your office. Maeve, sit down at your desk. And we'll all do our best to pretend this really freaky thing never happened.*

But, for the aghast witnesses, things only got worse. Matt also lifted his head, and the moment when his eyes met Maeve's, a jolt of energy passed between them with a crackle that was almost audible. With faces stunned with wonder, they gazed at each other, exchanging souls. Maeve lifted a hand to touch Matt's face, as if checking that it was real, that whatever was going on was actually taking place. Everyone around them knew that it was unseemly, being present at this moment of extreme intimacy, but no one could tear their eyes away.

It wasn't how Matt had planned to tell Nat that he no longer loved her, but she got the message anyway. Dignified as ever, she departed the compelling scene, left the office, drove into town, sat in her car in a parking garage and sobbed. Then she bought a new shower gel, got six inches cut off her hair, ate eleven macaroons, quite large ones, and felt ready to move on.

David's white face was the first thing Maeve

saw when she emerged. It was the face of someone she'd known a long, long time ago. In the course of forty-seven seconds, her whole world had shifted.

She needed to produce words to shift it back but none would come. Beseechingly, she looked at David.

What happened? his eyes asked.

I don't know.

I love you.

I know.

And I thought you loved me.

I thought I did too.

You've humiliated me.

I didn't know this was going to happen . . .

Around them, everyone except Matt had melted away.

"David, I —" But Maeve could think of nothing to say. David was watching her, waiting for her to fix things. "I'm sorry," she whispered. She couldn't bear the look in his eyes, the shock, the grief, the anger. "I'm really, really sorry."

"You're not good enough to lick her boots," David said to Matt, his voice trembling. "You're nothing but . . . but a *suit*." He turned his fiery-eyed gaze to Maeve. "As for you, I don't know what you're doing and I don't think you do either. This isn't over yet and don't for one minute think that it is."

DAY 58 . . .

Katie had had a challenging day, trying to drum up media interest in a little-known, singer-songwriter "next big thing." She'd finally got home and was half asleep on the couch, watching *The Gilmore Girls,* wondering if she should just get up and actually go to bed, when her landline rang. Suspiciously, she checked the number. Almost no one rang on the landline any more. Except her mum. And sure enough, that's who it was. She thought about not answering but past experience told her that the calls would just keep coming until she eventually buckled.

"Mum?"

"How did you . . . ? I wish you wouldn't keep doing that. It's unnerving."

"How are you, Mum?"

"I'm ringing now to wish you happy birthday because I've a busy day tomorrow."

"Okay. Thanks. Thanks for the breadbin."

"Not as glamorous as a platinum watch, of course. But useful."

"Useful is right."

"Forty, Katie. Isn't it hard to believe? Where did the years go? Now, while I have you, you'd want to start thinking about your hair."

"What about my hair?"

"It's very long."

"It's only just past my shoulders."

"But you're forty now. You'll have to start acting it."

Penny Richmond lived her life by a rigid, fear-filled code. She had all these *rules* and Katie was never quite sure where she got them from. (Examples: if you didn't get the facade of your house painted every four years, the residents' association could rightly authorize a public flogging; if you heard your next-door neighbor beating his wife to a pulp every night, you would sooner nail your tongue to the wall than mention it; you went to every event you were invited to, even if you loathed the other guests, because rudeness could kill.)

"And the color, Katie. You'll have to stop getting it dyed so dark."

"But it's my natural color. I'm just covering the roots."

"It's well known that as you age, your skin color fades and —"

The words tumbled from Katie's mouth. "Look, I know you're meant to go lighter as you get older but I like my hair the way it is!"

A screechy gasp came down the line, followed by a long, outraged silence. Katie was baffled by her own audacity: you tussled with Penny Richmond, arch-martyr, at your peril.

"Sorry, Mum," she said awkwardly. "I don't know what happened there."

In a trembly voice, Penny said, "I don't know what happened either. I won't pretend I'm not hurt, Katie. But because it's your birthday, I'll do my best to forget it."

As soon as Penny hung up, Katie rang Mary-Rose. "Pick up, pick up," she urged, but it went to voice mail. That's what happened when your best friend accidentally had a child by a married man. Her availability to listen to Katie bitch about her mum suddenly shrank dramatically because she was running around sterilizing things or mashing sweet potatoes or pacing the floor with a screaming teething child.

Katie didn't know how MaryRose coped and MaryRose herself had threatened to jump off the bridge over the Stillorgan dual carriage-way when she'd found herself pregnant at the age of thirty-nine. She was so *old*, she'd said — she'd be forty and a half when she gave birth. And how had it happened? It seemed like every woman in the world was having to try IVF and here she was, practically menopausal, having taken one, *one* condom-free risk, only to find herself pregnant. It was all wrong!

But within days of the terrifying blue line appearing on the stick, MaryRose had changed her tune. Proudly, she told Katie that she'd just been reading about herself in *Vogue*: there was a trend of single, first-time, forty-year-old mothers. "I don't mean to boast but I might be the first one in Ireland," she'd said. "How cool is that? I'm part of the zeitgeist. I don't think that's ever happened to me before. And I've been spared IVF or sperm donors or trying to adopt from China. I'm one of the lucky ones."

Katie had been flabbergasted. "I didn't even know you'd wanted a baby," she'd said. To which MaryRose had replied, "I didn't want one. But I do now."

Pregnant-women hormones, they'd both concluded.

Katie left MaryRose a quick message, then wondered who she could ring. No point trying Conall. He'd rung earlier, before going back to his desk, and she didn't want to disturb the slashing. Sinead, she'd try her. But Sinead was in some bar and could barely hear her, and refused to move because "some likely lad is giving me the eye." In the end, Katie had no one left to ring but Naomi. She wouldn't be sympathetic, but at least she understood their mum.

"I've just had a scrap with Mum."

"About what?"

"Nothing."

"Get used to it," Naomi said. "The minute you turn forty, you'll start having confrontations left, right and center."

"Oh God! It's going to make life so awkward. And I'm not even officially forty until tomorrow."

"That's because you've been a good girl and done your groundwork." Naomi had told her to start preparing at thirty-eight. "Keep saying to yourself, I'm forty, I'm forty, I'm forty, so that when it happens, you won't be so devastated."

But Sinead had advised the total opposite. "Denial, that's the way to go. Even when it happens, pretend you're still thirty-nine. Pretend you're thirty-nine for ever. Until you die. Of course, they'll find out then that you lied and they'll be shocked, but you'll be dead so what will it matter?"

"I'm glad you rang," Naomi said. "Your birthday dinner on Saturday night . . . can Dawn come? It's just that in the seven months since she's had her baby, she hasn't been out once."

Dawn was Naomi's friend, not Katie's, but she was okay. "Ah I suppose, yeah, why not?"

"Who else is coming?" Naomi asked.

"MaryRose, Sinead and Tania."

"Tania is coming!" Naomi sounded glad. "I'll have something in common with someone." Tania was married with two children. "Instead of all your bitter single friends."

"They're not bitter! No more bitter than you married women going on about how much you despise your husbands. And Mary-Rose isn't exactly single!"

"Her boyfriend, the father of her ten-month-old little girl, lives with his wife and four children and makes sporadic maintenance payments and hasn't seen Vivienne for nearly four months. Oh believe me, Katie, MaryRose is *definitely* single."

A period of silence followed, in which Katie regretted the way she could never keep anything, *anything,* from Naomi. (Except for one spectacular secret about her brother Charlie — which had come to her courtesy of Conall — and she was saving that up for when she really needed to reveal it.) Then she said, "You'd want to keep an eye on that, Naomi, you're turning into Mum."

DAY 58 . . .

They met the stag party of Sikhs in the queue outside Samara and it was one of them who suggested they hijack the Viking Splash. Lydia was all for it because she hated queueing, it was demeaning.

"You're too impatient," Shoane had said earlier, when they joined the queue. Shoane had wanted to see the inside of Samara; she was showcasing new red shoes, which most of Dublin had seen, and she wanted to include the people inside Samara. "It's Poppy's hen night," she'd said. "You have to do everything she wants."

"I just hate wasting time," Lydia had said in frustration. These days she got so few nights off . . .

"We're queueing as fast as we can," Poppy'd soothed. "We'll be inside in ten."

"Ten minutes!" Lydia had exclaimed. "This poor man —" she'd indicated the great-grandfather of the Sikh party, a hale but aged gentleman sporting an impressively Old Testament-style beard and a turban the size of a small car — "he could *die* in the next ten minutes. No offense," she'd added to the man.

He'd replied that none had been taken, that he agreed with her, that at his hour in life, aged eighty-one, he liked to maximize every second. "I had always hoped to die nobly," he'd said. "To die in the early hours of the morning while waiting to be refused entrance into a Dublin super-bar would not be noble. The obituary would have to be deliberately vague."

"It could say you died among family and friends," Lydia had said. "That part would be true." She'd gestured at the many turbaned men present. The stag party — who had come from Birmingham — numbered seventeen and there were four generations present: the groom-to-be, his father, grandfather and great-grandfather, plus assorted cousins, brothers and uncles.

"You seem like a resourceful young woman," the elderly man then said. "If you could extricate me from this queue, I'd be grateful."

"Okay." Always one to step up to a challenge, Lydia had raised her voice and yelled,

190

"Hey! Pops here is looking like he might snuff it."

Several people seemed to take this seriously, then someone — they tried to piece it together the following day but no one's memory was reliable enough to identify the ringleader — yelped, "Let's hijack the Viking Splash!" And the suggestion met with everyone's approval, even Shoane's.

The Sikhs, Lydia and her three friends, and sundry hangers-on surged from the queue and swarmed up Dawson Street, through the reveling throngs, to where the Viking Splash awaited.

This was an amphibious vehicle, popular with tourists. Its route took in many Dublin landmarks and as an electrifying finale it plunged into the Grand Canal and pootled around sedately before returning to dry land. It operated only in daylight hours but — again details were sketchy — the Sikhs had accumulated some new friends, three blokes all called Kevin, one of whom was a Viking Splash tour guide who had filched the key from the office and was prepared to do a middle-of-the-night tour for a reduced and strictly off-the-books fee.

Alarmed at having no alcohol for the duration of the tour (forty-five minutes), Poppy managed to purchase ten cans of "psycho cider" from a cluster of homeless men, and distributed them to Lydia, Shoane, Sissy, the

191

three Kevins, the hilarious Bulgarian leg-waxer, her hilarious friend and the tall silent woman who, in retrospect, belonged to no one. ("I thought she was one of the Bulgarians." "The Kevins thought she was one of us.") The Sihks, bewilderingly, didn't drink.

Everyone clambered into the vehicle — the orange life jackets wouldn't fit over the Sikhs' turbans but it didn't matter because they were breaking so many laws anyway, one more wouldn't do any harm — then they whizzed off into the night.

This was more like it, Lydia thought happily, as the buildings whipped past her. If she had to lose her income from Thursday, one of the most lucrative nights of the week — and she *had* to, she'd been best friends with Poppy since their first day at school so she could not miss her hen night — she wanted it to be a good one.

Thursdays were big party nights, perhaps even more so than Fridays, and Lydia was used to spending them ferrying around parties of drunken girls who spilled into the back of her cab in a tangle of bare legs and glittery toenails and blow-dried hair, singing and crying and muttering into their chests. Her plan for tonight was to be one of them.

She'd left the house in heavy eye make-up and high heels and a short dress. It was so short that Jan had pressed a tea towel to his eyes with one hand and blessed himself with the other. Andrei had watched her but said nothing.

"Go on," she'd said to him.

"Go on?"

"Say whatever's on your mind. I can see you're bursting to."

He'd shrugged indifferently. "You look good."

She'd waited. There had to be more.

"Slutty but good."

Bad feeling had blossomed between them.

"Better than looking like I keep my lady-garden in the deep freeze," she'd said.

Andrei had seemed to swell in size. "You talking about Rosie?"

"Who else do we know who keeps their lady bits in the deep freeze?" Lydia — well, there was no other word for it, really — Lydia *hated* Rosie. All that demure country-lass thing Rosie went on with, with her modest skirts and her white wine spritzers and her buying good leather boots in the sales. Lydia never found anything but shite in the sales, and if you got boots, by the time it was cold enough to wear them they'd be last year's boots and no one with any common sense would go out in last year's boots.

Lydia had swiped her lip gloss across her mouth, flashed Andrei a look of contempt that had an extra witchy effect because of her glittery dark-green eyeliner, and left the flat.

■ ■ ■ ■

There were eleven of them at the start of the night and the chances that it would be sedate were never high.

"Give me four units of alcohol," Lydia said to the barman. "Any way you like. Surprise me."

When her surprise drink arrived (a black-currant daiquiri), she said, "We're binge-drinking. I mean, I know we're on a real binge, but even if we weren't, we would be. Two bottles of Magners counts as a binge these days."

"No wonder we go on proper binges if they're so mean-spirited about normal drinking," Shoane said and everyone agreed that if they were going to be accused of binge-drinking they might as well get the most out of it and get proper falling-down drunk.

"We're the kind of girls they mean in the articles in the papers."

"At least we're panties," Poppy said.

Although some of them had their doubts about Shoane.

"Another four units here or will we go somewhere else?"

Shoane decreed that they'd try another venue, so that the people there could see her new red shoes. Through the night they moved from pub to pub in great good humor, acquiring and losing people as they went. By the time they met the Sikhs it was just gone 2 a.m. and they were down to the hardcore of Poppy, Lydia, Shoane and Sissy.

The illegal jaunt in the Viking Splash was followed by an impromptu party in the Sikh best man's hotel room, then, after all the units in his minibar had been consumed, everyone drifted away home.

Sissy snogged her taxi driver. Shoane showed up at five in the morning at her parents' house, although she hadn't lived there for seven years, weeping and incoherent and minus her new red shoes. Poppy came to with flecks of matter in her hair, which she subsequently identified as vomit — almost certainly, she insisted with great hauteur, not her own. ("I'm many things but I'm not a puker.") And Lydia woke up in Gilbert's bed, where he explored her body with his beautiful hands and discovered three mystifying purple bruises on her left shin.

It was, by unanimous agreement, a great night.

DAY 57

"I'm not normally a dog person, but you're different. You're in a category of your own. I suppose I trust you and I don't trust easy. Can I get you anything? What are these things here? Dog biscuits. Have a couple, I insist. You deserve it. If you like, I'll have one myself to keep you company."

From her bedroom Jemima could hear Fionn in the kitchen attempting to sweet-talk Grudge. A mighty battle of wills. Grudge, a paranoid, vengeful creature who felt under extreme threat, loathed Fionn. But Fionn had to make everyone, even dogs, love him. If they didn't at first, he would stop at nothing, he would chip away and chip away with smiles and compliments and simply erode a person until they surrendered and wearily agreed to love him with all their heart. But considering what he'd come through, poor soul, he'd turned out very well. Perhaps a slight propensity for preferring the company of vegetables to that of human beings, but when one considered the wealth of potential dysfunctional behavior on offer — drug addiction, compulsive home decorating and so on — she had no complaints.

Jemima could still remember when Fionn, aged twelve, had arrived in Pokey with Angeline, his mother. Their arrival had taken the town by storm. Only on television had the townsfolk seen the likes of Angeline, with her glamorous, hollow-eyed, breathless beauty, and her stunning mini-me daughter. (Because of his tousled, shoulder-length blond locks and pretty, pouty face, it took about six months for people to realize that Fionn wasn't a girl.)

The story was that they'd moved from Dublin "for the climate." Naturally, this was accepted as a euphemism. Was Angeline on the run from the law? From a drug deal that had soured? Because who in their right mind would move to Pokey for the weather? Indeed, as many of the restless natives agreed, who would move to Pokey *at all?*

The mother and daughter took up residence in a one-bedroomed flat behind a bookie's, and almost as soon as they'd crossed the threshold they were behind with the rent. Angeline got a job, working in the pub, and lost it almost immediately. She found alternative employment in the fish-and-chip shop but got the sack within the week. A stint as a cleaner didn't last long either. The problem was that Angeline was often "sick."

Lazy, was the consensus. Or drunk. *A lazy drunken Dubliner. Who wears too much makeup. And gives our men the glad eye.*

And has a fake daughter, don't forget the fake daughter. (Angeline had never tried to fool anyone that Fionn was a girl but the towns-folk's mistake made them feel foolish and then resentful.)

Drugs, someone else whispered, behind their hands. *And no father for that ladyboy.* They loved talking about Angeline. Endlessly, relentlessly, they watched and talked and talked and watched and lost any interest in spying on the oddball Protestants in their preposterous glass home. Angeline's beauty, her kohl-rimmed eyes, her murky past — she was better than a soap opera.

No one could believe it when she died.

It turned out that she'd had emphysema. Her story about coming to Pokey for the climate was entirely true. She'd been seeking fresh air to mend her poor damaged lungs when what she'd really needed was medication. But because she was a fragile, impractical type, who was desperate for positive outcomes, without any understanding of how to make them happen, she hadn't asked for help.

Obviously, no one in the town had offered assistance. They *couldn't.* Although they'd noticed she lived her life in chaos — Fionn didn't go to school and there were often scenes in the supermarket because Angeline didn't have enough money — not until Angeline's descendants had lived in the townland for four generations could she be accepted as one of them. Harsh, perhaps, but rules were rules.

Everyone assumed that Angeline had been an amoral floozy with no idea who'd fathered her child, but Fionn produced details and one phone call from the Pokey police was enough to conjure up Pearse Purdue. A beautiful man, in Jemima's opinion. As handsome as Angeline had been beautiful and, like her, a free spirit. (Or, if you wanted to be uncharitable, which Jemima didn't, pathologically irresponsible.) A fisherman, Pearse had spent his life working the trawlers up and down the west coast. Fionn had been the result of a short-lived but very passionate marriage with Angeline, and although they hadn't stayed together — Pearse was at sea eleven months of the year and Angeline spoke just a tiny bit too slowly for Pearse to endure — relations had remained cordial. Pearse loved Fionn but acknowledged he was incapable of parenting him.

He'd have to be fostered.

Which is when Jemima and Giles stepped in. They were aghast at Angeline's death. "How could we have let it happen?" Jemima asked Giles.

"You brought her soup."

"But I didn't understand how ill she was. Fionn was giving her Lemsip. I thought she just had a bad cold."

"We weren't to know," Giles said, kneading her shoulders. "We weren't to know. But we can give him a home now."

"He'll be a handful," the man from Social Services warned Jemima. "He's inherited irresponsibility from both sides of the family. A double hit. He hasn't a hope. And he looks like a girl."

"Giles and I aren't daunted," Jemima said. "A well-balanced child will always get a home, but it's the poor damaged ones who really need it."

DAY 57 . . .

Today is Katie's actual birthday.

"Forty," Danno said when she walked into the office. "Next stop, death."

A small delegation of staff approached her desk. "Happy birthday, Ms. Richmond," Danno said. They presented her with a card and a gift-wrapped parcel. "It's only small, we could never compete with Slasher's loot, but we put a lot of thought into it."

It was a fortieth-birthday diary. On the cover it said, "Life Begins . . . A guide to what's left of your life." At the top of each day was an uplifting thought.

200

"But this is divine." Katie flicked through it. "Let me read out today's message. 'Dance joyously every day of your life. But don't let anyone else see you, not at your age.' That's beautiful. You shouldn't have, guys."

"Slasher Hathaway's here!"
Wildly surprised, Katie looked at Danno.
"I thought you said he was in Helsinki," Danno said accusingly.
"He was."
"He's flown back just to take you out for lunch," George said.
George was probably right, Katie acknowledged. Conall was a great man for the grand gesture.
"In a private plane with cream-leather upholstery and royal-blue carpet, ankle-deep," George said dreamily. "Drinking Krug and eating Beluga caviar although caviar is strange and disgusting. That popping texture . . . it's like Space Dust for gourmets —"
"Shut up, you nutter," Danno snapped. To Katie, he said, "He's waiting downstairs. Eating chocolate, as usual, trying to push down all that guilt he must be carrying. He's keen to see you."
She took her time. She'd had other things lined up for this, her birthday lunch hour, and she was pissed off at Conall's presumption. Okay, so she'd only been planning a visit

201

to the foot-protection section of Boots, but, for a woman who lived in high heels, it was where two of her specialist interests intersected. She was mildly obsessed with sole-protectors — invisible padded gel cushions which were meant to prevent that unpleasant burning sensation in the ball of the foot. She hadn't yet found a brand that worked for her, that didn't peel off the shoe and stick to her foot instead, but she remained hopeful. In addition, she'd seen an ad for a new product, a delightful see-through, wrap-around gel device to protect the little toe in open sandals, and she was keen for a look. And she was out of heel-guards, which she couldn't live without. Not only did they prevent naked heels from chafing against the back of shoes, but they also helped to anchor the foot in the shoe, preventing it from lifting out at pivotal moments in one's life, like crossing a stage to accept a prize in front of hundreds of people, as had happened to Katie when she had won PR of the Year some years back. The statue on her mantelpiece had eventually tarnished but that particularly humiliating memory had not. She would never permit it to happen again.

She made the four phone calls she'd been planning to make before Danno had announced Conall, then proceeded at a fairly leisurely pace to the ladies' and put on all the makeup she could find in her bag. Only then did she get the lift downstairs. There, as Danno had said, was Conall, clicking away on his BlackBerry, deep in thought and looking grim.

As she approached, he lifted his head and his entire demeanor softened. He jumped to his feet. She let him kiss her, not a full-on super-snog, they were in her working environs, after all, *and* he hadn't put up her mirror *or* replied to her text, then she pulled away.

"Happy birthday," he said, his eyes shining into hers.

"What happened to Helsinki?"

He shrugged, still smiling. "It's your birthday."

"You mean, negotiations briefly broke down but you're going back tomorrow?"

"Yeah." He sighed. "I can get nothing past you. I don't even know why I try. Can I take you to lunch?"

She waited. She thought about her mirror. "Probably."

"Then will you take the afternoon off work and spend it in bed with me?"

"I've got a press conference."

"I've missed you," he said softly.

"I've got a press conference." She set her jaw. She would not let herself say another word.

He was unhumanly persuasive. He didn't even have to speak to exert his will, all he

had to do was look at her with those gravel
eyes, eyes that said he was an unhappy man
and all that made life bearable for him was
Katie.

It was a measure of just how persuasive he
was that, after the terrible first date at Glyndebourne, Katie ever went out with him again.
She was adamant that she would have nothing further to do with him, but somehow he
talked her into giving him one more try. On
the second date, which was entirely different
from a trip to the opera but probably as risky,
Conall took her to meet his family. It was his
nephews' birthday, Laddie and Hector,
fourteen-year-old identical twins with identical hostile haircuts growing down over their
eyes and an identical absence of interest in
Katie when she was ushered into their small
sitting room. Only at Conall's instigation did
they grunt a greeting, but they remained
slumped immobile, one on the couch, the
other on the floor.

Katie was mortified. No one but a headcase would think this was a good idea. But
Conall's brother, Joe, a balding sandy-haired
man, was friendly enough, as was his wife,
Pat. Then a little girl bowled into the room
and declared, "I like your shoes."

"Are you talking to me?" Katie asked.

"Who else here has wicked shoes?"

This was Bronagh, Conall's seven-year-old

niece, who looked so astonishingly like Conall that Katie actually laughed.

"I know," Joe said. "You'd think the missus was diddling me brother behind me back, but she swears she wasn't."

Pat rolled her eyes. "I'm mad but I'm not that mad." Too late, she realized what she'd said.

"Thanks, Pat," Conall said. "Like I'm not having enough trouble trying to convince Katie I'm normal."

"Show us the new car!" Joe said, kick-starting a stampede to the front door. Even the Surly Twins were roused from their torpor at the idea of test-driving Uncle Conall's new Lexus. They piled out of the house and Pat melted away to the kitchen, leaving Katie alone with Bronagh, who sighed extravagantly. "Boys and their toys. Give me a try on of your shoes and I'll paint your nails silver."

By the time the men returned from their trip around the block, Katie had been ferried upstairs by Bronagh, who confided that she had taken to her.

Conall's risk had paid off: the warmth of his family had convinced her that he might just be semi-sane.

"You can take me for lunch," she said to Conall. "Then you can feck off. You can't just —"

"I know, I can't just waltz in here, expecting you to up-end all your plans when they've been in place for weeks and it's all my fault anyway for signing up for an unpredictable takeover which overlapped the week of your birthday and to add insult to injury I didn't put your mirror up."

She opened her mouth, then closed it again. He'd said it all. "Exactly."

"Exactly," he agreed. "But you can't blame a man for trying."

On their way to the restaurant, a cyclist zoomed toward them, scattering Katie and Conall to opposite sides of the pavement.

"Jesus Christ!" Conall said. "They're bloody everywhere."

"They make me feel guilty. I keep thinking I should start cycling to work."

"The environment?" Conall opened the restaurant door.

"Mmmm . . ." That and her thighs. "But I'm so lazy. Funny, because I loved my bike when I was a kid."

A managerial-looking type had recognized Conall and they were led straight to their table.

As they sat down, Katie asked Conall, "Did you have a bike?"

A shadow passed over his eyes.

"What?" she asked. "You twitched or something."

"I had a bike."

"So why the twitch? Tell me why. It can be my birthday present."

"I already gave you a watch!"

"Tell me."

He paused. "You know the upbringing I had?"

Conall had grown up without much money. Not abject *Angela's Ashes,* drunken-father/mother-on-the-game poverty, but fairly hand-to-mouth. His dad had been a plumber, his mum a dressmaker. All through his childhood, their front room had been Mrs. Hathaway's work space, covered with bolts of fabric and strange off-cuts and half-finished wedding dresses. He grew too fast and his mum was always worried about new shoes for him.

"There wasn't any money for bicycles."

Katie put her hand over her mouth. "I shouldn't have asked. I'm sorry."

He waved away her apologies. "It's okay, it's okay. But Spudz did this offer where, if you collected five thousand chip packets, you'd get a free bike."

"Who could collect five thousand chip bags?"

There was an odd little moment, then he said, "I did."

"How?"

"I needed somewhere where they ate chips in huge quantities. So I went to the local pub and did my pitch."

"What age were you?"

"Nine. No, ten. No, nine."

"And what happened?"

"They had a good laugh at me, the barmen. But they said they'd collect them for me."

"And did they?"

"Yeah. And in three other pubs too."

"Three others!" Even aged nine he'd been an entrepreneur. What was she doing with this man?

"It took me nearly four months, but I got five thousand chip bags and I got the bike."

"What are you trying to tell me?"

She watched him retreat back into himself. "That I got a free bike when I was nine."

That he never gave up? That if he wanted something, he got it? That he was driven in ways she would never understand?

"My mirror —" she said.

"It's on the wall."

"Since when?"

"Since . . ." He took a look at his watch. "Since an hour and forty-four minutes ago."

"Jason's wedding?"

"I'll be back for it. I swear on my life."

"On your life?"

"On my life, I'll be there. Everyone in Helsinki knows about it."

She exhaled slowly, wondering if it was okay to relax.

"I'm sorry," he blurted out. "For your mirror. For the way I am. I know you're holding back on me . . ."

She was startled. Yes, she'd taken care not to fully surrender her heart and her hope and her future to a man who mightn't be capable of caring for them. But she hadn't realized he'd noticed.

"Who knows what's going to happen with us," he said. "But whatever it is, it won't work if only one of us is into it."

He'd never been so forthright before and she wasn't sure how to reply. "But Conall, you're a workaholic. It makes you unreliable."

He flinched. "I'll change. I'm trying. I turn off my phone when we're together, haven't you noticed?"

She had but . . . She took a risk and jumped into virgin territory. "I've been heartbroken before. I really don't know if I have the energy for it again."

"Who's to say that that's what would happen?" He was earnest. "You could just as easily get sick of me."

"Maybe," she acknowledged.

"Please don't."

He sounded unexpectedly anguished and suddenly the word *LOVE* was hanging in the air, looping them together, garlanding them with flowers and hearts and lovebirds and pink mist. *I love you.* It was there, all that was needed to breathe life into it and make it real was for one of them to utter it. *I love you.* But Katie wouldn't.

Even though she had fallen in love with him, just a bit. You couldn't not. He was sexy, sexy, sexy.

It was up to him.

He looked at her, an eyebrow raised questioningly. She presented a bland face to him and he watched her for a little too long. "Okay." He sighed. "Let's order."

DAY 57 . . .

"Hi, Maeve."

"Hi, Doreen."

"What'll it be?"

"The usual."

"Ham salad on brown bread, no mustard? Despite there being a wealth of sandwich differentials to choose from in the modern Ireland?"

"I'm happy with the ham."

"A bag of plain chips." Doreen put them on the counter. "And a can of Fanta." But there was no Fanta on the shelf. "Where's the Fanta?" Doreen called to some unseen person behind a door.

"We're out of it," the unseen voice said.

Maeve became aware that the next girl in the queue seemed almost as distressed as she herself was by this news.

"Maeve, I don't know what to say, but we're out of Fanta," Doreen said.

"Ah feck!" the girl beside Maeve groaned.

"I love my Fanta!"

"Hi, Samantha. Sorry, girls." Doreen looked grim. "Heads will roll for this, is all I can say. I'll do my best to have it in again by Monday."

Suddenly, there was some kerfuffle at the storeroom door and then a hand was extended, holding one can of Fanta. "Last one," the voice attached to the hand said.

"You're in luck, Maeve," Doreen said. "Sorry, Samantha."

This was Maeve's chance. An act of kindness, right there and then. She forced herself to gift it to this Samantha and it was *hard,* almost as hard as smiling warmly at random strangers. But Samantha was effusive with gratitude and Doreen gave Maeve a free can of Lilt as a substitute, and Maeve tried to savor the warm glow generated by her own goodness. The thing was that she didn't like change. Any alterations to her routine, no matter how small, threw her, and refreshing and all as the Lilt was, she felt quite off-kilter for the rest of the day.

DAY 57 . . .

Lydia, hungover and exhausted, had just pulled in to eat her lunch, a strawberry yogurt and a banana — it was all she could trust her stomach with after the number of units she'd consumed the previous night — when her phone rang. It was a County Meath number, one that she didn't recognize — then she did! *Shite.*

"Lydia? Flan Ramble here —"

"Hello, Flan." She spoke quickly. A low, dready feeling swamped her. He only ever rang with bad news. In fact, he seemed to delight in it.

"Don't call me Flan. I'm Mr. Ramble to you."

"What's up?"

"There's been a bit of a . . . an incident —"

"What?" *Just tell me.*

"If I was to say the words *a small house fire,* would you get my drift?"

"A fire? In the house? A small one?"

"Got it in one! A pot was left on the ring too long, the curtains went up, blew out the windows. No real damage, but you'll have a fair old job dealing with the scorch marks." He chuckled. "You'd better get down here pronto with your paintbrush."

"I'm in Dublin, Mr. Ramble." *Flan, Flan, Flan.*

"I've tried to get hold of Murdy or Ronnie, but I can't run either of them to ground."

Surprise, surprise. "I'm in Dublin," Lydia repeated. "Fifty miles of road between us. With very heavy traffic."

"Someone needs to be here," Flan said, sounding uncomfortable.

Irkutsk, Irkutsk, Irkutsk.

Much as she disliked Flan Ramble, and she disliked him a lot, he was just passing on information. "Okay, thanks. I'm on my way."

No time for lunch now. She switched off her For Hire light, agonized by losing half a day's income, and headed for home. While she drove she rang Murdy who, to her surprise, answered.

"I thought you were the bank," he yelped. "I'm in crisis here! They've stopped my credit line. I'll be shut down if I don't come up with thirty grand by close of business."

He hung up on her! Hung fecking up! She was used to him doing that but didn't he realize that this was different? Worse. A fire. Flames. Burned curtains. Serious stuff.

Immediately, she rang Ronnie who — to her disbelief — refused to get involved. "You're making a drama out of a crisis," he said, with infuriating calm. "Again."

"The house went on fire!"

"If you're that worried why aren't you here?"

He — too — hung up on her. *Ssskkkk!* This was mad stuff. Why was she the only one . . . ? With shaking fingers, she rang Raymond but his phone was switched off. Why would his phone be off? Because he knew. He'd been tipped off.

Fuck him. Fuck the lot of them, the selfish useless crowd of fucking fuckers. May they perish in Archangelsk. May they find themselves in Murmansk in the depths of winter with no gloves. May they fall off the side of a ship in dry dock in Gdansk. She'd have to drive to Boyne, County Meath, and she'd have to leave now if she wanted to beat the Friday-night exodus out of Dublin. Twenty minutes later would add three hours to her journey, most of them spent sitting on the N3, inhaling exhaust fumes and facing due west as a mad-shiny sun blazed down on top of her, in a car with no air conditioning.

Grimly, she fashioned some plans. When she got to Boyne, she would descend upon that gobshite Buddy Scutt and she wouldn't leave until she got what she wanted, what she should have been given months ago.

Her final call was to Gilbert. The phone rang for a long time and eventually his voice mail kicked in.

"I won't be round tonight. Maybe not tomorrow night either. Call me," she said. But she had a feeling he wouldn't. He'd probably sulk, in a childish attempt to punish her for abandoning him at such short notice.

At times she had her doubts about Gilbert.

As Poppy said, "Never trust a man with two mobile phones."

And Gilbert had three.

That she knew about.

At 66 Star Street, she bounded up the stairs and ran into the kitchen to stick her yogurt

214

into the fridge, but it was full — completely full — of neatly stacked cans of beer, funny Polish stuff they bought in the Polish shop. Jan was going to visit his girlfriend for the weekend, so Andrei was obviously planning a wreck-fest with his pals. There was literally no room for her strawberry yogurt. A single strawberry yogurt! Many was the girl who'd need space for soya milk and broccoli and flax-seeds and other bulky items. They had no idea how lucky they were to have her.

She yanked one beer from its plastic holder, perched her little pink yogurt amid all that brownness and carefully placed the can of beer right in the middle of the kitchen floor, where hopefully Andrei would trip on it.

Then, clear-headed from adrenaline, she began flinging things — underwear, spare jeans, iPod — into a zippy bag. What else did she need for this impromptu mini-break? Deodorant, toothbrush, makeup wipes . . . The downstairs buzzer rang; it was probably someone from one of the other flats who'd forgotten their key. She pressed the door open.

Through the living-room doorway, she caught a glimpse of the computer. Should she go online? Just for a quick look? The urge was suddenly almost irresistible. No, no time. One final, eagle-eyed scan of the bathroom, just in case she'd missed something; of course, they had shops in Boyne, but there mightn't be any time for — What was that? A knock on the door of the flat. Irkutsk! She shouldn't have opened the front door without checking who it was. But no harm, she was in a very speedy groove and whoever these interlopers were — Mormons, politicians — she'd make short work of them. She'd bounce them back down the stairs in . . . how quick could she do it, she asked herself. Fifteen seconds, she decided.

She wrenched open the door. "I'm a devout Christian, I don't vote and I have no money to buy anything."

Standing there was a girl — so probably not a Mormon — and she looked nothing like a politician. The absence of a big fake grin plastered across her mug was the clue. But she might be flogging something. Crap makeup was Lydia's guess.

"I seek Oleksander," the girl said.

"Do you mean, you seek enlightenment?" The girl was clearly not Irish; she could have her words mixed up.

"No. I seek Oleksander. A man."

"You'll have to seek him somewhere else. There's no one of that name here."

"Ukrainian man."

"I can do you a couple of Poles, if that's any good."

"But this is the flat of Oleksander!"

"There's no Oleksander and I'm in a hurry."

The girl — slippery as an eel — slid past Lydia and into the tiny bedroom. "He lives here."

"This is my room. Ah! You must be talking about the previous tenant." Now that she thought about it, Lydia had seen a couple of envelopes addressed to Oleksander someone. Andrei had organized a little pile of them in the kitchen. "You had me worried, there. I thought you were a madzer."

"Oleksander is gone!" the girl cried. "But where?"

"I haven't a scobie."

"I must speak with him! Oleksander is sexy, beautiful man."

"Ring him."

"I deleted number!"

Lydia stared helplessly, scouring her brain for a solution, something to get rid of this girl so she could get on with her packing. "He'll probably come back at some stage to collect his mail. Write him a note. I'll give it to him."

Already the girl was scribbling on a piece of paper. "I am Viktoriya. Please tell him he must ring me."

"I will, I will, now I must —"

"Also please tell him I made big mistake. Man from Department of Agriculture was stupid, and had a smell of cows."

"Had a smell of cows. Gotcha."

"You promise you will tell him?"

"Yes, yes, yes, I promise."

But still Viktoriya lingered, giving the impression that she thought if she hung around long enough, this Oleksander would clamber out from under the bed, covered with dust balls.

"He's really not here. You must go. I have my own situation going on."

DAY 57 . . .

"Drink, Maeve?"

They were nice to keep asking, her co-workers, even though she'd never yet joined them for the end-of-week happy hour. "I'm grand, thanks." She smiled. "Have a good one. See you Monday."

Maeve had a regular appointment on Friday evenings. It was a good night for it because Matt was out too, on the jar with his team for their end-of-week wind-down.

On the dot of six, Maeve finished up and began cycling through the bright evening, heading south. After eight minutes of pedaling, it suddenly hit her what date it was. Hard to believe that she'd only remembered it now, considering she'd spent her entire day working with days and dates. She spent a few shocked seconds just coasting, then surprised several people — four drivers, seven pedestrians and most of all herself — by making an abrupt U-turn. She was moving with purpose in a different direction. Not back toward work — so it wasn't as if she'd just remembered that she'd left something like her phone or her wallet behind and was nipping back to pick it up — but down toward the river, to the docklands. The roads got narrower, but she zigzagged her way through them, bumping over cobbles, like a woman who knew exactly where she was going. Then she slowed and stopped. In a side street, she propped her bike against a wall and fired off a quick text.

Sorry. Sik. C u next week.

Half-hidden by a building, Maeve peeped out at an office complex across the road. No Brainer Technology. An IT company, yet another one; this city was overrun with them. People were streaming out through the front door, nearly all of them young and casually dressed.

Maeve watched and watched and her face displayed no emotion, even though she'd bent her right ankle until it was facing the wrong way, as if her leg had been put on backward. It was an agonizing maneuver, by the looks of things, but she was feeling no pain, even her breathing had almost stopped. And then she was ablaze with a dazzling cocktail of emotion. She released her ankle and it spun round, back to its correct alignment. Some bloke had just emerged from the building. Long and thin and handsome in a disheveled, unkempt fashion, he had the demeanor of a poet.

He was walking away from where Maeve was secreted, but something stopped him in his tracks and made him twist his head round and look back over his shoulder. He saw her. Their eyes locked and a cable of white-hot energy snaked forth to unite them. It pulsed for some seconds, sparks and stars fizzing, then his eyes went dead and his face became blank as if his plug had just been pulled. He dropped his head and stumbled away.

This was the man who was present in Maeve and Matt's flat. *This* was the person who had inveigled his way in, corrupting the perfect two-of-this and the perfect two-of-that.

All of a sudden Maeve was desperate to be somewhere, *any*where else, but her legs were shaking so much she couldn't trust herself to cycle. Slowly, placing her feet carefully on the uneven streets, she wheeled her bike and wheeled her bike and wheeled her bike until the trembling left her.

DAY 57 . . .

Andrei and Jan made their way along Eden Quay. They were supporting a large, burly man who appeared incapable of walking or

220

even standing upright. A Friday-lunchtime drinks session that had gone too far, one could only presume.

They caused quite a commotion as they proceeded, an unbreakable wall of three, along the pavement. Pedestrians were compelled to step out of their path, then would turn to stare with hostility after them. However, on closer inspection, it became evident that the middle person was not an obese man, made heavier by virtue of being stupefied by drink but, in fact, a very large teddy bear. Larger, actually, than either Andrei or Jan.

The trio continued to bump their way down Eden Quay, making for the bus terminal.

Jan was about to board the bus to Limerick, where his sweetheart, Magdalena, was currently billeted, working on reception in a big hotel. It would be her birthday on Sunday and Magdalena was very much a teddy-bear kind of girl.

"Limerick?" the ticket-selling man asked. "One person?"

"One person."

The ticket-seller, one Mick Larkin, leaned forward on his high swivel chair to get a closer look. "Is he going?"

"Who?" Andrei asked. "Bobo?"

"Is Bobo the bear?"

"Yes."

"Bobo needs a ticket. He's too big. He

needs a seat of his own."

"He is going to visit his sweetheart," Andrei protested.

"Who? Bobo?" Mr. Larkin was a bureaucrat who liked to know exactly what he was dealing with.

"No. Jan. This man here. It's Magdalena's birthday, she's high-maintenance." (Actually, Magdalena was sweet and easy-going but Andrei adored that phrase and used it every opportunity he got.) "Jan has budgeted carefully and he needs all the money he has with him."

Mr. Larkin shrugged. "Bobo needs a ticket."

"You have no romance in your soul," Andrei complained.

"Neither have you. You're Poles, not Italians."

Ire rose in Andrei. Everyone misjudged them. They thought Poles were simply hardworking but passion-free builders. They had no idea of what they were really like.

Jan was doing a quick calculation of his funds and the outcome compelled him to say, "Andrei, I am glum."

"You see?" Andrei pointed at Jan's pitiful face. "You see how glum you have made him!"

"Glum," Andrei heard someone further back in the queue say. "Now, that's a word you don't hear very often these days."

"No, and it's quite a good one," another

voice replied.

"It sounds like what it is. Glum!" The first voice again.

"Glum! I wonder why it went out of fashion." A new voice. Several people were in the discussion now. "Glum, glum, glum, glum. What do we say instead?"

"Pissed-off."

"Bummed-out."

"A bit down. Low. Depressed. In the horrors. Buzz-wrecked. Head-melted."

"Ah, no *wonder* glum went out of business! The market has been flooded with all these new words. The laws of supply and demand, they'll get you every time."

"What's going on up there at the front with the teddy? I'm going to miss my bus," a man, six people back, said. "Although it might be a blessing. A weekend with my family, you know yourself . . ."

"I do, yeah," the girl in front of him said. "Low. Depressed. In the horrors. Buzz-wrecked. Head-melted."

"Glum!" he countered with, and loud laughter rippled through the queue.

"I don't want to miss my bus," another woman said. She walked to the front of the queue and suggested, "He could put the bear on his lap."

Mr. Larkin shook his head sorrowfully. "Bobo's too big."

"Is Bobo the bear? Okay, your *man* could

sit on Bobo's lap."

"Actually, he *could* . . ."

As Andrei waved them off, Jan perched high on Bobo's lap, he mouthed through the window of the bus, "You're a hero." As soon as they were out of sight, Andrei went to the gym where he spent sixty-seven minutes lifting weights, then he hurried home to admire his beer. He rubbed his hands together with the glee of freedom. Andrei carried many burdens: he was the main source of income for his parents and younger sisters at home in Gdansk; he felt deeply protective of Jan, who seemed to find life in this country even harder than he himself did; and he had started to worry about Rosie getting home safely from night shifts, even though she still wouldn't sleep with him. At times Andrei felt he was responsible for keeping the world turning. But today all his liberations had come at once. He had sent a wodge of money home, which had lifted the harried feeling that perpetually dogged him; for the duration of the weekend, Jan was the responsibility of Magdalena; Rosie was in Cork on a hen weekend and therefore out of his jurisdiction; he had a fridge full of beer and a coterie of male friends coming over later; but, best of all, the evil pixie had gone on a trip. He knew this because his zippy weekend bag had disappeared. So had his deodorant.

She was usually gone at weekends, off tormenting Poor Fucker, but he hugged a small warm secret hope to himself that the missing bag might signal a longer absence.

Nothing, not even stumbling over the can of beer she had left in the middle of the kitchen floor, could dilute his happiness.

DAY 57 . . .

More things Lydia hates:

Magazines that are more than eight years old
Saucepans that have had the arse burned off them
Doctors' waiting rooms
The smell of rotting food
Doctors' receptionists
Homes without broadband
The smell of rubber gloves
Doctors
Her brother Murdy
Her brother Ronnie
Her brother Raymond
Dr. Buddy Scutt
Homes with no internet connection, not even dial-up

Please note: this is not a complete list.

DAY 56

Matt and Maeve tried to move their cart through the gridlock of the meat aisle.

"Pizza, Sunday night. Lamb on Monday," Maeve was muttering and counting out days on her fingers. "Fish, Tuesday and Wednesday. Beef, Thursday, takeout on Friday. So what'll we have tonight?"

"Maeve . . ."

"What?"

"We're going out tonight."

"Oh."

"Mum's birthday. Her sixty-fifth. Maeve . . ." He shook his head. This was almost funny. "You couldn't have forgotten?"

"I haven't forgotten," Maeve admitted. "I've tried my best but how could I forget when you've reminded me every day for the past month. I've just been in denial. Hoping that if I pretended it wasn't happening, it wouldn't."

"It's happening."

"So we don't need to get something for our

dinner tonight?"

"No. We'll be getting top-notch grub at l'Ecrivain."

"What time are we meant to be there?"

"Seven-thirty."

"Then there's probably no point going on our hike this afternoon. We'd have to cut it short to get home in time."

"You're right. Pity, though." Matt tried to pretend he wasn't relieved.

He and Maeve went hiking in the Wicklow Hills every Saturday afternoon. Except they hadn't been in weeks. And weeks. Now he could lie on the couch and watch the rugby instead.

Ireland was in the process of suffering a humiliating loss to England when Maeve sidled into the living room. "Maaa-aaaat?"

"Hmmm?" He couldn't tear himself away from the screen.

"Matt. I feel sick."

That got his attention. He twisted round to look at her. "What sort of sick?"

"My stomach. I feel really pukey. I don't think I can go tonight."

Matt gazed at her. He suddenly felt like crying. "Please, Maeve. Can't you try? They haven't seen you in ages. They'll think I've murdered you and buried you in the back garden."

She hung her head.

"It won't be so bad," Matt coaxed. "It'll

227

only be the six of us. It could be worse; they could be having a party."

But parties were better. You could disappear into the crowds at parties and, if you played your cards carefully enough, you could talk to almost no one.

"Okay," she said. "I'll come."

"Thank you."

"How posh is this place we're going to?"

"You know Mum. She likes them posh."

"Can I wear my jeans?"

"As far as I'm concerned, you can wear whatever you want. But I suppose if you had a dress . . ."

When Matt and Maeve arrived at l'Ecrivain, Hilary and Walter Geary were in the bar, already well into their first drink. Hilary, a petite, stylish woman in a pale-pink tailored dress and a perfectly matched lipstick, was wittering away to Walter, a large, taciturn man in a yellow golfing sweater. Hilary was on the gin and Walter on the neat whiskey, Matt noted with a heavy heart.

"Happy birthday, Mum. Sorry we're late," Matt said. Maeve had had to try on everything she owned before she found a dress she felt comfortable in.

Hilary sprang up to administer fragrant hugs. "You're not late!" she scoffed. "We're early."

"They're late," Walter said, into his drink.

"But not as late as his brother."

"Ignore him." Hilary enfolded Maeve in a perfumed embrace. "Lovely to see you, Maeve."

"We were beginning to think Matt had done away with you," Walter said, then threw back the last of his drink.

"Shush!" Hilary gave Walter a playful cuff with the back of her hand. "Don't mind him. We know Maeve is busy. And no one can help getting sick. We all get sick from time to time."

Walter raised his glass at the barman. "Another of these."

"Here's Alex and Jenna," Hilary said.

A good-looking pair: Alex was a taller, leaner, slightly older version of Matt, and Jenna was summery and fresh, with long, shiny blond hair and cornflower-blue eyes. Tonight she wore an eye-catching coral sundress and sexy slingbacks.

"You got the dress!" Hilary exclaimed, pointing at Jenna.

Jenna shook her head ruefully. "I should have listened to you, Hilary. I couldn't stop thinking about it and in the end I went back."

"I told you!" Hilary laughed. "If I know anything, I know clothes, and that dress was made for you."

"I'll know the next time."

"Where's my hug?" Walter groused.

"I'm not hugging you." Jenna laughed.

"You're too cranky." Then she relented and gave him a kiss on the forehead.

"Hi, Matt." Jenna gave him a quick peck and moved on to Maeve.

Matt didn't miss the lightning-quick once-over that Jenna gave Maeve, taking in Maeve's rumpled, roomy dress, her Birkenstocks and her tangled curls. Not a bitchy look, Jenna wasn't bitchy; the expression on her face was more like . . . well . . . *pity.*

"Now that you're all finally here, can we go to the table?" Walter said. "I want my dinner."

"But what about Hilary's birthday presents?" Jenna was carrying an elaborately wrapped polka-dotted box, with ribbons and stars hanging from it.

"After we've ordered," Walter said, lumbering toward the tables.

"Long time no see," Alex said pointedly to Matt.

Matt forced a bark of laughter. "You know how it is, work and all that."

"Still busy?"

"Great!" No way would Matt mention that two members of his team had been made redundant in the last month. Alex was his older brother and trying to impress him was as automatic as breathing.

"Even in the CEC?"

"What — Oh the Current Economic Cli-

230

mate? Yeah, we're doing okay." A big sale would be nice, but they were holding their own.

"I heard they let two of your people go."

Shit. How did Alex know? That was the thing about Ireland, everyone knew everything.

"Yeah, but the rest of us are fine." Paradoxically, the jobs of his remaining four staff felt safer since the redundancies. The worst time had been waiting to see who'd be shown the door.

"No chance you could be made to walk the long walk?"

Matt shook his head. "I'm Head of Sales so without me they've no sales force. How're things with you? Busy?"

"Never better. Credit crunch, my arse." Alex was a rep for a medical-supplies company. "Sickness is recession-proof. Better, if anything. Everyone on antidepressants."

"Any new updates on the wedding plans?" Hilary asked Jenna. Alex and Jenna were getting married in October.

"No change since I saw you, Hilary."

"I suppose it was only a couple of days ago." Hilary was disappointed.

"But the stag night," Alex said, "now that's coming along *very* nicely. Has Russ been on to you?"

Russ was Alex's best friend and joint best man with Matt.

231

"No."

"No? He said he was going to email you. Anyway, it's all set up. We're going to Vegas."

"Vegas! What happened to Amsterdam?"

"Everyone goes to Amsterdam."

"We'll never do Vegas in a weekend."

"That's right, my man. That's why we're going for a week."

A week? Matt and Maeve exchanged a look.

"Last week in August," Alex said. "Make sure you've got the time off work."

"Look . . . Alex . . . I'm your best man. I'm in charge of your stag night. Not you."

"You're my *joint* best man. You couldn't make the last two meets to organize stuff, so we went ahead without you and organized Vegas. Which suits the rest of us down to the ground."

"But what would we do in Vegas for a week?"

"I can think of plenty," Walter said.

"Are you coming?" Matt asked his father.

"Of course I'm coming! It's my oldest son's stag night, stag week, whatever you want to call it. I believe there's great golfing in Vegas, that'll keep us all occupied."

"I don't play golf," Matt said.

"So take it up," Alex said. "You've a couple of months before we go. Anyway, about time you started, it's one of the few things yourself and Maeve haven't tried. Horse-riding, ski-ing, mountain-biking, hill-walking . . . ?"

Speaking of which, how's your hill-walking going?"

"Great. Great."

"Were you out today? A perfect day for it."

"No, we thought the place would be overrun with schoolkids and we needed to be back in time for tonight."

"And last weekend?"

"I think we were out last weekend? Were we, Maeve?"

"I think we were," Maeve said.

Alex gave them a look: he knew they were lying.

Suddenly, Hilary clapped her hand over her mouth and said to Maeve, "God above, I've just remembered. We forgot your anniversary."

". . . Anniversary?" Maeve asked.

"Your wedding anniversary? Two weeks ago. I'm so sorry, but in all the excitement with Jenna and Alex . . . Are you okay, Maeve? You've gone a bit pale."

"I'm grand."

Hilary studied Maeve's face. "You *are* pale." Realization moved behind Hilary's eyes. "Oh my God! Is there something you'd like to tell us?"

"What?"

"Special news for us?" Hilary's face was radiant with hope and gin.

"Muu-uum." Matt buried his head in his hands. This was what happened when Hilary

233

didn't stick to the wine. "Maeve isn't pregnant. If and when it happens, we'll tell you. You don't have to keep asking."

"But I can't help it!" Hilary was slightly slurring her words. "You've been married for more than three years and I'm the only woman in the tennis club without a grandchild. It's embarrassing!"

"Sorry, Mum," Matt said quietly.

Maeve gazed at her thighs, her face burning.

"Because there are things you can do," Hilary said. "If you're having 'difficulties.' "

"God," Alex groaned. "Who let her at the gin?"

"Tests and things. They'd start with you, Matt. You'd have to go into a little cubicle —"

"Stop! Stop right now!" Alex said.

"No son of mine is going into any little cubicles," Walter rumbled. "No son of mine is firing blanks."

"A week in Vegas?" Maeve said, in the taxi home.

"I'm not going."

"He's your brother, you're his best man, you have to go."

234

Less than thirty yards from l'Ecrivain, Katie was in another restaurant, celebrating her fortieth birthday with five other women.

"Poor Katie." Dawn sighed drunkenly. "You never got to have children."

"I'm not dead yet."

"As good as," Dawn said. "There's no hope for you now. This Conall, he doesn't want kids, does he?"

Katie looked at Naomi, who had obviously been spilling the beans. "How do you know he doesn't want kids?"

Naomi flushed. "I just said he wasn't domesticated."

"Why?"

"He didn't put your mirror up."

"It's up."

"He took his time about it."

"It's up now."

"He'd better be back from Helsinki for Jason's wedding," Naomi blustered.

"He'll be back."

"And if he isn't?"

And if he isn't . . . ?

"He's very fond of his niece, Bronagh." Katie shouldn't have to defend Conall to Dawn. "She's his god-daughter and they get on great. And she's a kid, she's only seven."

"Really? That doesn't sound like him."

"But you've never even met him!"

"Here come the martinis!" Sinead said desperately. "Lovely strong drinks. Just what we all need!"

It was turning out to be a very strained night. Normally, they all got along great, despite their different circumstances: Naomi, married with two kids; MaryRose, a single mother; Sinead, single and childless; Tania, married with two kids; Katie, girlfriend of Conall and therefore in some twilight no-man's-land where she wasn't exactly single but she definitely wasn't locked into something secure and permanent.

It was Dawn. Dawn was the source of the trouble and she wasn't even Katie's friend; she'd only been allowed to come out of kindness.

"I bet you haven't met his parents," Dawn said.

"Who? Conall's? I have."

"Did they hate you? Did they think you were after his money?"

". . . Ah, no." She'd met Ivor and Ita a few times and they'd been friendly — but not creepy. They didn't treat Katie as the savior, the woman that might finally force their oldest son to settle down. "And I've met his brother and his kids tons of times." Well, maybe *tons* of times was stretching things a little. "I was at Bronagh's First Communion last month."

Dawn took a gulp of her pomegranate

martini. "How will you cope when he dumps you?"

Tension froze the table. Dawn was simply articulating what everyone else thought, but all of a sudden it was starting to annoy Katie.

"Dawn . . ." Naomi said anxiously.

"You'll end up in the nuthouse," Dawn decided.

"That's enough," Katie said sharply. "You don't know what you're talking about."

"But I —" Dawn looked horrified. Katie was normally so . . . nice, pleasant.

Katie felt as appalled as Dawn looked. This was the second sharp exchange she'd had in the last few days. The first was with her mum about her hair color, and now this. God. It was true what Naomi had said: now that she was forty she was suddenly going to be super-touchy and she'd have no choice about it. She'd make enemies everywhere.

"Dawn, look, I'm sorry." She couldn't hold it against Dawn. Dawn had a young baby, she hadn't had a night out in seven months, and she'd lost both her social skills and her tolerance for strong liquor.

"I haven't had sex in two years!" Sinead declared, diplomatically trying to plow a new conversational furrow. "Last time was Katie's thirty-eighth birthday. That was a great night. Remember the crowd of Slovakian fact-finders we met —"

"I haven't had sex in eleven months,"

Naomi said.

"But you're married! I'd give anything for regular sex," Sinead said.

Naomi tisked. "I wouldn't care if I never did it again."

Katie sighed inwardly. She knew where this was going. The chocolate conversation. All the women present who had long-term partners (Naomi, Dawn and Tania) were about to start complaining about how their men were always badgering them for sex but how they'd happily do without it for the rest of their lives if they could have a bar of chocolate every evening instead.

Sure enough, they went into a big long love-in about which chocolate they'd like: Mars Bars; Twirls; Twixes (unpopular); Bounties.

"Sex with Ralph once a month or a Twix every night?" Tania challenged Naomi.

"The Twix, the Twix! And I don't even like Twixes!"

"Neither do I. Why is it?"

"The shortbread," Naomi said knowledgeably.

"You're right! It *is* the shortbread."

Then Dawn mentioned Green & Black's and the discussion became so high-pitched that one of the waiters had to ask them to quiet down.

DAY 55

Andrei was in bed, crying softly. The combination of homesickness, the comedown from the weekend of heavy drinking and it being Sunday evening, the worst night of the week, was just all too much.

When he heard the key in the door, he was surprised because he wasn't expecting Jan back from Limerick until the following morning. But he wasn't expecting the evil little pixie either. She always spent Sunday nights with Poor Fucker. But it was definitely her, he could hear her, moving lightly around, spreading her unique brand of vileness throughout the flat.

He buried his face in his pillow, trying to stifle his sobs. The pixie must not hear him.

Lydia wasn't exactly in top form either. Drained and depressed by the weekend, she was facing a five-thirty start in the morning followed by a seventy-hour week. And from the grumpiness that pervaded the air, at least one of the Poles was home. Andrei probably.

Gilbert would fix her. She'd missed him this weekend. She rummaged for her phone, hit redial and irritation rose as she got his voice mail — again. He'd blanked her since Friday, obviously pissed off by her abrupt disappearance. Weekends were their time together. They both worked Friday and Saturday nights, usually into the early hours, finished up around 3 a.m., then spent Saturday and Sunday together, luxuriating in Gilbert's big bed.

"Stop sulking, you big baby," she said. "I'm home and I want to see you."

For a moment she wondered, *really* wondered where exactly Gilbert was right now, and what he'd spent his weekend at. There was no evidence that he was off with other girls but she was surprised by a queasy wash of some sort of emotion. Not nice, not nice at all.

She should eat something. Or maybe get some sleep.

Poppy was always saying that Gilbert probably had a wife and six children stashed away, back home in Lagos. It was a running joke among Lydia's friends, this thing about Gilbert's other life. Lydia always scoffed at it. A person supporting seven other people wouldn't spend as much money on clothes as Gilbert did.

But he *might,* she acknowledged. It wasn't

impossible.

Gilbert was secretive.

Dishonest, if you prefer.

When they'd met he told her he was thirty, but a few weeks later he'd let slip that he was only twenty-seven. There were things she knew about him — for example, that he owned a share in a small restaurant in North Great Georges Street — that she'd learned from Odenigbo. Gilbert had never mentioned it to her. Then again, why should he? She didn't own him and there was plenty he didn't know about her.

But she had to admit that some of Gilbert's claims seemed bafflingly gratuitous. He'd told her he was allergic to eggs. Insisted on it. A morsel of meringue could kill him, he said. However, she'd seen him happily eat an omelette and he hadn't swelled up to seven times his normal size and rolled around on the floor, gasping for air and wheezing for an adrenaline injection.

She understood that he lied to muddy the waters, to keep her from knowing exactly who he was. Gilbert was his own man and he needed to keep part of himself entirely for him. This was who he was and better, in her opinion, than a sap who insisted on giving her full and frank disclosure and then insisted that she return the favor.

All the same, tonight she wished her boyfriend was a little less mysterious. It was a bright summer evening and she was going mad at the thought of being trapped in this flat. Desperately, she fired off a few texts but no one would come out to play. Shoane was still in bed, nursing last night's hangover, and Sissy was on a date! Some man she'd met in the ticket queue at BusAras. Poppy was sitting before a spreadsheet, trying to do a seating plan for her wedding. Apparently, it was complicated, with various members of the family not speaking to other members and having to be kept well apart from each other.

"Let them sort it out themselves," Lydia advised.

"I can't." After a pause, Poppy said tearily, "But sometimes I feel like just running away from it all."

Lydia fully understood. If she was having to get married at the age of twenty-six, she'd be frantic with fear. She couldn't understand why Poppy was signing up for it. She was so young, there were so many years left in her life and she'd have to spend every single one of them with Bryan, who was nice enough but could Poppy sustain an interest in him for the next fifty years? The thought of having to do it herself made her insides go cold with terror.

"Come on out tonight. A few drinks will relax you."

"Lids, I can't." There was an edge of hysteria to Poppy's voice.

"I could come and help you with your plan."

"But you wouldn't help me. You'd put thoughts in my head, that I'm a madzer to be getting married at twenty-six, and telling me that Bryan is boring —"

"I never said Bryan is boring —"

"Steady! You said he's steady. That's the same thing as boring."

"I like Bryan!"

"But you don't want to marry him."

"Because you're marrying him."

"You don't want me to marry him either."

"I want whatever makes you happy." That was one of the most useful lines she'd ever learned in her life, Lydia thought. Diplomatic without being dishonest. It wasn't good to lie outright. A girl needs a code to live by.

"But you don't think being married to Bryan will make me happy."

"I do, Poppy, I do, I do, I do."

"But —"

"Really, I do. Look, I'll go now, leave you to it. Good luck and all."

She hung up, hugely relieved to have extricated herself from that downward spiral. Getting married sent people *mad.*

Gloomily, Lydia considered her options for the evening. She could work — in fact, she *should* work to try to recoup some of the revenue she'd missed out on this weekend. She visualized herself going down the stairs and getting into the car and switching on her light and seeing what happened — but every cell in her body revolted. She simply hadn't got what it took to endure a round of "Thanking you's" and "*Muchas gracias*'s" Not tonight.

She could go online and do some research but even work would be preferable to that. Paralyzed by the array of unpleasant choices on offer, she lapsed into a reverie, trying to decide which of her brothers she hated the most. How lucky she was, absolutely *spoiled* for choice. Murdy was obviously a total gobshite, you only had to look at him. He'd shaken off his taxi-driving roots and gone on to head up a bathroom-fittings empire, now boasting two showrooms in the county of Meath. He lived like a man of means, in a brand-new colonnaded mansion on the outskirts of the town, with a blond, jeep-driving wife and two chunky discontented children. He drove a Beemer and went on sunbeds and had people over for "supper" and teetered daily on the edge of bankruptcy. Only last night his golf clubs were repossessed. Pascal Cooper of Cooper Sports ("For all your sporting needs.") had arrived at the house and there was a short muttered discussion at the double-height front door. Lydia had overheard a couple of terse phrases from Pascal: "It was a special order from Jackson Hole," then, "We do this quietly or I send the sheriff — Ah howya, Lydia! You're looking well. That's a grand head of hair you have. How's the smoke treating you?" "Hello, Mr. Cooper." "Pascal, Pascal! This mister business makes me feel old. Right, Murdy, the clubs!" The clubs had been lifted out from the trunk of Murdy's Beemer and into the trunk of Pascal's ten-year-old Civic and, with a couple of loud backfires that Murdy perceived as a deliberate show of disrespect, Pascal roared away down the drive.

Ronnie, Lydia's second brother, was different. He lived from hand to mouth, was secretive, mysterious and had at least two unknown women on the go. ("His right ball doesn't know what his tallywhacker is doing," to quote Raymond.) Frequently, he'd go missing, anything from a couple of days to a week at a time, his mobile turned off, and when he reappeared, would offer no explanations. He had a black beard and thick black hair and he looked vaguely satanic. His personality was sort of satanic also, Lydia mused. Strong-willed, like, *abnormally* so. He never got angry, he could argue his case for ten years without ever raising his voice, and yet she was pretty sure that inhuman quantities of rage burned somewhere below the surface. Poppy used to say that Ronnie was half creepy, half sexy. She'd often said — this was in the days before Steady Bryan appeared on the scene — that she had a compelling curiosity about what sex would be like with him but suspected she'd feel quite sullied afterward.

Then there was Raymond, who'd run away to Stuttgart as soon as he was old enough. As kids, Raymond had been Lydia's favorite brother, the most fun. But over the last year and a half she had come to absolutely *hate* his fun-loving nature. Every time she tried to talk to him about something serious he twisted the subject away with another "funny" anecdote.

She jumped to her feet. She wanted to get drunk and if it had to be alone, then so be it. Lone drinking wasn't yet illegal. She went out and bought savory snacks and a bottle of wine and lined them up on the kitchen counter.

For her starter she'd have the Sour Cream and Onion Pringles, she decided, and for her main, the Texas BBQ Pringles . . . *What was that?*

Strange noises. She strained to listen. Coming from the Poles' room. A sort of a quiet whimpering. She moved closer to the door.

Was someone having sex in there? But who? Jan was away and there was no way Rosie would have dropped her panties for Andrei unless there was a ring on her finger. Lydia took a moment to savor her hatred of Rosie. She couldn't abide her and her ironed clothes — she was only twenty-one, what twenty-one-year-old ironed her clothes? — and her neat ponytail and her fake air of injured innocence and the very *un*innocent way she used sex as a bargaining tool . . . Maybe Andrei had finally got sick of her and was in there riding someone else? But that was almost as hard to believe as him riding Rosie; he was so right-and-wrong about everything . . . Then she heard the noise for what it was: crying! Andrei (or possibly Jan, but for some reason, despite his stoical nature, she suspected Andrei) was crying! Well, it was too funny for words. This she must see.

She knocked on the door and opened it before Andrei (or possibly Jan) could shout at her to go away.

It was Andrei, who, aghast at her presence, jerked around to face the wall, wiping his eyes furiously.

"Oh hello, Andrei. Do you have a cat in here?" she asked. "I heard funny noises."

"No cat." His voice was muffled.

"You're crying."

"Not."

"You are, you are. I heard you. What's up? Did Rosie break it off with you?"

"No." That really would have been reason to cry.

"Get up. Come out. I'm bored."

"No."

"It's got to be better than boo-hooing in here on your own, like a girl. Come on, I've got wine and chips."

He wasn't going to get any peace. She would keep at him and at him until he caved. Reluctantly, he swung his feet on to the floor.

"So why were you crying?" Lydia asked.

He thought about it. It was difficult to describe the bleakness that sometimes overtook him, but homesickness probably had a lot to do with it. Admittedly, he'd experienced similar bouts of despair while he'd actually been living in Poland, but he wasn't going to think about that now.

He shrugged. "I wish I could live in my own country."

"I wish you could too."

He lifted his head. Was she being kind?

No.

"It was a joke," she said, almost in amazement. This had gone on for too long. "Don't you have jokes in Poland?"

"Of course!" They had everything in Poland and all of it much better than what was provided in this benighted country. "But you . . . when you say it, it is not funny."

"Right back at you, crybaby."

With great dignity, he surrendered the four Pringles he held in his hand and got to his feet. "I'm going back to bed."

"Stay where you are. This will cheer you up: I'm going to tell you about my weekend."

■ ■ ■ ■

Well, he cried again. He was in a teary mood and it was all very sad. Such a story, he could hardly wait to tell Jan.

And he saw Lydia with new eyes.

"So this is why you are this terrible person!"

"Ah, yes . . . I suppose." Was she that terrible? "So what's your excuse?"

DAY 54

Lydia's dad used to joke that she could drive before she could walk. Not that he was given to joking much. Too busy setting up unsuccessful businesses and inventing new political schools of thought and having heart attacks.

Poor Dad, she thought. She didn't really hate him. He'd done his best, he'd worked very, very hard and tried to hold it all together, it was just that he had whatever the opposite of the Midas touch is called and then he had to go and die at the untimely age of fifty-nine, leaving a big, fat mess behind him.

Lydia was fifteen the first time she'd driven a fare. She was uninsured, unlicensed, but there was no one else available to do it and Peggy Routhy had gone into labor and needed a lift to the hospital and there was a spare car sitting outside the Duffys' house, wasting money with every second that it wasn't on the road, and Lydia's dad was on the radio, shrieking at her to get behind the wheel and drive the fucking thing, how hard could it be, and to be sure to charge extra for soilage if Peggy Routhy broke her waters on the good upholstery.

The Duffys were a taxi dynasty. Auggie had been the town taxi-man, with another three or four freelancers connected to him — and, more importantly — his radio. The radio of power. He who controls the radio controls the roads. And he who controls the roads controls the world. It sat in the Duffys' front room emitting static and kept the Duffys constantly on their toes. They were never free from its intrusion but sometimes they picked up the frequency of the local police and would invite the neighbors in to listen and mock.

Running a taxi business from the family home was chaotic. A call could come in or a hand might rap on the sitting-room window at any time of the day or night. (Respecting the divide between the public and private lives of the Duffys, those seeking a taxi knocked on the window while normal visitors came to the door.)

It was always a struggle to pay the tax, pay the insurance, pay for anything, and Auggie Duffy's income was never high enough to qualify for a mortgage.

All the same, things had been scrappy for the Duffys, *but not disastrous,* until Auggie Duffy read *The Communist Manifesto.* It had a profound effect on him. The key to making money, if he had Karl Marx right, was to own the means of production. But he, Auggie Duffy, would subvert the basic teachings of communism and use them in the successful pursuit of capitalism. Oh-ho! They'd have to get up early in the morning to get one past him!

Armed with his new theory, he somehow persuaded a bank to loan him enough money to buy four cars, then informed his drivers that from now on they'd have to lease a car from him. But why, these men wondered, would they lease a car from Auggie Duffy when they had a perfectly fine one of their own? Auggie reminded them of the small matter of the radio. He who controls the radio controls the roads, remember? But — and Karl Marx would have been thrilled — the workers revolted. These men had mobile phones and one of them had the bright idea of printing up little cards (Corinne's Stationery would do a thousand for a tenner) bearing their numbers. They distributed the cards around the town, in pubs and drugstores and on the church notice board and, undercutting Auggie Duffy's rates, business was soon coming their way.

Auggie found himself in the unexpected position of having a massive bank loan, five cars (the four new ones plus his original) and no one to drive four of them. His sons,

Murdy, Ronnie and Raymond, and his wife, Ellen, were press-ganged into service. Every second that one of his cars was sitting unused, Auggie felt it like an ache. No job was ever turned down.

So when Peggy Routhy showed up and Auggie, Ellen, Murdy and Ronnie were all out on jobs (by this stage Raymond had run away to Germany to escape the stranglehold of the radio), Auggie was convulsed at the thought of losing a fare. Lydia was only fifteen, but she was a great little driver. Well able. "Do it," he ordered.

"I haven't got a license."

"Good point. Make sure you don't get caught by the police."

"I'm not insured."

"So don't kill anyone. And remember what I said. Watch out for soilage."

Peggy was on her hands and knees outside the Duffys' front door, roaring with pain, and Billy Routhy was banging on the window, shouting, "Lydia, would you come *on,* she's going to have the baby right here on the path!"

So, with a sense of destiny, Lydia took the keys to the Corolla from the hook and stood a little taller; she got into the car and drove seventeen kilometers to the hospital, breaking the speed limit all the way, Peggy groaning and shouting, on all fours, in the back. At their destination, the Routhys hopped out of the car and made straight for the doors of the hospital but Lydia called a halt and requested her fare. She even insisted on an extra twenty because, yes, Peggy's waters had broken all over the back seat. Billy was hostile as he handed over the money and Peggy, crippled with pain, her face contorted, shouted, "That's mean of you. I thought we were all in this together, like a film. I was going to call the baby Lydia."

Lydia shrugged. Business was business. The back seat was destroyed. And what if the baby was a boy?

That was the start. When she turned sixteen, she got a license and began working full time for her dad. Just for a couple of years but it was enough to ruin her for any kind of regular work. When she moved to Dublin, she got a job in an office, until she discovered that if someone was annoying her, she couldn't simply open the door and tell them to get out.

Inevitably, she got the sack; they told her she had an attitude problem. To make ends meet, she went back to cabbing. Only temporarily, until her attitude changed. But the attitude change was taking longer than she'd expected and until then she was doomed to drive a taxi.

DAY 53

"Jemima, what's keeping you?" Fionn called. "The car is here."

"I'm coming." She was struggling to close the button on the waistband of her skirt. How infuriating. Her skirt had unaccountably become too small. But she had no plans to purchase a new skirt, not at this stage of her life. She didn't indulge in squanderbug behavior (could it be described as "squanderbuggery"?): she was eighty-eight years of age and, although she came from excellent stock, she was unlikely to get forty years' wear out of a new skirt before she died. Which, incidentally, she had no intention of doing any time soon, regardless of that wretched presence hanging about.

Nor did she intend to go on a reducing diet. That sort of thing was the province of other women, women different to her, those poor creatures who couldn't control their corporal urges, who ate entire cartons of ice cream in one sitting. Food, she had always understood, was not to be enjoyed. It was simply there to fuel one's body, in order to have the requisite strength for do-goodery. Since the age of seventeen, she'd been a stringy ten stone — except for a short spell four years ago, when she'd dropped to nine and a half stone during a clash with cancer, in which the cancer came off as the definite loser and had to limp away bruised and humiliated — and she did not intend to alter now, no matter what this recalcitrant button was trying to tell her —

"Jemima, are you *right?*" Fionn called. "The driver keeps ringing me."

How entertaining! Fionn, the most unreliable creature alive, chivying Jemima Churchill, who had Punctuality Is Next To Godliness running through her bone marrow, like a message through a stick of seaside rock.

Her hands slippery with effort, she forced the button into its hole and exhaled with triumph. But the enthusiasm of this breath proved too much for the waistband and the button pinged from its moorings and shot across the room like a bullet, catching Grudge bang-slap in the right eye. A great, high-pitched howl issued from Grudge, who was secretly delighted. The slap in the eye hadn't hurt — it looked far more dramatic than it was — but it meant he had a grievance he could work for days.

"Jemima!" Fionn roared. "Fecking Grainne's after ringing. We have to go!"

Jemima had to smile. Grainne Butcher ran a tight ship. This was only the second day of Fionn's television career and already the early starts and long hours were taking their toll on him. He wasn't used to having to be places at a certain time and then having to stay there once the novelty had worn off. Nevertheless, experiencing a schedule with a certain amount of rigor might do him some good.

Jemima kissed Grudge again, smoothed her cardigan down over her gaping waistband and picked up her ancient brown handbag. Fionn was pacing in the hallway, looking cranky but so dazzlingly handsome that it lifted her game old heart just to look at him. Grainne Butcher's stylist had brought pressure to bear so that he had washed his hair, his jeans and his many-pocketed jacket. He was a prince, thought Jemima, a beautiful clean prince.

Today is a very special day for Fionn. Except that Fionn doesn't know it. Not consciously, anyway. Several layers down in his subconscious, continental plates are starting to shift, creaking apart, clashing, promising forthcoming upheaval.

Today Fionn has been alive for 36 years and 128 days. He is a day older than the age his mother was when she died. He has outlived her. Up until this day, Fionn has had to work at keeping himself alive. So much energy had to be put into protecting himself that there was none left over to give to another.

But today marks a new dawn.

Today, for the first time in his life, Fionn is free to fall in love.

Frankly, I'm on the edge of my seat . . .

Like a grayhound out of the traps, Fionn was. Not a second to waste in this new exciting phase of his life. He hurried down the stairs, Jemima and Grudge, who were accompanying him on today's shoot, bringing up the rear. He opened the front door . . . and a few feet away, standing in a pool of yellow light, was the most exquisite woman he'd ever seen. Stunned, he came to an abrupt halt, Jemima and Grudge tumbling into the back of his legs. He gazed at this woman's succulent rosebud mouth, her pink and white skin, her tumbling blond curls, her freshness, her innocence, her bicycle, her —

Alerted by the intensity of his gaze, the woman lifted her head sharply and an expression of frozen awe appeared on her face.

Fionn bounded down the last few steps to the street, his hair flashing golden in the early morning sunlight. "I'm Fionn Purdue." He extended his hand to her.

The woman ignored Fionn's hand. She remained silent and motionless and continued to stare at Fionn as if she'd been turned to stone.

A man appeared from nowhere, young, be-suited. Fionn hadn't noticed him until now.

"Matt Geary," he said.

Once again Fionn thrust his hand forward, but once again it was ignored.

"And —" Matt leaned much closer to Fionn and bellowed these next words — "this is MY WIFE."

"What's your name?" Fionn breathed at the beauty. But she didn't answer.

Fionn turned to Matt, his radiant face eager for knowledge.

Seconds ticked by, then Matt admitted with reluctance, "Maeve."

"Maeve," Fionn said, with wonder. *Maeve.* What a beautiful name, possibly the most beautiful name he'd ever heard and entirely suitable because it belonged to the most beautiful woman alive. "Maeve, the warrior queen. I'm your new neighbor. I'm on the first floor, with Jemima Churchill. Do you know Jemima?" Frantically, he flapped his hand, urging Jemima to step forward. He looked over his shoulder and glared at her. "Come on," he hissed. "Come and say hello to Maeve!"

"I already know *Matthew.* And Maeve," Jemima said politely.

"I'll be living here for a while." Fionn addressed this solely to Maeve. "A couple of months or thereabouts."

The beeping of a car horn interrupted his reverie. "Fionn, would you come on!" It was Ogden, the driver. "Grainne's going mental!"

All of a sudden, Fionn was delighted to be making this television show. The horribly early starts and the stupid hair conditioner and the gay new T-shirts unexpectedly seemed worth it. It might impress Maeve. "I'm starring in my own gardening show," he blurted eagerly. "Called *Your Own Private Eden*. Channel 8." He half-noticed that Jemima had grasped his elbow and was determinedly leading him to the car. "Thursday nights," he called over his shoulder to the vision, who remained rigid and mute. "Coming soon! Watch out for it!"

Doors slammed shut, Ogden floored the accelerator and Fionn gazed in rapture out of the back window until they turned a corner and he could no longer see her.

"Who was *she?*" he asked Jemima.

"Leave her alone." Jemima sounded uncharacteristically sharp.

Fionn laughed happily. "You've nothing to be jealous of! I'll always love you the best. What can you tell me?"

Jemima's lips tightened. She didn't engage in scuttlebutt. Although she wished she did. During the course of her life she'd experienced many pleasures of the flesh: sixty-seven glasses of sweet sherry (one every Christmas from the age of twenty-one to the present day); she'd smoked two lungfuls of a cigarillo given to Giles by a client; at Fionn's behest she'd tasted a toothsome confection called Death by Chocolate in a charming place called TGI Friday's; and, obviously, she'd enjoyed sexual relations with her late husband. But nothing had hooked her the way that speculating on the lives of others had. She yearned to have what women's magazines called "A Good Gossip." To learn a secret gave her a pleasure rush that was almost alarming in its intensity and to pass it on was even more enjoyable. But she couldn't indulge in tittle-tattle. Good-living people didn't. However, there were times, she thought wistfully, when she wished she hadn't been brought up as she had been, when she wished she wasn't so good.

Matt stared after the car ferrying Fionn away. He was almost sick with rage. "Who the *fuck* does that wanker think he is?"

Maeve stared anxiously at him. "I'd better get going."

"Did you see him?" His voice was several octaves higher than usual. "Did you see the way he was *blatantly* —" He stopped. Of course she'd seen.

"I'll be home at the usual time," she said.

"Okay." He kissed her but he was so angry he could hardly bear to touch her.

He watched her cycle away, then found his

car and drove past crowded bus stops, ignoring all the people he could have offered lifts to. What would be the point? They'd just accuse him of being an ax murderer.

In the hallway of Edios, he bumped into Niamh, one of the brightest members of his team. She looked upset. And different in some way, a bad way.

"What's wrong?" he asked.

"Isn't it obvious? My hair. I got it cut after work yesterday. It's a disaster."

That was what was different about her.

"I look like a transsexual," she said.

That was exactly what she looked like, Matt realized. Something about the short blunt cut turned her into a very mannish woman, a person who was halfway through the hormones and surgery transition. Here was Matt's opportunity to get his act of kindness out of the way before 9 a.m. It would absolve him from the commuters he'd abandoned at the bus stops.

"Nail on the head, as usual, Niamh." She had a gift for cutting through the dross of any situation. "Go back to the salon. Get something else done. I don't know what to suggest, hair isn't my thing. But you can't go round looking like this —"

. . . The look in her eyes. She was staring at him, like a puppy he'd just kicked. She was shocked to her core. *I thought you were lovely,*

262

her eyes said, confused and piteous. *I thought you were one of the nicest men I'd ever met. How could you be so cruel?*

He nodded curtly, itching to get away. Something had gone badly, heinously wrong.

Before he'd moved ten paces, he saw his mistake. His act of kindness should have been to *lie,* not to be honest. All she'd wanted was some reassurance.

"Niamh," he called.

She turned round.

"Niamh, I'm sorry," he said humbly. "I've had a chance to think. Your haircut. It's nice. It just needs a bit of getting used to."

She nodded, her chin trembling. "Thanks." Her lips were wobbling.

"I'm really sorry if I upset you."

"It's okay."

But it wasn't. She'd lost faith in him. She'd never trust him again.

Deeply depressed, he made his way to his office. Fucking Acts of Kindness and Trios of Blessings and the whole fucking thing. Nothing worked. Nothing helped.

Today could be the day he closed the sale to the Bank of British Columbia. They'd asked for yet another meeting and there was nothing else left to discuss. Nothing! Not even Wimbledon tickets. They weren't getting any, because he couldn't pour any more money into this without a result. Once, in the past

— only once, mind — he'd got to this point with a client and they'd bailed. It had been a blow that had almost unmanned him. He'd put so much work into the wooing and spent so much of Edios's entertaining budget that when he got the phone call delivering the bad news, a roaring noise had filled his ears, and his vision went tunnelly, then completely black. The colleagues at nearby desks had told him that he had fainted, but he hadn't fainted. Of course he hadn't fainted! He'd dropped the phone, his legs stopped supporting him for a moment or two and he'd gone temporarily blind, but he hadn't fainted!

It was possible that the Bank of British Columbia had called this morning's meeting to tell him they weren't buying the system. It was possible that they would extend the courtesy of letting him know in person, instead of a snippy two-line email. But perhaps they were going to make the purchase. And if they did, if he pulled this off . . .

There would be commission. There would be kudos. And there would be something else — he didn't exactly know how to put it, but it would sort of remind him of who he really was.

First, though, he'd have to be enthusiastic. He'd have to be upbeat. Driving through the city, Salvatore, Cleo and Niamh crammed into the back of the car and Jackson in the front, he told himself: You're a salesman. Be

264

a salesman.

But at the bank, as he led his team to the meeting room, where the fate of this deal would be decided, his confidence once again faltered and he paused.

"Group hug?" Salvatore asked archly.

". . . No. Good luck, everyone. Here we go." Pasting on the biggest smile he could manage — he couldn't remember ever having to force himself to smile before, the smiles had always happened automatically — he burst into the room where the men were waiting and launched into growly, good-humored noises. "Yah-haaahh! How's it going?"

"Excellent, Matt, and you?"

"Great. Eee-yahhh!" He was grabbing shoulders and giving them friendly shakes and doing gentle shoving and pushing. That was the way Matt did business. Mates, yes, everyone was mates. Best friends, plenty of body contact, none of this boundaries mullarky. Discussing hangovers. Discussing cars. Discussing sport. Ireland had done badly in the rugby. "Ouff! Not our finest hour."

"Ouff, indeed!"

"But we'll be back to fight another day! Yah-haaaghh!"

"Yah-hahh!"

"Eden is everywhere." Fionn smiled warmly into the lens. "Even in a small city-center flat like this." He waved his arm to indicate the space and the camera panned around to show a cramped mini-kitchen.

"Good, Fionn," Grainne said. "Just a bit more enthusiasm. Eden is EVERYWHERE. Like, how amazing is that?"

"Eden is EVERYWHERE." Fionn smiled warmly into the lens. "Even in a small city-center flat like this." He waved his arm to indicate the space and the camera panned around to show a cramped mini-kitchen.

"Good, Fionn. Just a bit more amazement. EVEN in a small — actually, let's say tiny, tiny is better." Grainne adjusted her script. "Even in a TINY city-center flat like this."

"Eden is EVERYWHERE." Fionn smiled warmly into the lens. "EVEN in a TINY city-center flat like this." He waved his arm to indicate the space and the camera panned around to show a cramped mini-kitchen.

"Getting there. Go again."

Oh dear, Grudge thought, smiling spitefully to himself. Fionn wasn't very good at this, was he? How many times had he done this little pantomime already? Frankly, so many that Grudge had lost count.

"Fionn, I just want to let you know that there's nothing unusual in doing this many takes," Grainne said. "It doesn't mean you're doing anything wrong."

Oh dear, dear, Grudge thought, studying his nails and hiding another smirk. They were patronizing him now, they were actually *pitying* him. It could only be a short while before Excellent Little Productions realized what a terrible mistake they'd made and Fionn Purdue would find himself back on the Monaghan Meteorite and on his way home to Pokey and shameful ignominy, never to return.

Not that the idiot seemed to have any idea what a disaster he was. He was saying his lines and waving his arms on demand, but he was thinking about that Maeve girl. *Loved up*, Grudge thought with distaste. Between takes, Fionn lapsed into a moronic state, a languid half-smile on his face, repeating the word *Maeve* over and over again in his head. *Maeve, Maeve, Maeve, Maeve, Maeve, Maeve, Maeve, Maeve, Maeve, Maeve, Maeve, Maeve, Maeve, Maeve, Maeve, Maeve, Maeve, Maeve, Maeve.* Grudge could hear it quite clearly even if no one else could.

"Okay, Fionn, go again," Grainne said.

"Eden is EVERYWHERE." Fionn smiled warmly into the lens. "EVEN in a TINY city-center flat like this." He waved his arm to indicate the space and the camera panned around to show a cramped mini-kitchen.

Grainne shook her head. "Sorry, Fionn. It wasn't you that time."

For once, Grudge thought, with savage pleasure.

"Picking up something on the sound." A muttered conversation ensued between Grainne and the soundman, who had supersensitive headphones. "Bus down in the street, going over a manhole."

"Can we ask them to stop?"

"We can try."

The runner, a young pierced creature called Darleen, was ordered downstairs with instructions to divert all buses until further notice.

"That's impossible," she said.

"In your interview you told me you wanted to work in television," Grainne said. "You said you were prepared to do whatever it took." She shrugged. "This is what it takes."

A tough nut, that Grainne, Grudge thought, with reluctant admiration.

Darleen must have accomplished something down in the street because after two more takes Grainne was satisfied with Fionn's delivery, the sound, the light and all the rest of it.

In the next scene, the camera followed Fionn as he moved toward the kitchen wall, wrenched open a window and smiled at the camera. "Ladies and gentlemen, I give you Access to Eden." Tenderly, he laid his dirty hand on the outside ledge. "Otherwise known as a windowsill." He smiled again, as if sharing a secret with the viewers, and Grudge swallowed anxiously. Fionn had looked a bit like a star there. Just for a moment. Quickly, he looked at Jemima. Had she noticed?

But Jemima had spent the entire morning gazing at Fionn like he was Daniel Day Lewis giving an Oscar-worthy performance. She had no discretion when it came to Fionn, Grudge acknowledged. She thought every single little thing he did was astonishingly wonderful. In fairness, she extended the same generosity to himself, Grudge. But he was different.

At the end of the day, Grainne Butcher was quite pleased. For someone who'd never done this sort of thing before, Fionn Purdue really wasn't bad. And he looked great — the face, the body, the hair, the *hands*. The dirty, loving hands. They'd got lots of lingering close-ups as he tamped down earth into window boxes and tenderly repotted sprigs and gently rubbed leaves between thumb and finger.

Grainne, who was never keen to give credit unless she really had to, was forced to acknowledge that Fionn was as patient as he was handsome. She didn't think she'd ever worked with someone so good-humored about the constant retakes. Obviously, Fionn Purdue wasn't overburdened with ego.

She wondered how long that would last. The first time they saw their photo in the paper was when the diva behavior tended to kick off. And Fionn was going to get plenty of attention; she'd already had four interview requests for him and it was only a day since the press release had been sent out.

Of course, there was a *small* chance that Fionn might stay humble. Mind you, he'd further to come, ego-wise, having been sequestered in the bleak back-arse-of-beyond of Pokey, with no ambitions whatsoever, beyond keeping the desperate housewives weed-free.

"We'll call it a day," Grainne said. "Good work, Fionn. See you in the morning. Will, ah . . . will Jemima and Grudge be coming tomorrow?" It was a strange thing to say but she felt that the dog had an attitude problem.

"I don't know yet," Fionn said. "What if I invited someone else instead? Would that be okay?"

"Sure, grand, who is it?"

But Fionn didn't seem to hear her. He had gone way inside himself. Artists! Fey! It was the characteristic that exasperated her the most. She could take people being bent out of shape by all kinds of demons from rage to stinginess to pathological jealousy, but, as a master pragmatist herself, feyness (if that was the word) drove her wild. Fionn's eyes refocused as he reemerged from wherever he'd been. "Grainne," he said, "what's the name of that emotion where you can't stop thinking about a particular person?"

". . . Erm . . . Obsession?"

Fionn clicked his fingers in gratitude. "Obsession! Bang on!"

DAY 53 . . .

Matt left work ten minutes early. The morning meeting with the Bank of British Columbia hadn't brought about any conclusion. They'd been friendly and had asked more questions and said they'd be in touch, and his head was downright melted from it. Back in the office, he had a manic moment when he considered picking up the phone and ringing them, telling them that he was refusing to sell them the system, just to put an end to the agony of waiting.

He spent his lunch hour alone in the office, reading *Top Gear.* When he'd finished that — and it seemed to end far too soon — he found himself grabbing Cleo's paper and, in a kind of frenzy, doing the three sudokus, one after the other. But the very second he'd filled in the last number and laid down his pen, guilt overwhelmed him. Doing another person's sudokus was very wrong. It was *stealing.* The same as eating a slice of cake that someone had been saving in the fridge.

He'd just have to come clean and offer to

271

buy her another paper. He refolded the pages, to hide his crime from himself and, as he did, he noticed a short paragraph about the random lumps of ice falling from the sky. Just a roundup of what he already knew, but it was still enjoyable to spend time on. He narrowed his eyes as he realized that the locations where the ice had landed were all capital cities. Had any of the experts clocked that? What did it mean? Was it the start of an apocalyptic meltdown in which capital cities around the globe were targeted? He could already hear CNN. "Gigantic hailstones are battering Buenos Aires . . . breaking news from Washington, D.C. . . . panic in the streets of Tokyo . . ." Like a good movie.

What were the chances of one of these ice boulders landing in Dublin? And if so, where would it land? Whose car would it squash or whose roof would it damage or — daring thought — whose life would it end? For a moment, the image was so delicious that he closed his eyes, to savor it even more.

But resentment curdled this glowing vision. It would never happen. There was no justice. None. None at all.

He couldn't pull himself out of the slump. Nothing, not even Cleo cheerfully absolving him from the sudoku theft, could hoist him out of the pit and back to his normal self. He was unable to do any work. He should be tracking down new business, pestering more companies to buy Edios's software, but right now he had no heart for it.

He was having a bad day, everyone had them sometimes. Maybe tomorrow would be different, but he might as well give up on today.

"Gotta go. Dentist appointment," he said casually.

Noises and sympathy and surprise followed him as he left. Brave Matt, knowing all day that he had a dentist appointment hanging over him and not even mentioning it. What a great guy he was. Even Niamh (who'd gone out at lunchtime and had another, healing haircut) wondered if she should reassess her opinion of him.

Matt got in his car and shot out of the parking lot — but he didn't drive toward home. I followed his route, trying to make sense of it. For a moment I wondered if the dentist story had been true and not just a pretext to spring him from the office early. Then I noticed that he was headed for the docklands. Did this mean what I thought it meant?

. . . It did.

In the same side street where Maeve had parked her bike four days earlier, Matt parked his car. He put enough money in the meter for two hours, then stood directly opposite the main doors of No Brainer Technology — brazenly, not hidden like Maeve had been — and watched the people leaving, just like

273

Maeve had.

And here came the bloke, loose shirt tails and missing buttons and long, uncombed hair, a satchel with a fraying strap stretched across his long torso. When he saw Matt, fear pulsed from his ashen face but almost immediately his equilibrium was restored and he laughed — *laughed* — at Matt. The chuckling sound floated across the road, and rage roared from Matt's center, pushing and swelling into every cell in his body. Lanky-boy ambled away with exaggerated insouciance and Matt wanted to punch a wall.

He got back into his car and pummeled himself five times in the gut and felt a bit better: his anger had reduced and he had hurt himself. Which was appropriate, because this was all his fault.

. . . There's no point asking me, I'm all at sea.

DAY 53 . . .

"What am I to wear?" Conall asked, when he called from Helsinki. He checked in most nights before Katie went to sleep.

"Your Tom Ford suit and that shirt I bought you."

"The pink one?"

"It's not pink, it's lavender. Very pale lavender. Almost white." Not really; it was full-on girlie lavender, which paradoxically made him

274

look extra manly. But there was no point trying to explain that; there were times when it was better to simply insist on something. "And I've left out the tie I want you to wear. It's on your bed."

"And I'm to pick you up at one?"

"That's my flat at thirteen-hundred hours, just so we're clear. Is your car clean?"

She detected a slight hesitation. "It will be. We could always go in yours."

No, they couldn't. Her car was nice but not impressive. Not like his Lexus. Call her shallow but this was her ex-boyfriend's wedding they were attending. She was happy that Jason was happy and all that blah but *nevertheless* . . . she didn't want to look like it was hurting.

"And your flight?" she asked. "Finnair, is it? Gets in at ten-fifteen on Saturday morning?" She knew this already, every single detail, but there could be no room for misunderstandings. This was very, very important.

"Ten-fifteen."

"You couldn't come on Friday night, just to make sure you'll be here?" She'd asked this several times before but she was so anxious she couldn't stop herself from asking again.

"I will be there."

"Okay."

"I promise."

A moment of silence.

"I promise. I will not let you down on this."

I will not let you down on this. What more could he do to convince her, she asked herself. And at least he wasn't in Manila or Saigon, like he sometimes was, with so many more possibilities for flights to be delayed and connections to be missed. Helsinki was a direct flight, only a couple of hours away. It would all be grand.

Very obviously changing the subject, Conall asked, "Now, what's the thought for today?"

"Hold on." Katie reached for the diary Danno and the others had given her for her birthday. She flicked to the right page. "Today's uplifting phrase is, 'Love your body exactly as it is. You think it's imperfect and you're right, but it's only going to get worse.' "

"Your body is perfect," Conall said softly.

Katie snorted, but he'd got her . . .

After she'd hung up she wondered if he'd know which shoes to wear. Should she ring him back? Maybe not. He was unreliable but he was well dressed and perhaps she'd hounded him enough about this wedding.

Instead, she decided to put her trash out.

Fionn stood up.

"Where are you going?" Jemima asked sharply.

". . . Ah . . . nowhere." He resumed sitting on the antimacassar-covered armchair and directed an expression of fake concentration at Jemima's small, very old television.

In silence they drank their tea, then Fionn clattered his cup into his saucer to signal a change of activity. Getting to his feet, he said casually, "I think I'll stretch my legs."

"They're long enough already. Sit down."

"I need to get out, Jemima. A country lad like me, I'm no good cooped up in a small flat. I need a stroll."

"It's ten o'clock at night. The streets will be littered with scofflaws and stumblebums."

"So what?"

"You may not be able to hold your own," she said archly. "A simple country lad like you."

"Just for a few minutes . . ." He was already at the door.

"She's married," Jemima said, in ringing tones.

"Who?"

"You know who. Maeve."

She didn't *feel* married, Fionn thought.

"As I understood it, you've heretofore given married ladies the widest possible berth."

He had, of course he had, any decent person would. But Maeve was different. He didn't know how, he couldn't say in what way, all he knew was that she was.

"You were brought up to respect married women." Jemima was trying to shame him into forgetting about Maeve, but he would not. He could not! He was stunned by the intensity of his feelings for her. She'd been in his head all day, an unbroken background hum. It was the first time a woman had affected him in this way and, if he was to be really honest, he didn't care that she was spoken for. He wanted her and he was going to get her.

"I feel . . . how can I put it? That she's not really married." He shook his head, his eyes narrowed in suspicion. "That Mark character —"

"His name is Matthew!"

"— something's wrong there, it's like he's keeping her prisoner."

"Have you taken leave of your senses?" Jemima inquired, her eyes bright as a bird's. "I beseech you to listen to yourself."

"I'm telling you, Jemima, something's not right."

"This is balderdash! You're simply trying to absolve yourself from a terrible thing. Which I will not permit you to do."

"How're you gonna stop me?" Suddenly, all a-swagger, he was fifteen again.

"I forbid you to leave."

She glared at him. He'd forgotten about the power of her glare. The irresistible force, he and Giles used to call it. It pinioned him like a laser beam and he found himself being moved bodily across the room and shoved back into his armchair, where he slumped, spent and limp.

Jemima fixed him with a polite smile. "More tea, dear?"

You can stick your tea up your bony Protestant hole.

"Okay," he mumbled.

"Do tell me," Jemima said tartly, as she lifted the teapot. "What were you planning to do? Knock on her door and ask her out, with her husband sitting two feet away?"

"I thought I'd invite them along to the set," Fionn said, with icy dignity. "*Both* of them. People seem to like that sort of thing."

"I think they'll manage quite well without a trip to a television studio, thank you verrrry much!"

DAY 53 . . .

Less than ten feet below Fionn, Matt and Maeve were at their usual lark, twisted around each other on the couch, watching some home-improvement program. They were very much creatures of routine. Every day they awoke at 7:30 and sat down to a civilized breakfast of porridge and honey and a vitamin pill. At 8:30 they left for work and returned at 6:30. Every evening they cooked a robust dinner, anchored by potatoes, and this was always followed by something sweet — they were fond of refined sugar, baked goods, Cornettos, apple turnovers and similar. When they'd eaten their fill, they twined around each other on the couch and watched television, regardless of what was on, and snacked further on confectionery. When the clock struck 11, they put on several layers of clothing, went to bed and wrote their Trio of Blessings in their notebooks.

They were made for each other, Matt and Maeve.

The irony was that even though David — like Maeve — was a Galwegian and Matt was, to quote David, nothing but "a suit," Maeve had far more in common with Matt than she'd ever had with David. She laughed with Matt, she laughed a lot. Something that hadn't happened much with David, who found the world so outrageously unjust that laughter seemed like the act of an insensitive and frivolous person.

But even though she and Matt were made for each other, she was eaten up with guilt about David. All he had ever done was love her and be good to her, and she was appalled and ashamed by how publicly she'd humiliated him. From the perspective of her new relationship, she could see what had been wrong with herself and David, a lot more than she'd acknowledged when she'd been with him. She'd been so flattered by David choosing her above all the other girls in Goliath — David so clever and passionate and charismatic — that she'd never really stopped to ask herself if David was the person she wanted.

She was desperate to explain things to him, to somehow take away his hurt, but David wouldn't permit Maeve to "explain" anything. Mind you, Maeve acknowledged, she'd have her work cut out. She hadn't a clue how it had happened. One minute David was her boyfriend and she'd been vaguely fond of Matt and the next she was violently in love with Matt and David had been relegated to a bit player.

She tried to get David to meet for some sort of talk, but it was impossible. He hung up on her phone calls, bounced back all her emails and, with melodramatic dignity, took to crossing the road when he saw Maeve coming. In inter-team meetings he made murky references to how other staff members couldn't be trusted, and once, when she accidentally brushed by him in the games room, he hissed, "Don't touch me."

Matt's innate optimism insisted that David would get over Maeve and soon move on to someone new, but Maeve wasn't so sure. David felt things deeply, and the traits she had once so admired about him, like his passionate objection to all injustices, suddenly seemed like impediments. David still held a grudge against Henry Kissinger for orchestrating the coup in Chile that overthrew Allende, even though David hadn't actually been born at the time.

Natalie was a different story. With admirable pragmatism, she accepted the new Matt'n'Maeve configuration almost overnight. "You guys —" she waved a smooth brown hand at them — "just look at you, you're the real deal, you're meant to be together. I didn't like it at first, but what could I do?"

"What should we do about David?" Maeve asked Natalie.

But Natalie was from the same optimistic school as Matt. Airily, she advised, "Just give him time."

So a month passed, then two months, but David remained cut up and Maeve remained riddled with guilt, and all in all, it made work a little awkward. And, indeed, their leisure time also. Matt was keen to be with Maeve at all times, he was happy to fall in with her usual pursuits, to eat falafels in the rain, to be jostled and splashed with beer at Gogol Bordello or to repeatedly fall off a surfboard and into the freezing Atlantic. But Maeve couldn't do it to David. She'd hurt him so much, it was only fair that he get custody of their friends and their social life.

Hopefully, it wouldn't be forever and, in the meantime, she and Matt forged a new path, finding a middle ground between their two different lifestyles. She made him read a Barbara Kingsolver book and he persuaded her to spend a weekend in a hotel with a spa, even to partake of a couples massage. And although she'd been sure she'd feel guilty about the demeaning work the poor masseuse had to do, she found that giving a hefty tip went a long way to clearing her conscience.

In fact, she had to admit that she found the whole weekend delightful. As Matt did the Barbara Kingsolver. But then again, they found everything about each other delightful, so it was hard to be sure.

DAY 53 . . .

Fionn shifted in the little armchair and thought, aha! Yes, aha! Jemima would have to go to bed at some point. He would bide his time. She was a powerful woman and at times a terrifying one, but everyone had to sleep. So he drank his tea and watched the silly little television and at eleven o'clock, when Jemima announced she was turning in, he did a big stretch and faked a long yowly yawn and agreed that it was time for bed. He kissed her goodnight at her bedroom door, then waited and waited until he heard regular little whistling sounds coming from her bedroom, and even though he forced himself to wait another fifteen minutes, when he opened the front door he was sincerely afraid that she would appear before him like an avenging angel and order him, shamefaced, to return to bed. But it went off without incident. She must be losing her touch.

He tiptoed down the stairs and slipped a note under Maeve's door. Nothing controversial, nothing controversial at all. At all. Addressed to both of them, inviting them along to the set. *At your convenience.* His mobile number. Jemima's mobile. Jemima's landline. All very casual.

Katie, dressed in pajamas and high heels, was returning from putting out her trash. The ability to do everything in life in four-inch heels was a gift similar to having a beautiful singing voice, a gift that had to be respected, that had to be kept oiled and toned. In the same way that singers worked their voices every day, doing scales and whatnot, Katie too was diligent in her practice. If she lost her gift, if she began to tilt forward and go over on her ankle and complain about the balls of her feet killing her, she'd feel like she'd lost a part of herself.

She was running up the stairs and had

almost reached Lydia's flat, when she heard Jemima's door open below her.

Curses! Like any normal person, she lived in dread of having to speak to her neighbors, but she was too near to Jemima's flat to escape. With huge misgivings she turned, bracing herself for a few minutes of polite nocturnal chat with the old woman. But, to her great surprise, it was not Jemima who emerged into the hallway, but the most stunning-looking man. A golden god, with long hair and perfect bone structure and a jaw set with purpose. A phrase of her mother's spoke in her head: His beauty would take the sight from your eyes.

Who was he?

Though she was frozen to the spot and openly gaping, he didn't see her — proof that she'd become invisible now that she was forty. Fascinated, she leaned over the banister and followed his glowing progress as he tiptoed furtively downstairs and slipped a note under Matt and Maeve's door.

What was the story there?

Then, assailed by a mild reeling in her head — the heels, the heels — she realized she'd topple over the rail and down a flight of stairs if she wasn't careful. She pushed herself back into a vertical position and continued upward.

DAY 52

Matt was stumbling and yawning along the hall on his way to make the coffee — he always got up before Maeve — and was doing a quick recce, just to check that it was safe to be alive, when he noticed the piece of paper lying on the floor. It was immediately obvious it wasn't a flyer; it was a handwritten note and it had to be from one of the neighbors. He was mildly curious. What had they done? Had their telly on too loud? Then he read it, and even as a boiling rage lit up his every cell, he stepped into the kitchen and closed the door to protect Maeve from the strength of his feelings.

The dazzling morning light poured through the kitchen window and hurt his eyes, and the blood was pounding at such a rate through his body that his ears felt hot and sore. He leaned his hands on the kitchen counter and bowed his head. Such *disrespect!*

Would he tell Maeve? Like fuck he would! He thrust the note into the compost bin, where it belonged, where it would rot with vegetable peelings and discarded food.

When he brought Maeve her coffee, she was still in bed, lying flat on her back and looking particularly leaden. "Matt . . . ?"

"Mmm?"

"I feel . . . like someone is watching me."

For the second time in ten minutes, Matt was assailed by emotion. A dense lump of doom hurtled into him and at high velocity pulled him toward the center of the earth. He was appalled at his own recklessness: that detour he'd made yesterday, what had he been thinking? He should have left well alone. He'd stirred stuff up; he'd drawn your man on them. Unless it was that Fionn bloke . . . ?

"Watching you how?" he managed to ask. "Through the windows?"

"No, not like that."

"Watching you at work?"

"Maybe."

"Waiting outside work for you?"

"No, more like . . . this sounds mad, watching me through the walls."

"Through the walls?" *Through the walls?*

"I don't know, Matt. I'm sorry. I just feel it."

They had their showers, prepared their porridge and poured their honey but Matt couldn't eat. His throat was so closed he could barely force down his vitamin pill.

287

Eventually, they leave for work, but I stay in the flat. I'm looking for something. But what? Nothing awry with their tea bags; their underwear drawer holds no secrets, just jockey shorts and knickers that are long past their prime; and in the bathroom, an unopened cellophane-wrapped box of Coco Chanel body lotion is covered with a thin coating of dust, which strikes me as sad but not exactly revelatory. Then I return to the kitchen cupboards and see what I'm supposed to see, and entre nous I'm actually quite ashamed. I've been watching Maeve and Matt for over a week and it's taken me until now to notice that their daily vitamin pill is not, in fact, a vitamin pill. It's an antidepressant.

Day 51

Upward, upward, she was meant to rub it in *upward.* She'd put it on downwards so, in an attempt to cancel out the damage, Katie slapped on more night cream, this time rubbing it in the right direction — against gravity. Suddenly she felt a presence and seized up with fear. The hairs on the back of her neck lifted and goosebumps puckered her arms.

"Who are you?" she whispered. She'd closed her eyes tightly because she was afraid that if she looked in her dressing-table mirror, she'd see a figure sitting next to her.

I'm good at this. So good that sometimes I even scare myself.

"Who are you?" she repeated.

Me? I am the wind in the trees, the dew on the petals, the rain in the air.

Ah no, only joking.

"Granny," she said. "Is it you?"

No, Katie, I'm not your dead granny.

Katie had been very fond of Granny Spade, her mother's mother. In a way, Granny Spade had been the saving of Katie in the wake of the breakup with Jason. Initially, the split had been fairly unacrimonious, no third parties involved, precious little wrangling over CD collections; Katie was sad but hadn't lost her faith in hope, happiness and the triumph of the human spirit.

Until . . . yes, until, four short months after their tearful farewell, word reached her that Jason had a new girlfriend (Portuguese) and — astonishingly — she was pregnant. In the twinkling of an eye, like milk curdling, Katie went bitter. Indeed, her condition got so bad that she had to go to a de-bittering course. (Called Beyond Bitterness: Letting go of blame and learning to love again.) Granny Spade had suggested it on her deathbed. "You've become very sour, Katie," she said. "Go to this course." She pressed a leaflet into Katie's hand, then promptly snuffed it. Well, a deathbed request was a deathbed request and Katie was not the kind of person to run the risk of being haunted by an unquiet spirit. It was hard enough to keep her flat tidy without her dead granny flinging eggs around and smashing mirrors and generally making a shambles of the place.

Every Friday night for four weeks, Katie had to attend and the gist of everything she learned could be reduced to one sentence: the only way to get past bitterness is not, as she had expected, to go and burn down Jason and Donanda's house but — could you credit it? — to wish them well. In the course of the four weeks, she was encouraged to do impossible things like visualize Jason and Donanda having everything she, Katie, had ever wanted: three children, a flat stomach, someone to do her ironing. The first time she tried it, she dry-retched.

It was very, very difficult. But, spurred on in no small part by fear of the ghost of Granny Spade, she kept at it and, by the end, she was different from the person she'd been when she started.

Of course, there were still times when she took pleasure from having lively conversations in her head with all the people who'd ever done her wrong, in which she won every verbal joust and reduced them to remorseful wrecks, but for much of her life she was free.

Day 50

"Well, excuse *me*." Lydia barreled into the bathroom, in her nightdress (actually, a T-shirt, an old one of Gilbert's that he'd been about to give to the charity shop and she'd rescued) and collided with Andrei, who was cleaning his teeth.

She'd overslept. How, when she'd lost so much work lately, could she have overslept? Every second that passed without her being on the road, she was losing money. In a panic, she needed to shower and get moving *fast* but there was a half-naked Pole in her bathroom. There he was with his bare chest and his muscly arms and nothing but a small towel wrapped tightly around his narrow waist. The . . . the *cheek* of him.

"What are you doing here?" she asked, flapping her arms impatiently.

He raised an eyebrow in sarcastic query: what did she *think* he was doing?

"Whateves," she said. "Just get out. I'm late. I need to shower." There was a very brief window of time in which she could bear to wash herself; she had to maximize her chances.

But why should he get out, Andrei asked himself. He too had a job. He too had ablutions to perform. And — not to be childish about things — he was here first.

"Outttt," she repeated, with menace. "*Tttettte.* And," she raised her voice in wild irritation, "would you fecking dress yourself!"

Andrei had thought that Lydia had already left for the day; she usually started work at some ungodly hour. He'd assumed he was within his rights to be in his own bathroom wearing only a towel.

Surprising them both, he reached out his right arm, his shoulder shifting like there were ropes under his skin, and pulled her to him. Her feet resisted, but he was too strong for her and she found herself pressed against his bare chest. His arm felt rock-like against her back, so hard it didn't feel human.

Like the metal bars to stop you falling out of roller coasters.

Speechless at his audacity, that he'd had the nerve to touch her, she moved her eyes past his smooth pectorals to gaze up at him. Frozen in the moment, he gazed down at her. His minty breath was fresh on her face and his eyes blazed blue. She was close enough to see that he hadn't yet shaved.

Heat blossomed between them and they

both became aware of a growing hardness beneath the towel, then she shook herself free and he gave her one last, puzzled look, before turning away.

DAY 50 . . .

Maeve was crouched over on herself, her hand in front of her mouth. "I just keep thinking . . ." she eventually said, then meandered off into silence.

Dr. Shrigley gazed calmly at her.

Dr. Shrigley was a psychotherapist. Tall, lean and beautiful in a bony-faced way, she was wearing penny loafers, a navy eco-cashmere cardigan that she might have stolen from her husband, and buff-colored, fair-trade chinos that might also have been stolen from her husband. A calm, intellectual lefty, she wore no makeup, had no time for any silliness. You need only look at her to deduce that she read hardback biographies of worthy women and stayed up late drinking red wine and arguing about deconstructionism. There was also a decent chance that she might be good at sailing.

Her kindly trade was purveyed from a clinic in Eglinton Road, from a small plain room furnished with two comfortable-but-not-too-comfortable chairs. A box of tissues sat invitingly on a self-effacing little table.

As Maeve contorted herself into a

294

miserable-looking pretzel, Dr. Shrigley presented a wonderful expression: concerned but not patronizing; patient but not martyred; interested but not prurient. She gave the impression she could wait all day, or at least until the hour was up, and that it wouldn't matter a whit if no one said anything. But if Maeve *did* open her mouth, well, then she'd be delighted to hear whatever she had to say.

No wonder people have to study for so long to be therapists; it could take years to accomplish that look.

Dr. Shrigley was a good woman. Behind her mask of professional detachment, she pulsed on a loving, caring frequency. Although she knew it was a gross violation of boundaries, she couldn't help worrying about Maeve. She thought of her often, between their weekly sessions. She could see the person Maeve had once been and sometimes she caught glimpses of the person Maeve could become if she stuck with things, but she was afraid that Maeve would run out of hope and abandon the process before she was healed and whole again.

After some time, Maeve spoke. "I always thought the best of people. I thought the world was a good place. But now . . ."

"Your trust has been violated and recovery takes time."

"But how much longer? It's taking so long!"

Dr. Shrigley tried to smile reassuringly but

her mouth trembled a little. "This is your journey, Maeve. It's hard, but you are doing it. Putting one foot in front of the other, moving forward."

"Will I ever feel okay again?"

"Yes. But there's no time frame."

"I'm still doing my daily Act of Kindness and I write my Trio of Blessings every night. I've been doing it for months now. That's got to count for something, right?"

Dr. Shrigley nodded. She feared that Maeve put too much faith in those practices, but at the same time it probably didn't do her any actual harm. "That's certainly one way to try to regain your faith in the goodness of the world."

Maeve nodded.

"Time's up now," Dr. Shrigley said. "Same time next week?"

Maeve nodded again.

"And your cancellation last week . . . ? You were just not feeling well? That was all?"

Maeve couldn't make eye contact. "That was all."

Maeve needed to cycle fast, to cycle away the feelings. She got a lovely long run of it along Ranelagh Road, her legs pumping, her lungs taking in gulps of air, and when she saw that the lights up ahead were red, she couldn't bear to stop. She'd take her chances. She shot out into the danger zone, and suddenly a car was there, about to sideswipe her. She pedaled faster and the car swerved and, with lots of beeping behind her, she crossed to safety. It had taken only a second or so. Her heart was beating like the clappers. That had been really, really risky, but she hadn't been able to stop herself, and she was safe now, wasn't she? For a moment, she was actually elated, but that feeling began to drain away the closer she got to home. It was that Fionn. She didn't want to bump into him. She'd seen him again this morning when she'd come out of the house with Matt. He was getting into a car and he'd stopped and stared at her with such . . . such . . . If the driver hadn't hustled him into the back seat, he might have come over to her, and even as the car had driven away Fionn had gazed out through the back window until they turned the corner at the end of the road.

Day 49

Katie had spent a fortune on her dress. And a fortune on her shoes — gold sandals, Dolce & Gabbana, very glamorous. And a fortune on her hair. And now she was having a deluxe pedicure. Conall was picking her up in an hour, which gave her plenty of time to get home, change into — Her phone double-beeped and she *knew:* he was canceling on her.

Still in Helsinki. Emergency. Very very very sorry.

She read it again, wanting it to say something different, then she swallowed hard and her throat tightened with the onset of angry tears. She wanted to kick something but her toenails weren't dry and she wasn't going to risk her pedicure. He wasn't worth it. If she had to go to her ex-boyfriend's wedding on her own, at least she could hold her head up, secure in the knowledge that her feet were second to none.

As it happened, the pedicure was a godsend, especially during the church bit. It took her mind off the radiant beauty of Donanda, the sincerity of Jason's vows and the pitying sidelong glances from those who'd been friends of Katie'n'Jason but who had backed the winning side after the split. Indeed, her embellished feet were nothing short of a lifeline when Jason and Donanda's little girl presented the rings on a white velvet cushion. *You may have a delicious toddler daughter wearing a crown of flowers, but I have beautiful pink toenails.*

However, when she got to the restaurant, her poise faltered: the room-plan revealed that she was seated at TST — The Shit Table.

She gave herself a pep talk, counseling against paranoia. She and Jason were fond of each other, why would he insult her? But her table was right down at the back, with a wall on two sides — one beside her, one opposite her. The other guests, all Portuguese, clearly part of Donanda's extended family, were four ancient, black-clad women and a burly man in his fifties who sported a magnificent mustache and a shirt opened to mid-chest. They didn't speak a word of English. Yes, undeniably the shit table.

There was one empty space — apart from the seat that Conall wouldn't be filling —

and Katie hung all her hopes on it. She couldn't believe it when she saw a dishevelled, very attractive man approaching. What had he done to merit a place at TST? Obviously, some family black sheep. Drug problems. Embezzlement, perhaps. They'd decided to put him somewhere he couldn't do much damage.

As he got closer, the alarm on his face became visible. He picked up his name tag and read the gold calligraphy as if he couldn't believe it was true then, with eyes that bulged with panic, he scanned the six eager faces, slipped his name tag into his pocket and scarpered.

"They never saw him again," Katie said.

Joking aside, this was it. No one else would be joining them. She was stuck.

With exaggerated gallantry, the man with the mustache moved places so that he was beside Katie.

"Ohhh-hooooh!" All the old women egged him on. Clearly they doted on him.

He hit his chest and said, "I, Nobbie."

"Katie."

"You har bee-oodiful kwoman."

"You have a magnificent mustache. You must be very proud of it."

"Donanda great-aunt." One of the women pointed at herself. Then she indicated the other three women. "Great-aunt, great-aunt, great-aunt."

Katie poked a finger at Nobbie and said, "Great-aunt?"

Well, how they laughed!

"Oncle, oncle," Nobbie said, in his deep, macho voice. "You?"

"Ex-girlfriend of Jason's," she explained, as if they spoke perfect English. "Probably the love of my life." The Portuguese people nodded politely. "From thirty-one to thirty-seven. I'll tell you what was gas." She crossed her legs and leaned forward in a confiding manner. "We decided it was time to have a baby and it was only when we had to have lots of sex that we discovered we didn't fancy each other any longer! Terrible, as you can imagine. For a while I thought I was going to lose my reason." The Portuguese people were starting to look nervous. But, in fairness, Katie thought, they *had* asked. "Then Jason met Donanda."

"Donanda." They nodded to each other, relieved to understand something. "Donanda."

"When she got knocked up I was devastated. Then after a year or two I met Conall, who sadly couldn't be here today because he's slashing jobs in Helsinki. So I'm here on my own to celebrate the marriage of my ex-boyfriend!" The moment she finished, shame washed over her. These poor people were only trying to make conversation. What was she like? She had been a far nicer person when

301

she was in her thirties.

Instantly, she resolved to be extra-polite and kind but making small talk across a language divide was hard work and it was a long reception, with rambling speeches and terrifyingly lengthy gaps between the courses. And there was no respite. The few familiar faces in the crowd no longer counted as allies; they'd cut off all contact with her in the wake of the split. Indeed, they were the only reason she didn't simply get up and leave — she could just hear their fake pity: "Poor Katie, poor, poor Katie. Her imaginary boyfriend couldn't make it and she had to come on her own. And did you see her shoes? Can you imagine what they cost? Well, when you're childless, you might as well try to fill the hole in your heart with gold sandals."

Funnily enough, the most painful emotion she was feeling was boredom. It was just so bloody *tedious.* She would have loved a magazine to flick through. Now and then she'd stick her foot out and admire her toenails: they were still nice. Then she'd get up and go to the ladies, just for the laugh. On one of her excursions, Jason lunged at her.

"Is your table okay?" he asked. "Because your boyfriend speaks Portuguese we thought it would be a good idea . . ."

Conall spoke Portuguese? News to Katie. That was because Conall was a liar. A liar

302

who had promised he would definitely be here with her today and who wouldn't shame her by coming up with some urgent work thing at the last minute.

"Yes, Jason, Conall is accomplished at many things."

Most of all *lying.*

"I must be off now. Enjoy being married to someone other than me."

Up to that point, she'd gone easy on the drink because a) she was driving, b) she didn't want to get scuttered and start crying and get Jason in a headlock and slur at him, "Remember the time you made the picnic for me in bed? And remember the time we . . . And remember the time I . . . Six *years,* Jason, six YEARS. And here you are, getting married to a Portuguese woman and I'm going out with a liar."

But when she got back to the table, all her resolve was gone and she drank four double rum and Cokes in twenty-three minutes (curiously, a drink she'd never before had in her life), then she was drunk, then she wanted to go home and she was unfit to drive and had to get a taxi.

To her surprise, her taxi driver was a girl. And Katie knew her! They lived in the same house!

"I never knew you were a taxi driver!"

"You know now."

After driving some distance in silence, the girl asked, "Nice night?"

"No."

"Good."

"I was at my ex-boyfriend's wedding."

"Who? The testy looking bloke who comes with the flowers?"

"Who — ? Oh you mean Conall. No, another ex-boyfriend."

DAY 48

Lydia slammed her door shut and cantered down the stairs, deep in thought. It was a fairly new thing for Lydia, *loving* her mum. Not that she'd previously disliked her or anything; if she noticed her at all, it was with a vague, fuzzy fondness. Ellen had always been a warm, capable presence in the background, the glue that held things together; she calmed down Auggie's scattergun anger and quietly provided high-quality catering and laundry services even though she was also a full-time member of Operation Duffy ("Wheel get you there!").

Now and again, like when Lydia witnessed Poppy in tears because *her* mother, Mrs. Batch, a sour, disappointed woman, was making her feel like a failure for not getting married at nineteen to a dentist, the way her perfect cousin Cecily had, Lydia realized that, as mums went, she'd got herself a good one. But she and Mum, they weren't, like, best of friends or anything. Not like Shoane and her mum, Call-me-Carmel. But Call-me-Carmel was freaky; she dressed just like Shoane — they swapped clothes — and she'd come out drinking with them one car-crash night and got into a face-lock with a bloke who couldn't have been more than twenty-seven. It had been unbelievably horrific and it had plunged Lydia into deep gratitude for Ellen. Ellen would never, *ever,* behave like Call-me-Carmel. Ellen was the best mum in the world! But the moment passed and all the other stuff in Lydia's head rushed back in — hair care and hangovers and flatmates and boyfriends and overdrafts and nice trainers — and her mum sank back to where she usually lived, buried several layers down.

Even after Auggie died so unexpectedly and Ellen became a widow at the age of fifty-seven — and, worse, a widow with a mountain of debt to pay off — she didn't go greasy-haired and crying-at-the-kitchen-table maudlin. She just got on with things. Although her empire had been reduced to a single car, she'd continued to work all the hours, a reliable and pleasant driver, whose only fault, if one were to look for fault, was that she took the roads a little too cautiously. *You wouldn't want to have a train to catch,* as her loyal customers would say. (Which was their little joke, because they usually employed Ellen to drop them at the station in Mullingar to get the Belfast Express.)

The only time Ellen had allowed herself a good old cry was whenever Lydia was on one of her short, infrequent visits home. They'd take it in turns to impersonate Auggie Duffy pacing up and down in front of the mantelpiece and beseeching God to send through a job. "Poor Dad," Ellen would say and Lydia would reply, "Poor Dad." They'd shed a few tears together, then Lydia would sniff loudly and say, "Gimme a tissue. Anyway, he was an eejit and we're well rid of him," and half-mean it and Ellen would cuff her and say, "You're very bold."

Lydia was so deep in thought that she didn't see the man on the next landing until she had crashed into him.

"Hey," he said, eyes sparkling, teeth gleaming. "I'm Fionn, your new neighbor."

A good-looking sort who wanted everyone to love him — Lydia was on to him immediately.

"Oh yeah?" she said, with an extra dollop of sneer. "What's with the smile?"

DAY 47

Conall took it hard.

"But Katie, I love you." It was the first time he'd said it.

"You don't."

"I do. I'm sorry about Helsinki. I'm sorry about Jason's wedding. I know how much it meant to you. But we couldn't get the take-over signed off without losing another twelve staff —"

"I don't want to know."

"I will work less." He grasped her hands. "I will. I promise you."

"You've said that before, Conall."

"But this time I mean it."

"No." She pulled her hands away from his. "You're too unreliable and I don't want to do it any more."

The strange thing was that she meant it. She wasn't playing games nor was she being torn apart by a conflict between her head and her heart in which her head was telling her she had to end things but her heart was kicking and screaming.

Conall was sexy, he was powerful, he was rich, he had a beautiful mouth, he smelled delicious, he had perfect skin, he had stubble, he was a good kisser — and it didn't matter. She could no longer do the dance of Conall, one step forward and one step back, and she'd never felt this way before: sad but certain she was making the right decision. So certain that in fact there was no decision.

Was this what turning forty did to a person? Removed your tolerance for bullshit? Did people run out of patience? Could it be that you only get so much in a lifetime and hers was all used up? Whatever, it was very awkward, very, very disruptive.

"I'm serious," she said.

From his stunned expression, he was starting to realize that, actually, she was.

"You can't help it," she said. "I know you never meant to hurt me. You're not a bad man."

"Pity!" he exclaimed. "You pity me."

"No . . . I . . ." God, maybe she did.

"But what will I do without you?"

"Try a younger woman," she said.

He was aghast. "I don't want a younger woman. I want you."

"A girl in her twenties." She carried on as if he hadn't spoken. "They usually can't tell the difference between challenging and fucked-up."

She should know. She'd wasted her twenties unable to tell the difference.

"But what happened?" he asked. "What changed?"

She didn't know. It wasn't as if she'd had a massive infusion of self-esteem and was strutting around the place shouting, "I'm fantastic and deserve better. R.E.S.P.E.C.T.! R-E-S-P-*EEEEEEEEEE*-C-T."

"I just . . . can't be bothered any longer."

"Can't be *bothered?*"

"Conall, I've always believed in love, that love would conquer all. But it doesn't. Because here I am, at forty, and love has conquered nothing. Except my common sense over two and a half decades."

"But Katie . . ."

"I want you to go now. And remember what I said: a girl in her twenties."

Conall's and Katie's heart vibrations are no longer in harmony. Something has jolted Katie's heart off course — it could be that bloody milestone birthday — and Conall's heart knows this. It's all over the place, trying to adjust itself in his chest, trying to latch on to the new beat, trying to find the way back.

DAY 46

Matt and Maeve's clock started its gentle plinky-plonky chiming and Matt tumbled out of bed, making for the kitchen. He wasn't exactly sure why, but he was expecting to find another note from Fionn on their hall floor this morning.

He and Maeve had seen him a few mornings now, being driven away in his Merc and staring at Maeve like he wanted to eat her. Maybe he and Maeve should change the time they left for work, he thought. Then a worse thought occurred to him: maybe Fionn wouldn't send another note, maybe he'd just show up at their door and ask why they hadn't been in touch and then Maeve would find out that Fionn had sent a letter and that Matt had put it in with the vegetable peelings . . . So it was almost a relief when he saw the white envelope lying on the floor beside their front door.

He whipped it up and threw a quick look over his shoulder to make sure Maeve hadn't seen anything, then hurtled into the kitchen and tore it open. Just like the last letter. Filming a garden show. Please come along. This phone number. That phone number. Whenever suits you.

Rage boiled in Matt's stomach. The *cheek* of the man. Maeve was his *wife.* He'd have to do something. But what? In theory, Fionn had done nothing wrong. He'd invited both of them to the filming. Not just Maeve. Although they all knew that it was only Maeve that Fionn was interested in. What the hell was he to do? Well, he'd destroy this fucking letter, for starters. He tore it into a hundred little pieces and stuffed it deep into the trash.

DAY 46 . . .

Katie wasted no time breaking the news about the demise of herself and Conall — the more people who knew, the more real it became — and, considering how everyone had always thought she was punching way above her weight with him, they were surprisingly shocked. And when they discovered that Katie had been the one who'd administered the fatal blow, they were utterly floored.

"You?" Naomi yelped. "I thought he'd improved recently. Switching his phone off when he was with you, that sort of thing."

"I suppose he had."

312

"So what the hell . . . ?"

"I can't really explain, Naomi. I'd just had enough. He's driven in a way I'll never understand. He told me once that work was the force at his core. Apparently, we all have one."

"Bollocks. I certainly haven't got one. Have you?"

"The only thing I could come up with was food–clothes–exercise. The blessed trinity. How much can I eat while still looking half-decent in my clothes? How much exercise must I do so I can eat as much as I want? Obviously, we were very different."

"But he was just starting to come good. All that work you put into him, all that patience!"

Don't. "The next woman will benefit."

Naomi could hardly bear it. "But it's not fair! Won't you miss him?"

"Hard to miss a man I never saw."

"You did see him!"

"God, you've changed your tune."

"I know you think we all hated him —"

"But you did!"

"— and yes, in a way, we did. But it was because he gave the impression that it wasn't serious to him. He didn't seem long-term enough about you."

"And because he was flashy."

"Only Dad. And only because he's jealous."

"I'm not saying Conall's a bad man," Katie said. "Because he isn't. But you know what,

313

Naomi? If he wasn't a workaholic, if he'd been reliable and . . . and . . . *normal,* he wouldn't have bothered with me. He'd be married to someone like Carla Bruni."

"You've become very philosophical. So let me get this straight, you don't even miss him? Mind you, it's only been one night. Let's try you again in a week."

"Naomi, please . . . I'm trying really hard to not think about it. The idea of him with another girl . . ."

"And he'll get a new one fast, won't he?"

"Would you stop? I know all of this, there's no need to spell it out."

"But if it hurts you so much, then why —"

How could she describe it? The certainty that it was less painful to be without Conall than with him? That loneliness was preferable to chronic disappointment?

"Because . . ." Well, yes, it was true! *Say it, go on say it.* "I thought I deserved better."

Naomi made a strange little squeak. She tried to push the terrible words back into their box, but they erupted with force. "Deserve? You're forty, Katie! That's really quite old. I grant you, we're living longer these days, better diets and all, but even so you're still probably halfway through your life. Deserve has nothing to do with it. You take what you're given and you should be grateful for it."

"Maybe it's Conall who should be grateful.

Did you ever think that actually he was the lucky one? I gave him a lot of happiness. More than he gave me."

Empty space hissed on the line: Naomi was dumbfounded. After a long pause, she asked, "Have you done another course? Did Granny Spade appear to you in a vision and send you to another of those mad places?"

"No, but I do sound quite weird. Not like myself."

Naomi sighed. "It's a disaster."

"I thought you'd be glad he was gone."

"Not when he was *just starting to come good.*" Naomi seemed dangerously close to tears.

"Naomi, just because I think I deserve better doesn't mean I'm going to get it. Like, I'm sure I *won't* get it."

"You won't?" Naomi sounded mollified.

"No."

Well, that was all right then.

Day 45

"Gilbert, I slept —" Lydia paused. If she was going to tell the truth to Gilbert she might as well do it properly. "I had sex with Andrei."

She waited for thunder to fill his face, but apart from a little flicker behind his eyes, Gilbert's expression remained blank. After staring at her for some moments he asked, very politely, "Which Andrei? This flatmate of yours?"

"Yes."

"The one you dislike so much?"

". . . Ah, yes."

"Perhaps," he said, in his dark-chocolate voice, "you will have the courtesy to tell me what happened."

She opened her mouth, then closed it again. It was very hard to say.

"There was this pot," she started.

"A pot?"

"You know, a saucepan, a small one. We were in the kitchen. He wanted to use it but I hadn't washed it. He was annoyed. Is he

316

ever any other way?"

She wondered how best to describe what happened next. Andrei had banged the saucepan down hard on the kitchen counter and he'd glared at her, his eyes burning blue, a muscle working in his jaw, and she'd glared back at him, and suddenly — and quite genuinely she was at a loss to describe how it started — they were kissing frantically, ferociously, and it was such a relief. Then she was tearing at his clothes, desperate for more of him, and he was steering her to his bedroom and, locked in his steely embrace, she tumbled on to the bed, and he was muttering endearments in Polish and distributing small frenzied kisses along her hairline, and she stretched out her arm, which had become inexplicably naked, and swept the bedside photo of Rosie onto the floor and that made him laugh. And despite the narrowness of the single bed and the fact that she disliked Andrei so strongly, it was the best sex of her life.

But she couldn't tell Gilbert any of that.

"The flat is too small," she said, the only explanation she had come up with that had made any sense. "I don't think men and women were meant to live so closely together. When lots of women live on top of each other, their periods get synchronized. When men and women live together they end up having sex —" She stopped. This was convincing no one. "It meant nothing," she said.

317

Admittedly, it had been the most intensely experienced fifteen minutes she had ever lived through; she had never been so grateful to have been born, to have skin and nerve endings and the sense of touch and smell and taste, but it had *meant nothing.*

" 'It meant nothing'? You sound like a man." Gilbert's face was cold and unimpressed.

"It meant *nothing.* It will never happen again. I don't even like him . . . and I like you very much."

"So, Lydia." He tapped his long elegant fingers on the table. "I am asking myself a question: why are you telling me this?"

"Because it's right. I have to be honest. I respect you, Gilbert."

"You respect me? You sleep with another man and show me disrespect by telling me?"

"No! I sleep with another man, *by accident,* I might add, and I respect you enough to tell you the truth. You think I wanted to tell you? It would have been far easier for me to say nothing, to treat you like a sap, a sappy sap who'd get upset, but that would have been wrong. Honesty is important. If we haven't got honesty, we haven't got anything."

But even as she was saying it, she was asking herself if she was wrong.

"When did this *accidental* event take place?" Gilbert asked.

Lydia looked at her watch. "An hour

and . . . thirty-seven minutes ago."

"You have come straight from his bed?"

"I had to tell you." She'd felt that every second that had passed without Gilbert knowing was a further insult to him . . .

"How thoughtful you are."

. . . although Gilbert was so angry that now she wasn't sure. But she couldn't have lived with a cover-up. What would have been best was if she hadn't had sex with Andrei, but unfortunately that wasn't an option.

"You think you have been my only woman?" Gilbert asked softly, sudden spite in his eyes.

She swallowed away a lump in her throat. "Yes," she said. "Actually, I did."

"But you were not."

She swallowed again. "Grand. I see. Right."

"There have been others."

"Okay." She heaved a huge breath from deep in her gut. "Just as well we're having this little chat, then, no?"

"But these other women —" with a triumphant glint, he sarcastically mimicked her earlier words — "it meant nothing."

"It meant nothing? Just like mine meant nothing? But funnily enough," she said, as she got up to leave, "the last thing you sound like is *a man.*"

319

DAY 43

The years have been good to you.
It's the weekends that have done the damage.

Katie was so surprised and entertained that a
little noise escaped from her throat. Could
she be said to have laughed out loud, she
wondered. Did that make the quote count as
"laugh-out-loud" funny? Automatically she
went for her phone: Conall would love this
one.

Then she remembered that she couldn't
ring him. Not now, not ever. Another little
noise escaped from her throat and this one
definitely wasn't a laugh.

The days when she could casually pick up
the phone and read out that day's bitter little
bon mot from her diary were gone forever.

Oh. Now that didn't feel at all nice. She
wasn't feeling too good this morning. Monday night, the night she'd broken it off with
him, had gone okay. Tuesday night had gone
okay. Wednesday night had gone okay. Last

night had *not* gone okay.

Because she'd made the terrible, terrible mistake of reading an Anita Brookner — she didn't know the name, they were all the same — and it had put the fear of God in her. She was convinced that for the rest of her life she'd have to spend her holidays with some woman she barely knew from work, someone with repressed lesbian tendencies, and together they'd visit cathedrals. They'd wear stout shoes and carry guide books and spend entire days admiring fifteenth-century naves. In the evenings they'd go for a prix fixe and have one glass of house red each and the repressed lesbian would say, "Men, nasty brutish creatures. We women can provide comfort for each other."

That's what happened when you were forty and alone.

In fact, she would probably die alone. She'd be dead for eight days before she was found, and only the mewing of her twenty-seven hungry cats would alert her cold-hearted, uninterested neighbors.

But she didn't care too much about that; after all, she'd be dead. It was just the holidays she was worried about: the stout shoes, the cathedrals, the cheapo stuff on the prix fixe (soup of the day, melon) and all the lovely things on the à la carte — the prawns, the sea bass — forbidden to her. And what if she wanted a second glass of wine, would her lezzery companion permit such debauched bacchanalia?

She rubbed her hand over her eyes. What a bleak picture of a life . . . *And* — she just thought of something else — they'd have a box of chocolates, some dreary brand like Milk Tray, and every night before they climbed into their narrow single beds to read four pages of their improving books, her companion would invite her to select a sweet. To show her appreciation, Katie would be obliged to spend hours reading the guide, and even longer savoring the one piece, the only piece, of pleasure in her life, then the box would be replaced in her companion's suitcase — and locked! — until the following night.

Oh God! God, God, God!

The problem was that she hadn't been realistic enough in the beginning. Conall was a special man, with a big presence; he'd taken up a lot of space. You didn't cut someone like him out of your life without undergoing some adjustment. She'd been mildly delusional thinking that it would be easy. Coupled with the fact that this was her first break-up in her forties, was it any wonder she was struggling?

But, on the positive side, other than this newfound fear of holidays with a repressed lesbian, she was coping. Drinking a bottle of wine a night, admittedly, sleeping very badly, admittedly, picking up the phone to ring him twelve times a day, admittedly, but *coping.*

DAY 41 (EARLY
HOURS OF)

"Three double espressos," Lydia said.

"There's only one of you," Eugene said. She could hardly see him through the steam of the cappuccino machine.

"I'm knackered," she said. "I've got to last through till nine."

Eugene looked at the big greasy clock on the wall. It was 4:20 a.m. "You've a while to go yet. Anything to eat?"

"Something loaded with sugar."

"Grand, I'll bring it all over."

She turned, looking for a free seat. The place was crowded with taxi drivers tucking into middle-of-the-night breakfasts and — Gdansk! — she saw a familiar friendly face. "Hey, Odenigbo!"

Odenigbo jerked his head up, looked alarmed, then smoothed all expression from his features and gave her a short, cool nod before, very deliberately, twisting away.

Irkutsk! Not Gdansk at all. "It's full in

here," she muttered to Eugene. "I'll be outside."

Closing the door on the noise and the steam, the night air cool against her hot face, Lydia swallowed hard. Odenigbo blanking her, now that was harsh. But only an eejit would expect that Gilbert's mates would stay friends with her. Loyalty and all that. She understood it. She'd done the dirty on Gilbert; of course his compadres would close ranks. But she minded. She missed the other Nigerians, they were fun. And what about Gilbert having done the dirty on her! The unfairness of it!

She needed to talk to someone. It was twenty-five past four in the morning — what were the chances that Poppy was awake? Quite high, actually. She was getting married in five weeks; she hadn't had a full night's sleep in months.

R U awake?

Ten seconds later Poppy rang. "You got me at a good time. I've just had a nightmare about the flowers and I'm lying here *shaking*. What if they're mortifying?"

"But they're flowers. How can they be mortifying?"

"Mum was at a wedding last week and she said the flowers were hideous."

Yes, but Mrs. Batch was a sour old boot

who found fault with everything. If she was admitted into heaven, she'd kick up a stink at reception and demand to speak to the manager and complain at the top of her voice that everything was too radiant and blissful.

"Your flowers will be cool, cop on, Poppy! I'm never getting married if this is what it does to you. I just got blanked by Odenigbo."

"Oh! That's harsh. But you wouldn't expect me or Sissy or Shoane to play nice if we bumped into Gilbert."

A little silence followed. They both had their doubts about Shoane.

"You're right, yeah, I'd go mad. I just got a . . . you know, it was a reminder, I suppose. Do your test on me, Poppy!"

"Just yes or no answers, right? Question one: Your life is over?"

"No."

"You'll never meet another man again for as long as you live?"

"No, no, I will, I'd say."

"When — and I say when and not if — you think of Gilbert being with the other girls, you want to tear your skin off?"

"Yeah."

"You're sorry for all those times you told your good friend Poppy to shut up when she said he had a family and six children back in Lagos?"

"No."

"Oh. Sure?"

"Would you stop!"

"Moving on. You keep fantasizing about him arriving at your door and offering to do anything —"

"— to burn his Alexander McQueen jacket, the one that cost over a thousand euro, to show how sorry he is."

"I'll take that as a yes. You told him you loved him?"

"You know I didn't."

"He told you he loved you?"

"No, I'd have told you."

"*Did* you love him?"

"I don't know. I was hoping the Poppy Test would tell me."

"Did he love you?"

"Well, obviously not if he was riding other girls."

"Had you made plans to go on holiday together? Maybe a mini-break in Barcelona?"

"No, but not because he wouldn't. Because I can't —"

"The Poppy Test deals only with yes or no answers. So that's a no. Let me add up your scores. Okay. There was very little to this rel— Well, I'd hardly even call it a relationship. It'll hurt for a short while, quite badly, but there's no depth to the wound. Like a paper cut."

"A paper cut!" Lydia was liking the sound of this. "I know what you mean. Really, really sore, *surprising* like, especially because it was only a bit of fecking *paper.* Not like a huge big sword that they execute people with in the Al-Qaeda videos."

"For a few days every single thing you do will hurt."

"Then it'll stop?"

"And you won't even notice it going. You're not thinking you might get back with him?" Poppy asked delicately.

Lydia snorted. "No way. I wouldn't take him." Anyway, it was complicated. It wasn't like other breakups where only one person was in the wrong and the other could wait like a smug martyr for pleas for forgiveness. They were both wronged and in the wrong and it meant they were stuck.

"Good. You'll be grand and there's plenty more where he came from. Lagos," Poppy added.

Poppy was right about one thing: there were always more men coming on-stream. Even if Lydia was still waiting to meet one who didn't eventually disillusion her with his sappiness or his faithlessness or his outrageous stupidity. "You know what, Poppy? With men? It's not the despair that kills me —"

Together, they chanted, "— it's the *hope.*"

"When will I be over Gilbert?" Lydia asked.

"It's been three days? Give it a week. Can I go back to my nightmares now?"

Lydia wanted to keep talking. She wanted to blurt out how she hated herself for think-

328

ing Gilbert was worthy of her. But if she said that, Poppy would bollock her for having abnormally high self-esteem and that other girls wouldn't like her if she went around saying that sort of thing.

And there was something else.

"What about . . . him, the other . . ." Lydia choked on the word, ". . . man."

"Andrei, the flatmate you accidentally slept with? This is not an area the Poppy Test covers."

"But what do you think?"

"I think that every time you look at him you'll feel guilt, confusion —"

"Revulsion."

"*Revulsion?* That bad?"

"I haven't been able to be in the flat with him since . . ."

Since that moment — well, mo*ments* — of nutjobbery. As soon as it had ended, she'd legged it out of the flat and hotfooted it over to Gilbert, trying to convince herself that if she fessed up, it might make it not have happened. Christ, how wrong could you get? She discovered that yes, it *had* happened and, worse again, that she and Gilbert were no longer a going concern. The very thought of Andrei had been so repulsive that she literally hadn't felt able to breathe the same air as him. But there had been nowhere she could go — Gilbert's house no longer being an option — so she'd cruised around all night, picking up a fare here and there. When she eventually came home, at around 8:30 in the morning, Andrei had left for work. And in the few days since then she'd slipped into a different work schedule, driving through the night and coming home to sleep only when she was sure Andrei had left for the day. In a few weeks' time, he was going to Poland for his summer holiday; maybe she could avoid seeing him until then.

"Personally," Poppy said, "I think Andrei's quite ridey. I can see why you —"

"Please! No! Stop!" Her skin crawled at the thought that they'd — arrgh! — had sex. Sex! Arrgh, arrgh, arrgh!

"Okay, revulsion. You'll blame him for the breakup with Gilbert. But you'll have to suppress it until one of you moves out. Learn to live with it."

"Maybe I shouldn't have told Gilbert."

"Wouldn't change the fact that he was cheating on you."

"Yeah. I'm better off knowing." For the millionth time, fury rose in a big red wave.

"Lydia, I must go back to sleep now. Forget Gilbert. Laters."

Poppy vanished, leaving Lydia alone with her thoughts. She couldn't believe how quickly everything had changed. This time a week ago, even four days ago, her life — almost all of it — had been great. She'd had a hot man and he had friends she liked and together they'd formed a little community, almost a family, then that mad business with Andrei happened and suddenly everything was arseways. If only she'd known how good things were.

Irkutsk! She kicked an empty can, and it bounced a few times along the pavement, the noise ugly in the peaceful night air. She really didn't feel good. She and Gilbert, they'd had a connection. It had felt pretty solid but all it had taken was one short conversation to destroy it. They'd both come out of it looking bad — selfish, disloyal and shallow — and that was enough to put the brakes on any chances of dramatic jacket-burnings and getting back together. Not that she'd have him back, she thought, as her imagination kindly provided a couple of pornographic images of Gilbert riding some mystery girl and another wave of red fury rolled upward from her gut. Fuck him.

A loud rapping noise made Lydia jerk awake. Her face was slumped heavily on her steering wheel, her tongue was stuck to the roof of her mouth and her heart was racing. She lifted her head to see Jan's startled face peering in through her car window.

"What you doing?" she heard him ask.

What indeed? She was too stunned from the abrupt awakening to speak. Anyway, she didn't know what was going on. Confused, she took stock of her surroundings. She appeared to be in her car. Parked in Star Street. It was daytime. Sunny.

"I thought you have heart attack." Jan sounded hopeful.

Clumsily, she unwound the window. "What time is it?" Her tongue was thick.

"Nine-thirty."

"In the morning?" Since she'd switched to night duty, her body clock had gone haywire.

"In morning. I work now. Late shift."

It was all coming back to her. After her three coffees and doughnut, she'd got the fare of her dreams, taking her all the way to Skerries. But that was where her luck had run out. When she returned to the city center she'd spent over an hour waiting behind countless other taxis at a stand, and at about seven o'clock had given it up as a bad job. She'd driven home and parked in Star Street, then realized it was a Sunday and far too early for Andrei to have woken up and gone out, so she'd settled down to wait. At some point she must have fallen asleep.

"Do I have a mark on my face?" she asked. "From the steering wheel?"

"Yes. You are a Toyota person now and forever."

"Is . . . ah . . . who's at home?"

"No person. Andrei is out."

That was all she needed to know.

She let herself into the empty flat and

though the need to go on the net came upon her suddenly and urgently, she had to have a shower first. She still didn't like washing herself, but over these last few days, for the short scalding seconds she was under the water, she scrubbed until she was red and tingling, trying to erase Andrei's besmirching touch. Aaargh!

DAY 40 (EARLY HOURS OF)

Katie was helping Keith Richards put his socks on. "That's the boy, that's it, now the other foot," when stumbling, scuffling noises at her front door woke her from the dream. She lay on her side, frozen in her sleep pose. It was twenty-nine minutes past five, according to the red devilish numbers on the alarm clock, and she was being broken into. She listened hard and, once again, heard a series of stumbling noises, like a body falling against the wood of her front door. Shouldn't she be doing something? Like ringing the police? Like darting into the kitchen and getting something to protect herself?

But she couldn't believe it was happening. And she couldn't believe a burglar would be so unstealthy. She was amazed at how unprofessional they were being.

Louder noises this time — her front door was being pushed and shoved — then came the most frightening sound of all: the metallic scratching of a key seeking the lock.

Had someone stolen her key and had it copied? Almost delirious with fear, she flicked back through her recent life, searching for a moment when her bag was unattended, when it could have happened.

There was one other explanation for this person at her door.

It could be . . . Conall.

With a click and a shove, the door opened and the person, whoever it was, was in her hallway.

"Katie," she heard Conall ask in an urgent whisper. "Katie."

Should have changed that stupid lock.

He knocked lightly on her bedroom door. "Katie. Are you asleep? Wake up."

Should have made you leave your key.

The light clicked on, nearly blinding her. Conall, looking a little disheveled, was swaying at the side of her bed. "Katie, I'm going out of my mind."

"Why?"

"Because I love you. Sorry for this," He waved his hand to encompass him standing in her bedroom at five-thirty in the morning. "I should have rung, but it's so late. Or maybe it's too early."

"So you thought it was better to come in person."

"Absolutely!"

He was, she realized, quite drunk.

"Katie, I want to marry you." He dropped

335

to one knee and wobbled slightly but managed to maintain his balance.

She stared at him, wondering if she'd actually woken up, or if she'd simply moved sideways into one of those dreams where you dream you're awake.

"Marry me," he urged.

"Is this a proposal?"

"Yes."

She was electrified with sudden insight. This was one of the most important moments of her life. She would marry Conall Hathaway, she would put up with his workaholism and his unreliability because there was a lot that was great about him, and every positive choice in life brings a commensurate loss. And, of course, there was the added bonus that he might change.

Yes, she thought, secure in her decision, she would be the wife of Conall Hathaway and live with all of the pleasures and unhappiness that that would guarantee if, *and only if,* he had brought a ring with him.

"A ring?" She prompted.

It would be a sign that their week apart had altered him, that he would be more amenable to making concessions in their future.

Conall patted one jacket pocket then another and rummaged around in his trouser pockets, then admitted the unpalatable truth. "I didn't bring a ring . . ."

Well, that was it. The decision was made

for her and the vision of her life as the wife of Conall Hathaway dissolved and disappeared.

"I would have got one but I came over here in such a rush —"

"It's not a proper proposal if there's no ring," she said.

"I can get one." Already, he had his mobile out. "Trevor, Conall Hathaway here. Did I wake you? My apologies to your good lady wife." He was definitely drunk, Katie thought, he didn't normally speak as if he'd wandered out of a Dickens novel. "Listen, I need a diamond ring. Right now. High end. Open up the shop, I'll make it worth your while."

Conall put his hand over the speaker and asked Katie, "Is it diamonds you want?" Like he was ordering a takeout.

She shook her head.

"Emeralds, then? Sapphires. Anything you want, just say."

She shook her head again. He couldn't buy his way out of this.

"Trevor, I'll call you back." Conall was confused. "Katie, what *do* you want?"

"Nothing."

"But . . ." He was stymied. People always wanted something. "I've changed. I'm already different. I'm going to get a deputy. I'll start looking tomorrow. No more long trips away from home. No much rush jobs, no more twenty-hour days."

She shook her head again.

"But . . . why? I thought this was what you wanted?" He couldn't make sense of this. There could be only one explanation. "You've met someone else?"

". . . No . . . I . . ." Of course she hadn't met someone else, but for whatever reason, a picture of the golden-haired man from downstairs appeared in her mind's eye — and Conall, being the astute machine he was, felt it.

"You have!" he declared, appalled.

"I haven't."

But it was enough for Conall. Like a wounded animal, he had to be alone.

A taxi was approaching. A gift from the gods, he thought and stuck his hand out. It pulled up beside him and he tugged at the handle of the door and climbed into the front seat.

"Get out," the taxi driver said. "I'm off duty."

"Take me to Donnybrook. Quick as you can."

"I'm finished for the night. My light's off. Get out."

"So why did you stop for me?"

"I didn't. I was parking." With an efficient screech forward, then a perfect reverse curl, she — for the driver was a she — had maneuvered the taxi into a tiny space, in one of the neatest pieces of parking he'd ever seen.

"There we are, parked," she said. "Out you get."

He reached for his wallet. He had to get away from this terrible place, the site of his shame. For the second time in five minutes he said, "I'll make it worth your while."

"I'm not for hire, I'm actually asleep with my eyes open, I shouldn't be on the road, I'm a danger . . ." Then she looked at him carefully. "What's up with you?"

"Nothing."

"There is. Your tie is crooked and your hair is a mess."

"I don't need your sympathy."

"You're not getting my sympathy. Put your fat wad away. I'll drive you metered rate if you tell me what's going on. I'm always uplifted by the misery of others. Where to?"

"Wellington Road."

She tightened her mouth and put the car into gear. "That was a good spot, the best I'll ever get, and it'll be gone when I get back. This'd better be good. Is it to do with the sexy schoolteacher?"

"Who?"

"The woman with the knockers and the shoes? Your girlfriend? Gdansk!"

"Do you mean Katie? How do you know her?"

"I live in the same house. The flat below hers."

"You do? Number sixty-six? Small world.

But she's not a schoolteacher."

"Governess, then? So she's dumped you, yes? Why?"

"Because I work too much."

"Why? Short of money? Saving up for when your mother turns into a nutbar and you've to stick her in a home?"

"No."

"Demanding boss?"

"I work for myself, essentially."

"So, *essentially,* you work too much because you like it?"

". . . No, not *like* . . ."

"Because you need to keep proving your-self?"

"I guess. That's what my girlfriends keep telling me anyway. How did you know?"

She waved her arm, airily. "I'm always driving the likes of you. Emotionally crippled overachievers. Gdansk."

"But I'm going to change."

"If I had a euro for every time I heard that I'd probably live in Wellington Road, next door to you."

"Why do you keep saying 'Gdansk'?"

"I like to say 'Gdansk.' "

A prolonged silence followed.

Eventually, Conall asked, "Why?"

"The beginning is cheery, it sounds like 'G'day' but the end has the 'sssskkkk' sound. I love the 'sssskkkk' noise. It's like the beginning of 'skedaddle.' You can say it to get rid of people. Like this." She turned her attention away from the road and hissed at him with venom, "Ssssskkkk!"

Conall recoiled.

"Now, do you see?" she said. "It's a great word. Gdansk! If you want to use it in your own life, work away. It's my free gift to you."

Conall was looking at her with sudden interest. What a funny, acerbic little creature she was . . .

"You'd probably charge people for the use of it," she said. "I suppose that's why people like me are living in Dublin 8 and people like you are living in Wellington Road."

. . . and now that he looked at her properly, he saw how very pretty she was, those flashing eyes, that sexy mouth, the mass of dark curls . . .

"Then again," she said thoughtfully. "I'm not an emotionally crippled overachiever and you are."

. . . and out of nowhere, he was remembering the advice Katie had given him . . . and Katie's advice was always on the money.

Slowly, he asked, "What age are you?"

"Not that it's any of your business . . ."

"Not that it's any of my business . . ." He was liking her more and more.

"Twenty-six."

Suddenly, Maeve was awake. She didn't know what time it was but, from the color of the morning light, it was early, so early that the alarm clock hadn't started its gentle chiming. What had disturbed her? Whatever it was, it hadn't woken Matt. He was snuffling in slumber, snuggled up behind her, his front against her back. And then she felt it. His erection. Firm and springy, even through the layers of clothes they were both wearing. Insistent against her lower spine and bigger than she remembered. She had to get out of the bed.

Quickly but silently, she slid from under the covers and made her way into the hall and began to breathe again — but when she saw the piece of white paper lying on the floor beside the front door, the fear came flooding back. It so obviously wasn't a flyer from someone offering to clean their gutters. All mail from the outside world was left on a table in the communal hall so this must have been hand-delivered from inside the building. She was afraid to pick it up. Then again, she was afraid of everything.

Dear Maeve and Mark,
   I'm beginning to think you're ignoring me! Maybe you didn't get my other notes.

What other notes?

For the third time, I'd like to invite you along to the set of Your Own Private Eden. (Will be on Channel 8 soon.)

A plethora of phone numbers followed.

Give me a shout. Let me know when it suits you to come.

All the best,

Fionn

Fionn. From the instant she'd clapped eyes on the note, lying so innocently on the mat, she'd known it was from him. And what about the other notes he mentioned? Matt must have done something with them. Well, she'd do something with this one. She folded it in half, then in quarters, then in eighths, then in sixteenths, and would have kept folding forever except that it got too fat and refused to bend itself any smaller. Then she tiptoed into the living room and secreted it in her change purse, in her wallet, in the inside pocket of her satchel. She'd shred it when she got into the office.

Thoughts of Fionn followed her all day, like a shadow. He came with her to work and stood beside her as she destroyed his note, and he walked next to her when she did her

343

act of kindness by going to the pub and retrieving the phone that her colleague had forgotten, and there wasn't a moment all day long that she wasn't aware of him.

When she let herself into the flat, she hoped she could leave him outside in the hallway but he slid in with her. He accompanied her to the kitchen to discuss dinner with Matt, and it was only when she was stretched out on the sofa in the living room, idly flicking through the paper, working her way to the television pages, that he gave her some peace.

But, suddenly, there he was! Fionn. In the paper. A color photograph smiling out at her. Goosebumps shrank her arms and cold tingles danced around the back of her neck. *It's not real. My head must have made this happen.*

She touched the paper with her fingertips and the picture didn't disappear. There was great detail; you could clearly see the individual strands of his golden hair and the fair-colored stubble on his jutting jaw line. At least, she *thought* she could see it. She would have given anything for someone to confirm that she wasn't imagining this, that she wasn't getting worse and going entirely mad, but the only person in the flat was Matt, and obviously he was the last person she could ask. The words near the photo jumped around like a flea circus, so it was impossible to discover why this man would have leaped

344

from her head to the page in front of her. Eventually, the little black shapes organized themselves in neat lines and told her that Fionn would be presenting an upcoming gardening show — it must be the one he'd mentioned in his note.

She began to breathe more easily. This was normal. Coincidental but normal. People got their pictures in the paper when they were going to be on telly. And there were facts in there that she hadn't known, like Fionn being from Monaghan and that the show was going to run for six weeks. No, she hadn't imagined this.

But to see his photo, when she'd been thinking of him all day . . .

She braced herself to do the one thing she hadn't done yet: to look into his eyes. He gazed back at her . . . and slowly he winked. She threw the paper away from her in a sharp rustle and shoved her hands between her thighs to stop them shaking.

Day 39

"What film have you got us?" Lydia's mum asked.

"*Pirates of the Caribbean.*" Lydia was up to her elbows in sudsy water and her red face was wreathed in steam. Her hair would be destroyed. She'd look like Sideshow Bob.

"I've seen that before. A musical."

Lydia paused from her energetic scrubbing. "I think you must be thinking of something else, Mum, it's not a musical. It's got Johnny Depp in it."

"Johnny Depp. Oh yes, he's lovely. Tormented. I do like a tormented man."

Lydia agreed grimly. She had a couple of men in mind and, as far as she was concerned, the more tormented the better. Suddenly, she realized that this particular pot was done for; no amount of effort was going to shift the burned-in food. It had been heated and reheated so many times that the old food was actually welded to the aluminum and had become part of it. She hauled it out

346

by the handle, shook off the worst of the bubbles and made for the garbage.

"Lydia, what are you doing with that pot?"

"Throwing it out, Mum. It's done for."

"That's a good pot."

"It's burned to fuck."

"Do you kiss your mother with that mouth?"

"Haha." Lydia lunged, her tongue extended, and her mum beat her back.

"Get away, you filthy creature."

Lydia picked up another saucepan and clattered it into the sink. She'd been scouring till her shoulders hurt for the past twenty minutes and the mountain of food-soiled cookware hadn't seemed to diminish at all. It was like the Mad Hatter's tea party — as soon as one pot or plate or cup was used, her mum simply moved on to the next clean one, washing nothing, and when she'd worked her way through everything, she began using and reusing at random.

"How will I cook a dinner if you keep throwing my saucepans out?"

For a moment Lydia considered chucking them all into the bin. No pots meant no cooking meant no smelly, stinky pile awaiting her every time she arrived from Dublin. It also lessened the risk that the curtains might go on fire again.

. . . But it would unsettle Mum too much if all her pots suddenly disappeared. And Lydia was still determined that she could force Murdy and Ronnie, the lazy bastards, to do their share.

"We'll get a takeout tonight, Mum. Chinese, you like Chinese."

"Do I? And then will we go out dancing?"

"We've got a DVD. Remember? We're watching a movie."

"What movie?"

"You know what movie." *Please know.*

"How would I know?"

"*Pirates of the Caribbean.*"

"Oh that old yoke." Her mum sounded disappointed. "I don't like musicals."

Lydia swallowed. "It's not a musical, you're thinking of something else. This is good, it's got Johnny Depp."

"Johnny Depp! I like him. Soulful. I feel he couldn't be happy if you put a gun to his head, do you know what I mean?"

"I do, Mum."

"When will you be finished with the washing-up?"

Lydia surveyed the horror of the kitchen, the precarious-looking heaps of plates and pans and half-eaten food. "I'll be a while yet."

"I'm hungry," Ellen declared.

"Okay, I'll order the takeout soon."

"Are we getting takeout? Goody!"

"I'll just put on a machine-load of laundry first."

In the bathroom, going through the linen

basket, Lydia was surprised to find some male underwear. On closer examination she deduced they must be Ronnie's. The stunning . . . the *outrageous* . . . cheek! No girl should ever have to eyeball her brother's worn jocks! It was fundamentally wrong. She flung them back into the basket as if they were radioactive (and with Ronnie's lifestyle, you never knew).

Carefully, she made her way back down the narrow stairs, an armload of laundry almost obscuring her vision. She kicked opened the kitchen door and Ellen was sitting in the chair exactly as she'd left her. She glared at Lydia. "This is no life for the pair of us. Sitting in on a Saturday night."

"It's Tuesday."

Her mum jumped to her feet in a girlish fashion. "We should *do* something." She twirled around, her arms outstretched. "Don't you feel it, Sally? Oh Sally, life is out there, hot and hungry and vibrant. We're letting it slip away from us!"

Lydia spent a lot of time on websites, inputting her mum's symptoms — confusion, forgetfulness, abrupt abandonment of all housekeeping duties — and looking for a disease that would fit. But these symptoms, like Mum was channeling some shitey black and white film, what diagnosis could be made of them?

"Sally, do my hair."

Should she? Helpless and frustrated, Lydia didn't know if it was best to humor her or guide her back to reality. No one would tell her. No one would even admit that Mum had become a bit of a madzer.

"Put it up for me on top of my head."

Ellen's hair was short and had been for as long as Lydia could remember, so that made the decision.

"Mum, you know I'm not Sally, don't you?"

Ellen studied her cautiously. "You're . . . Lydia?"

"But you keep calling me Sally."

"Sorry, love, it's just you look so like her."

"Ah Mum!" She couldn't stem the rush of tearful exasperation. "That's no excuse. I mean, Ronnie looks exactly like Satan but you don't call him Lucifer."

"Maybe not out loud," Ellen admitted, a sudden twinkle in her eye. "But in my head I do. Beelzebub."

"You don't!" It made Lydia laugh. "Beelzebub."

"I'm not saying he is Beelzebub, just that —"

"— he looks like him, yeah, I believe you." Lydia flicked her with a tea towel.

"Oh Lydia, your own brother! He doted on you, used to call you his little doll. You were just this tiny wee thing, but you had him wrapped around your finger. He'd have done anything for you."

350

Yeah, well, that was a long time ago. He'd do nothing for her now.

"Eat up," Mum urged.

"Yeah, okay." With a marked lack of enthusiasm Lydia shoved another forkful of fried rice into her mouth.

"It's delicious!" Mum exclaimed.

It wasn't. It wasn't revolting either, just all a bit bland. But when the double-chocolate ice cream also tasted a bit nothingy, Lydia acknowledged what she'd already known: it wasn't the food, it was her. The flavor was gone from her life.

Without Gilbert, there was nothing to look forward to. This paper cut was taking too long to get better. Idly, she picked up her phone.

"Who are you ringing?" Mum asked sharply.

"No one."

"Watch Johnny Depp."

She was just checking to see if Gilbert had left a message — even though she knew he hadn't. Just like she wouldn't. She had two more days before Poppy's stipulated Week of Grieving was up. Then that would be it: no more thinking about him —

"Oh Mum!" Chocolate ice cream was smeared all over Mum's chin, dripping on to her skirt. Lydia reached for a tea towel. "Here, let me wipe your face."

Her mum twisted away, slapping her hands

at Lydia's. "Stop treating me like a *child*. And why did you come to see me if you're not going to watch the film with me?"

"I am!"

"You're not. You're thinking about other things."

You see. There were times when Mum made some sort of sense, and in those moments Lydia told herself that maybe there was nothing wrong with her at all.

She ousted Gilbert from her head then stretched out her legs and put them in Mum's lap, and gave Johnny Depp her full attention for the next two hours. Even Mum stayed agog until the credits began to roll.

"Did you like that, Mum?"

But Ellen fixed her mouth into a sullen line.

"What's wrong, Mum?"

She wouldn't even look at Lydia.

"Mum? What's up?"

"You said we were having takeout. When are we getting it?"

DAY 39 . . .

Doll houses and mini-stables and tiny glittery sewing machines — so much *pink*. Katie was looking for a gift for MaryRose's little girl, Vivienne. MaryRose had been very good to her this past Conall-free week and she wanted to show her appreciation but MaryRose went weird if you gave her something for herself.

She actually seemed confused, as if she'd forgotten she was still a person and not just an adjunct of Vivienne, so all gifts had to be funneled toward the child. Katie dawdled beside the shelves, sightlessly picking things up and putting them down again.

Curses on Conall Hathaway!

She'd been grand last week. Well, not *grand,* obviously. Drinking too much and unable to be on her own and very bad company and full of fear about lesbian holiday companions. But she'd been protected by an unshakable conviction that if she kept putting one foot in front of the other, marching forward through the grief, one day it wouldn't hurt so much.

She had lived through an entire week, including working days and the weekend and those empty little pockets of time and loss that loom at you when you least expect it, and she'd been okay. In fact, and she blushed to admit it, but last week she'd actually been a little *smug.* Watching approvingly from the outside, as she lived her life having made the tough choice, but the *right* choice. She had even been — God, she was mortified — *proud* of the centered, grown-up person she'd become. (And closed her eyes to the bottle-of-wine-a-night scenarios because they took the gloss off things a little.)

But now it had all gone messy. When Conall had tumbled through her door yesterday it was like he'd taken a big stick to a settled pool and stirred it furiously, churning up all the mud that had settled at the bottom.

She hadn't been able to go back to sleep after he'd lurched off in a drunken huff, and last week's steely certainty had steadily eroded as the day had gone on. *Maybe I was too judgmental, maybe I shouldn't have insisted on the ring —*

Her phone chirped and she jumped — sleep deprivation was playing merry hell with her nerves — and sent a pink replica service station, with miniature pink petrol pumps, clattering to the floor.

It was Naomi. "Katie, where are you?"

"Toy shop. Want to get something to say thanks to MaryRose." Slowly, she retrieved the station from the floor.

"Will I be getting a present too?"

"Haha." The Richmonds didn't give spontaneous presents. It might smack a little too much of kindness. "So what's up?"

"Just checking in. Making sure you're not still obsessing about your one chocolate a night. You can bring your own chocolate, you know, on your lezzery holiday. Or you can come away with me and Ralph and the kids."

"I'd rather go with the lezzer."

"Well, feck off so."

"Not like that, Naomi. It's that single-person thing. I don't want to be an add-on to other people's holidays, like they've taken pity on me. Imagine you and Ralph, all sun-kissed and having your grilled fish and carafe of sangria, and me sitting at the table with the two of you, like a big, interfering romance-wrecker. At least the lezzer would want me there."

"It's not like Conall ever took you on holiday."

That wasn't true, as it happened.

"And I wouldn't mind having you along. Ralph would be less likely to badger me for sex if you were there. In fact —" Naomi was suddenly excited — "you and I could share the double room and we'll stick Ralph in your single bed."

"Grand. That's all set. I'll cancel my trip to Chartres cathedral, so. Hortense will be disappointed."

"Never mind her."

"She's already bought the guide book and she's really stingy."

"She can go on her own. Anyway, she shouldn't be preying on the likes of you, you're straight."

"Listen . . ." Katie was bursting to tell all about Conall's visit, even though she knew she shouldn't. But how could she stop herself? "I've a slight update on events."

"Oh yeah?"

"Conall called around in the middle of the night."

"Booty call? Cheeky bastard. Doesn't surprise me, though. Highly sexed. God, what a nightmare. Although I wouldn't mind so much if it was him who was on top of me instead of Ralph —"

"He asked me to marry him."

"*What?* Whhell!" Naomi sounded wildly impressed. "You're the wily one, playing the long game, calling his bluff by breaking it off with him, all the time holding out for the big prize."

"I'm not the wily one." Whatever that was. Hortense might know. "I wasn't calling anyone's bluff."

". . . You mean . . . ?" After a long, shocked pause, Naomi said, "Christ on a bike, Katie, don't tell me you said no."

"He didn't mean it, Naomi. He was a bit pissed and he hadn't brought a ring and —"

Naomi began to wail. "I don't believe it, I do not believe it. What do you want, jam on it?"

"He didn't *mean* it. He'd have sobered up and changed his mind."

"Why would he have asked you if he didn't mean it?"

"Because he doesn't like losing. Even when he doesn't want the prize."

"Right, that's it. I can't talk to you. I'm too upset. But think on this, Katie, how can I help you if you won't help yourself?"

Noisily, she hung up, and it felt like an assault. Suddenly, Katie couldn't think straight, everything around her was too fecking pink.

For a few seconds she shut her eyes, and when she opened them again she stepped away from the toys. Anyway, MaryRose, being a short-of-funds single mother, needed practical stuff. This new canyon of goods featured buggies and blankets and baby gadgets. Katie picked up a white plastic something, but when she couldn't identify it she shoved it back on the shelf. The sheer volume of baby paraphernalia was starting to overwhelm her. She should just ring Mary-Rose and ask her what she wanted, but baby instructions got very complicated. MaryRose would say something like: Not the one with the pale blue attachment, but if it's red it's okay. And it *must* say MM. Got that? MM. It means medium medium. Ordinary medium won't do. They'll tell you that ML is the same, but it's not . . .

Retreating to the baby toy section, she picked up another random object. What on earth was this? Some sort of animal . . . Oh right, a hedgehog, a multi-textured one, to introduce the baby to different surfaces. And this squeezy flower here made eight different sounds. And what was this little device? According to the packaging, it would reproduce the vibrations of the womb. Katie fell on it and clutched it to her chest. She was buying this one. For herself.

Then, reluctantly, she replaced the little gadget. It couldn't help her. Even when she'd

357

been in the womb her mother had probably said things like, "Sit up straight, stop kicking, don't stick out so much, no one likes an attention-seeker."

DAY 38

First thing in the morning, I popped in to see how Matt and Maeve were getting on and, yes, I admit it was my fault. Maeve was lying in bed, waiting for Matt to bring her coffee, and I suppose I got a little too close, just trying to see if I could get in there, you know? Maybe winkle something out of her, find out some of her secrets, because of all the people in Star Street, she was the one putting up the most resistance to me, and it was driving me mad. I swirled my way around her head — and she felt me . . .

Suddenly everything in Maeve was going at ten times its normal speed. Her heartbeat went into overdrive and her blood was pumping hard and fast through her arteries, bottlenecking at the other end, anxious to get back into the heart and get going again. Her body was flooded with adrenaline and her skin was prickling with the need for fight or flight. She clambered to a sitting position, her back against the wall, her head jerking from corner to corner, her eyes scudding wildly, trying to see everywhere at once, patroling for all possible danger. She began to sob with terror. It was happening all over again. Something was wrong with her chest, a terrible weight pressed on her lungs and she could barely breathe. Air was being pulled in through her open mouth, making an awful creaky sound, and her eyes bulged with fear. She had to call for Matt, who couldn't be far away, he'd only gone to the kitchen, but she was paralyzed, held in a never-ending spasm, like one of those nightmares where you know you're sleeping but you can't wake up.

"Wake up and smell the — Oh Christ!" Matt dumped the two cups on a shelf and rushed to Maeve. "Breathe," he urged. "Just breathe. You're okay, you're not going to die. It's just a panic attack. Just breathe."

He squeezed his arm around her shoulders, so she could have the comfort of physical contact but without her airways being blocked. "In through the nose, out through the mouth, that's it."

In the past, Maeve had tried to describe the terror that overtook her during an attack. "Imagine being locked in a car trunk with a dog, one of those horrible fighting ones, and he's been given speed. Imagine how scared you'd be. That's what it's like."

"Keep breathing," Matt urged. "You're

okay, you're safe, you're not going to die. In through the nose, out through the mouth."

After ten or fifteen minutes of wheezy inhaling and exhaling, Maeve said, "I think I'm okay now." Then she promptly burst into tears. "Oh Matt, I'm so sorry."

"It's okay, it's okay, don't be sorry."

"It's been ages since the last one. I thought I was better."

"It's probably just a one-off," Matt said.

"You think?"

"I do."

He didn't.

Day 37

Lydia could see that Ellen's slide had a tame enough beginning. One night, about a year and a half ago, Ellen had rung Lydia and went into great detail about a local funeral: the widow's elegant black shoes, the fanciness of the coffin and the confused old priest who kept referring to the deceased by the wrong name. It was what passed as entertainment in Boyne while they were waiting for the building permit for the cinema and, only half listening, Lydia had let her chatter on. The following day Mum had called again — an unusual enough event in itself; normally, they didn't speak more than once a week — and while she chatted away, Lydia downgraded her attention and began to paint her toenails. She was paying so little notice that it took her a while to realize that she'd already heard this conversation.

"Antoinette O'Mara," her mum was saying. "Yes, even on this, her saddest day — because she and Albert loved each other no matter what people said about him and that woman from Trim — she was turned out like a fashion plate. Her shoes, Lydia, her beautiful shoes —"

"Wait, I know —"

"— black, of course, they had to be, but the softest-looking leather and a good high heel on them. You might have thought she'd have picked something more practical for a funeral but she's a lady to the tips of her fingers. And —"

"I know —"

"— even when that old eejit Father Benedict kept calling poor Albert by the wrong name, she didn't flicker. "Our brother Horace has gone to his reward." The whole church was looking at each other and saying, "It's all very well for this Horace, whoever he is, but what about poor Albert O'Mara? Has he got any reward at all?""

"I know, Mum, you told me all this last night."

"When last night?"

"On the phone last night."

"I wasn't on the phone to you last night."

That was the start of it.

Except, of course, it wasn't. It had being going on for a while — Lydia wasn't sure how long, maybe two years, maybe even longer — but it was the first time she'd noticed and, all of a sudden, memories of other odd things bobbed to the surface: the time she'd found Mum's watch buried deep in the sugar bowl; the way Mum kept talking about "the thing you use to clean the inside of your mouth" because, inexplicably, she couldn't remember the word *toothbrush;* the times when Mum called her Sally. (Sally had been Mum's younger sister, who'd died at the age of twenty-three.)

Each of those episodes had made Lydia exasperated and mildly touchy, especially the Sally thing — "Stop it, Mum, you're freaking me out. She's *dead!*" — but this was different. This time Ellen had forgotten an entire conversation and it caught Lydia's attention.

"Mum, you can't have forgotten! We were on for ages."

"Lydia, I don't know what to say . . . You must be thinking of some other time . . ."

"Oh, you mean the *other* time Albert O'Mara snuffed it and his fancy woman from Trim turned up at the graveyard wearing a black hat with a polka-dot veil."

"How do you know about that?"

"Because you *told* me. Last *night.* On the *phone.*"

". . . I . . . ah . . ."

Mutual incomprehension fizzed on the line.

I am the daughter, Lydia thought, oddly wounded. You are the mother. It is my job to neglect you and to forget to phone you for weeks on end; it is your job to be thrilled to see me, to get chocolate in especially for me, to tickle my feet and to never, ever worry me.

Eventually, Lydia extended an olive branch. "Were you drinking at the funeral, Mum? Maybe you don't remember ringing because you were scuttered."

"I wasn't scuttered."

"What did you have at the do?"

"Two Baileys."

Lydia was inclined to believe her. Ellen was an amateur drinker who got flush-faced and giddy after a couple of glasses. Then Lydia had a dreadful thought. Perhaps Ellen was necking tranquilizers. "God, Mum, you haven't started on pills, have you?"

"For the love of the lord, I don't even take aspirin."

Quite true and, more to the point, Ellen was a steady stoic who had endured thirty years of marriage to Auggie Duffy and his radio and his ambitious, disastrous schemes. Her central nervous system was made of cast iron. A Valium wouldn't have known what to make of it; it would have lain down and cried.

"Right, I've had enough of this," Lydia said. "Next time I talk to you, try not to be so mad."

She hung up and promptly forgot about it.

But she remembered it again, during brief breaks in time when she was stuck too long on a red light or having her arse bored off by a particularly tedious fare. *The watch in the sugar bowl. The milk in the microwave. A hole in her memory where a conversation about Antoinette O'Mara's funeral shoes should be.*

What did it mean?

Tentatively, Lydia asked her brothers, "Do you think Mum's losing it a bit?"

"*Mum?* Do you mean Ellen Duffy? Ellen Duffy our mother? She's as sharp as a tack and she'll outlive us all!"

And then came the first phone call from Flan Ramble.

"Who? Oh, Mr. Ramble, a few doors down from Mum?" Lydia's heart plunged. Flan Ramble hated her, always had done, since she was a little girl who laughed at the hair that grew out of his ears, so he was hardly ringing for a neighborly catch-up.

"I won't beat around the bush, Lydia. Your mother went walkabout last night. She was found on the Mullingar road in her nightie. The guards brought her home in the squad car."

". . . She was sleepwalking?"

"That's one way of putting it . . . except that she was awake."

"Awake-walking?"

"She was confused."

". . . I . . ." It was too weird. Even though she'd half-expected a call like this, Lydia felt, well, *surprised.* Her mother wasn't normally a selfish person who caused trouble.

"Lydia, is it the sauce?"

"No."

"She's losing it, so."

But Mum was only sixty-five, far too young to be going in the head. And Lydia was also too young for this aged-parent business. At some time, far, far away in the misty future, she knew that Mum might go a bit quavery and shrunken. On the very rare occasions that she even considered such a possibility, a picture of a little pull-out seat in the shower would appear in her head. A man would have to come and install it. But that was fecking *decades* away!

"If she's going soft," Flan Ramble warned, "she shouldn't be driving that taxi."

"Our mother is the most capable woman I've ever met."

"She *used* to be, Murdy, but not any more. This is what I'm trying to tell you. Things have changed. She's not well. She's *gone in the head.*"

"She's grand," Murdy said.

"She's grand," Ronnie echoed, when she eventually ran him to ground.

Maddened with frustration, she rang Raymond in Stuttgart, who said, "She's grand."

"She went wandering the streets in her nightdress!"

"So did half the town. It was Good Friday,

drink was taken." Then he went smoothly into his chortley, I'm-telling-a-funny-story voice. "Did I ever tell you about the time I got locked out of a hotel room in the nip in the middle of the night? I'd thought I was going to the john and I ended up out in the hallway, the door slammed behind me And this Italian couple got out of the lift and saw me, me tallywhacker swinging free and easy for all the world to see, and the woman, a well-made specimen too so she was, says —"

"Christ, would you shut *up?*"

"All I'm saying," he sounded wounded, "is it's the same sort of thing with Mum."

"It isn't. She needs to see a doctor."

"Work away."

Ellen begged Lydia not to bring her to Dr. Buddy Scutt, GP of Boyne. "You'll only offend him and I've to live in this town."

"I won't offend him."

"You will. It's your way. You can't help it."

"Come in, come in, come in!" Dr. Buddy Scutt greeted Lydia and Ellen with what Lydia considered to be unprofessional bonhomie. (Ellen and Buddy played on the same team on Thursday night's table quiz at the Condemn'd Man.) Buddy dragged a chair around to the public side of his desk and the trio sat in a little circle, their knees almost touching. Way too pally for Lydia's liking.

She cleared her throat and tried to create a more somber atmosphere. "I'm sure you heard, Dr. Scutt, about the guards having to bring Mum home in the middle of the night."

"Sleepwalking," Ellen said. "Buddy, I went sleepwalking."

Buddy nodded at Ellen, flashing a message: "Let's humor the little missy, then I'll make short work of her."

"But there's other things. She puts the milk in the microwave, she forgets conversations —"

"And you're perfect, are you?"

"No, but — look, sorry, Mum," Lydia said. "I'm really sorry." She didn't know if Ellen minded being humiliated like this but it was a surprise to find that it was killing her to do it. Unfamiliar emotions — compassion, a tender painful love — were squeezing the breath out of her. "Could you refer her for a scan?" Lydia's internet research recommended it. "An MRI scan?"

"What for? MRI scans cost a fortune and there's nothing wrong with your mother."

"I'll pay."

"That's not how it works. You can't go round having MRI scans willy-nilly. There's a huge demand. Only sick people should have them."

"But she *is* sick. Sorry, Mum!"

Buddy Scutt shook his head. "There's not a bit wrong with her. I've known this woman

369

all my life."

But what did that mean? "So if you've known a patient all their life they can't get cancer?"

"Have I cancer, Lydia?"

"That's not what I meant, Mum. You're just a bit . . . senile or something."

"Senile, my sweater!" Buddy interjected. "When I need to catch a train, who do I call? Ellen Duffy."

"Look, about the taxi," Lydia said awkwardly. "I'm not sure she should be driving at all."

This was the hardest thing Lydia had ever said. If Ellen stopped driving, someone else would have to become responsible for her financial upkeep. It opened up a whole new world of worry.

"Let's ask the woman herself. Ellen, are you worried?"

"Ah, sure, I'm just getting old," Ellen said.

But Lydia saw the little flicker. Ellen knew that something somewhere was gone a bit wonky, but like everyone else — Murdy, Ronnie, Raymond, Buddy here — she didn't want to know what it was.

"You heard your mother. I've a waiting room out there full of real sick people so don't be wasting my time."

"Look, just send her for the scan and then we can see."

Buddy rolled his eyes at Ellen. "Kids! Sent

to try us. See you Thursday night, Ellen."

"Please," Lydia said. "Please would you refer her for a scan? She can't have one without a letter from you."

"And I'm not writing it because there's nothing wrong with her. Good day to you."

Lydia walked away. A doctor with decades of experience had said that Mum was okay. But she knew he was wrong. He couldn't bring himself to tell Ellen she was losing it in case he was bounced from the quiz team. Since his wife had died, he was lonely. Thursday nights meant a lot to him.

What else could Lydia do? Wait until Mum got worse, then try again?

And lo and behold, Mum got worse. She had always been house-proud and germ-aware but, overnight, she abandoned all cleaning duties. Lydia arrived one icy Sunday afternoon to find every pot and pan and plate and cup her mum possessed piled in higgledy-piggledy, teetering stacks. There was a strange smell — a *smelly* smell. Gone-off meat or something. Christ! And there was no reasoning with her. It was like *Invasion of the Body Snatchers.* Her mother seemed to have been replaced by an entirely different woman. And Ronnie and Murdy did nothing — nothing! — to help. It was amazing to her, fucking *amazing,* that they would let their mum live in this squalor. But what was worse was that

Mum didn't mind. She didn't even notice.

To prevent an outbreak of bubonic plague Lydia drove down from Dublin every five or six days and cleaned like a fury.

Fury is right. Now I understand why she wouldn't wash up after herself. Which hardly seems fair to poor Andrei and Jan. Not that I'm here to judge. Or am I . . . ?

The next thing to go was Ellen's grip on numbers. Not always, some days she was grand, but on other days her understanding of decimal points went haywire and a five euro note became the same as a fifty. A bad business when you drove a taxi and had to deal with money. Heated exchanges ensued when Ellen vastly overcharged customers. Worse again, certainly as far as Lydia was concerned, was when Ellen started giving change from a hundred euro to those who'd proffered a tenner. (Flan Ramble was particularly gleeful about this glitch in Ellen's sanity. "I could have come home that night ninety euro to the good. Only that I'm an honest joe. But there's plenty knocking around town who're buying drinks for everyone in the house.")

Ellen stopped paying her bills. Because she stopped being able to write her signature. Because she was no longer convinced about who she was. ("Is that my name, Lydia? It doesn't feel right.")

Lydia brought each new set of problems to her brothers and laid them at their feet like a cat with a dead crow, and they responded to each offering with a variety of deflections: that Lydia was a drama queen; that Ellen was menopausal; that care of the sick was women's work.

"You should come home and mind her," Raymond said. "You're the only one with no ties."

"Fecking Ronnie has no ties!"

But Ronnie was a man.

Lydia spent most of her waking life being eaten up by corrosive rage. She was twenty-six, she wasn't meant to have these sorts of worries, it was all wrong. She was the baby of the family, the only girl; her brothers were meant to be sappy and dotey about her. Bastards.

Now and then, just for the variety, she'd swap feeling homicidal with resentment for feeling sick with dread, wondering what form Ellen's next caper would take and when it would hit. The only thing that stopped her going mental from fear was the certainty that sooner or later something freaky enough would happen to make the lads take notice.

Sure enough, the kitchen curtains went up in smoke a couple of weeks back and it was a proper fire: the window panes had cracked from the heat, the ceiling paint had blistered so badly it would have to be redone and the walls were as black as pitch. If it hadn't been for beady-eyed Flan Ramble, who spotted it before the whole house took, who knew what would have happened. But Murdy, Ronnie and Raymond (*and* Ellen, actually) insisted that no, the house had never been in danger of burning down, and Lydia realized that it was time for a fresh assault on Fuckbucket Scutt.

"A letter for a scan," Lydia told his receptionist (Peggy Routhy, as it happened). "I'm not leaving until he writes it. And I'm good at waiting. All taxi drivers are. In Dublin, sometimes I have to wait eleven hours before I get a fare."

Peggy Routhy entered the inner sanctum and, in ringing tones, urged Buddy Scutt to let Lydia "whistle." Clearly, Peggy still held a grudge over being charged for the trip to the maternity hospital while she was in labor. Small towns, Lydia thought, with contempt. No such thing as professional detachment, personal relationships colored everything.

Peggy returned from the office and smirked at Lydia. "No go."

Grand. She could wait. "Hello, Mrs. Tanner," she said loudly. "What's up with you? Bad chest? Don't know why you're here to see this gobshite. He hasn't a clue. He should be struck off. STRUCK OFF, I'm telling you. Wait till I tell you how he misdiagnosed my poor mum —"

Peggy Routhy got buzzed into the office, and after an absence of several minutes she reappeared with an envelope, which she handed to Lydia.

"For Mum's scan?"

"No."

Lydia jumped to her feet and barged into Scutt's office.

"You can't go in there without an appointment!"

Scutt was behind his desk.

"What's this?" Lydia waved the envelope.

"Sending her for a second opinion," he said. "If he thinks your mother needs a scan, which I very much doubt, he can refer her. But I'm not doing it."

The scan had become a point of principle, Lydia realized. A personal struggle between herself and Scutt. He wouldn't give in. He couldn't. It would mean that he was admitting he'd been wrong.

"Who are you sending her to? It's got to be an expert." Someone who knew about memory loss, confusion — yeah, okay, *Alzheimer's,* she may as well admit it, because even though the word terrified her, her internet searches kept coming back to it. "A doctor who knows about mums turning into madzers. And not anyone who knows Mum personally. Not some fool like you."

"William Copeland is his name," Buddy

said unpleasantly. "Consultant neurologist, a whiz with madzers."

DAY 37 . . .

Katie turned the page of the storybook and kept reading and, in her crib, Vivienne sighed with sleepy pleasure.

. . and the king of the fairies said to Killian, "You have succeeded in your task. You may have your wish. You can become all-knowing."

"Now I will leave this place," Killian said. "And show everyone my great knowledge."

The king said, "Not so fast."

Katie stopped reading and looked doubtfully at the cover of the book. *Celtic Myths,* it alleged. Something called *The Man Who Knew Everything.* Not a story she'd ever encountered before tonight.

Vivienne stirred in her crib — why had the story stopped? — and hastily Katie continued reading.

"Only as a spirit can you be all-knowing. You must surrender your life."

Killian was angry. "You have tricked me," he said. "And how come, if I am all-knowing, I did not know about this?"

The king of the fairies was compassionate. "You did not read the small print. Never was it said that you would know everything. It was said you would have *the ability* to know everything — but you would have to work for it."

This was the oddest bloody story, Katie thought, looking again at the cover. It was unbelievable the kind of shit that got published. But she might as well finish it. Vivienne seemed to be enjoying it.

"I do not wish to surrender my life," Killian said.

"You must. Human beings cannot know everything," the king of the fairies said. "The burden would be too great to be carried."

"Let me live."

In sorrow, the king said, "The time for that is passed, your life is claimed. You may choose to be born into a new life, but when you become mortal again all your knowledge will vanish. What do you choose? Knowledge or Life?"

Killian considered, but the choice was an easy one. "Life."

"You may decide whom you wish to be born to. Use your great knowledge. Choose wisely."

There were many people, the length and breadth of Ireland, whom Killian could choose from. He visited the north, the south, the east, the west, calling upon the blessed, the beautiful, the rich, the clever. But his heart led him to one couple, humble, good people, who loved each other deeply, so much so that their souls had merged and become as one. "This man and this woman have the purest hearts in all the land. They have endured much sorrow but I could make them happy."

"Go."

When Killian's spirit had become housed within his new mother, the king of the fairies tapped Killian on the head. "With this touch, I retrieve your knowledge and gift you with innocence in order that you may be born again."

Killian began to tingle and spark. Like an incoming tide washing away traces on the sand, he disappeared little by little, clearing the way for his soul to be rewritten by a brand-new person.

And the man and woman, humble, good people, kind and loving companions who shared the one soul, who had endured many sorrows in their lives, who had lived through times of fear and loneliness and despair, were full of heart and restored to happiness and love when they learned that their baby had finally been sent to them.

And that was it. Katie flicked forward a few pages, wondering if she'd missed something, but it didn't look like it. How . . . *odd*. Despite the strangeness of the story, Vivienne had fallen asleep, her face sweet and peaceful in the glow of the pink night-light. Katie tiptoed from the room and hurried to the kitchen, ready for her glass of wine.

"*The Man Who Knows Everything?*" she said to MaryRose. "It was really weird."

"Never heard of it. She has so many books in there."

"Nothing like what we were told as kids."

"Because we were told the one about the good girl with long hair who gets rescued by a prince with a company Lexus and a job in the finance sector."

Katie's face crumpled and slowly she lowered herself into the sofa.

"Have wine, have wine." Anxiously, Mary-Rose thrust a glass at her.

"I'm drinking too much."

"Good, good. At least you're taking care of yourself."

"I was doing okay, you know." Katie looked up beseechingly. "I was doing grand. The first few days I was downright fecking blasé. I'd got so sick of being let down, I was *certain* I was doing the right thing. But I hadn't thought it through. Every morning, no matter where he was, I used to read out my thought for the day from my diary . . . and now I can't any more."

"Here's my phone. Ring him. Just say yes."

She'd told MaryRose about the proposal. She'd told everyone because she wanted them to talk her into it.

"But he was a little pissed off. If I'd said yes, we'd have gone right back to me being number five or six on his priority list. Wouldn't I?"

"Maybe he's learned his lesson."

But what if he hadn't? "I'd have had to go through all this again at some stage. I've already done ten days of agony. I can't waste them."

MaryRose tried to top up Katie's glass, even though it was brimming over.

"I just have to keep going." Katie managed a watery smile. "When you think about it, my life is so good. I have my friends and my sister and my job —"

"And shoes! You have such beautiful shoes."

"Yes —"

"And cake! Not much in life that can't be fixed by cake."

"Cake, yes, cake."

But after an uneasy pause, Katie toppled forward until her forehead was almost on her knees. "I'm always going to be the childless woman who has to read bedtime stories to other people's kids."

"You could have a baby! If that's what you wanted."

"It's just that now there's no chance of . . . anything." Katie addressed her lap. "I might as well be dead."

"But you don't have to be childless or dead or in Nantes with that Hortense — Conall asked you to marry him! He's learned his lesson, he loves you, he's serious about a future with you."

"But what if he isn't, MaryRose? What if I'm just fooling myself? And I think I am, you know. Fooling myself, I mean. Oh God, I don't know *what* to do!"

DAY 37 . . .

Dinner, telly, cookies, more cookies, bed — didn't they ever get bored, Matt and Maeve? No wonder Maeve had to risk her life every day on her bike; it was the only way to ensure she got a bit of excitement.

They were lying on their couch, watching a holiday-home-in-the-sun show, but Maeve's mind was far away, thinking, for some reason, about when she and Matt had got engaged.

Before they told anyone, Natalie had guessed.

"Fast work!" she said.

"It's been five months."

Indecently soon, perhaps.

"But when you know, you know, right?"

Maeve said.

"Congratulations." Nat grinned. "Throw the bouquet my way."

"You're a star, Nat, so you are," Maeve said.

"Poor David's not going to be happy," Nat warned. "He's still waiting for the two of you to break up."

"Oh *God.*" Maeve shoved her face into her hands. "You know, I think I'm going to leave Goliath and try to get a job someplace else. It's too tough on David, seeing Matt and me every day."

"He really hasn't forgiven you." Natalie made it sound almost funny.

"I know and the guilt is wrecking my head." David was still refusing to talk to Maeve — and, of course, Matt — and he showed no interest in hooking up with any other girls.

"It's his ego," Natalie said. "He just couldn't believe a newbie like you would dump him."

"Don't say that. He's entitled to his feelings. But I want to keep this engagement business as low key as possible, I don't want to be rubbing his nose in it."

However, all that changed when Hilary Geary insisted she absolutely *must* throw an engagement party in her gracious Carrickmines home. "It would be a *sin* not to mark this happy, happy occasion!" Hilary said. "We'll greet the guests with champagne cocktails," she said, writing in her notebook.

"And we'll have a full bar in the dining room. And you must invite everyone from your work! It's not every day that the most beautiful girl in the world agrees to marry your son!"

Maeve had a pretty good idea that she wasn't exactly the kind of girl that Hilary Geary would have picked for her son (she'd probably have preferred someone who was more into clothes and manicures and table arrangements), but if Hilary had reservations about Maeve, you'd never know. Hilary kept going on about how gorgeous Maeve was, what wonderful skin she had, how perfect she was for Matt and how beautiful she'd be in her wedding dress.

Maeve quite liked the idea of a party — except for the worry of David.

"We can't," Maeve told Matt. "It would upset David too much."

"We have to. We haven't a hope of stopping Mum," Matt said. "Any excuse for a drink. I mean it — I know what she's like. That party is happening, one way or the other."

So should they invite David or should they not? Maeve *agonized.*

"It'd be a right poke in the eye not to invite him, but will it look like we're gloating if we do?"

"Look, just invite him and let him make up his own mind," Matt said.

"No, Matt, please . . . it's not so simple.

He's upset."

"It's like this, Maeve: he wanted you, I wanted you, I got you. End of. Time for us all to move on."

"You're too pragmatic."

"That's right. I'm brutal." He nudged her and she smiled in response, then said ruefully, "Matt, have a heart, think of his feelings."

"I *have* been thinking of his feelings. I've done it for the last five months. And, actually, for the three months before that as well. That's enough."

"Okay, I'll invite him."

When he hadn't responded one way or the other by the day of the party, Matt said, "I guess we can take that as a no." Maeve wasn't so sure. She half-expected the guests to arrive and find their way into Hilary and Walter's beautiful detached home barred by David and a group of his sympathizers, carrying pickets and noisily urging them to boycott the event.

But it all went off fine. David didn't come and Maeve didn't know whether to be sorry or relieved.

DAY 37 . . .

The real pisser, Lydia felt, was that Ellen had the ability to hold it together for short periods of time. When she guided her mum into the office of William Copeland, she almost had to stop herself from saying: Here's my mum, just give us the referral for the scan and we'll be on our way. But the neurologist insisted on "drawing out" Ellen, who responded by chatting charmingly. In response to his gentle questioning, she correctly name-checked the president, then — and this is what killed Lydia — she could *do basic sums.* The woman who was lining the pockets of half of Boyne by not being able to recognize a tenner, was able to multiply six by twelve. Then, oh fecking *then,* she aced a short — very easy, Lydia noted anxiously — IQ test.

"Everything looks good here," Dr. Copeland said.

"The test was very simple."

"It's standard."

"But Mum, she's been so . . . different."

"Example, please."

"She doesn't understand money any more."

"She's just demonstrated that she does."

"She's only being polite. Because you're a doctor —"

"Consultant."

"Consultant, then. When we leave here, she'll turn into a madzer again."

"Madzer isn't a term I'm comfortable with."

"Nutjob, then." When he didn't show any sign of warming up, she said, "Can we send her for a scan?"

"I see no reason."

"She thinks I'm her dead sister."

"Do you think that?" He addressed Ellen.

"Lydia looks almost identical to how Sally looked when she died," Ellen said quietly. "Sometimes the wrong name slips out."

Dr. Copeland nodded. "Sometimes I call my son Sophie. The dog's name."

"She's stopped cleaning the house," Lydia said. "It was always, like, perfect, really clean and that."

"She's entitled to kick back a little. Don't you think she worked long enough taking care of you and —" he consulted his notes — "your brothers?"

That's just what Ronnie had said.

"But the place gets disgusting. Sorry, Mum, but it does. Like, *abnormal.* I'd be worried about rats and things."

Ellen chuckled gently. "I've seen your flat. Yourself and Sissy live in a pigsty."

"But Mum, I'm twenty-six. I'm irresponsible. I don't care about things being clean. That only happens when you get older. And," she added, in distress, "I don't live with Sissy any more. I moved out two months ago. That's another thing you've forgotten."

Dr. Copeland was doodling on his pad. He seemed to be wrestling with an unpleasant choice. Eventually, he looked up and spoke. "Lydia, let me tell you something. I get adult children in here, worried because their parents are suddenly going on a trip to Australia and, quote, 'spending their inheritance.' They tell me their parents have taken leave of their senses."

It took a moment. "I'm not trying to get Mum sent to some bin so I can steal all her money! There *isn't* any. Mum doesn't even own the house she lives in."

Copeland gazed hard, like he was trying to mind-bend Lydia into confessing to the crime of false accusation, and Lydia suddenly remembered what everyone knew: all head-doctors were nutters, far madder than their patients.

After another long pause, Dr. Copeland said, "Lydia, what do you want for your mother?"

"I just want a name. Like, of whatever is wrong with her, then she can be given tablets and she'll be grand again."

"And start cleaning the house again?"

"Be back to her old self."

DAY 37 . . .

Naomi was wrong to say that Conall had never gone on holiday with Katie. There had been a weekend in Budapest, four days in a fabulous hotel in Ibiza (which ended up being only two because of a delayed flight), but Katie's fondest memory was of their first trip away. They'd been going out with each other less than a month when Conall showed up with tickets to Tallinn. He was still trying to make amends for the Glyndebourne fiasco. "I picked Tallinn because they have a six-hundred-year-old apothecary," he explained. "And I know you love drugstores."

They'd arrived late on a Friday night and the very first thing they did the next morning was go directly to the apothecary. Actually, it was more like the third or fourth thing they'd done, she remembered. They'd woken up in the curved, carved bed and had long, languorous sex, then they'd had breakfast with champagne and strawberries, because, say what you like about Conall, call him flashy if you must, but he knew how to do things in style. Eventually, they'd got dressed and had a chat with the concierge about maps and locations. Well, Conall did. Katie had no interest in that sort of stuff. She thought it was only for men: they loved it — highlighter pens, x marks the spot, all that. When the discussion ended, Katie headed toward the door and the sunlight outside, only to discover that she was being steered by Conall back toward the stairs.

"A few moments of your time," he'd murmured, a gleam in his eye.

They'd tumbled back into the suite they'd just left, falling noisily across the room and on to the bed, where they had an unexpected but very sexy quickie.

"Okay." Conall had got Katie to her feet and helped her to put her bra back on. "Visit to the drugstore, take two."

It was the Taj Mahal of dispensaries, a beautiful, old-fashioned apothecary. The walls were lined with small square wooden drawers, and high up on shelves were brown glass jars labeled with chemistry symbols. The light, reflected by fly-blown mirrors, was dim and respectful. But this was a working drugstore and, to Katie's pleasure, a plethora of modern-day products were also on display.

"Come on," Conall asked, "please walk me through this." He pulled her to him. "Are you . . . look, don't be embarrassed."

"Of course I'm embarrassed," she said. "I'm the only person I know who browses in drugstore."

"But I browse in hardware shops. For our next holiday we'll be going to the world's biggest widget outlet. And we both browse in stationery places."

"Are you really sure you're interested?"

"I swear to God. I want you to show me the things you love." He picked up a box. "So what's this here?"

"A special soap to prevent acne." Nothing special.

She didn't linger on the skin and hair products — no matter how energetically he nodded, she suspected he was faking it.

Anyway, her favorite was the first-aid section. They were so cunning, all these developments.

"What's this?" He picked up a plastic cylinder.

"Oh Conall." She couldn't prevent her enthusiasm spilling over. "It's a wound wash, and it's brilliant. Remember when you were a kid and you'd fall and cut your knees and there'd be bits of stone and grit, and how awful it was, having it cleaned with a disinfectant. None of that now. You just spray this on, and I think it must have a mild local anesthetic, and of course it's antibacterial."

Conall studied the instructions. "I see, it washes out 'foreign matter'. Is that —"

"— the stones and grit. Exactly!"

"Christ, I actually wish I was injured so I could give it a go."

She flicked him a glance and they both began laughing and he exclaimed, "Katie, I'm not making fun. I do think this is interesting. And what's this here?"

"Spray-on plaster. For awkward areas, where you can't get one to stick. All you have to do is just spray it on."

He pressed the nozzle and a drop of liquid hissed on to his finger. "It's dry! Already! See." He waved his hand at her. "And that acts just like a Band-Aid?"

"It seals it from infection."

"I see what you mean, this *is* exciting."

"This must be new." She'd picked up something that she'd translated as echinacea gargle. "Sometimes you see things abroad that you wouldn't get at home. This would be brilliant for the winter . . . like, if you thought you were getting a sore throat."

He insisted on buying it for her.

She knew he didn't really get it, the whole drugstore thing, no one really did. But the point was, he'd been willing to try.

DAY 37 . . .

Four hundred euro it cost. Four hundred euro to be practically accused of trying to get Mum committed so she could get at her money, like they were in some nineteenth-century novel, maybe by one of the Brontës. Lydia wasn't a reader, so she couldn't be sure, but they'd made her read something at school and this sort of reminded her of that.

William Copeland, what a fool.

But the thing was, Lydia acknowledged, that in a way this whole Irkutsky mess *was* about money. As soon as Mum had started to go off-side in the head, Lydia had been seized by fear — fear of Mum changing and fear of Mum disappearing and fear of Mum dying. And working her way down through her fears, through all the different levels, she found that underlying every other fear, the way it had been her entire life, was the fear of

391

not having enough money. What if Mum had to go into residential care? Someone would have to pay for it and, unlike other families, the Duffys had nothing.

Mum didn't own her house, Lydia had no money, Murdy had no money, Raymond had no money, Ronnie *behaved* as if he had none, but he was the sort of person who, after he'd snuffed it, would be discovered to have assets of millions; but even so, he wasn't the type to share it in the here and now.

As her brothers had become more and more shouty that nothing was wrong, Lydia had gone the other way and started planning for a catastrophe. She'd launched into working flat-out, she'd stopped buying cute trainers, she'd moved into a cheaper flat, she'd started doing the lotto.

She'd even visited a couple of nursing homes, and love of God, the horror! Wall-to-wall crocks, everyone was *ancient*. She'd never seen old people before, not in real life, and this crew were the living dead. Never smelled the likes either! It was all true what they said about those places smelling of pee. I mean, *Jesus*. When the time came, Mum couldn't be put into one of those homes. Not that Lydia could afford to. In both cases the astronomical cost had been the decomposing cherry on top of the maggoty cake.

"Get in the car, Mum."

"No."

"Come on, we've to go home now."

Ellen struggled out from Lydia's hands. "Sally, will you let go of me!"

"Oh now you decide to be mad again. Hey!" Lydia yelled up at the second floor of the building they'd just exited. "Hey, your Godness, Copeland, my mum's gone again. Come down and do your IQ test now."

"Sally! Hush, Sally! Stop shouting!"

"My name's not Sally! I'm Lydia, your *daughter!*"

Ellen's eyes were huge and her bottom lip trembled. She looked like a chastised child and guilt almost brought Lydia to her knees. "Sorry, Mum, sorry, sorry. You can't help it, I know you can't help it."

"I'm sorry too."

They fell, weeping, on to each other.

"Don't be cross with me," Ellen said, her voice muffled against Lydia's shoulder.

"I'm not cross. I'm sorry, Mum, I'm so sorry."

"You're my own girl, Sally, my pet, there's nothing I wouldn't do for you."

Lydia stared ahead without seeing the road, way too crushed to care about her driving.

She'd had to fight so hard for today's appointment, and she'd had high hopes that a real doctor would see what she saw, that Mum would be sent for a scan, that whatever had happened to her brain would become evident and she'd be cured.

What could Lydia do now? Go back to Buddy Scutt and ask for another referral? Stupid old gobshite probably wouldn't give one, or else he'd just send them to another one of his mates, who'd sing from the same prescription pad. What did you do when doctors couldn't — or *wouldn't* — see that someone was sick, ill, losing it, whatever you want to call it? Maybe she could try to get Mum to see a different GP, a doctor who wasn't an old pal, a doctor who wouldn't be worried about the fallout of giving an unpleasant diagnosis. That would be some job. Mum was terrified of causing offense in the town by switching loyalty; she still went to the same butcher who'd sold her a pound and a half of gone-off ham for Murdy's confirmation party, twenty-five years ago.

She wouldn't think about it now, she decided. She'd think about something else, something nice. But her brain wouldn't stop. It kept throwing up more and more horrible scenarios. What if things got worse? What if the time came when Mum couldn't be left on her own? Apart from Flan Ramble, most of the neighbors from the old days were gone. Nearly every house in their crescent had been sold to young suits who commuted to Dublin and were gone all day and had no interest in taking care of a senile woman.

And why should Mum be dependent on the goodwill of neighbors when she had four children? But the lads wouldn't agree to a schedule and Lydia couldn't make them. She could force most people to do almost anything, but her brothers were cut from the same cloth as her.

They kept saying she should move back to Boyne if she was that worried. But she was better in Dublin; she could make more money there . . . And, actually, she didn't want to move back to Boyne. To put it mildly. She'd go *out of her mind.* It would be like being buried alive. She'd be as mad as her mum within a month.

Oh Christ, the regret she felt for the person she used to be — before she'd had to live with this huge big shitey worry. She'd been shiny and hard and immune to pain, and everything was possible because she was afraid of nothing. Now she was crisscrossed with wounds, and as raw and vulnerable as meat.

She was too young for all of this. Mum wasn't going to get better, but no one would share the burden and you shouldn't have to endure that love and pain and fear and loneliness when you were a selfish, irresponsible twenty-six-year-old.

In her lap her phone double-beeped and her nerve endings frizzed. *Gilbert!* But it was only a text from Poppy. Right! That was it! It had been eight days now and eight days was long enough. Gilbert wasn't going to ring her; she wasn't going to ring him. Line in the sand and all that. No more checking the phone. No more being sappy and hopeful. And even if he were to prostrate himself with some gesture of remorse, she wouldn't take him back.

She pulled over to the hard shoulder.

"Sally, what's happening?" Ellen was confused.

Quickly, Lydia deleted Gilbert's number. There! Gone, now. Even if she got smashed she wouldn't be able to ring him. There was a tricky little moment when she wondered if she might cry again — the business with Mum was really taking its toll — but she leaned her head back against the headrest until the squeeze of eye water went away.

Then she set her sights on Boyne and pulled back out into the traffic.

DAY 37 . . .

Matt and Maeve got dressed for bed, then it was time to write their Trio of Blessings. Matt was enjoying a great run on them at the moment. Tonight, like he'd done every night for the past ages, he just scribbled down:

A mysterious lump of ice didn't fall on my car.

A mysterious lump of ice didn't fall on my flat.

A mysterious lump of ice didn't fall on my wife.

Ten seconds it took him to write this; no agonizing, no soul-searching, just bish-bash-bosh and it was done. Maeve didn't even inspect it any more. He tossed the notebook across the bed and returned to his magazine.

Long after Matt had finished, Maeve remained in deep thought, doodling spiky mountain ranges in her notebook with her gold-colored pen. There *were* good things, there *were* blessings.

Eventually, she wrote, "Today's first blessing: Matt didn't leave me."

After another long pause, she wrote, "Today's second blessing: I didn't leave Matt."

Her third blessing? She couldn't think of anything. She closed the notebook to study its cover, the Chagall painting. All that was keeping the woman earthbound was the man, but his grasp on her fingers looked so tenuous. It would be so easy to let go and, if he did, she'd rocket skywards, lost forever.

She opened the notebook again. Today's third blessing? Come on, third blessing, she urged herself. Finally, and with an air of defeat, she wrote, "I didn't have a panic attack." Then she snapped the notebook shut and turned the light off.

Just one thing that I feel I should mention because it's so bloody peculiar — when Maeve has her morning shower, she wears her swimming costume, like she's in Big Brother.

DAY 36

On my way, keep dem talking.

Late for work, Katie galloped down the stairs, trying to text Danno at the same time. Then, probably because she had the phone in her hand, she addressed head-on the thoughts that had burgeoned and grown more real over the last three days. *Conall has learned his lesson, he loves you, he's serious about a future with you.* She'd been too harsh, insisting that he had a ring on him there and then — it was a spontaneous act, he'd acted out of irresistible emotion. And what she kept coming back to was this: he had asked her to marry him. And he had said he loved her . . .

She was almost at a breaking point. Why suffer the pain any longer?

Maybe she'd just ring him, have a conversation, see what came out of it and — Hold on a minute! She knew that van! The one that was parking outside her house and that she'd expected never to see again. It was Cesar, the flower-delivery guy.

Oh Conall.

Cesar jumped out of his seat. "Morning, Katie." Conall had sent so many bouquets over the past ten months that she knew Cesar quite well by now.

Cesar went round to open the back of the van and Katie followed. Her heart was rising, rising, rising. The sun had burst free from behind a blanket of cloud.

Cesar reached into the interior and Katie leaned around him, trying to see. Just how big would the bunch be, she wondered. The size would be an indication of the seriousness of Conall's intentions.

With much crackling of cellophane, Cesar drew out the bouquet and it was a monster, right enough. But there was something odd about it, it was made up of strange spiky blooms, sharp, almost aggressive. Was that . . . *a thistle* . . . lurking in the middle of it? Conall usually sent lilies — stargazers, tigers, callas, elegant and fragrant. Why was he sending these ugly, pointy things?

With some misgivings, Katie stretched out her arms to accept the thorny-looking bundle. But Cesar was consulting his clipboard. "Have you moved flats?"

"No."

"But this is for flat three."

"It must be a mistake, I'm flat four."

"This is for flat three. It says it here." He indicated his worksheet.

"It's just a mistake, Cesar. I'm sorry, but I'm late for work." And she was going to be even later because she'd have to run back upstairs with the flowers, so if Cesar would just hand them over . . .

She had a thought. "Unless they're not from Conall."

"They're from Mr. Hathaway, all right."

"Then they're for me."

"Hold on a minute." Cesar had his mobile out. "I'll just give the girls a shout."

After a short conversation, he snapped his phone shut. "It's for the taxi-driver girl, who lives in the flat below Katie Richmond."

"Oh." Katie couldn't think of anything else to say so she said it again. "Oh."

All the breath had been knocked out of her. What was Conall up to? How did he know Lydia? How did he know she drove a taxi?

"I'll, ah . . . just . . ." Cesar indicated that he needed to get past to reach the doorbell — in order to give the flowers to the right person. He looked a little mortified. Eye contact wasn't what you might call *full*. "Right, ah . . . Good luck, Katie, have a nice day."

"Yes, ah, Cesar. Yes, right, you too."

DAY 36 . . .

Lydia tumbled into the flat, every sense on red alert, seeking Andrei's presence. Or

401

rather, hoping not to seek it. *Don't be in, you miserable Pole, be at college, be at your creepy girlfriend's, be out drinking, but don't be here.*

She stuck her head around the sitting-room door and there he was. Shite. The first time she'd seen him since . . . Since nothing. Since the thing that hadn't happened.

"Where's Jan?"

"At work."

"When will he be home?"

"After ten."

"Are you in for the evening?" Maybe he'd be going out with Rosie.

"Yes."

Minsk.

"Rosie is coming over," he added.

Oh no! Worse and worser! Rosie was the pits. Whenever Lydia was with her — not often, which was just the way she liked it — Lydia always got this mad urge to start yelling that Rosie was a total faker, that she was only pretending to be virtuous and that she was actually calculating and cold and probably had a plan for world domination. Not that Lydia minded anyone being calculating and cold. Be as calculating and cold as you like, just be honest about it; and if you've got a plan for world domination, at least have the decency to live in an underground lair and wear a white suit and stroke a fat white cat, don't be skipping round the place going on about pretty flowers and fluffy bunny rabbits and pinkness. The only thing that stopped Lydia from thrusting a fork into Rosie's eye was that Rosie clearly detested Lydia as much as Lydia detested Rosie and she made no attempt at all to hide it, none whatsoever, and Lydia respected that because for once Rosie wasn't faking.

"Andrei, how long more before you go on your summer holiday?"

"Four weeks, six days and sixteen hours."

Further away than she'd thought. Much further. Shite. "Oh, I borrowed your bag," she said. "Your overnight bag."

"It's okay," he said. "Where were you? You see your mum?"

She gave a curt nod.

"Sad?" he asked.

Feck off with your sad, *you love-wrecker. Gilbert would still be my boyfriend if it wasn't for you.*

Naturally, she was prepared to take the rap for whatever part she'd played in herself and Gilbert being trashed but, come on, when you thought about it, it was all Andrei's fault.

She went into the kitchen and came to an abrupt halt. Instantly, she returned to the living room. "What's with all the bunches of flowers? The kitchen's fecking full of them! I can hardly get in."

"They are for you."

"Haha."

"Truly. They are for you."

403

"For real?" She'd assumed he had bought them to give to drippy Rosie. "Who are they from?" Then she had a dreadful thought. "Not from you?"

"Haha. Funny joke." His sarcasm was quite impressive.

She returned to the kitchen and gazed with confusion and irritation. There were four bundles of blooms, each of them humongous. One in the sink, one lying on the draining board and two standing upright on kitchen chairs, looking like they were about to tuck into their dinner. Even then she knew they weren't from Gilbert. He wasn't that type of man, and just as well he'd slept with other girls because this sort of cheesy gesture would send her right off him.

What was she meant to do with them? Like, what was the use of flowers? Chocolates she could understand, but flowers were just pointless bloody things. Hadn't Poppy got a bouquet when she'd left her last job . . . ? Lydia had a hazy, drunken, late-night memory of all of them trying to snort the life-extendy powder, but they hadn't got a hit. Like she said: pointless bloody things.

She spun on her heel and returned to Andrei. "Who sent them?"

"Man in van."

"Yeah, but who *sent* them?"

He shrugged. "Open envelope. There is envelope with each collection."

"The word is *bunch.*"

Cautiously, she approached the bunch in the sink. As Andrei said, there was a little white envelope on a stick, in the middle of the foliage. As she reached for it, something stung her. "Ow! Christ!" What happened there? Were those green fronds . . . *nettles?* They fecking were! In fact, all the plants — you couldn't really call them flowers, they were mostly thistles and thorns — were spiky and aggressive and dangerous-looking. They were held together by a neat little bow, very cute, except that it was made of barbed wire. She tore open the envelope and written on a little white card was:

I saw these and thought of you

It was so unexpected that she actually laughed. But the card wasn't signed so she reached into the heart of another bouquet, this time the one lying on the draining board. Large, closed, flesh-colored buds crowded together, sinister-looking, like they could open their jaws and savage you with serrated teeth. She whipped the card out quickly before they came to life and snapped her hand off.

. . . and these . . .

Love of God!

She rounded on one of the bundles on the chair. A cluster of pointy, orange things, as long as razor shells and just as sharp, it bristled with malign energy.

. . . and these . . .

The last bouquet was different. It had proper flowers: round smiling blooms in blocks of bright color — vibrant yellows and reds and pinks — like a child's drawing.

. . . and these. Conall Hathaway. Give me a call.

Who? Aha! She had it! Mr. Wellington Road. The old rich guy. She'd been so tired doing that drive she only half-remembered it. But she remembered that he'd asked her out.
"*Out* out?" She'd been gobsmacked.
"Yeah. On a date."
Then he'd asked her if she liked stationery shops. Or drugstores. He was really weird. She didn't think she'd ever been in a stationery shop in her life.
"No thanks," she'd said.
"Why not?"
Why not? She'd turned to stare at him. "You're not my type." Then she'd added, "To put it mildly."
"I'm fucked-up," he'd said enticingly.
Perplexed, she'd asked, "Since when was

that a good thing?"

"I'm told that's what the girls like. The young ones, anyway."

"Look, just pay up and get out of my car."

"I'm hard to get."

"You're not! You're offering yourself on a plate! You couldn't be *easier.*"

"Only now, just to get the ball rolling. But in a month's time you won't know which end is up. How much do I owe you?"

"Eight euro forty. I'll call it eight if you'll just get out."

He'd handed her a tenner. "Keep —"

"— the change? No thanks. Here's your two euro. Please get out. I've to go and see my mum." She'd looked at her watch. "I need a few hours' nap first."

"One of my girlfriends, the one before Katie, parked outside my house for sixty-seven hours when I broke up with her."

"I would never go out with someone like you. You're too old. You're too . . . You'd bore me senseless . . . Look! You're upset about the sexy governess, but she'll take you back, her type always does."

"I'm Conall Hathaway. I like you. Expect to hear from me again."

"Feck off, you stalker. I suppose you'll be wanting a receipt? Your type always does."

"Who send flowers?" Andrei asked.

"Some lunatic."

Andrei smirked.

"What?" she demanded.

"I did not say word."

"Yeah, but you were thinking that a man would have to be a lunatic to send me flowers."

"I said nothing," he said, over-innocently.

She glared but let it go.

DAY 36 . . .

Fionn was outside on the front step, the blue door swinging open behind him. He was pretending to study the stars while trying to catch a glimpse of Maeve through the gap in her sitting-room curtains. But all he could see was Matt sitting on the floor, steadily eating his way through a box of — Fionn couldn't be certain, it was too far away — but it looked like a box of blackcurrant flapjacks. Maybe not blackcurrant, they could be blackberry, or even blueberry, but definitely some sort of rectangular bun with a purplish jam.

"What are you up to, son?" A duo of passing policemen interrupted his beady-eyed squinting.

"Standing outside my own dwelling place looking at the stars."

"Stars are that way." The bigger of the two pointed at the sky and only when Fionn turned his face upward did they lumber on.

Fionn gazed up into the royal-blue dusk, waiting for the boyos to disappear, resenting every second that he wasn't keeping tabs on Maeve. And it wasn't like he could even properly see the stars, not in this city, which blazed artificial light everywhere and dimmed the wonder of nature. *Arm-wrestling with nature.* He liked that phrase. He wondered if Grainne would let him use it. She might, you never know. Then again, she might not and Grainne was a tough nut . . . Something compelled him to turn his head, and through the dim light he saw a female creature walking along Star Street toward him. All at once his vision filled with comets and stars, colors and spirals — Fionn had fallen in love again.

Like someone who'd discovered a new skill, perhaps like making pancakes or riding a unicycle, Fionn was keen to keep trying it out. Even as he was stunned with love for this new woman, this bandbox-fresh little delight, he was kind enough to consider Maeve and he knew he would always think fondly of her, his first love. But, all of sudden, Maeve seemed raw and disheveled — *What was with the baggy cords?* — and the type of woman a youngster, inexperienced in the ways of love, would fall for. This new emotion was different, infinitely more sophisticated, because Fionn was more mature now, more of a man.

He fastened his loving gaze on the vision's

swinging skirt, her narrow waist, her swishing ponytail. An expression that Fionn didn't even know that he knew spoke in his head: *matchy-matchy.* Shoes, belt, handbag. An embroidered blouse. A modest girl, like something from the olden days, the early eighties, perhaps. He knew with profound certainty that she could sew a button on to a shirt. He pictured her, pulling a length of thread along her plump lower lip and expertly snapping it with a bite of her little white teeth.

Fionn stepped forward to impede her progress along Star Street. He was powerless to stop himself. "Hello," he said.

She stopped. She stopped! "Hello."

He was close enough to see she was wearing a delicate gold cross on a chain around her slender white neck.

"I'm standing here looking at the stars," he said.

"We all have to have a hobby."

"See that one." He pointed toward a pinprick of intense light. "That's the planet Venus. It's not actually a star at all."

"Would you credit it? It looks just like a star. Only brighter."

"The brightest star in the sky. They call it the planet of love." Was he going too far? "I'm Fionn Purdue."

"Pleased to meet you, Mr. Purdue."

Oh the modesty, the sweetness! "Fionn, Fionn, Fionn. And what do they call you?"

"Rosemary Draper."

"Rosemary," Fionn murmured. God, it was beautiful. Rose, Rose, Rose. Mary. Mary. Mary.

"My friends call me Rosie."

"May I . . . ?"

"Are you my friend?" Oh flirting! Flirting from the little madam who looked like butter wouldn't melt.

"I'd like to be."

"Oh stop that now, you brazen pup!" But she smiled. A prim little smile, somewhat lacking in warmth, but a smile nonetheless.

Already he knew so much about her. Their home would always be neat and pretty, far more charming than the identical ones their neighbors had; she'd be a marvel with money, making a little go a long way; she'd be a gifted cook, working alchemy with cheap cuts of meat; they'd be the only people in their street to go on a foreign holiday; she'd keep her figure even after countless babies and she'd always be delightfully turned out in skirts and blouses that she'd fashioned herself at her sewing machine. Fionn wasn't sure why their life together would be lived in the mid-fifties, but there you are.

"What do you do for a crust, Rosemary?" He was planning to land it on her that he was shortly to be a star of the small screen.

"I'm a nurse."

A nurse! She seemed too, well, *prissy,* to be

411

a nurse. The nurses Fionn knew were earthy raucous creatures who spent their days tending with great compassion to the sick and the dying and their evenings drinking vast quantities of alcohol and dancing the night away in Copperface Jacks with policemen and firemen.

"Now, if you'll excuse me." Rosemary — dare he call her Rosie? — made to get round Fionn. She seemed to be aiming herself at the open doorway.

"You're coming in! You live here too? I'm on the first floor!" What was it with this house that it was riddled with beautiful women? Sirens! Temptresses! Then it occurred to him that perhaps the only reason she had stopped to talk to him was because she was trying to gain ingress into the house and his great joy dimmed a little.

"I'm visiting my boyfriend. Andrei Palweski."

"You have a boyfriend?" It was a blow.

"I have a boyfriend."

But of course she did. Never mind. He'd make short work of that arrangement.

"What hospital do you work at?" he called, as she climbed the stairs away from him.

Her lower legs — all he could see of her — hesitated. Then the magic words floated down to him. "St. Vincent's." And her legs began to climb again.

"I've no food in and I'm starving," Lydia said. "Do you mind if I eat some of your funny Polish bread?"

"No problem; but it is old."

"Stale. Can I eat some of your funny Polish cheese?"

"For sure."

She slapped some white cheese and two slices of stale bread together, then flung herself on the couch. Amazing what tasted nice when you were starving. Some program was on, about a house being exorcized of its ghosts. She let it wash over her, too tired to ask that they watch something good.

She flicked a glance out of the corner of her eye, just to see if Andrei was showing signs of effing off to his room. As if he felt her eyes on him, he turned and looked at her and they exchanged a moment of hearty, mutual dislike. Naked antipathy. Then one of them, probably Andrei, she decided afterward, made a small movement and everything went blurry. They both moved, a twist of the body toward each other, and then they somehow launched themselves at one another, kissing and pulling and tearing, caught in a frenzy of want.

It was like the previous time, except that now she had the pleasure of anticipation. She knew how fabulous it was going to be. She knew how his skin would feel — hot and cold and smooth and rough — against hers. She knew how he would press her hips flat against the bed, his biceps bulging. She knew she would arch herself upward to meet him. She knew how he would move himself, rock hard, back and forth into her, smooth and fast as a piston. She knew she would wrap her legs around him and come again and again.

It was an absolute revelation, to discover so much pleasure available to her, right in her own home. Right in her own body. The skin of his back beneath the palm of her hands, the resistance of muscle as she pressed her heels into his buttocks. If she could spend the rest of her life doing this, captured in the moment, with Andrei's mouth on hers, his body moving in and out of hers, she would happily live forever.

It was different from Gilbert; Gilbert was slow. If the phrase didn't make her want to puke, she would say that he made love. But with Andrei there was no finesse, it was wild and intense, the volume of every nerve ending turned up to ten, like a roller-coaster ride, a short, thrilling burst of out-of-control sensation.

Harmonious heart currents? It's all such a wild lustful flurry, everything beating in such a frantic, deafeningly loud cacophony that it's impossible to tell.

On paper, Andrei and Lydia don't look like the perfect match, but you've got to stay open-minded, no?

DAY 36 . . .

Rosie knocked softly on the door of flat three, then stood back and smoothed her skirt and fixed a sweet smile to her face.

But the moments passed and the door remained unanswered and she was surprised. Vexed, in fact. Obliging her to knock for a second time was . . . well, it felt disrespectful. As she rapped once again, a frosty persona began to steal over her, one that Andrei would have to work hard to jolly her out of.

And still — astonishingly — no one appeared. How unexpected. Andrei and she had arranged that she call at eight-thirty and here she was now, ten to nine.

Was she expected to knock again? A third time? Seriously?

She considered simply flouncing away down the stairs. She was wearing a good skirt for it. But a flounce was no good if there was no man to suffer from seeing you do it.

She rapped once more, quite angrily this time, enough to hurt her little knuckles — and the seconds ticked by and the door remained impassive. This was entirely unacceptable. Rosie Draper was not the kind of

415

girl you left standing outside an unanswered door.

This wasn't a deliberate snub; Andrei had the total dotes for her. Something must have happened with his job or the van or that cretin Jan to derail his plans. Nevertheless, if Andrei couldn't organize his life adequately, in order to fulfill his obligations to her, a price had to be paid.

Already she was planning how to punish him. She might cry; that just about killed him. Or she could go the icy route. Do tell me, she would say with frightening froideur, why no text arrived to advise me of the change in plans?

No matter which way she went, she would make it very clear that this slight had added several more weeks to the endurance period before — indeed, *if* — she went to bed with him. Already his longing for her had him unraveling with despair, and to tighten the screws further would be fun . . .

Gosh, she was still outside the door and it still hadn't been answered. It seemed that he actually really wasn't here. She could phone him. But she would not. She, Rosemary Draper, making calls, trying to track down a man? I don't think so!

On the floor below, she heard the Fionn hunk going into his flat and calling out, "I'm back." Then came the sound of frenzied barking and shouting. "Shag off, you mad bastard of a dog!"

Fionn must have had his fill of star-gazing.

A dreamboat, no one could deny it, one of the most handsome men she'd ever seen. Quite full of himself, though.

But he'd asked for her number, and Andrei had seriously blotted his copy book and Rosie was a great believer in safety nets, Plans B and contingency arrangements.

She reached into her handbag and fetched out a pretty little notebook, the pale yellow pages patterned with buttercups. With the matching yellow pen, she wrote:

Dear Andrei,
    I called at your flat like we arranged but you're not here. I can't understand what I have done to you that you would need to humiliate me so badly.

She considered adding, "I have only ever tried to be good to you," but suspected that might topple things into overkill. Less is more. Sometimes.

She tore the page out and shoved it under the door, then skipped down a flight of stairs and reached once again for her notebook. Neatly, she printed her name and work number, eased the page out carefully, folded it tidily and slid it smoothly under Fionn's door.

They lay in each other's arms, Lydia's head on Andrei's buff chest, his fingers tangled in her springy curls.

"I do not understand," Andrei said thoughtfully, "I dislike you very much."

"Mmmm, and I hate you."

"You have these bad manners."

"And you've no sense of humor."

"So can you explain me why did this happen?"

"Haven't a clue."

"What?"

She sighed. "Probably because your girlfriend is a professional virgin and this flat's too small."

The spell was wearing off.

She clambered from the bed and gathered up her clothes from the four corners of the room and stopped at the door. She refused to cover herself. Let him look. In fairness, he wasn't covering himself either. He lay on the bed, the duvet flung to the floor, an arm behind his head, his hard muscular body fully on show. "Never again," she said. "D'you hear? If this happens again I'm moving out. Outtttt," she emphasized. "You'll have to get a new flatmate and think of how hard it was the last time. You'll have to put an ad in Midget Times."

He shrugged. "Never again is okay with me."

DAY 34

Katie stuck her head around the sitting-room door. "Hi, Dad."

Energized by the sight of her, Robert Richmond dusted the newspaper off his lap and on to the fireside rug. "How's Miss Havisham?"

". . . Do you mean . . . me?"

"Ah Katie, Katie, what were you at? He arrives in the middle of the night, jarred by all accounts, gets down on one knee and you think he means it?"

Silently, Katie cursed herself for having told anyone about Conall's middle-of-the-night visit. Especially bloody Naomi! Naomi — even though she professed to hate their mum — told her everything. In the Richmond house, there were never any private places in which to lick your wounds.

"I didn't think he meant it." She worked hard to keep her voice steady. "I didn't say yes."

"I hear he has his eye on some young one

now," Robert said, almost cheerfully. "Naomi said he sent her flowers. And you're all upset."

In a sick, strange way, Dad's cruelty was a form of concern. Robert and Penny Richmond had worked hard to instill a powerful value system in their children: getting ideas above your station could only end in tears; hubris would always be punished. Low expectations were the key to happiness.

Penny darted in from the kitchen, a vision of domesticity in a Simpsons apron. Clearly, she'd been listening. "You should never have gone near him."

"Why not?"

Katie's mother stretched her neck to ten times its normal length and reared back in shock. "Are you raising *your voice* at me?"

Robert, never one to miss an opportunity to take offense, rose halfway out of his chair. "Are you raising your voice at your mother? In her own house? While she's cooking you Sunday lunch?"

A long, tense stand-off ensued. From the kitchen Katie heard Naomi ask, "What's going on in there?"

Nine-year-old Nita answered, "I think Auntie Katie raised her voice at Granny."

And Ralph's voice said, "Oh Christ, Naomi, your family. Where's the wine?"

Penny glared at Katie, her mouth trembling with woundedness. Her neck was still abnormally long and her chin was tucked into her chest so she looked like an aggrieved goose.

"Why shouldn't I have gone near him?" Katie heard her voice quiver. Then she answered her own question. "Because I wasn't good enough."

"I don't know what's got into you." Penny stared at Katie.

"Don't mind her, love," Robert urged his wife. "Just get on with the lunch."

Rain beat against the windows and the only sound throughout lunch was the clinking of cutlery on plates. Penny Richmond maintained her martyred air for over an hour and even Naomi's kids, Nita and Percy, were silenced by the toxic atmosphere. The lone bottle of wine disappeared in seconds and when Katie realized that there wasn't any more, silent tears began to course down her face and plop onto her plate.

"Why are you crying, Auntie Katie?" Nita asked.

"Because all the wine is gone."

Nita patted her knee.

As soon as the torturous meal ended, Naomi pulled her out into the garden.

"I told you not to tell her," Katie said.

Naomi made an apologetic face, but they both knew that when Penny Richmond sensed a story, no one could withstand the interrogation.

"You could kill that thing with the taxi-driver girl with one call," Naomi said.

"Why would I do that?" What would be achieved? In her heart of hearts, Katie had known she shouldn't ever have taken Conall's 5 a.m. proposal seriously. She'd tried to talk herself into believing it. She'd manipulated her friends into convincing her it was real, but she'd always known. Nevertheless . . .

". . . Why did he have to pick someone *where I live?*"

Naomi sucked her teeth and narrowed her eyes. "He's one vicious bastard." She waved a lit cigarette at Katie.

"He's just clueless. But it's all gone so messy. In the beginning it was a neat surgical strike, now the wound has become infected."

"You do love a medical analogy. So what you need is a painkiller." Naomi thrust the cigarette again. "Take this, would you? I'm after lighting it for you."

"For a clever man he can be really stupid — Would you stop with that thing? I don't smoke."

"You do today."

Katie accepted the cigarette. TLC at the Richmonds? This was as good as it got.

"Don't let her see us," Naomi said.

"You're forty-two." Katie inhaled. A bad idea. She'd been feeling sick anyway, now she was sure she was going to throw up. "What age do you have to be before your mum will let you smoke?"

In silence, they sat on wet garden chairs and listened to the raindrops dripping from the branches.

"Death by Sunday lunch," Naomi said moodily.

"Fecking torture."

"How does Charlie get out of having to come to these bloody things?"

Katie paused, afraid that the secret about Charlie would just tumble out of her mouth, then she carried on. "He's got a stronger sense of survival than either of us. He knows Mum will make him feel like shit, so he won't put himself through it."

"Yeah."

"I hate her," Katie said suddenly. "I hate them both. Why couldn't we have had parents who told us we were great?"

"Well, you choose them."

"Excuse me?"

"This book I'm reading. It's one of yours, actually. Louise L. Hay. I took it off your shelf the night of your birthday. It says we choose everything we get in life. Even our own parents."

"We *choose our own parents?* Before we're born?"

"Before we're conceived, actually."

"But how could we do that? That's just . . . *shit.*"

"I know. They're all shit, all those books. I'm only saying."

Day 33

Maeve's phone rang. "Emerald Hotels reservations, Maeve Geary speaking, how may I help you today?" She had to say the full mouthful every time she answered. Sometimes they monitored her calls and unpleasantness could ensue if they found out that she was cutting corners on her intro.

"Maeve, it's Jenna."

"Oh. Jenna. Hi." Why would Matt's brother's fiancée be ringing her? She liked Jenna but they weren't what you might call close. This must be hen night–related, Maeve realized. Oh cripes!

"Sorry for ringing you at work."

"It's okay," Maeve said cautiously.

"I just wanted to talk to you about something a little . . . delicate."

"Okay." No!

"Your honeymoon . . ."

"My *honey*moon?"

"Am I right in thinking Hilary and Walter paid for it?"

"Yes, it was their wedding present to us."

"Well, it's the same with Alex and me, they're paying for ours."

"Where . . . ?"

"Antigua."

"Oh right, I knew that."

"The thing is, Maeve, that they're insisting on paying for business-class flights and Alex and I, well, we don't know if we should accept, it just seems a bit . . . you know, lavish. But if they paid for business-class flights for you and Matt, then it's appropriate that we accept."

Maeve gave a little laugh. "Sorry, Jenna, it was cattle-class for myself and Matt. But take the nice flights, for the love of God. Why not? Go on, if they've offered."

"Yes, but . . ." Jenna was in a knot of anguish, desperate to do the right thing.

"Matt and I won't mind, if that's what you're worried about."

"I see, well, I'll talk to Alex, and we'll have a think, and thanks, you know."

"No probs. See you soon."

Maeve hung up and for a moment she felt awash with sparkling, crystal light. It had been a while since she'd thought about her honeymoon, the most glorious fortnight of her life. A sybaritic fourteen days and nights in a lush-gardened, all-inclusive Malaysian resort, with air conditioning and Evian ice cubes and obliging staff and private, dark-wood, thatched-roofed dwellings. So different from the kind of holidays Maeve used to go on before she'd met Matt, when she'd go off the beaten track, hitching lifts with locals, eating from street stalls and getting the outlandish diarrhea that was the badge of the authentic traveler.

When she'd first arrived at the honeymoon resort (which seemed to have been entirely and intricately carved out of teak), she'd felt slightly like a sell-out — but the guilt had lasted just as long as it took to wipe her travel-stained brow with the deliciously icy-cold, lemongrass-scented cloth that was presented to her by a smiling man in an embroidered dress: she'd taken to a life of luxury with unexpected ease.

The beauty of everything — the triumphant yellow morning light, the flashes of intense color from the exotic flowers, the luminous blue water, twinkling silver in the sun. She and Matt had passed their days lying on indecently comfortable sun loungers and having massages and ringing for room service and sleeping and swimming and, above all, having sex. Every afternoon, while Maeve had rocked gently in a hammock in the shade of their own personal trees, eating sliced mango and humming happily to herself, Matt had read aloud to her from his new James Bond book, the kind of thing Maeve would normally have no interest in, but, with Matt doing accents and voices and music, she'd been enthralled.

Every night after dinner, they'd tumble back into their adorable little house, where some invisible, lovely person would have lit dozens of candles and created a heart-shape with rose petals on their enormous bed.

It had been wonderful.

DAY 33 . . .

"You mean you were there all the time?" Rosie asked. "In your flat? While I stood outside knocking for hours?"

"But you did not ring buzzer. Buzzer is loud. Knocking with your little hands is not loud. I did not hear."

Andrei was distraught. He had completely forgotten about his darling Rosie; all thoughts of anything had been annihilated by the force that was Lydia.

When he'd found that fragrant yellow note in the hall . . . ! The shame had cut him like knives, flaying him bare, right down to the bone.

It was days before Rosie would speak to him and even then it was a humble whisper. "Obviously, I mean nothing to you, Andrei. I just wish you could have told me. But I want you to be happy. I hope you meet a really nice girl, who cares for you as much as I did."

He'd had to launch a full-on apology offensive, involving countless texts and phone calls. He'd had two or three Rosie-style girlfriends in Poland and he knew the precise price you paid for this sort of misstep. Flowers, obviously. But they could only be roses and they could only be red and they had to number twelve. No more, no less. A dozen red roses — any variation in the formula could actually make the situation worse. Then a piece of jewelry. But this was not the time for an engagement ring, because the girl would cry and say, "Whenever I'll think of us getting engaged, it'll bring back unhappy memories of me standing outside that door like a . . . like a . . ." Words would become incoherent, then cease as the storm of weeping disabled her entirely.

A charm for her charm bracelet, a little gold and ruby heart, would be just the thing. Finally, a promise of a weekend away, when no one would be left waiting outside any doors.

Andrei knew Rosie was milking it somewhat, but he wanted to go along with it. Rules were rules and restoration was necessary.

But Jesus Christ and all the angels! If Rosie only knew what he'd been up to while she'd been standing a few short meters away. He kept having moments when his head reeled and his skin became drenched as he remembered his act — *acts* — of betrayal. He'd be driving the van, or taking the back off a PC,

430

and the next thing the horror would sweep over him and he would want to fall to his knees and pray for forgiveness.

He cared for Rosie. He thought he might actually love her. So what was he doing with Lydia?

DAY 32 (VERY EARLY IN THE MORNING)

They all looked the same, those tall, posh Georgian houses. Lydia parked outside number eleven and reached for her mobile. She refused to get out of the car and ring the doorbell because it was drizzling and she had her hair to think of. "Taxi for Eilish Hessard." Lydia left a message on the mobile contact. "I'm waiting outside."

Over the years she'd discovered that there was no pattern to where she could be taken by the forces that governed taxis. She might never have visited a road and then she could find herself driving there five times in the one week . . .

. . . so to find herself picking up on Wellington Road could be a meaningless co-incidence.

But she didn't really believe it. Not after those bloody flowers. And it wasn't much of a surprise when the passenger door was wrenched open and the rich old guy, whatever his name was, jumped in beside her. "Morn-

432

ing, Lydia!"

"Out," she said. "This is Eilish Hessard's car."

"She's my assistant. Subterfuge. I booked you. Did you get the flowers?"

"How did you track me down?"

"I thought at the very least I'd get a call thanking me for the flowers."

"I didn't ask for them. There should be a law against sending things to people that they don't want. So how did you book me?"

"Very easy. Luckily, there aren't many girls who drive taxis. Eilish rang all the taxi companies."

"You got your assistant to ring?"

"Because she's a woman. I didn't think your controllers would be too keen to hook you up with a man."

They were nothing like as noble as that, Lydia thought.

"Eilish said you'd driven her and that she'd liked you. The guy seemed to find it hard to believe but . . . joke, Lydia."

"I'm doubled-over laughing. So where to?"

"Nowhere. I just thought we'd sit here and talk. Why don't you come in for some breakfast?"

"The neck of you! I've a living to earn. I'm not your . . . plaything."

"I'll pay you."

"I don't want you to pay me." She shuddered. "This is really creepy. You're turning my stomach. Please get out."

He stared at her, aghast. "I've handled this all wrong," he muttered. "How can I make it better?"

"By getting out of my car and never contacting me again. That way I won't press charges."

"Give me a chance."

"Please get out of my car."

"When's your next day off? What would you like to do? Say anything you want. Anything, and I'll go along with it."

"Yeah, grand, so. I'd like you to drive me to Boyne in County Meath, help me clean a really nasty kitchen, humor my not-very-well-in-the-head mum, visit an old people's home with me and threaten one of my brothers. I don't mind which one. I've got three, so you can have the pleasure of choosing."

"Wouldn't you prefer something more . . . you know? We could drive down to Powerscourt and have lunch at —"

"Don't start negotiating. It's my day off, that's what I'm doing."

"When?"

"Tomorrow."

"Tomorrow? I've to go to work tomorrow."

"So go to work. I couldn't give a shite."

Dispirited, Lydia stomped up the stairs to her flat. Thanks to that madzer Conall Hathaway, her night's take was down at least thirty euro. She couldn't take his money, it felt trashy. When she'd eventually managed to oust him from her car, she hadn't got it in her to go after another fare. It was 7:30 a.m. and all she was good for was home. She'd have a shower, she decided, and wash away her night's work, and then she'd go straight to sleep. And when she woke up she'd go to the supermarket and buy proper food, fresh stuff, with vitamins and enzymes; no more living on chips and chocolate. Maybe then she wouldn't be so knackered all the time . . .

She let herself into the flat and, as she shut the door behind her, she heard a noise. It was the sound of Andrei and Jan's bedroom door opening. Andrei appeared, bare-chested, in a pair of sweats, as if he'd been waiting for her. Without thinking, she moved to him and he took her in his arms and wordlessly unzipped her hoodie and she let him. She surrendered with relief to his hard body, to his smell, to his sure, confident touch. Suddenly, all her tiredness had disappeared and she was tearing off her clothes and pushing him toward his bedroom, and when she met a wall of resistance she realized that Andrei was steering her to her own room. Jan. She'd completely forgotten about him.

"Jan? He's here?" she gasped.

"Sleeping. We must be quiet," Andrei whispered urgently.

But it was impossible. As he covered her

body with kisses, she couldn't stop little whimpers escaping. When he entered her, he groaned long and hard, and when she came, he clamped his hand over her mouth and she stared at him, bug-eyed, as his blue eyes burned into hers and her body exploded in ever-increasing circles of pleasure.

"What about Poor Fucker?" Andrei asked, cradling her body in his arms. "You still . . . ?"

"No. Gone."

"You tell him? About this?"

"Yeah." She felt him tense up. "You worried about a posse of Nigerians coming round to kick the crap out of you?"

"Not worried."

"What about Rosie?" Her instinct, as always, was to add some insulting description like "Rosie, the last virgin in Ireland," but it didn't feel right. *I mean, I'm sleeping with her boyfriend. I couldn't insult her any more than I already am.*

"Do not speak her name."

He was rolling away from her and getting out of bed and leaving the room, and she was glad because now she could go to sleep.

Matt walked into his office and Salvatore said, "Didn't know you'd got the morning off."

"Haha."

Yes, so it was 11:15. Yes, so Matt was late. But Maeve had had another panic attack this morning, the second in less than a week, and it had taken a long time to calm her down and to persuade her that they could both go to work. It was like a return to the bad old days, and it was all Fionn Purdue's fault.

"So what's up?" Salvatore asked.

"An emergency."

"How thrilling! What kind of emergency?"

Matt looked at him carefully. Salvatore had always been a smart-arse, but this was a bit much.

"A private emergency," Matt said slowly. "And I'm here now."

And it wasn't as if he was exactly snowed under with work. He and the team were keeping a steady flow of cash coming in, by flogging upgrades to those companies who already had Edios — no mean feat in the current economic climate — but there were precious few proper prospects on the horizon. What they really needed was to land a big fish, to persuade some company, preferably a giant conglomerate, to change their software to Edios. Amazingly, there was still no movement on the Bank of British Columbia. They hadn't agreed to a sale but neither had they pulled out of negotiations and all progress had stalled, bogged down in the mud of their poker-faced inscrutability. Sign of the times, Matt knew — people were terrified of spending money — but the stalemate was chipping away at everyone's morale.

He wondered if his team was losing faith in him. Salvatore's disrespect wasn't a good sign. But, looked at another way, he was probably lucky to still have a team.

Looked at another way, a dark voice said in his head, *he was probably lucky to still have a job.*

Quickly, he turned away from that unthinkable thought and faced into his emails. Nothing of interest, except one from his brother, Alex, subject matter: TONIGHT!!!!

Matt, Alex and the second best man, Russ, were due to meet after work to finalize details on the Vegas stag week.

6:30 The Duke. Do not cancel again! Alex

Matt fired off a breezy reply:

I'll be there. Should be early. I'll have the pints waiting.

As if. Not with Maeve the way she was. Briefly, his life seemed to tighten around him

438

— Maeve, the job, the stagnation of everything — choking off all light and hope . . . Then he had a fantastic idea! There was a way out of this!

Energized and hopeful, he was keen to get going right away. When could he nip out? When could it be called lunchtime? Noon, that would do. Less than forty minutes.

"Thanks for dropping by," Salvatore called after him, but nothing could puncture Matt's buoyant hope.

A new home, Matt had decided. That was the answer! A fresh start in a new place would fix everything. He spent a few moments in the street outside the real-estate agent's, glancing from photo to photo, wondering what form his and Maeve's new life would take, then he stepped confidently inside, all set to make it a reality.

The girl at the desk — Philippa — looked up expectantly when Matt came in, then he saw something behind her eyes die a little.

"Can I help you?" She managed a professional smile.

"Ah yes. I'd like to move home."

"Take a seat. You've been in before?"

". . . Er . . . I have."

"Matt, isn't it?"

"Matt Geary."

"That's right, I remember. So we'd have your details on file. What's your address?"

"Sixty-six Star Street. The flat on —"

439

"— the ground floor. It's all coming back to me." Philippa started clicking. "You were last in, in March."

That recently? It felt much longer ago to Matt.

"We did a home visit this time last year," Philippa said. "And did a valuation. But in the current market, that figure would have dropped substantially."

Matt swallowed. "By how much?"

"We recently sold a very similar flat to yours, ground floor, back garden, central location, for —" She did a bit more clicking and named a sum that was so low it scared Matt. Even lower than it had been the last time he'd been in, which, if Philippa was right, was only three months ago.

"So we'd be looking for another home in or around the same price region?" Philippa asked. "You haven't won the Euro Millions or anything?"

Matt shook his head.

"And what were you thinking of? A flat in a similar setup to your current home? A flat in a new development? There are some really good deals in a magnificent gated community in CityWest. Incredibly high-spec. The apartments are spectacular, and there's a gym, sauna, Jacuzzi, a sunken yoga garden —"

"In each *apartment?*"

"Oh no. Communal. Shared."

"Right. Well, I was thinking more of a

house. Somewhere private. You know, where you wouldn't meet other people in the hall."

"You certainly wouldn't get a house this close to the city center. Not with the equity you have."

"Okay. Well, show me what you've got."

"Just out of curiosity," Philippa asked, "what happened the last time?"

"My wife didn't like the ones I picked out."

"Right. Well, let's see if we can find something she likes this time."

DAY 32 . . .

Lydia didn't recognize the number on the phone but, what the hell, she answered it anyway. Live a little.

"This is Conall Hathaway."

"Ah, for the love of — How did you get my number?"

"You rang this morning to tell me you were outside my house."

Her hair! Her bloody needy hair — she should have just got out of the car and rung the doorbell.

"I've decided to take you up on your invitation," he said.

"What invitation?"

"Tomorrow. I'm taking the day off. We're spending it together. We're going to drive somewhere and — what did you say? Do some cleaning? Meet your mum?"

"I only said it because I knew you wouldn't be into it."

"But I *am* into it."

"You're not coming."

"What time will I pick you up?"

"No time. You're not coming. Get used to it. Go into work, make another million quid."

"I'm coming."

He sounded firm and convincing and she realized it was a good thing she'd met his type before. She'd driven a fair few of them over the years. Those men — and they were nearly always men — with their confidence and their vision and their complete lack of interest in what anyone else was looking for. They wanted what they wanted and then they went and got it and they didn't care what mayhem they caused. There was a phrase that army blokes used when they were trying to explain away a load of dead civilians. *Collateral damage,* that was it. Yeah, the Conall Hathaways of this world had no interest in their collateral damage.

"I reckon about ten o'clock," he was saying. "You won't want to go any earlier because of the traffic. But any later and too much of the day will have gone."

If he was doing this to anyone else, it might even work. But it wouldn't work with her.

"So . . . see you at ten?"

"See you at ten," she repeated, with great sarcasm.

She'd go at nine.

DAY 32 . . .

As he was driving home, Matt passed the woman who'd accused him of being an ax murderer a few weeks back. The memory filled him with surprising bile. Which only intensified when he remembered that he hadn't done today's daily Act of Kindness. Bollocks. Between the late start this morning and then the distraction of all that Philippa, the real-estate agent, had had to offer him, he'd clean forgotten. But the thought of having to be kind to some random stranger met with shocking resistance. He couldn't do it. No way. He'd just lie to Maeve, he decided; and the idea sat so comfortably with him that suddenly he was scared. No, he'd tell the truth and simply ask her for a day off. Then he had an even better idea: hadn't he done today's AOK by visiting Philippa? By finding Maeve a potential new home, he'd done an AOK for *her*. Or indeed for himself. But that was such a novel notion, he moved on quickly. Yes, an Act of Kindness for Maeve. And by not going out with Alex tonight, he was doing Maeve yet *another* AOK. Speaking of which . . .

As soon as he was parked — in a stunning stroke of luck, right outside 66 Star Street — Matt fired off a quick text to Alex.

Mergency at work. Cnt mke 2nite. Cary on widout me!

Then he hurried into the building, as if he could rush away from the guilt.

Maeve was on the couch, watching *South Park.*

"Take a look at these." Matt poured a bundle of glossy brochures into her lap.

"Again?" she asked.

"It's ages since we looked and I just think . . . like, it's not good here, Maeve. Too many people in and out. We'd be better off in a house of our own. Just take a look, and keep an open mind, that's all I ask."

Maeve nodded. "Okay. Open mind. I will." She glanced at the first one, saw the address and said, "No. Cripes, no, Matt."

"Why not?"

"It's less than five minutes' drive from Hilary and Walter. They'd be round the whole time. Well, Hilary would." There was a high likelihood that Walter would never visit. "I know she's your mum, Matt, and she's a dote, but we'd never get rid of her. She'd be sitting at our kitchen table, drinking wine and talking shite, till the cows came home."

"We wouldn't give her any wine."

"She'd bring her own."

"Okay." Matt sighed heavily. "Scrap that one. Next!" A two-story box on a housing estate in suburban Shankill.

"Shankill?" She turned a despairing face to Matt. "When did we become Shankill people?"

"I thought it would be nice, it's a community —"

"In suburbia, no one can hear you scream."

"All right, forget that one." It was obvious she already had her mind made up. "Look at the one in Drumcondra. It's nowhere near my parents, it's not in suburbia, it's perfect."

Maeve gazed at the photo of the house and Matt gazed at Maeve.

Eventually, she spoke. "Twelve," she said.

"Twelve what?" But he could guess.

"Five on the ground floor, six on the first story and an attic skylight. Windows. No way. What else have you?" She moved on to the fourth and final brochure. "Cripes, Matt? A gated community?" She read through the spec. "Coded gates, coded doors, a *communal Jacuzzi?*"

"I know it's not for us. I didn't even want to take the brochure but the girl made me."

"And the people, Matt, could you imagine the type who'd actually want to live in a place like that?" Soulless professionals with Thai-food fixations, acting like fish sauce had just been invented. "They'd be out at work all day."

The cluster of glassy towers would be like a ghost town.

"I know this place is full of comings and

445

goings . . ." Maeve said and Matt saw her point. Unexpectedly, it seemed safer to live in a ground-floor flat in Star Street, even with creepy Fionn sniffing around, because at least there were always people nearby.

Maeve gathered up the brochures and handed them to Matt. "Trash."

Day 31

Conall Hathaway had to circle the block four times before he found a parking space with a good view of the front door of 66 Star Street. He switched off the engine and reached gratefully for his BlackBerry. The red light was flashing. Lovely. New emails.

Seven in total and nothing exciting in any of them, but still, communications were like oxygen to him — urgent phone calls, cryptic texts, detailed emails. He couldn't let too much time elapse between them or else he might die.

He drank his coffee and flicked through the radio stations and watched the blue front door and shifted in his seat and looked at his BlackBerry and wished the red light would start flashing again. He was feeling edgy. He couldn't remember the last time he'd rung Eilish and said the words *I won't be in today.* Naturally, he'd been absent from his desk many, many times, but only because he was sitting at another desk in another company, in the process of taking it over. And he went on corporate jollies, champagne-soaked days in Monaco or Ascot, but that was in order to stay on the inside track with those shadowy figures in the financial markets who knew when a company was failing long before the company itself knew. It was still work.

He'd never before just called Eilish and said he wasn't coming in because . . . well, he just *wasn't coming in.* It didn't feel good, it didn't feel right, but it had to be done.

He'd been fond of Katie, very fond if truth be told, and he hadn't been at all prepared for them breaking up. A woman finishing with him was a radical mutation in his pattern of romance. It hadn't happened in a long, long time, perhaps never, and it had shaken him. Not to his core, no; his core was sealed in titanium. But to quite *near* his core. Enough to cause the coffee cups on the tables of his core to rattle.

Worse than Katie dumping him was that she refused to be won back. He'd offered her the ultimate prize — marriage — and she'd spurned it. Spurned *him.* But instead of wasting time in hand-wringing regret, he asked himself what he could learn. That always worked when things veered off course in his job. He'd devised his own formula, "The Three As and the One M":

Assess the situation.

448

Acknowledge where control had been compromised.
Adapt with a new, more appropriate response for the next set of dynamics.
Move forward.

He wished it was a catchier slogan. Four As would have been ideal. The first three were perfect but he just couldn't find an A that encapsulated the last point.

With Katie, he'd Assessed the situation and wasn't afraid to admit he'd made a mistake — it was what made him so good at his job — and he was man enough, in his opinion, to Acknowledge that being dumped was *his fault*.

Now it was time to Adapt: he'd have to become more flexible about his devotion to the job. Adapt to survive. He didn't believe in fate but he believed in maximizing opportunities, so when Lydia appeared and challenged him to take a weekday off work, he moved on it. Give it a go, see if the world ended; and if it did, well, he was always on the BlackBerry.

Even his clothes this morning had been chosen with a view to his survival. Lydia had accused him of being "too old" so he'd had a pair of fashionable jeans biked over from Brown Thomas and — after a lot of deliberation — he'd matched them with a Clash T-shirt, because the Clash were ageless. Weren't they?

Speaking of the Clash, he stuck in his ear buds and listened to half a verse of "Rock the Casbah" before getting bored and changing to Johnny Cash. He sang along with "Walk the Line" and stared at the door of number 66 and eyed its banana-shaped knocker with irritation. He'd never liked it. Now that he and Katie were kaput he wouldn't have to look at it ever again. Unless, of course, things worked out with Lydia . . .

He couldn't explain why but he was extremely taken with her. Her beauty wasn't the first thing you'd notice because she was so angry but, actually, she was a doll. He liked her angular little face and her scornful eyes. He liked seeing her, small and furious, behind the wheel of her taxi. He liked her "Gdansk!" and "Outttt!" and all that mad stuff. She was a one-of-a-kind.

And she was the right age. Katie was spot-on: a girl in her twenties would suit him. The two girlfriends he'd had before Katie had been in their early thirties, and they'd been . . . how could he put it? *Expectant.* Yes, expectant and watchful. He'd thought of both those relationships as a straight line; he'd found a level he was happy with, and was comfortable with it continuing like that, unfurling out in front of them without any changes, forever. Well, perhaps not *forever.* But indefinitely.

Whereas, with the benefit of hindsight, he

saw that both Saffron and Kym had visualized the relationship as wedge-shaped, like a piece of Cheddar. Starting from a small point, they expected things to improve exponentially, expanding outward and upward, three-dimensionally, with bonus add-ons every month or so. Add-ons such as: meeting their friends; meeting his friends (the few he had); accompanying them to a charity ball and bidding in a flash fashion at the auction; listening to their suggestions for how he should decorate his house; agreeing to let them do one room; fighting his way through the cluster of beauty stuff that appeared overnight in his bathroom; being persuaded of the wisdom of leaving a couple of ironed shirts in their wardrobe; then the big cheese itself: talk of moving in together.

As for Katie? How had she visualized their relationship? He hadn't felt the same pressure from her. Some, certainly, but perhaps the angle wasn't so steep. More like a slice of Brie, than a wedge of Cheddar.

And Lydia? Christ alone knew. She probably had no angle of expectation. Hers might be totally flat, like a packet of Easi-slices. In fact, and he wasn't sure how comfortable he was with this realization, it mightn't be cheese at all.

It was coming up to 8:30 and if Conall had read Lydia right, she'd exit the house soon, looking to put many miles of road behind her before he showed up at ten o'clock. But he was already here!

He lifted his coffee and was shocked to discover it was all gone. Maybe there was a can of Coke somewhere. A thorough foraging in the side pocket of his door yielded nothing more exciting than four squares of Honeycrisp and seven green American Hard Gums. He ate them without enthusiasm; green was his least favorite flavor and he'd obviously left these for dead when he'd eaten all the other colors from a full bag. He'd love a full bag now. He was bored and Johnny Cash was no longer doing it for him. He whipped out the ear buds and scrolled down his screen, reading bulletins, checking sites, assessing the financial markets, looking for anomalies in share prices. Who was underperforming? Overperforming? A bulletin popped up with a rumor that H&E Enterprise, a large clothing company, was about to announce quarterly losses. Nothing too catastrophic and they'd turned in profits for the last eleven quarters. But Conall had been watching the rise in the cost of the raw materials they sourced in the Far East and he'd been made aware, discreetly, that their fourth biggest customer was making overtures to someone else. To have one loss-making quarter was no cause for panic but Conall was getting that tingly feeling. Two of H&E's biggest competitors had been circling at a distance for over a year and if there was to be a takeover or a buyout, he wanted in. Especially because H&E had most of their operations in Southeast Asia, his specialty. He'd do Eastern Europe or Scandinavia if necessary, but the Philippines, Cambodia and Vietnam were where he did his best work.

He looked at his phone, then he looked at the blue front door. Could he make a quick call to one of the shadowy figures to assess H&E's damage and risk Lydia coming out at the same time?

He made the call. He couldn't help himself. The coffee was gone, the sweets and chocolate were gone, the music wasn't working; he needed *something,* so a quick shot of adrenaline would have to do. Saffron used to say that he should pretend he was allergic to wasps and would go into anaphylactic shock if he got stung, because then he could get adrenaline injections from his doctor, which he could administer himself whenever he got bored. She didn't say it at the start of their two years together, she was happy back then; she only said it toward the end when she seemed considerably disillusioned with him and his devotion to his work.

He listened to the ringing tone and idly kicked his accelerator. Answer, for the love of Christ! God, he was bored.

Someone picked up. "Hello?"

"Shadowy Figure?"

"Conall?"

"Where are you?"

"Playing golf."

"Where?" He was in the mood for a chat.

"Syria. What do you want?"

"Story? H&E? Buckling?"

"Could be. I'm waiting to hear. I'll let you know."

The shadowy figure hung up and Conall's ennui dissipated. He was always on the hunt for the next project. It was imperative to have a new job lined up before he finished the current one because the gaps between his projects made him very unhappy. He needed new challenges. And yet whenever a fresh prospect hove into view, his fear was as strong as his excitement.

Every takeover was different. Experience from previous jobs was useful but there always came a point when he had no idea how to proceed, when he had to build the path he had to walk on. People thought it was easy, doing what he did. That he just went in and sacked all around him and made the staff move to a building with much cheaper rent. They assumed he was paid his vast bundle to deal with the guilt of having to ruin people's lives.

At a dinner party, when he'd still been with Saffron, Conall was asked by another man, "That job you do? How do you sleep?"

Before Conall could defend himself by offering his — sincerely held — belief that if he didn't sack some of the staff, then, sooner or later, all of them would be out of a job, Saffron jumped in. "We find that a million euro a year helps greatly," she had replied. Of course, those were the days when she had celebrated his ability to make far-reaching decisions free of emotion.

In the middle of a project when he was trying to visualize a complex enterprise in a three-dimensional way, in order to make the right decisions, Conall sometimes wished he was a postman like his brother. Every single judgment he made had huge financial implications but he never had the time to follow all possible permutations down to ground zero because, more important than anything else, decisions had to be made fast.

With each evaluation he signed off on, he felt the fear. Had he sacked the wrong people? Closed down the wrong office in the wrong country? Sold off the wrong assets? What if this was the one where he removed the vital organs and the whole thing died?

So far it never had. But it felt like playing Ker-Plunk! Every time he removed a stick he held his breath and waited for a massive avalanche, signaling that it had all collapsed on him.

And when everything was completed, the satisfaction of having done the best possible job, of having dismantled a company down to its bare bones and reconfigured it into a new sleek, streamlined entity, lasted only for an evening, before the hunger started up again. Kym had said he was like a shark, always moving, always hunting. (She'd also said he'd stolen the best years of her life.)

Conall didn't know why he worked like he did. It wasn't for the money. He probably had enough money now, whatever enough was. He didn't do it for the respect of his peers because he had all that. He did it because he did it.

He was prepared to admit that his work/life balance wasn't perfect — he had very few friends. But then most people had very few friends. He had Joe, his brother, of course, but he suspected his success was a barrier. That's why he needed a girlfriend.

DAY 31 . . .

Get up, Katie urged herself. *On your feet and face the world.*

She'd just emerged from one of the worst night's sleeps of her life, the genesis of which could be traced back to last night, at a launch, when she'd jettisoned all pretense of professionalism and attached herself to the free bar. She drank grimly and with purpose until the hard edges slipped off life.

She had a fuzzy recollection of standing way

too close to Danno and saying, "Really am quite spec*ta*c*u*larly drunk. It'll garntee me good ni'sleep."

Somehow she'd got home and tumbled way down into a drunk, dreamless coma.

Then, in the dead of night, she'd jerked awake. She'd been having a terrible nightmare in which she had landed on a deserted planet, a lump of barren, gray rock, swept by howling, perishing winds. Alone, all alone, stranded for eternity.

She waited for the terror of the nightmare to disperse, but it didn't — because, she realized with a terrible thud, it was all true. She *was* alone, all alone, stranded for eternity. No one would love her ever again.

Every time a romance had ended, she'd been genuinely convinced that she'd never fall in love again. But this time it really *was* the end. Forget forty being the new eighteen and all that. You could be Botoxed to kingdom come, you could jostle with fifteen-year-olds in Topshop, but forty was forty.

Just when she thought she couldn't feel any worse, she remembered something appalling: she'd commandeered one of the artistes' limos to take her home.

She'd lurched out of the nightclub, seen it idling at the curb and hijacked it. The driver hadn't wanted to take her, he was on-call for Mr. Alpha, he kept repeating, but she'd pulled rank, threw her weight around, threatened him with his job.

Oh no! The memory was so shaming that she whimpered into her pillow. Not only was she stranded on a lump of barren rock for all eternity but she'd stolen a car from a visiting superstar, *an international household name.*

She got up and puked and crawled back into bed, desperate for sleep to release her from her tormented thoughts, but she was still awake when the birds started singing. She didn't know the time because she'd been too afraid to look at the clock, but obviously it had to be bad. At some stage she passed into a light anxious doze, and when her alarm started beeping at 7:30, she wanted to slit her own throat.

Makeup wasn't helping. She painted epic quantities of concealer under her eyes and still she looked like Sylvester Stallone. Eventually, furtive and jumpy, already anticipating pain, she was ready to bolt from the building (she was so frightened of bumping into Conall romancing Lydia that, whenever she had to leave her flat, she sprinted down the three flights of stairs and into the street with her eyes closed and her breath held).

But it had been five days since he'd sent the horrible flowers — they'd come on Friday and now it was Wednesday. She'd seen no sign of him hanging around over the weekend and a tiny bud of hope, like a snowdrop after an unforgiving winter, broke through: maybe it had just been a one-time thing.

She was out the front door, the gallop was over. She could open her eyes, she could inhale. Then she remembered that there was no point jingling her car keys because there was no car. After last night's stunt with Mr. Alpha's limo, her ride was still in the parking lot in work. But hey! There was Conall's car. Right there! Just parked, waiting! Without thinking, she made for it.

"Conall?"

He looked up from his BlackBerry. Jesus Christ, it was Katie! Standing there in the street! He clambered out from the car and reached down to kiss her politely on the cheek.

"What are you doing here?" she asked.

"Ah . . . waiting for someone." He was very, very embarrassed. He should have known this might happen. *Unless, of course,* a little voice prompted, *unless he* had *known.*

Her face tight and closed, Katie backed away on her high heels. All of a sudden, the door of 66 Star Street opened and a large donkey-like dog bounded out, followed by the old woman who lived on the first floor, and then came this . . . *man* and it was the man who caught Conall's attention. Saffron used to accuse Conall of being an emotion-free automaton but, actually, Conall quite prided himself on his intuition. He'd intu-

459

itively known the time Arthur Andersens had beaten him in the bid for Jasmine Foods — he'd bumped into their head of acquisitions one Sunday afternoon in the pliers aisle of the Hardware Hut, and although the man had been amiable enough, Conall *knew.* Now he was alerted by the same sense of threat. This blond-haired, sloppily dressed, idle-looking . . . *gobshite* was the one who had replaced him in Katie's affections.

Katie was still backing away from Conall, then she collided with your man. Speedily, she turned round and Conall heard her say, "Sorry," and your man said, "No, *I'm* sorry," then came the sounds of laughter, then more conversation, too low for Conall to hear properly, followed by more laughter, then Goldilocks lifted Katie's hand and kissed the back of it with fulsome tenderness. *Prick.* The dog, the old woman and the man piled into a Merc and sped off, Katie walked away into the distance and Conall was left alone.

With great contempt Grudge watched Fionn gaze out through the rear window as they drove away from Katie. "Now," Fionn asked, "who was *she?*"

Jemima rested her head back and closed her eyes. "Fionn, dear heart, truly I find I'm quite wearied by your wayward affections."

"Ah Jemima!"

Fionn was sparkly-eyed and skittish and

460

Grudge shook his hairy head in disgust. Jemima wasn't as young as she'd once been and it wasn't appropriate — *appropriate* was Grudge's favorite word; he'd heard it on *Dr. Phil* — it wasn't *appropriate* for Fionn to involve her in such adolescent . . . silliness.

"First poor Maeve, then Rosie . . ."

Grudge attempted to tut but his tongue was too thick. That had been an appalling episode, the little nurse sliding her phone number under the door of the flat and urging Fionn to call her. Jemima had become terribly distressed, beseeching Fionn to stay away from girls who were spoken for. "She and Andrei are a good match." But Fionn had disregarded Jemima's distress and rung Rosie anyway. An assignation had been arranged for this very evening, but would Fionn proceed with it now that his attentions had been caught by Katie?

"Katie? Is she married?" Fionn pressed. "Or what?"

Jemima exhaled. "Not married. That dark brooding creature in the Lexus was in attendance for many months, but I sense there has been a sundering recently."

"So she's single!" Fionn rubbed his hands together in glee.

"Don't they have women where you come from?" Ogden eyed Fionn in the rear-view. "I never met such a randy article."

Yeah, Grudge sneered at Fionn. *Randy.*

"Ogden makes a good point, Fionn. Perhaps you should consider returning to Pokey. I fear you're finding city life rather overstimulating."

DAY 31 . . .

Just as Conall had anticipated! Only five to nine and here was Lydia, leaving earlier than she'd said, just to avoid him.

He stepped out of the car, into her path. "Going somewhere?"

First she looked incredulous, then a thunderous rage appeared on her little dial. "Right, that's it," she said. "I'm calling the police."

He couldn't stop laughing. "Lydia, I just want to go on a date with you."

"You're stalking me!"

"I'm wooing you."

"What kind of stupid word is that?"

"I mean, I like you, I'm trying to get you to come out with me. Since when was that a crime?"

"Listen to me, if I was the type to get scared, you'd be scaring me."

"The girlfriend before Katie told me this was her favorite fantasy, me turning up unexpectedly."

"My condolences to her." Lydia pressed a couple of buttons on her phone, then nodded, looking satisfied. "It's ringing."

"Emergency Services?"

"The Kevin Street cop shop."

"You've the police station on speed dial?"

"I'm a taxi driver. Me and the cops are in regular contact."

Alarm overtook him. Her phone was pressed to her ear and her head was cocked to one side. "Are you really trying the police?" he asked.

"I really am. Don't worry, they often take a few minutes to answer. They're busy."

"Hang up, Lydia." *Hang up, hang up, hang up.* "Hang up, Lydia." Their gazes were locked. Fire burned in her eyes but his will would prevail . . .

Hang up, hang up, hang up.

. . . yes, prevail. Except that it was taking a little longer than usual to prevail . . .

Hang up, hang up, hang up.

. . . aaaannnddd . . . prevail it did! Gotcha!

"Love of God!" Lydia snapped her phone closed. "What is it you want?"

"One chance. The day you suggested. We go to that town in Meath, I clean a dirty kitchen, talk to your mother and put the frighteners on your brother."

"But I don't want you to come."

"We'll go in my car. I'll drive you."

She wasn't happy but it was the offer to drive that swung it in his favor. His consummate skill was in finding a weak spot and he'd assessed, correctly, that she was sick to the back teeth of being behind a wheel.

I'm Conall Hathaway and I always get what I want.

DAY 31 . . .

Danno missed nothing. Katie hadn't even opened the office door fully before his eyes locked with hers. "What?" he asked.

"Nothing."

He unfolded himself from his chair. She watched his snake-hips cross the office floor and she was powerless to stop him.

"Go back to your desk, Danno. Do what you're paid to do."

"It's okay about Mr. Alpha's car," he said quietly. "I sorted another one."

She swallowed. So much had already happened this morning, she'd almost forgotten how she'd disgraced herself last night.

"What's Slasher done now? Did he *hurt* you?"

It was Danno's concern that broke her.

"I think . . ." She shouldn't be telling Danno. She was his boss and he already did everything in his power to ignore hierarchy. "I think Conall is seeing the girl who lives in the flat below me."

George gave a theatrical gasp and placed his hand on his chest. "*That's* a bit close to home."

464

"What makes you think that, babe?" Danno asked.

Without inflection, Katie related Friday's events with the flowers, then finding Conall waiting in his car outside the house this morning.

"It could be just a coincidence." Audrey had crept closer to Katie's desk. They all had, like little woodland creatures emerging from their hidey holes.

"No coincidences in Slasher Hathaway's life," Danno said. "Nothing happens by accident. You!" He pointed at George. "She's had a shock, go out and get her a bun."

"So you think he's seeing her to hurt you?" Danno asked.

"Do you?"

"Yes," Tamsin said

"No," Lila-May said.

"But how would he know she'd see him this morning?"

"Because she goes to work every day!"

"Okay, how did he know she'd meet the flower-delivery man?"

"Maybe he told him to deliver them at the time she leaves for work."

They squabbled with quite vicious acrimony among themselves for a while but no conclusion was reached.

"But something else happened?" Danno said.

Katie hadn't been expecting that. "How do

you know?"

"Because you look so . . . something."

"I met a man." Even to her own ears, she sounded faint and strange.

"Ooooh." She had the rapt attention of all her staff, something that didn't happen often.

"No, not like that. Not like, *I met a man.*" Their faces were baffled. Kindly, but baffled. "I don't mean, like a potential boyfriend."

"No, no, bit old for that now." Danno chortled. Then he rounded on George. "Are you still here? Didn't I tell you to go out and get her a bun?"

"I bumped into him," Katie said, unable to stop herself from talking about Fionn. "I actually literally bumped in to him. I was backing away from Conall's car and smacked into him and he was so nice —" She stopped. The expression on Lila-May's face said, *Pathetic,* so she definitely couldn't splurge how she really felt: that Fionn had healed her pain. The shock of seeing Conall waiting for another girl, the agony of her jealousy, the aching, gaping sense of loss — it was as if she'd been in red-hot torment with a toothache and suddenly, with Fionn smiling and speaking, the pain was wiped clean and she was flooded with its absence, like it was a force in itself.

"He must live near you if you bumped into him," George said. "Maybe on the same road."

"Same road? He lives in the same house as me. Two flats below."

"What?"

"What's going on in that house?" Lila-May asked sharply.

"What do you mean?"

"Something's happening. Something weird. That's too much of a coincidence. Slasher's new girl, your new man."

"You read too much Stephen King," Danno said.

Suddenly, Katie remembered the terror she'd felt one night recently, maybe a couple of weeks ago, the absolute certainty that some person or presence was in the room with her, existing like a single note held on a violin. She had almost been able to feel it breathing and she didn't think she'd ever been so frightened. But what did it have to do with Conall or Fionn? Nothing probably.

"He'll only be living there for a couple of months. He says he's making some gardening program."

"It's not that guy?" George widened his eyes. "Finn something."

"Fionn Purdue."

"Yes! Google him!" George stood up. He was actually shrieking. "Google him. Google him. I saw him in the paper. Google him!"

They clustered around Katie's screen and watched in awe as Fionn's picture appeared, pixel by pixel.

"Is he that beautiful in real life?" Tamsin asked. "Or has he been Photoshopped?"

Katie swallowed. "You probably won't believe me, but this isn't a great picture of him."

"Christ!"

"He kissed my hand."

"Lucky hand!"

They studied Fionn's square jaw line and golden glow, trying to decide what, if any, color he had in his hair when a twinkle of light sprang from the screen and the five of them reared back.

"Did he just . . . wink?" Danno asked, faintly.

No one spoke.

"Power surge or something."

"Yeah. Power surge." A little bit rattled now, the exodus back to their desks began. They needed to put some distance between themselves and Katie's freaky goings-on.

"He said he's coming to see me tonight."

"What the hell . . ." Lila-May furrowed her forehead. "Why you?"

"I honestly have no idea."

DAY 31 . . .

Maeve was sitting on the steps of the Central Bank, eating her sandwich, alert for AOK opportunities. It was the bag she noticed first, a colorful embroidered mini-rucksack that she'd have loved. It was attached to a girl, a slight little thing, with short black hair, ordinary-looking in every way except for the air of isolation that surrounded her. She was alone, very alone, glowing her way darkly through the aimless shoals of shiny people, and the rigid immobile cast to her face was one that Maeve recognized. Though she wasn't close enough to see the girl's eyes, she knew what she'd find if she looked in there. *This* was today's act and Maeve so didn't want to do it. She'd rather lug twenty buggies up twenty flights of stairs than this. But what choice had she? Suddenly aware of Maeve's scrutiny, the girl twisted her head, and when their gazes met Maeve forced herself to smile. Really smile, right from the heart. The girl looked puzzled — she was wondering if she knew Maeve because why would a total stranger be smiling at her with such warmth? Maeve kept smiling, kept sending out love, but the girl looked at her in alarm, almost fear. *Keep smiling, keep smiling.* Then Maeve's mouth began to wobble and she had to look away. When she looked back again, the girl had gone, and Maeve felt worse than she would have thought possible. Acts of Kindness were meant to make her feel better, not plunge her into despair. What was the point of doing them? The panic attacks were back, she'd had another one this morning.

She might stop the Acts of Kindness and Trios of Blessings, she decided. They weren't working. But how would she break it to Matt?

DAY 31 . . .

Conall pulled in outside 74 Star Street, an impressively adjacent parking spot for number 66. How did he manage it, Lydia wondered. How did people like him always get what they wanted?

"Today went quite well," Conall said.

She already had her seat belt off and her handle on the door but she paused. "I hate the way you do that. Always assessing things and putting values on them."

"So what'll we do for our next date?"

"Bye."

"Describe your perfect night."

"Have you gone deaf?"

"Go on. Your perfect night."

"You're unbelievable. You only hear what you want to hear."

"Describe it. Everything you've always wanted."

"There you are, doing it again."

He shrugged.

"Arrgh!" She put her head in her heads. "You're one of those people who use silence like a . . ."

Still he didn't speak and eventually she said, "I don't know how you do it. I'll de-

470

scribe it if you swear that I won't have to do it."

"Your perfect night. You don't want to do it?"

"Not with you."

"I hear you."

"You don't. Okay, I'd love to go —"

"Hold on a moment, just before you get started, describe a night that's humanly achievable. There's no point saying you'd like to go to the moon —"

"I won't," she said shortly. Who'd want to go to the moon? "I'd like to go to Float. It's this club with a swimming pool on the roof and —"

"I know it."

"But you have to be a member —"

"I'm a member."

"*Mr.* Hathaway! Are you really? Savage!" Her face was transformed with a luminous smile.

"We can go there, no problem." He looked happy to have pleased her.

"With Poppy, Shoane and Sissy."

"Who are they?"

"My friends."

His face hardened. "So . . . what? I come too? And pay for everything?"

"Thanks very much, Conall. We like pink champagne."

He watched her, without comment.

"Oh." She furrowed her forehead and shook

471

her head sadly. "Mr. Hathaway no happy?"

He certainly didn't look happy.

"You asked me what my ideal night was," she said. "I told you. Simple as."

He shrugged and wouldn't meet her eyes.

"Are you *sulking?* At your age? You wanted my perfect night to be something you wanted to do too. But I'm different from you, Hathaway. You can't *make* people want the same stuff as you."

Something in her words . . . Suddenly, he was hearing echoes from the past, from the day he'd taken Katie to Glyndebourne. What she'd said to him then. *I think you're slightly insane.*

Adapt! Adapt in order to survive! "Okay. Bring your friends. When do you want to go? Tonight?"

"God, no. We need to get our hair blow-dried. We need time to look forward to it. It's all right for you, going to fabulous places every night of the week, but it's a big deal for us."

"Saturday, then?"

"Saturday!" Such scorn. "Every gobshite goes out on Saturday. We'll go on Monday, that's when the cool people go out."

Monday wasn't ideal. He was meant to be going to Milan on Tuesday. Maybe he could change that to Wednesday. "Right, Monday."

"And Conall?" she said softly.

He looked at her, ready to accept her gratitude.

"You'll be the oldest of us by about sixty years. Just so long as you're cool with that?"

Matt and Maeve's wedding had been the full traditional job — a white Rolls-Royce, a sit-down meal for a hundred and fifty, the usual arguments about which cousins to invite. They themselves weren't that bothered about having a big shindig, but both sets of parents had lobbied hard so they went along with the plan to keep the peace.

"I don't care how we do it so long as we do it," Matt said.

"To be honest, I could do without the whole song and dance," Maeve admitted. "Fecking photographers and bridesmaids' dresses and all. But Mam and Dad . . ."

"Yes," Matt was in firm agreement. "Make your peace with it. Reenee and Stevie Deegan's only child — that's you, by the way — is getting a massive white wedding whether she likes it or not."

"I *don't* like it," Maeve said gloomily, then, almost instantly, she brightened. "Sure, what the hell, it'll be a great party."

Naturally, organizing a big wedding in six months was not without its challenges. Hilary and Walter Geary claimed to find Maeve's parents' accents impenetrable. Meanwhile, Reenee and Stevie Deegan, solid country people, who'd been putting money aside for this event almost since the day Maeve was born, were unimpressed with sophisticated Hilary and Walter.

Tricky as things were when the in-laws weren't meshing, they became a lot trickier when, unexpectedly, Hilary and Reenee formed an unholy alliance whereby Hilary dripped notions into Reenee's ear and Reenee, who was absolutely awash with cash, received them eagerly.

Suddenly, Reenee Deegan was insisting that Maeve have a makeup artist, a wedding hair-specialist, acrylic nails and a dress from Harrods.

"Harrods?" Maeve said helplessly.

"Yes, Harrods," Stevie Deegan said, planting his feet firmly on the floor to deliver his piece. "We're all going to fly to London. Nothing's too good for our Maeve."

"But Harrods is a . . . a . . . *joke,*" Maeve exclaimed.

"It's the most exclusive shop in the world," Reenee said.

"It *isn't.*"

"Hilary says it is."

"And so does Walter," Stevie threw in.

"And you're to have fake tan," Reenee said. "We're all getting it. Hilary knows a woman who'll come and spray us. She brings a little pop-up tent so the bathroom doesn't get destroyed."

"No," Maeve said, with rising panic. "Not fake tan. I wouldn't feel like me."

"Don't shame us, Maeve," Stevie said. "Hilary knows her onions. She says there isn't a bride in Ireland who doesn't get fake tan these days. She knows what's what and we're blessed to have her."

But dresses from Harrods and her mum getting sprayed with Sun FX weren't Maeve's only worries. There was David. His displays of wounded emotion weren't as dramatic as they'd been in the early days, but he still wouldn't talk to either Maeve or Matt. Sometimes, at work, Maeve would find him staring sadly at her, but he'd look away hastily as soon as she noticed him.

"Should we invite David?" Maeve asked Matt, holding a pen and a list of possible invitees in her hand.

"Sod him," Matt said cheerfully.

"Oh Matt."

"He's not my friend. He's not your friend."

"But we hurt him so badly."

"It's been nearly a year now. Time he got over it."

"Don't be so mean." Maeve put a tick beside David's name. "We'll invite him."

"He won't come.'

'He might."

Maeve wasn't sure which would be worse — if he came or if he didn't and she had no idea which way it was going to go because, just like he had with the engagement party, David ignored the invitation, not bothering to reply one way or the other.

The wedding itself was beautiful and Maeve found herself enjoying it even more than she'd expected she would, especially as she'd got her own way on the fake tan and the dress from Harrods. But beneath her joy ran a tiny hum of dread, so faint that she was barely aware of it. Throughout the happy day — and it really was happy — she was waiting for *something*.

Her dread reached its zenith during the part of the ceremony when the priest asked if anyone knew any reason why she and Matt should not be joined together. *David,* she thought, and had a sudden, horrible vision of him storming into the church, waving placards and shouting about Matt having colonized Maeve. He might fling paint or cry or . . . or . . .

But the moment passed without incident and Maeve began to breathe again.

And then it was all done. The vows had been said, the rings had been exchanged, and she and Matt were walking back down the aisle, through a sea of smiling faces, while triumphant chords swelled from the organ. Just for a moment, a thought took her away from the present: when she got back from honeymoon she would start looking for another job. It wasn't fair to David, to have his nose rubbed in things, day in, day out.

The decision was made and suddenly Maeve's happiness burst into full flower.

DAY 31 . . .

Katie knew how these things worked. Television: they did long hours. Fionn hadn't said what time he'd visit her but it could be as late as nine. Maybe even later, depending on where they were shooting.

She dressed in casual, hey-just-hanging-out stuff. It took several attempts before she got the right combination and even then she worried about her feet. She couldn't wear her gold sandals because who wore four-inch heels at home? But when she put on her flip-flops, she had to take them off immediately, appalled at how stumpy they made her legs look.

The lovely pedicure she'd had for Jason's wedding had worn off and the hard skin on her soles had crept back, but she'd done nothing about it. Just let it happen!

By the time I've scrubbed my feet raw with my diamond foot-smoother, he'll be here.

She knew Fionn would come. She was certain. There had been something strong and sure between them that she couldn't explain.

"You can depend on me," he'd said, when they'd had their first conversation this morning. "You can depend on me for your life." And although it was a frankly ridiculous thing for one stranger to say to another, she knew it was true.

The balls of her feet were pretty smooth but he still hadn't arrived, so she scrubbed a bit longer, then she stopped. She wouldn't be able to walk tomorrow if she continued eroding her soles like this.

She was too agitated to eat. She paced between the living room and the bathroom, checking her makeup, checking it again, standing on the loo-seat and holding the hand mirror up high, because that was where the best light in her flat was. Pleased, but also frightened, she saw a largish not-rubbed-in patch of foundation on her right jaw. What if she hadn't spotted it? What if she'd just relied on the light from the ordinary down-low mirror? And did that mean that most days she was walking around with the kind of makeup that made other people nudge and snigger? Should she ask Danno? Or perhaps Lila-May was a better bet: she was horribly honest. Seized with panic, she raced to the bedroom and changed her top. It was wrong, all wrong.

What was she *thinking?*

A quick flick at her watch. It was suddenly a quarter to ten, and dread began a slow slide inside her.

Katie knew how these things worked. Television: yes, they did long hours, but the unions had them in a stranglehold. As soon as they'd worked a certain number of hours, the technicians' hefty overtime rate kicked in. No director went there. Fionn should have finished work ages ago.

Suddenly, she was hungry, hungry, hungry, craving baked goods in sizable quantities, but there was nothing in her cupboards. She couldn't keep confectionery in the flat, it would torment her and she'd eat it all, just to give herself some peace. She ate a banana and instantly wanted twenty more. It was imperative that she leave the kitchen *right now*.

She would watch a DVD, something short, only half an hour, and by the time it was over, he'd be here.

She watched an episode of *Star Stories,* the Simon Cowell one, her favorite, and when that was over she watched the one about Tom Cruise.

Maybe she'd give him until eleven.

He wasn't coming.

She was a cretin to have thought he would. That's it then! Cleanse, tone, moisturize and into bed! But should she go to bed still made-up? Just in case he called in the next five minutes . . . No! Without mercy, she scrubbed her face bare, until she was pink-eyed and raw-looking.

Bastard, she thought, with such a backwash of bile that she shocked herself. She'd better watch it. She couldn't go the way she'd gone after Jason had met Donanda. She didn't want to have to do another course. Or to be haunted by Granny Spade on Bitter Watch.

She turned off her light and, almost instantly, noises started up in the downstairs flat. Grunting and the slap of wood against something. Were they moving furniture? So late? . . . Oh no! It was people having sex!

An unbearable thought struck her: it wasn't Conall, was it? With little taxi-driving Lydia? That would finish her off entirely. She would get out of bed and go downstairs in her pajamas and go out into the street and lie in the middle of the road and wait for a bus to run over her. There was no way on earth she could endure hearing Conall having sex with someone else. She switched the light back on, got out of bed and put her ear to the floor, listening hard. She didn't recognize the grunting. Conall *was* a grunter, but a different kind. This must be one of the Polish guys, she reckoned. What was his name? She couldn't remember . . .

"Andrei! Oh Andrei, Andrei!"

"Thank you," Katie yelled at the floor. "I wouldn't have slept a wink trying to remember. I'm very fecking obliged to you!"

Angrily, she thrust earplugs into her ears with such force that they almost lodged in her brain, and eventually she fell into a troubled but deep sleep.

DAY 31 . . .

"You're breaking up with me? On our first date?"

"The thing is, Rosemary, I've met someone else."

"How? You only met me five days ago."

Fionn shrugged helplessly. How could he describe how he felt about Katie? Unlike the first time he'd seen Rosie, with Katie there had been no spirals and color. Instead, he'd had an abiding, irresistible sense of safe harbor. Of docking. Of everything — *everything* — clicking into place. He was powerless over it and his short-lived fancy for Rosie had immediately seemed silly and skittish.

"Sorry," he said, hoping he could go now. It would take him forever to get back to Star Street and Katie.

Rosie had chosen a spot far, far across the city for their first date. A pub in Greystones overlooking a little harbor. Very scenic. Also — Fionn suspected — handily placed so that it was unlikely she would bump into anyone she knew.

Fionn hadn't wanted to go. Now that he'd met Katie, what would be the point? But the only number he had for Rosie was the one at the hospital (cagey creature that she was, she hadn't given him her mobile), and she wasn't on duty. He had no way of canceling and he couldn't simply abandon her to sit in the Harbor View in a pretty lemon-colored cotton dress, sipping her West Coast Cooler all by herself, looking up hopefully every time the door opened. He'd loved her once.

He wanted a quick in and out — thanks for coming, sorry and all that, let's move on — but he lost valuable time by getting a Dart going in the wrong direction and was twenty-five minutes late when he arrived.

"This is not acceptable." Rosie quivered with affronted dignity. "You do not leave a lady sitting alone in a public house. You should always arrive fifteen minutes early."

". . . Um, sorry." Fionn was suddenly afraid to admit his error with the Dart. "My job, it ran over and it's television —"

"Television? I'm sure we're all impressed. But I'm never impressed by bad manners."

He had to suffer through a short lecture on etiquette and then found himself trying to talk Rosie out of her grump. The problem was that he wasn't sure how to break up with her because he'd never had to do it before. It had always been done for him. When he'd

483

refused to fall in with his girlfriends' plans for the little van with his mobile number on the side, tears, shouting, perhaps throwing of objects would ensue. Finally, the girl would leave and he'd be alone for a while with his potatoes and courgettes until a new one showed up.

"Rosie, you're a lovely girl," he said, trying to feel his way through this.

She nodded. She knew that.

"I'm sure you're a great girlfriend."

"I'm a prize, Fionn."

"And I'm sorry if I misled you —"

"Misled me?"

"— but I'm not sure this is working out."

That's when she realized what was happening. "You're breaking up with me? On our first date?"

But she didn't slink off in humiliated tears. She sat up straighter, seething with righteous indignation. "You can't do this to me. I'm not the type of girl you play games with."

Great alarm rose in Fionn. Was she going to insist on a relationship? Was she going to *force* him?

"Do you think I make a habit of giving my phone number to men? And meeting them in Wicklow? I've risked things for tonight. I have a boyfriend!"

"You still have him?"

Reluctantly, she nodded. Far too canny to dump one prospect before the other was a dead cert, Fionn realized. Thank God for that.

"Go back to your boyfriend, Rosie. Forget me." Fionn remembered a line that had sometimes been yelled at him as a parting shot. "I'm a fucking eejit. I'm not worth it."

They had to get the same Dart from Greystones back into town — Darts from Greystones were rare beasts and you missed one at your peril. Naturally, Fionn and Rosie occupied separate cars. When he got off at Pearse Street she stayed on the train, and as it pulled out of the station with its customary whine, her brightly lit carriage passed him. She lifted her little white chin and twisted sharply away from the sight of him, in an extravagant display of contempt. All very unpleasant.

Fionn bounded up the stairs to the top floor of 66 Star Street, but there was no response to his urgent knocking. Was Katie asleep? Or ignoring him?

It was imperative that he see her. She had to know that he wasn't a flake. Or a . . . ? He summoned further insults from past breakups. What else had been yelled at him before girls left for the last time? That he was a lightweight. A chancer. A messer. An immature moron. And most popular of all, by a long chalk, a fucking eejit.

But he was no longer any of those things; he was a man now, a man whose intentions were serious, and it was very important that Katie knew. But she wasn't answering the door.

A note. He'd write her a note and explain everything. His pockets yielded up a leaky pen and a few pages of the previous day's shooting schedule.

Dear Katie,
I'm sorry I didn't get here until now.

But he didn't own a watch, so he didn't know when *now* was.

I would like to see you. I will call again. Depend on it.

Yours,

Fionn

But words were frustratingly inadequate. He had to *prove* his regret. He searched his pockets for something and brought forth an ear of sage. No. What good was wisdom? Or gray pebbles? Or a torn Orbit wrapper? A deeper rummage unearthed a withered dark-green sprig. What was that? Then he identified it. Well, *perfect!* It was rue. Rue was very much a statement herb — God Almighty, he

486

was starting to think like Grainne Butcher's scripts — as it was bitter, poisonous stuff. In times past, people threw it at weddings, when their loved ones were marrying another.

Please accept this gift as a token of my rue.

He wasn't sure if that was grammatically correct, but it was from the heart, and Grainne kept saying that if it was from the heart it would work. Then he folded the sprig into the note and tried to shove it under the door — but it wouldn't go. Katie's door had something like a short sweeping brush fitted to the bottom of it. (A draft-prevention measure, but he wasn't to know, undomesticated animal that he was.) Reluctantly, he left the note outside and anxiously descended the stairs to Jemima's flat, where Grudge had spent several hours waiting to bite him, then pretend it was an accident.

Fionn was quite afraid. This evening he had learned that not all women were like the ones in Pokey, who, in retrospect, were sweet, malleable creatures, always cutting him plenty of slack, despite the insult-fest that usually signaled the end of their dalliance. Katie might be as tough and unforgiving as that Rosie.

Katie might never speak to him again.

You're right, Fionn, she mightn't.

DAY 30

Lydia's phone rang. She flicked it open and said, "Hi, Poppy."

"I got your message," Poppy said. "But who is this man?"

"No one. Just some rich old bloke who has me tormented."

"And he's going to pay for everything? As much pink champagne as we want?"

"As much as we want."

"Lydia, that's not right."

"He knows the score and he won't leave me alone."

"But it's like . . . he's buying you."

"He's not fecking buying me! I'm not for sale."

"Aren't you scared? Of him?"

"He's not like that. I sort of feel sorry for him. He hasn't a clue."

"The flowers were good, though. Funny."

"Yeah, the flowers *were* good."

"I don't know, Lydia, it all feels a bit sleazy."

"Do you want to go to Float or don't you?"

As Lydia had expected, Conall had been completely bloody clueless about cleaning. He'd emptied nearly a whole bottle of washing-up liquid into the sink and Ellen, Lydia and himself had almost been carried off in a wash of foam. The kitchen had looked like a Spring Break party.

But other than that, Lydia had to admit that he'd done quite well. Ellen had liked him.

"Are you Lydia's boyfriend?" she had asked him, as he'd pawed through the bubbles, trying to locate the sink somewhere beneath him.

"Ah, not yet, maybe. But working on it."

"An older man?"

"I guess I am."

"The boys always liked Lydia."

"I can well believe it, Ellen."

A sound at the door made the three of them turn round. It was Ronnie, his lips very red beside his black satanic beard. Lydia couldn't remember the last time she'd clapped eyes on him.

"What's going on here?" Ronnie spoke softly and with terrible menace.

"Oh, you know," Lydia said. "Cleaning a filthy house, taking care of our mum because —"

Ronnie ignored her and focused on Conall. "And who might you be?"

"Conall Hathaway." Conall wiped his sudsy hand on his jeans, pulled himself up to his full height and squeezed Ronnie's hand hard enough to hurt. Neither man spoke, but so much hostility passed between them that Ellen gazed anxiously at Lydia.

The deadlock was broken when a noise beyond the house made Ellen look out through the window. "Murdy's here!"

"It's like a sitcom," Conall said.

Ellen laughed with pleasure. "You should visit more often. Usually, the lads avoid Lydia like the plague."

There was a startled silence at the astuteness of this observation. Even Ronnie seemed surprised.

"If you stay long enough," Ellen's eyes twinkled, "Raymond will be getting on a flight from Stuttgart."

Murdy hurried in and fixed Lydia in his sights. "Flan Ramble's after ringing about the fancy car with the Dublin reg." He contorted his forehead and almost shrieked, *"Are you after buying a Lexus?"*

"No, it belongs to my friend here."

Murdy stepped back as Conall loomed over him.

"Conall Hathaway." Conall fixed Murdy with a flinty smile.

"Good to meet you, good to meet you."

Murdy was smiley and over-eager. He always went a bit mental when he smelled money. "Any friend of the sister's and all that, you know yourself. Do you work together or is it more of a personal thing?"

He bombarded Conall with probing questions and outrageously fulsome compliments. ("How tall are you, six five, six six? Only six one? You give the impression of a taller man." "Have you other cars or just the Lexus?" "What does your wife drive? No wife? By gor!" "Are you thinking of making sis here an honest woman?" "What wheels would you buy her if you tied the knot?" "Investment in small grass-roots businesses is the way to go in this current climate.") Murdy was desperate to piece things together: how much was Conall worth? How much power did Lydia have over him? What could he, Murdy Duffy, get out of it?

"What's brother number three like?" Conall asked Lydia, in full hearing of Ronnie and Murdy.

"Raymond? Great fun. Full of hilarious stories."

"I hate him already," Conall drawled.

DAY 30 . . .

Katie didn't want to wake up. She didn't want to go to work. Everything was shit.

If it wasn't for poor Wayne Diffney's career

relaunch she wouldn't bother.

When she saw the note lying just outside her front door, she deduced it was from Fionn but her heart didn't bother to lift. Her heart would never lift again. She unfolded the piece of paper and ignored the small dark-green sprig that floated from it.

I'm sorry

Yeah, right.

I will call again. Depend on it.

I don't think so.

Please accept this gift

Another Conall, thinking he could buy his way out of things. Anyway, what gift? Casting a glance around the landing, she could see no flowers or chocolates, no box of flimsy ridiculous underwear. It could have been stolen, of course, by someone else in the house, but that was unlikely. What was lots more likely, nay, *definite,* was that this Fionn was another flake. Conall all over again.

She crumpled the note into a ball and threw it over her shoulder into her apartment, then locked her front door behind her. There was a weed on the floor by the stairs. She should pick it up and throw it away but instead she flattened it to a pulp with the red sole of her Louboutin.

Why had she told everyone at work about Fionn? They'd be dying to hear how she'd got on with him. She couldn't handle the thought of their pity, so she decided she'd lie. Lie and be vague and airy. Yes, he called in, she'd say. Yes, he was very good-looking. No, he was a bit of a fool. No, she didn't sleep with him. No, she wouldn't see him again.

DAY 30 . . .

No special makeup tonight. All Katie wore on her face was an expression of lemon-sucking disappointment.

Shortly after nine, frenzied knocking started up at her door. It could be a balaclavaed man with a harpoon in his hand and evil in his heart, but Katie opened it anyway. What did she care? Invade her home, violate her person . . . she no longer gave a shite. Nevertheless, she wasn't exactly surprised to discover Fionn, golden and radiant, smiling a full beam of love right into her upturned face.

"I got delayed," he said.

By twenty-four hours and twenty years, she thought.

"Can I come in?"

"No. You could have come in last night, but sadly you didn't avail of that opportunity."

"Last night," he said, "I had something to

494

do and it took longer than I thought it would. But did you get the rue?"

"The what?"

"The rue."

Yes, that's what she thought he'd said.

"It's a herb. I left you a sprig last night."

She remembered the weed that she'd crushed with her shoe this morning.

"I don't know where it came from," he said urgently. "I don't grow it, it's poisonous. But when I was desperate last night, trying to write how sorry I was, it appeared in my pocket. You must forgive me. It's meant to be."

Tosh. "You're a flake."

"Yes! And a chancer, a messer, an immature moron and, most of all, a fucking eejit. But I'm ready to change. Because of you."

She was silenced. This was a really impressive apology. Way more anguished and convincing than anything Conall had ever rustled up.

"I'm really scared you won't forgive me," Fionn said. "I can tell you all about last night. I had to go to Greystones and I got on the wrong Dart, partly because, like you said, I'm a flake, and partly because I try to pretend Dublin doesn't exist even though I lived here until I was twelve."

He dropped to one knee.

"Get up," she said. "You've been doing well, but it's turning into a pantomime."

■ ■ ■ ■

". . . I'd convert an entire room into shoe storage — remember the one Big made for Carrie? No? I'll describe it so . . ."

". . . Jemima bought me a jacket — remember Harrington jackets? Just an ordinary jacket, but I tried to convince myself that when I wore it, I had magical powers. That I could make my dad come home from sea . . ."

Somehow they had ended up lying on Katie's bed, fully clothed, whispering into each other's face, revealing their secrets.

". . . my own little van and I'd go to festivals and injured people would come to me and I'd wash out their wound and I'd have all the different sizes of bandages because you need a tiny one to wrap it around your finger but if you cut your knee you need a big one, four inches long . . ."

He held her face tightly and kissed her again. Good job she was lying down, she thought, because otherwise she might swoon. She'd never been kissed like this, so slowly, so endlessly, as if kissing was their reason for existing.

"What happened to your hand?" she asked. "You cut yourself?"

"Jemima's dog bit me last night. He pretended it was an accident. He's not right in

496

the head."

They kissed again, and some immeasurable time later, Fionn spoke. "Didn't you feel it too?" he murmured. "As soon as I saw you, I knew. That you were the most important person I would ever meet."

"Why me?"

"Because you won't die."

"What do you mean?"

"I don't really know."

"But I will die. We all will."

"But you won't for a long time. You've got through the tricky part. Your thirties. That's when women die."

"Your wife?"

"No."

"Your mum?"

He nodded. "That's what I tried for the most when I wore my Jacket of Power. To bring her back."

Katie had to let a few moments elapse, otherwise she would have seemed unsympathetic. Then she asked, "So do I look forty?" She'd thought she was doing quite well, actually. Always wearing sunblock, drinking plenty of water, the usual.

"I'm not saying that. I never have a clue how old anyone is. But you felt safe."

"What sort of safe?"

"Safe for me. Safe from harm. Every kind of safe."

DAY 29

When Katie woke, her bedroom was flooded with early morning sunlight. She was still dressed, but her shoes had been removed. She felt as if she was lightly draped in cloths woven by fairies from gossamer. Who knew her trusty old duvet could feel so delightful?

"I've got to go now," Fionn said. "Work."

"Okay."

"Tonight?"

She nodded her assent.

"I have a present for you." He produced a green sprig.

"More rue?" She yawned. "Didn't I say I forgive you?"

"This is sage. I planted it months ago and didn't know why, but I can see now I was growing it for you. Sage is for wisdom."

"Thanks." She let him put it in her hand but she didn't want wisdom. Fionn was her adventure, her gift to herself; she was ready to embrace willful stupidity.

■ ■ ■ ■

"Well! Someone's getting some!" Danno exclaimed, as Katie walked toward her desk.

"Got a glow on, girlfriend," George said.

"Are you . . . thinner?" Lila-May narrowed her eyes in assessment. "Like, since yesterday?"

"Slasher's back?" Danno asked.

Katie almost stumbled. "No."

"So who? The celebrity gardener?"

Katie nodded.

"I thought you said he was a fool!"

"Yeah, well . . ."

DAY 29 . . .

Matt and Maeve were lying on their couch, miserably watching strangers fitting a new bathroom. Neither of them had spoken in twenty-six minutes, when Matt opened his mouth and said, "You'd think people would be suspicious if a man bought an ax."

"A what?"

"An ax. Wouldn't it send up signals that a person was planning to be an ax murderer if he came home with a nice shiny new ax? What else are they used for?"

"Chopping wood?"

"Who chops wood these days? We're not in Little Red Riding Hood."

"What are you talking about?"

"There was this woman at the bus stop —"

"Are you thinking of killing me?"

"Maeve!"

"Your subconscious must be trying to tell you something."

"I haven't got a subconscious! Dr. bloody Shrigley. Putting these ideas in your head. All I'm saying is there was this woman at the bus stop a few weeks ago and —"

"What would you do if I died?"

With visible effort, he calmed himself. "My life would be unbearable, as good as over."

"You'd meet another me."

"I wouldn't. How could I? There will never be another you."

"There are millions of girls like me, girls far better than me. You'd be happier with one of them."

"I wouldn't."

She laughed softly, almost contemptuously. "You used to say that you'd kill yourself if I died."

". . . I would. I *would* kill myself. That's what I meant."

"It's not what you said."

"It's what I meant."

A bristly silence ensued.

"Anyway," Matt said shortly. "You're not going to die."

I wouldn't be so sure about that, my cuddly *amigo* . . .

I've finally understood that Maeve isn't taking risks in the traffic just to counteract the tedium of her home life. I've been watching her, really watching her for the last few days. Despite the wall between us, one or two of her thoughts have been so intense and shocking that they've reached me.

If that truck skidded and plowed into me, it wouldn't matter, it wouldn't matter at all.

If I break this red light and I'm hit by a car, all I ask is that I die instantly.

She's not willing to take pills or cut her wrists — not yet, in any case. But if she cycles her bike long enough and recklessly enough, something will happen.

DAY 27

Two and a half days of foreplay. The entire weekend. They'd taken *days* to get undressed. It wasn't until late, late, late on Sunday night that Fionn finally unwrapped Katie, as if he were doing something holy.

Lean and long-limbed, he was naked before her. He kissed her everywhere, on her toes, behind her knees, at the base of her spine, parts of her body that she had never encountered before. When she'd reached combustion point, she rolled on top of him, but he stopped her. "Please," he said. "It's our first time and I don't want it to end."

She groaned. "No, it's got to be now."

She slid on to him and she was so drugged with pleasure, it felt as if his entire being had merged with hers. She'd never experienced sex like this, it was almost mystical.

When it came to an end it started again immediately, one continuous fluid act, and she was so blissed out, so deeply loose and free and adrift that she fell asleep with him still inside her. The sun had already risen.

Now, their heartbeats . . . I can't feel Fionn's at all. It's as if he has surrendered himself entirely to Katie. They have become as one.

DAY 26

Top of the day to you. I am after enduring a mighty trial and I reach out to you, my Irish brother, for your help.

Spam from some scam artist. Conall was reading his BlackBerry and had to admire how they'd localized their pitch for the Irish market. Idly, he scrolled down through the sorry tale of woe and assets tied up in foreign banks . . . then something made him look up. A young woman was being led to his booth. It took a moment for him to recognize Lydia. In her short skirt, high heels and heavy eye makeup, she was a totally different person. Sexier than he could have imagined.

He abandoned his screen and sat up.

Lydia was trailing three other girls, all of them shiny and fragrant and giggly, but none as sexy as her. Behind them were a couple of drab men, who barely registered.

"Mr. Hathaway. Your guests." The hostess smiled and withdrew.

Conall leaned forward to kiss Lydia on the

cheek but she had twisted her head round, deep in an assessment of how their booth measured up compared to every other one in the club. He watched her scanning the room, noticing their lofty vantage point above the dance floor and their proximity to the stairs for the pool.

"This is a good table," she concluded.

"The best in the place," he said. Because he'd requested it. And paid for it. No point leaving that sort of thing to chance.

Then she seemed to remember the other people she was with. "Oh yeah, Poppy, Shoane, Sissy, Conall."

They were sweet but showed little interest in him — very different from any other occasion when he'd met a girl's circle of friends for the first time. Those events were always characterized by excitement most tense and dreadful. He'd be presented and paraded like a prize bullock, his girlfriend so proud of him and so desperate for him to like her friends. Invariably, conversation would be too quick and in too high-pitched a voice; terrible bouts of near-hysterical laughter would erupt for almost no reason; jokey remarks would be misunderstood and any attempt to elucidate would only make things more excruciating.

This couldn't be more different. Meeting Lydia's friends had nothing to do with wedges of cheese and bonus add-ons. He was just a handy fool who happened to be a member of Float.

Lydia summoned the two lads forward from where they'd been lurking behind the girls.

They were cautious, even nervous. "This is Steady Bryan."

"Pleased to meet you, Steady Bryan."

Steady Bryan looked pained at being thus addressed.

"And this is BusAras Jesse."

"Good to meet you, man." Jesse was bright-eyed and eager. He sounded South African. No, slightly different accent. Probably Zimbabwean.

"Get in there," Lydia said, and there was an eager stampede into the booth. It was only thanks to some nimble footwork by Conall that he managed to insert himself in front of Shoane and thereby next to Lydia.

A hovering waitress, a tall blond girl with a yard of tanned leg on display, murmured, "Should I open the champagne now, Mr. Hathaway?"

He smiled his assent.

In silence, they watched the ritual of the champagne being removed from the ice bucket and opened and poured.

"Pink," Poppy remarked.

"Told you," Lydia said.

When all seven glasses were filled, the bottle was almost empty. The waitress eyeballed Conall: *Should I . . . ?* Did he want another?

He nodded discreetly, but obviously not

discreetly enough because he saw Poppy grip Sissy's forearm and Sissy grip Poppy's and they gave each other a hard, can-you-believe-this? squeeze.

Glasses were seized and much clinking ensued. "A toast," someone cried.

"To Lydia for getting us in here!"

"No, what's your man's name?" Conall heard Steady Bryan ask.

"Conall Hathaway," Lydia said, as though she wasn't sitting right beside him.

"To Conall Hathaway!"

"Okay! To Conall Hathaway!"

Conall permitted himself a small smile. He knew when he was being mocked.

"When are we going swimming?" Sissy asked, a few bottles later.

"I'm not drunk enough yet," Shoane said.

"Funny," Sissy said. "I think I'm *too* drunk. I might drown. God, I can't believe I'm here."

"I'm not going swimming." Lydia hated swimming. She hated getting wet. Her hair would go frizzy and her body bronzer would wash off. Nice to be in a place with a swimming pool but no need to actually *use it.*

"Your man Conall isn't as bad as you said," Shoane said, quietly. "The wheels haven't come off altogether."

"Stop."

"He's only forty-two," Poppy said. "Are you going to sleep with him?"

"Nooooaah!" Lydia guffawed. ". . . Ah sure, I probably will."

"Only fair."

"Only decent."

"After all that champagne he's bought us."

"Be nice to him."

"Make an old man happy."

"Why not? But for God's sake —" Lydia summoned the four heads together in a tight cluster — "don't let him dance."

"No, no. That would be horrific. One of us will keep him talking. How about Bryan?"

"Yeah, I don't want Bryan dancing either," Poppy said. "If I see him dancing I'm afraid I'll call off the wedding."

Conall fingered his BlackBerry in his pocket. Could he . . . ? Just a quick look? Would it be so bad? After all there was no one there to care. There was no one but him in the booth; everyone had peeled away. Within moments he was openly answering emails.

He hadn't seen Lydia in about an hour. She and the other three girls had swept off to dance and although he hadn't planned to dance himself — he had some dignity — Lydia had pressed her hand firmly against his chest and said, "You stay here and talk to Steady Bryan."

But Steady Bryan wasn't a scintillating conversationalist. He seemed so freighted by his forthcoming marriage that he could barely speak. He muttered something about a cigarette and that was the last Conall had seen of him.

Initially, BusAras Jesse had seemed a better prospect. He had treated Conall to an account of how he had met Sissy in the queue at BusAras. Something to do with a conversation about the word *glum* that seemed to have involved several hundred bus-goers. Then he'd heard about the many different countries that Jesse had bungee-jumped in. And about his plan to snowboard on some black run where people were always getting killed. "It's illegal, but I know a guy. Gaddafi's Praetorian Guard train there." What was it with people from the Southern Hemisphere and their thing for extreme sports? And did Gaddafi *have* a Praetorian Guard?

Then Jesse challenged him to a breath-holding competition in the upstairs pool, and when Conall declined, Jesse seemed surprised and offended. "Please yourself, man," he said, and stalked angrily away, leaving Conall alone with his BlackBerry.

"How are you doing for drinks here?" The waitress was back.

". . . Ah . . . another bottle, I suppose," he said.

"Sure thing. Anything else?"

Conall was sorely tempted. They did food here. But he couldn't go through with it — a grown man eating a bowl of chocolate ice cream in a nightclub would cut too risible a figure. *Cocaine,* that was what you did in nightclubs, not ice cream. "No, no, thanks. Just another bottle of that stuff."

As soon as she'd disappeared, Conall started to have serious doubts. It was so long since he'd seen Lydia, she and her friends could have left for all he knew. He stood up, trying to see her on the dance floor, and suddenly she appeared right in front of the booth.

"We were up at the pool," she said. "Very small." Then she flicked both her hands up at him, spattering him with water, and ran away, laughing.

Slowly, he wiped his forehead with his sleeve. He'd had enough. He didn't like it here. He was a member of every club in Dublin in case a visiting shadowy figure wanted to go, but he didn't normally frequent them and this place seemed worse than most. He'd noticed he wasn't the only man in Float with a posse of much younger women; the only difference was that his girls weren't Russian. All of a sudden, Conall felt foolish and exploited and exploiting, and really quite miserable. He was almost unable to consider failure but his heart wasn't in this. You choose your battles and he no longer cared about winning this one.

Out of nowhere, he thought of Katie.

Katie leaned forward in her seat as the opening sequence of *Your Own Private Eden* appeared on screen. Loads of them were crowded into the tiny edit suite: Jemima, Grudge, Grainne Butcher, Mervyn Fossil, Alina and any number of techies and runners. They were all squashed together on the couch, almost sitting on top of each other. This was just a rough cut — music still had to be added — but it was fairly momentous because until now no one other than Grainne had seen a full show.

And there was the first shot of Fionn! Standing on a hill gazing moodily at the horizon. Katie squeezed his hand, which was sweaty with nerves.

Fionn had called her earlier at work. "Grainne says episode one is ready. We're going to look at it tonight. Make a bit of an occasion of it. Will you come?"

She'd been surprised and touched, especially because she hadn't given him her office number. "Alina found it for me," he admitted.

Rigid with concentration, Katie carefully watched the monitor, praying that the program wouldn't be complete shite. What if it was? What would she say? *Brave*, that was a good word. *Astonishing*, that was another.

Anxiously, she had to admit that the camera

didn't do Fionn justice; he was far more beautiful in real life. And the piece about starting your own compost heap wasn't really for her. But when they moved to the next segment, Fionn rambling through a farmer's market, talking through seasonal produce, the screen filled with plenty of close-ups of him slowly handling and rubbing phallic vegetables with his big hands, Katie felt some interesting sensations.

"Wow," she murmured and Fionn looked at her gratefully.

Now and again the camera cut to scenes of Fionn spontaneously producing pebbles or herbs or crystals from his pockets and gifting them to random passers-by. The reaction of the recipients was variously startled, receptive and interested, and often the random gift would be curiously appropriate in their life. These little human vignettes became a recurring motif throughout the show, and when Fionn once again reached into his onscreen pocket, Katie found she was actually excited. What was going to emerge? What would it mean to the person?

"That jacket should have its own show," Katie said and the room exploded with good humor.

You couldn't fake that. From her own job, Katie could tell the difference between hype and genuine belief in a product. To her, *Your Own Private Eden* felt right. Obviously, its success would all depend on viewing figures, which depended on time-slots, which depended on advertising, which depended on viewing figures. A chicken-and-egg kind of thing. It was very tricky to make a success of a television show. There were an unquantifiable number of variables and so much of it came down to luck.

By the door, Mervyn was guarding three bottles of fizz. If he hadn't felt the show was working, he'd simply have put them back in the car and taken them home.

"Open them," Grainne barked at Mervyn. "All three."

A cork was popped and drink was poured and good wishes abounded. "Congratulations!" Katie stretched and ducked to touch her glass with Fionn's, Jemima's, Grainne's and with Fionn's again. Looking into Fionn's eyes, she threw back a mouthful of fizz. It wasn't champagne. It wasn't even Prosecco. It was just some cheapo sparkly stuff, but it tasted of happiness.

DAY 26 . . .

A home-improvement program. I mean, Matt thought afterward, with some acrimony, if that's not safe, then what is? She wasn't even particularly attractive, the presenter, Rhoda Stern. Well, obviously, she didn't have two heads either because, if she had, she'd never have been allowed to front up a show, but her shtick was plain-talking advice, where she spelled out — with what Matt considered unnecessary glee — every mistake people had made in their home decorating.

Matt and Maeve were lying on their couch, watching with some sympathy as a young couple — not dissimilar to themselves — had their bedroom decor mocked by Rhoda.

"I don't think it's so bad," Maeve said. "The curtains are nice."

"But!" Rhoda shouted. (Because presenters always shouted in those shows.) "There *is* something that saves this room from being a total disaster!" The camera panned back to show a super-king-sized bed. "Mmmm," Rhoda licked her lips, "I know what I'd like to do in that bed." She gave a suggestive, sidelong glance at the camera. "I'd like to sleep for twelve hours straight."

But it was too late. Something in that suggestive glance had awoken the beast. All of a sudden, Matt was aware of stirrings. *Down there.* In his groin. Swelling and thickening, it felt like liters of blood were gushing to the area. *Stop,* he ordered himself. *I command you to stop.* But it carried on, like it had a mind of its own, unfurling and becoming harder. He shifted slightly so that Maeve wouldn't notice, but that just gave it more room to expand and it began to jut against his underwear, making a bid for freedom.

Interest rates, Matt thought desperately. *Root-canal surgery.* Anything to stop his body from betraying him like this. *Mouse droppings. Gangrene . . .*

Beside him, he felt Maeve tense up. She'd noticed. Then she twisted herself round to see into his hot face.

"Matt . . . ?" She looked almost confused.

Without another word, she slid from the couch, taking care that no part of her body came into contact with his region, then, moments later, he heard the rushing of taps in the bathroom.

"I'm just going to have a bath," Maeve called, in a fake-cheery voice.

"Enjoy it," Matt called back, forcing similarly upbeat tones.

He heard the bathroom door being shut firmly, and he slumped back on to the couch, feeling quite hopeless. I am a man, he thought. I'm an animal. I'm programmed to respond in certain ways to certain stimuli. I can't help it. I've no control over it.

I've no control over anything.

I've just come to a shocking realization: Matt's and Maeve's heartbeats are in perfect harmony, but nothing of a sexual nature has happened between them for a long, long time.

Sitting on the loo, Lydia stared at her phone. Eight missed calls. Four messages. All from Flan Ramble.

Bollocks. Just when she was enjoying herself.

But no, she wasn't going, not this time. Murdy could deal with it. Ronnie could deal with it. *Mum* could deal with it. After all, if there was nothing wrong with her, there was no need for Lydia to leave Float and rush down to Boyne in the middle of the night. Anyway, she was way too pissed to drive.

Of course, they'd expect her to jump to it, to hop behind the wheel, but they could feck off this time. She'd done that drive too many times, for all the good it had done her, to be accused of trying to steal her mum's money. Let them try to manage without her for once. Let them find out that she, Lydia, was right and they were all wrong . . . Pleasantly adrift in her little reverie of self-righteous self-pity, she got a fright when her phone rang.

Flan Ramble again. But no, it wasn't. It was —

"Mum?"

"Lydia?"

"Are you okay?"

". . . Um . . . no." Her voice was small and pitiful. "I did something and I don't remember doing it and the police are here and I'm really scared."

"Oh God, Mum. You didn't kill someone, did you?"

"No. No." She sounded less than certain. "Flan is here. He'll tell you."

"It's all kicking off down here," Flan said loudly. "She was driving back into town from depositing a fare in the outlands and she must have misjudged a corner, because she went flying off the road into the reservoir, and instead of fleeing for her life, like any normal person, she stayed in the car, *laughing* as she sank into the ooze. When the cops showed up, they couldn't get over that she wasn't scuttered out of her brains, but stark-staring sober. I told you, Lydia," he said, sanctimoniously, "she shouldn't be driving that car. And she won't be after this. It's only because she's a well-loved figure in this town that she isn't spending the night in a cell."

"Okay, I'm on my way."

Conall was still in the booth. Sending emails, by the look of things. What a tool. "I've got to go," she said. "Something's after happening. Thanks for tonight."

"Wait, wait, what's going on?"

"Mum. She drove into the reservoir."

"Is she okay?"

"Yeah. But, like . . . upset."

"You don't need to go. Two of your brothers are right there."

517

"You saw what they're like."

"You're not planning to drive?"

"I'll get a taxi. One of the lads will do me a favor."

Conall stood up. "I'll drive you."

"You? Aren't you over the limit?"

"Pink champagne isn't my thing. Do you want to say goodbye to your friends?"

Lydia thought about it for a moment. But they were all so drunk; and the whole Mum thing — they'd never really got it.

"No, let's just go."

DAY 25

Fionn woke Katie early. "Have a bath with me," he whispered, helping her from the bed. He'd lit scented candles, the bath overflowed with foam and rose petals had appeared from somewhere. Katie was so floppy-limbed and giggly she could hardly stand. He lowered her into the warm water. Then he washed her, stroking her with the slippery lather until she was pink and swollen with desire.

"Gotta go now," he said.

"Thass right. Leave me for dead." She could hardly speak. It was like being stoned.

"Tonight?"

"Got a work thing. Launch party. Wayne Diffney. Poor Wayne." She laughed softly to herself.

"Why poor Wayne?"

"Oh you know." She was almost slurring her words. "When he was in Laddz, they made him be the one with the wacky hair."

"Like the Sydney Opera House?"

519

"Thass him."

"I thought I knew the name."

"After he went solo, his wife left him for Shocko O'Shaughnessy and his record company dropped him. Then he wrote an album about it all, and you know something, Fionn? It's really *not bad*. I've heard worse, a lot worse. Tonight's his big relaunch. Lot depends on it."

"I could come over after it."

"It'll go on late. Doesn't start till ten."

"Can I come?"

"What?"

"Was that the wrong thing to say? I've spent too long buried in the back-arse of nowhere and I don't know how things are done in the big city."

"No, it's just . . ." . . . that Conall had never once come to any of her launches. He'd used them as an excuse to work too.

DAY 25 . . .

Matt didn't recognize the incoming number but he answered anyway. In Sales, you *always* had to answer, just in case it was someone who'd decided on a whim to purchase a million-euro software system and this was the only time they might call. "Matt Geary speaking."

"It's Russ."

Christ! Alex's friend, the other best man!

"Russ!" Automatically, Matt forced exuberance into his voice. He'd heard nothing from Alex since he'd done a no-show last week and, in a way, Alex's silence was more shaming than if he'd rung in a rage. "So, Russ, how're things with you?"

"Not in a happy place. What's the story, Matt? Your brother is getting married —"

"It's work," Matt interrupted. "You know yourself. Challenging times!" He barked out a laugh. "Up to my tonsils in it!"

"I've booked the flights to Vegas."

"You have?" Shit! "Fair play. Thanks a million —"

"Twelve of us. We fly out on 23 August, back on 30 August. I need a check from you. I'll email the details."

"Hey, thanks, Russ."

"You've arranged the time off work, right?"

"Sure! Did it ages ago!" He hadn't even mentioned it to them.

"Good. We were a bit worried . . . Right. As well, I've booked the hotel."

"Have you? You've been a busy boy!"

"The Metro MGM. You're sharing a room with Walter."

"Dad? Well, ah —"

"Tough shite if it doesn't suit you. You should have come along last week to the Duke and staked your claim. Now, Matt, listen to me. Alex has done a lot of the work on this, but there are some things you and I

521

need to organize."

"Like what?"

"Surprises," Russ said irritably. "ATVs, that sort of thing. You can't make the poor bastard book his own treats. You and me need to meet up."

"Grand! Listen, I'll get back to you on that in the next day or two."

"No. We're fixing something now —"

"Great! I'll call you back." Quickly, Matt hung up. The phone slid from his grasp, his hands were so sweaty.

"So! Young Mr. Geary! How close are we to finalizing the deal with your Bank of British Columbia?"

The sweat from Russ's phone call had barely dried on Matt's hands before he'd received a sudden shocking summons to the Office of Fear, to account to Kevin Day, the MD, for all the money he'd spent trying and failing to flog a system to the Bank of British Columbia.

The trio of Edios bigwigs — the MD, the Finance Director and the Chairman — were gathered in Kevin's office and they were keen to talk to Matt. No warning had been given.

"You've shelled out a fair few bob," the Finance Director said, tapping a page in front of him and fixing Matt with an assessing stare.

"Gotta spend it to make it." Could they see

the sweat on his face, gleaming beneath the harsh overhead lights?

"How soon will it close?" Kevin Day asked.

How soon? It was over ten days since anyone at the bank had even returned his calls. "I reckon," Matt said, gazing up at a ceiling corner. "I'd say we should have it wrapped up in the next week."

"You do, do you?" More shrewd looks from the Finance Director. Matt's bowels spasmed. God, he was afraid. He should have been expecting this; he didn't know why he hadn't prepared himself.

"Good, good, within the week. Excellent," the Chairman said. "Tell me, Matt, how's morale?"

Morale was rock-bottom. Matt and the team had poured boundless energy into this deal without any sign of a return, yet they hadn't been cut loose to lick their wounds and move forward.

"Morale?" Matt flashed a cheesy grin and felt a line of sweat trickle down his back. "Morale is great!"

The perfect prospect was right there in front of Matt. An elderly man was all goofed up with the automatic check-out in Tesco. He couldn't get his barcodes to scan and he didn't know he had to weigh his apples. He looked confused and quite frightened by the hostile vibes from the arsey queue that had built up behind him. Absolute bloody god-send. Matt could go in and gently point out the apples on the screen and show him where the barcode on his cookies was.

But he kept right on going and waited for another check-out.

No Act of Kindness today. Or ever again. No point. Fucking things didn't work. And he was going to tell Maeve. When he got home tonight she'd ask, like she always asked, what today's Act of Kindness had been and he would tell her he hadn't done one. Just like that. No explanations, no anxious apologies. He'd make it way clear that he'd had a tailor-made opportunity and he'd walked right past it. Spurned it. See what she had to say to that.

"How was your day?" Matt asked Maeve.

"Oh, you know."

Go on, ask me, ask me.

He was ready, he was braced, he was pumped.

Go on, ask me, ask me.

But she didn't. Nor did she offer details of her own AOK and that was strange too. Things got stranger still when the time came for bed and they got into their sleeping clothes and she didn't produce their Trio of Blessings notebooks out of her drawer.

No explanation was offered and in the end Matt cracked. He had to know what was going on. "Er, Maeve, no Trio of Blessings tonight?"

"Nope."

"Are we giving it up?"

"Yip."

". . . Why?"

"It's not working."

And then he was really scared.

DAY 25 . . .

Conall pulled into a service station on the outskirts of Boyne. "We'll get some stuff for the drive home to Dublin."

They hadn't eaten properly all day, had just drunk endless cups of tea in Ellen's kitchen. Someone, probably Murdy's wife, Sabrina, had done a run to SuperMacs but had miscalculated the amount of food needed. The place had become Crisis HQ and had been overrun with people — Buddy Scutt and Flan Ramble and various cops, as well as Murdy and Ronnie. All very well, Lydia had thought, but they'd eaten hers and Conall's dinner boxes. The gall of Buddy Scutt, sitting there tucking into *her* crisis chicken pieces when he'd had the nerve to tell her nine months ago that there was nothing wrong with Mum.

Lydia had urged Conall to leave, had told him that she'd make her own way back to Dublin, but he'd said he had such a good signal on his BlackBerry that he'd stay. So she let him. She couldn't help but notice — and it was fiercely annoying — that everyone was taking her far more seriously now that Conall was hanging around.

He clicked away on his BlackBerry and nobody said he was rude, then, when Ellen went to the bathroom, he made an announcement to the full room. "Listen up. An MRI scan. That's what Ellen needs. That'll give a better idea of how things are."

"What's that you said? An MRI scan?"

"What does that do?"

"It gives a photo of her brain," Lydia said tightly. No one had listened when she'd asked for it, but because a rich man who drove a Lexus suggested it, suddenly everyone was all ears. "It'll show up the damaged parts, and then she can get treatment."

"How do we get one of them?"

"Her GP refers her."

"Except he won't," Lydia said.

"Can you sort her out with an MRI scan?" Ronnie narrowed his eyes at Buddy Scutt.

"Aaaah." Buddy shifted in his chair. "I suppose I could."

"Why didn't you do it before now?" Ronnie hissed.

"Yeah," Murdy sneered. "Why didn't you?"

"I didn't think there was anything wrong with her. Neither did you."

"I'm not a doctor."

"I'm not her son."

"We could sue you for this," Murdy said.

"Boys, boys, less bickering please." Conall shook his head. "You're all to blame. Lydia's the only one who's tried to help."

"I can fight my own battles," Lydia said hotly.

But, obviously, she couldn't.

Conall had dozed off in an armchair and slept away the afternoon, and only when the evening shadows began to fall, did Lydia wake him.

"We're going home," she said.

" 'Kay." A bit dazed, he stood up.

They'd driven less than a mile when he pulled into the service station. Lydia, still in her short tight dress from the night before, attracted a lot of attention, as she prowled the aisles, gathering up smoothies and bags of popcorn.

At the check-out she rejoined Conall, who was trying to control an armload of ice creams and sweets.

"Give me them," she said. "I'll pay. Least I can do."

They sat, parked outside, eating their Magnums. He crunched briskly through his, shattering the chocolate coating without a second thought.

"I like to eat mine slooowww." She flashed a glance from under her lashes — then she stopped. It wasn't right to torment him.

"Thanks, you know, for this. Driving me down and staying all day. How did you know about MRI scans?"

"I got Eilish to find out. Didn't take her long. Your mum should have had one months ago. I don't know why she didn't."

"Because her doctor is a gobshite and my brothers didn't want to know."

"They know now."

"Yeah, well . . . thanks for saying it. And thanks for last night."

"Did you like Float?" Conall started on his second Magnum.

She thought about it. "Not really. It was sort of sleazy. I just wanted to go because I couldn't."

"We always want what we can't have."

"Like you with me."

He laughed but didn't answer.

"You've money, you've a house in Wellington Road, you're . . . you know . . ." She waved a hand up and down his body.

"What?"

"For an old bloke, you're not bad-looking. You could get plenty of girls. Why are you hanging around, pestering me?"

"You're nice-looking." He paused. "*Very* nice-looking. And even though you're not pleasant, you're interesting. Like a David Cronenberg film. *Crash*." He crooked an eyebrow but the reference was lost on her.

"When will it all go weird and I'll suddenly

be mad about you?"

"Actually, I would have thought it would have happened by now. Most girls . . . me coming to see their sick mother. And rescuing you, doing the middle-of-the-night drive. That stuff is normally pretty effective."

"So when will you go off me?"

It was starting to happen already. Last night in Float — had it only been last night? — had shown him how mismatched they were. "When I've had sex with you."

She laughed. At least he was honest.

Eventually, she spoke. "All right."

"All right what?"

"Sex. Let's do it."

"You fancy me?"

She hesitated. "I think I might. A bit." She paused again. "I guess I'm curious." Suddenly anxious, she asked. "But you won't be all saggy and old-looking? I'm used to young, fit blokes."

"I'm forty-two, not eighty-two. I have good genes. And a personal trainer."

"But look at the crap you eat."

"I've a fast metabolism."

"Okay, just so long as it's not like *Night of the Living Dead.*"

"Let's just forget this. You're not into it —"

"No, I want to." Then she added, "I think."

Suddenly, she was being pulled toward him and his mouth lowered itself to meet hers. He smelled different. More grown-up. Gilbert

529

had been a great man for statement after-shaves, ones that surrounded him like a pungent cloud, base notes and top notes and God knows what else spattering everywhere. Andrei smelled of man-body and sweat and lust. But Conall smelled of . . . sophisticated lives. He smelled of old leather and wood smoke and parquet floor. He smelled of money. And ice cream, but only briefly.

Lydia waited. She paid attention to how she was responding. Yes, it was working. The smell of his skin and the heat of his hand on her waist.

"You've done this before," she said, when they broke away.

"So . . ." he said slowly, ". . . have you."

Right, she *definitely* fancied him.

Their heart vibrations are *not* in harmony. Lydia's beat is a nanosecond behind Conall's, so the end of hers bites off the start of his. But it's an interesting, edgy, overlapping one–two rhythm that in many ways is *more seductive* than harmony. Fascinating.

DAY 25 . . .

"Good evening," Jemima said. "Celtic Psychic Line."

"Mystic Maureen?"

"Speaking, my dear."

"Aha! It *is* you, at long last! I recognize that

530

posh voice. I've spoken to twelve, fecking *twelve,* so-called Maureens, trying to find you."

Yes, Jemima had to admit that the company liked to put about the fiction that there was just one wise old woman employed by Celtic Psychic Line instead of several appallingly badly paid women doing shift work on their own phone.

"I've rung loads of times trying to get you and all I got was these *liars* who know nothing about anything. I was afraid I'd never find you. I thought you'd, like, *died* or something."

Jemima had reduced quite dramatically her number of shifts. Fionn was the cause. Between accompanying him to the set and attempting to douse his out-of-control womanizing and keeping a lid on the enmity between him and Grudge, well, she was quite *sapped.*

"I spoke to you about a month ago and everything you predicted for me came true."

"Assuming it was happy events I foresaw, then I am overjoyed. But, as I'm sure I told you at the time, I have no psychic ability. There is no such thing."

"My name is Sissy? Do you remember me? You told me I'd meet a man in the ticket queue in BusAras."

"I assure you I most certainly did not. I would never say something as specific as that. As I remember, we did a quick overview of

531

your life, and I told you to brush your hair, smile at people and endeavor to see past the surface. That at first impression a man may seem like a . . . the word you used was *tool*, as I recall, and his hair may be, to fall back on your description, *gank* —"

"You said that a decent heart would beat beneath his hideous orange hoodie."

"I said that a decent heart *may* beat beneath his hideous orange hoodie. I offered no guarantees. I simply urged a more open-minded attitude."

"How did you know he'd be wearing a hideous orange hoodie?"

"I did not. The description was yours. I am eighty-eight years of age. What would I know of hoodies?"

"You said BusAras. That I'd meet him there."

"I acknowledge that we discussed that you take the bus for weekend trips to your family. I said, and I believe it to be true, that stations are places where romance tends to flourish, that travelers are less likely to be hidebound by their day-to-day identity. It's mere common sense."

"I brushed my hair, I smiled, I saw past the surface. I met a man! It all happened just like you said it would."

"Overjoyed, my dear." She would like to get off the line now; she was quite wearied by this silliness. She had only taken this job to save young girls from wasting their hard-earned cash. The last thing she had wanted was to convince them that it worked.

"Pick a card for me," Sissy said. "Is Jesse the man of my dreams?"

Jemima picked a card. Fidelity. "Yes."

"Will we have children?"

Jemima picked the next card. "Yes."

"How many?"

"Two. A boy, then a girl."

"What will we call them? Only joking!"

"Finian and Anastasia."

Sissy gasped. In an urgent whisper, she said, "Oh. My. God. How did you know that? No one could know that. You're amazing."

"I know nothing. I simply plucked two names from the ether."

"But they were my grandparents' names. My daddy's mammy and daddy. They were my favorites! Oh, I used to go and stay with them when I was small and I never had to eat proper food. They gave me Marietta cookies stuck together with butter for my breakfast and I used to squeeze them together and the butter would come out of the holes and — Oh my God, I've got tingles all over. It's not like they're regular names, like Paddy and Mary. It's not as if you could have taken a chance."

"A lucky guess." She was so very tired.

"*Not* a lucky guess. You're a genius. You should have your own show."

"Dear heart, you must go now. You've been charged so much money already. I bid you goodnight."

DAY 25 . . .

The drive took just over an hour, not long — it was ten in the evening and the traffic was light — but still long enough for Lydia to think about what she was going to do. It was a good thing, she concluded. She did fancy Conall, she was nearly sure of it, and it would cure her of Andrei. If she was sleeping with Conall, she'd stop sleeping with Andrei; that's just the way she was. She didn't multitask when it came to men. Some people, specifically Shoane, loved the intrigue of having two or three men on the go. She took great pleasure in going straight from one bed to the next and she set herself secret challenges, like sleeping with all three in a twenty-four-hour period. But, for some reason, Lydia didn't enjoy the complications. She wondered if you'd have to really hate men to behave like that.

But what would it be like with Conall? Because he'd had so much straightforward sex over the last eons would he have moved on to freaky stuff? Maybe he couldn't come unless he was being caned? Or asphyxiated? It would be fun, she supposed. In a way. Well, interesting, anyway. The only problem was that she wasn't sure how you'd go about asphyxiating someone, but she figured he'd show her.

Without consultation, Conall drove them to Wellington Road and although there was no way on earth Lydia would have let Conall into her cupboard at 66 Star Street, she was a bit miffed. He could have *asked* her.

"Jesus, the state of this place." Lydia gazed around Conall's hall, at the torn-at walls displaying their layers, like wounds.

"Yeah . . . it is a bit . . ." Conall seemed to be noticing it for the first time. "I've been so busy."

"Unbelievable." Lydia turned and caught her dress on a nail sticking out from a crate. "Get off me! And it's not a question of cash? Like, you have enough to do the place up?"

"A policeman wouldn't ask me that question. This way." He guided her up the wide splintery staircase and into his bedroom. Conall clapped his hands twice and suddenly a paradise was illuminated.

Stunned, Lydia stood on the threshold. She hardly knew what to look at first. The thick, thick carpet, spreading before her in a vast plain, in a color that she couldn't possibly name — not gray, not heather, not pale blue, but something else, something far more beautiful and unique. They must have invented a new color, just for Conall Hathaway's bedroom carpet. And the curtains, like curtains they had in expensive hotels, in some heavy silky fabric, tumbling twelve feet from the lofty ceiling, and gathering in a shimmering pool on the floor.

"What just happened there?" she asked. "Did we cross into another dimension?"

Oh the bed! Enormous. So wide. So *loooonnnngggg*. And there was something about the duvet cover. Even from a distance she could sense how delicious it would feel, how cool and smooth and kind.

"What a bed," she said, in awe. "I'll sleep well tonight."

"Not if I have anything to do with it," he said softly.

She turned toward the voice. Oh yeah. Him. For a moment she'd forgotten why she was there. "So how do you want to do this?"

"Do what?"

"This." She pointed toward the bed.

"I didn't realize . . . I thought we'd just wing it. See what happens?"

He kissed her and her body began to respond.

"How about I open this . . ." He played with the buttons on the front of her dress and when his hand brushed her nipple, braless under the fabric, it made her shudder

His eyes met hers and she shuddered again. "Good or bad?"

She wasn't sure.

He moved his fingers in a circular movement around the buttons, until she thought they'd never be opened, that she and her need would be locked in forever. Then, with a sudden, almost violent flick, all four buttons were opened and he slithered the dress off over her head. He lay her down on the bed and slowly removed her knickers. She was panting.

"Do you want me to cane you?" she gasped.

He broke away and looked at her.

"Or asphyxiate you?"

"No." He looked horrified. "Is that what you want?"

"No. I wondered if it turned you on."

"You turn me on." He took her hand and placed it on his groin. "So I do."

DAY 25 . . .

"Okay, boss?" Danno asked Katie.

Katie turned to Danno, her face ablaze with beauty. "Okay?" she asked.

"Yeah, like —" He gestured at the nightclub, at all the people, the journalists, the models and the celebrities who had shown up to help Wayne Diffney celebrate the launch of *Seven Vintage Cars, One Dart Ticket.* "Anything you need me to be doing?"

"Danno, I can quite honestly say that this

is the happiest I've ever been in my entire life."

Danno was suddenly deeply disillusioned. "I thought you didn't mess with that stuff."

"Not drugs. Just happy." She treated him to another luminous smile.

"High on life?" Danno distrusted nothing more than a natural up.

"I should be exhausted," she confided. "I got almost no sleep last night. But I feel like I'll never need to sleep again. I feel invincible."

"Sounds like happy pills to me," he said doubtfully. "You take care of yourself, Katie. Don't let your man play the eejit."

"Oh Danno, I'm fine! This is like a holiday romance. Either Fionn's show will fail and he'll go back to Pokey, or his show will be a success and it'll go to his head. There is no future in this *at all,* but for the moment it's perfect."

Wayne's launch had been a dream. Even before ten o'clock, guests had begun to arrive, so Katie didn't have to endure long, sweaty minutes, standing in an empty nightclub, Wayne gazing at her with wounded eyes, terrified that no one would show. And the people who came were proper guests. Wayne's many aunties and cousins were all well and good but Katie needed the media to appear for this to work and, to her great pleasure, they'd shown up in hordes. From chatting to them she understood that there was a great reservoir of goodwill for Wayne Diffney. "His wife doing that to him . . ." "Never mind the wife; it was the hair when he was in Laddz. My heart went out to the chap." "Do I understand it correctly, that the album title is about Shocko having seven vintage cars and Wayne only having a Dart ticket, the day Hailey left him?"

Katie was shepherding Wayne around, ensuring that he spoke pleasantly to all the social diarists and journalists, even those who had shafted him in the past — of whom there were many — and suddenly, there was Fionn, in his dirty boots and jacket of many pockets, standing in an empty space, smiling awkwardly and being ignored by one and all.

"Just wanted you to know I'm here," he called. "You do your thing. I'm here for you when you want me."

She snagged George, who was scurrying past. "George, this is Fionn. Mind him. Introduce him to a few people."

George swept Fionn away, and as Katie worked the room with Wayne, she caught an occasional glimpse of him. He seemed to be laughing and talking, which was a relief.

"Wayne, this is Catherine Daly from *The Times* . . ."

"Wayne, Casey Kaplan from the *Spokes-*

man. I know the pair of you go way back . . ."

Keith from the *Tribune* popped up in front of her. "Katie, give us a lend of Wayne for a second. Just want to take a couple of shots of him with someone." He seemed quite agitated.

"Who?"

"Just over here." Keith led them through the crowds. "Wayne, Katie, this is Fionn Purdue. Remember the name; you'll be hearing it again. Fronting up a new gardening show. Lot of heat around it."

Katie laughed in delight. "Pleased to meet you, Fionn Purdue."

"Pleased to meet *you,* Katie Richmond."

Neither Wayne nor Keith could see what was so funny.

"Katie." Danno appeared. "We're ready to start the speeches."

In honor of the occasion — and it *was* an honor — James "Woolfman" Woolf, the managing director of Apex Europe, had flown in from London, with his stunning wife, Karolina, and their equally exquisite daughters, Siena and Maya. Under usual circumstances, Irish launches remained untroubled by anyone from the London end of things.

Woolfman, blessed with extraordinary good looks and magnetic charisma, chatted with charming "just folks" humility about the times he'd met icons like Nelson Mandela, Robert Plant — and, of course, the Dalai

Lama. But who *hadn't* met the Dalai Lama, Katie thought absently. The brand was in danger of overexposure. A bit like Louis Vuitton. Outlets everywhere, even in duty-frees. She took a quick look at the faces around her: everyone was gazing with shiny, devoted eyes at Woolfman, and she was touched by the first prickles of alarm. They were so stunned with love for Woolfman that it seemed they'd entirely forgotten the reason they were there, to wit, Wayne Diffney. But . . . finally! . . . Woolfman said, "I can now add Wayne Diffney to the list of people I can boast about having met."

And the day was saved! Relief flooded Katie and she wondered why she had ever doubted Woolfman. He was a charm monster, a public-relations superstar, a hero.

Much clapping and whistling accompanied the appearance of Wayne on stage. His speech was brief and grateful and then, with prearranged spontaneity, someone (Danno) handed him a guitar and urged him to sing a few songs, which he promptly did. "The Day She Left." Then, "She's Having His Baby." And, of course, the first single from the album, "They Killed My Hair."

A tad mawkish, perhaps, but no one could deny he had good reason.

That was the work bit pretty much over for Katie, and for the rest of the night Fionn

541

never left her side. He generated a lot of interest. Time after time, Katie heard him being asked, "How do you know Wayne?"

"To be honest, I don't," he always replied. "I've never met him before tonight. I'm here with Katie Richmond."

"*With* Katie Richmond?"

"*With* Katie Richmond."

"Girlfriend's heading for a fall." George, watching from the shadows, shook his head gloomily.

"It won't last," Lila-May agreed.

"What's wrong with all of you?" Danno said, exasperated. "Can't you just let her be happy?"

"But what does he see in her?"

"What? You think it should be you? With your long hair and your pointy bazoomas and —"

Fueled by a sudden surge of rage, Danno lunged at Lila-May and engaged her in a hot, dirty kiss, which came as a huge surprise to her, but an even bigger surprise to him. He'd been pretty sure he was gay.

DAY 25 . . .

"Why don't you have a boyfriend?" Conall asked, into the silence.

They'd been lying without speaking, his leg thrown across Lydia's legs, the weight of it

542

pinning her to the bed. Lydia was speechless and happy, as much because of the size of the bed as the sex.

"What makes you think I don't have one?"

"We wouldn't be doing this if you had, right?"

"Is that how it works?" Even to herself she sounded hard done-by. Although she didn't care about Gilbert any more — and she discovered that she really didn't — her pride was still a bit wounded: who would have thought he was off riding other girls?

"What?" Conall was suddenly interested.

"I did have a boyfriend until about a month ago."

"But?"

"But I accidentally slept with my flatmate."

"What?" Conall sat up, he was so startled.

"Yeah, I accidentally slept with my flat-mate."

"How often? Just the once?"

"Just the once. Apart from one or two other times. It was like the damage was done, you know? We might as well. You know?"

Conall looked far from happy.

"So are you still sleeping with him?"

"Well, not right now, obviously."

When Conall made no pretense of a smile she said, "I'm not sleeping with him at all."

He nodded. He seemed satisfied.

"Except for when it happens." Lydia felt she'd better add that.

"What are you talking about?"

"Sometimes it just happens. If I bump into him in the kitchen . . ." She shrugged. "Or the living room. That sort of thing."

"How many times has it just happened?"

"Four."

"Four?"

"I think four. It might be a bit more."

She'd lost count after nine.

"He's your boyfriend."

Lydia laughed. "Listen to yourself, you're like a possessive . . ." She searched her head for the word with the correct quantity of scorn. ". . . girl. He's not my boyfriend. We don't have conversations. We don't even like each other. A bit like you and me."

"But I do like you."

"Well, I don't like you." Although that was no longer strictly true.

"When we had sex there, was it like you and . . . what's your man's name?"

"Andrei." No. Nothing could compare with the sex with Andrei. "Listen to me, Conall. Andrei and me, it's not real life."

"It's mind-blowing, isn't it?" Conall said.

She waited before replying, not sure what to say. But why would she lie? "Well, *yeah.* But I don't even like him. It's nothing. Nothing," she repeated. "Now let's go to sleep. I've to get up very early."

"So have I."

"How early do you have to get up?"

He eyed her. "Five-thirty. I'm going to Milan."

"So late? God, I'll have half a day's work done by then. What are you doing in Milan?"

"Taking over a company."

"Easy for some."

"Milan is just the first stop. Then I'm going to Malaysia."

"Taking over another company there?"

"Same company. Their HQ is in Milan but most of their operations are in Southeast Asia." He braced himself for a barrage of anxious questions: how long would he be gone? When would he be back? How was she meant to endure his absence?

"Conall?"

"Mmmm?" Here we go.

"How do I turn off your stupid lights?"

". . . Ah . . . clap twice."

"No. I'd feel stupid. You do it."

Conall clapped his hands and darkness fell.

"Can I say something?" Lydia said into the silence.

"What?"

"Oh nothing. Just that you looked quite stupid. Lying there with nothing on, clapping like a madzer."

"Goodnight."

Oh lovely sheet, Lydia thought, stroking it again and again. So cool and smooth and beautiful beneath my palm. Oh loads of lovely room to stretch out all my arms and all my legs, oh lovely marshmallowy pillows, so many of them —

"What age is he?" Conall's voice interrupted her reverie.

"Who — Oh, Andrei. Don't know."

"Twenties? Thirties?"

"Twenties. Maybe twenty-seven? Go to sleep."

"What does he do?"

"Computers. Fixing them, I think. I don't really know. Like I said, we don't talk. Go to sleep."

"So he doesn't own his own company or anything?"

"No."

"What does he drive?"

"Some sort of van. It's not even his."

"A van." Conall sounded scornful and pleased.

"But he does have a very big mickey."

Beside her, Conall went as tense as a plank of wood.

"A joke." Although Andrei *did* have a very big mickey. "Go to sleep."

It was the most delicious dream imaginable. She was bouncing up and down in a sea of feathers, the softest, the sweetest . . . then something was happening, someone was shaking her. Then she wasn't in the lovely dream any longer. She was fecky well awake, in Conall Hathaway's frankly magnificent bed.

"What does he look like?" a voice asked. Conall Hathaway.

"Who? Oh, for the love of God! Have some pride!"

"I just need to know what he looks like."

"Blue eyes. Very short hair, blondish."

"Tall?"

"Yes."

"Muscular?"

"Very. Sweet dreams."

Day 24

"Big night last night, Matt?"

". . . What?" Matt realized that Salvatore was talking to him.

"Where's my smile?"

"What?"

"Why the long face? One too many amarettos last night?"

"Nothing's up. Eee-yargh!"

Matt waited until Salvatore went back to his own desk, then let his face sink down again, until it was as gloomy as his feelings.

Doing the AOKs had been a pain in the arse, but Maeve nixing them was far more unsettling. Everything was moving in the wrong direction. Things were supposed to be getting better, but they seemed to have doubled back on themselves and started getting worse. He wasn't sure he could do this again; he didn't have it any more, whatever it was that was needed.

He picked up a newspaper that someone had left lying around and his heart lifted slightly when he read that another crater of ice had come crashing to earth, this latest one in Lisbon. Lisbon. See? Another capital city. Was he the only one who had noticed this fact? The very strange thing was that — as yet, anyway — no one had been hurt by these massive ice boulders. They came hurtling out of the sky and made shit of cars and roofs and public monuments, but no human being had strayed into their path. If — no, *when* — Matt told himself hopefully, *when* one landed in Dublin, it would definitely land on a person, a particular person, and it would knock the living bejayzus out of them. If there was any justice. Which, of course, there wasn't. The descent back into despair began again and intensified when he read that scientists were investigating the phenomenon (he rallied briefly at the word *phenomenon,* it smacked of science fiction, the kind of stuff he enjoyed; he could do with a bit more of that in his life), and they'd concluded that the icy missiles definitely weren't the opening salvos from a hostile alien race. The theory the scientists liked best was that the lumps of ice were coming from planes flying overhead.

Matt's phone rang and his nerves flared. With his heart banging in his throat, he spoke. "Edios. Matt Geary."

"Matt?" It was Natalie. "Are you leaving Edios?"

"No. Why?"

"I've been head-hunted."

The lizard part of his brain, the old instinctive response that alerted him to life-threatening danger, suddenly kicked into action.

"By Edios," she said. "Heading up the sales team, chasing new business, conducting negotiations until they sign."

"That's my job."

"That's what I thought. Sorry, Matt."

They were sacking him, there was no other explanation. They wouldn't be bringing Nat in to head up a second sales team, not in the current climate when there was barely enough work for one. Suddenly, Matt understood that yesterday's summons to the Office of Fear had been for the gruesome threesome to settle their heads on the matter.

It all came back to that Bank of British Columbia thing, Matt realized. Everything that had gone weird and wrong could be blamed on that. It was his own fault. He'd been affected by a perplexing paralysis whereby he didn't have the strength of will to bend the bank into buying and he didn't have the guts to call their bluff, and because of that everyone was stuck.

Christ, though. To be sacked. A wave of light-headed horror washed over him. He'd never before been sacked. It was always the other way round; employers loved him, and whenever he'd tried to leave they always begged him to change his mind. A sacked Matt? He didn't know that person.

Money. Without an income, what would he and Maeve do? Maeve's salary was a joke, like pocket money. He'd have to get another job but, for the first time in his life, he felt he wouldn't be able to. He wasn't the person he used to be. There was no way he could go into a room, the way he had once upon a time, and face down an interview board and convince them that what their business needed was him, Matt Geary.

It wasn't just the money that was a worry. It was Maeve. This would be the finish of her. She saw disaster in everything; one piece of bad luck was a sign that their life together was cursed.

He had a terrible sense that all control had long disappeared, that he and Maeve were heading toward some terrible dark finale. Goodness and happiness were gone for ever and nothing could be retrieved. This was going to end; and end terribly. The last three years had been spent trying to dodge their fate, but it was rushing up to meet them.

His phone rang. Feeling like he was in the middle of a bad dream, he answered and . . . oh the unbearable irony . . . it was Head of Procurement at the Bank of British Columbia. They were buying the system.

It was too late. He'd taken too long. He'd

spent too much money on the chase. But for the sake of the team he had to go through the motions. Yell. Punch the air. Shout "Ouff," many times. "For a minute there I thought the bastards were going to bail on us! Only for a minute, mind!" He had to pick up Salvatore and twirl him around. Send Cleo out to buy champagne. And at least when he started crying, heaving out some awful feelings from his solar plexus — and for a few petrifying moments, being simply unable to stop — it had been put down to tears of relief.

It was almost five-thirty before the call came: he was to present himself at the Managing Director's office asap. The old Matt would have made some quip to the others: "I may be some time." But the old Matt was no more. He said nothing to anyone. He'd never see them again; he wouldn't be allowed back into the office to say his goodbyes; he'd be escorted from the building without his special mug and his picture of Maeve. But it didn't matter. It was only stuff; they were only people.

At least, thanks to Natalie, he knew what was coming. Without her call he might be skipping off to the Office of Fear, thinking he was going to get a pat on the back for landing a big sale. And yet, as his legs moved forward without any input from him, it was impossible to believe that things had got so bad. He felt as though he was moving through mist and he couldn't feel his feet as they connected with the floor.

He'd arrived. He knocked, the door was opened and in he went. Serious faces all round. Matt bowed his head and waited for the executioner's ax to fall.

But it was worse than he'd expected. Oh far, far worse.

Matt wasn't being sacked. Oh no. Matt was being promoted.

■ ■ ■ ■

TWO WEEKS LATER

■ ■ ■ ■

DAY 10

Lydia's phone rang. It was Conall.

"Where are you now?" she asked.

"Vietnam."

She laughed out loud. "No? For real?" In the last two weeks he'd gone from Milan to Kuala Lampur to Manila. "Where's next?"

"Phnom Penh. Cambodia."

"You lucky bastard."

"It's not as nice as it sounds."

"Yeah, right. Flying first-class, staying in hotels, getting room service. I *love* room service."

"When I come back, we could go someplace. Like, with room service."

"Whateves."

"So what's going on?"

"The results of Mum's scan tomorrow. Dr. Buddy Scutt will explain all."

"Good luck with that. Let me know."

"Will do. Not much else to report. Poppy's wedding next Wednesday. She's cracking up."

"I keep meaning to ask, how come you're

not one of her bridesmaids?"

"Her mother hates me. And Poppy has Cecily, her perfect cousin. Since they were aged ten or something they swore they'd do each other."

"So who's your Plus One?"

Once upon a time it was meant to be Gilbert. "No one, I suppose. You're not volunteering, are you?"

"Maybe I am."

"You can come so long as I don't have to mind you. Does that mean you're my boyfriend?"

"I don't know. Does it?"

Then he was gone. Hung up on her! He was always doing that; he was an absolute bloody champion at getting the last word.

After glaring at the phone for some seconds, she rang Poppy. "Conall Hathaway wants to come to your wedding."

"Does that mean he's your boyfriend?"

"That's what I said."

"Maybe he is," Poppy said. "How're things with delicious Andrei?"

"I'm cured." She hadn't slept with him since the night she'd spent in Hathaway's supersized bed. In fact, between taking Mum for her scan and having summit meetings in Boyne, she wasn't sure she'd even seen Andrei for at least a week. More, actually. "And don't call him delicious."

558

Jemima tossed and turned in her bed, trying to find a position that didn't hurt. Grudge clambered up beside her and lay his head on her stomach. The heat he emitted was a great painkiller, so Jemima frequently told him. But she wriggled and couldn't settle and he wasn't surprised when she said, "Forgive me, my darling Grudge, but I'm finding the weight of your head quite uncomfortable."

Not surprised, no. But wounded, oh yes, very wounded. He bounded off the bed and stalked, rigid-necked, from the room to nurse his grievance in his basket. Then he tensed. Fionn! So finely tuned was Grudge's hatred that he could sense him even at a distance.

Fionn was down in the street with Katie. They were getting out — nay, *tumbling* out — of a taxi and trying to get their key into the front door; and here they came, padding up the stairs, giggling and mumbling. Coming home with the milk, to use a phrase of Jemima's, which Grudge didn't understand. Fionn and Katie didn't bring milk. They didn't bring anything, only sadness to his poor old mistress. Grudge shook his woolly head in disgust.

Until now, he had liked Katie — well, as much as he was able to like anyone — but her dalliance with Fionn showed a regrettable lapse in taste and judgment.

Trying to curl his lip in contempt, Grudge listened to the sniggering and whispering as the loved-up pair ascended the stairs in their stockinged feet. Lots of "Sssh's and stifled laughs. Unseemly. "Stop it, you *brat!*" Katie commanded in a hoarse whisper and Grudge wondered what Fionn had done. Stuck his hand up her skirt? Shoved her hand down his pants? A muffled bumping noise ensued. Fionn must have pushed her against a wall for a snog. Dear God, the carry-on!

They tiptoed past Grudge, hidden behind Jemima's door, growling softly. Now they would go into Katie's flat at the top of the house and have noisy relations.

Fionn hadn't slept a night in Jemima's flat for almost three weeks. He was practically living with Katie. This development had thrilled Grudge to his angry marrow — not only did he have Jemima all to himself again, but he could indulge in long sessions of sanctimonious disdain. What a fickle feckless creature Fionn was. What a disloyal ingrate. Jemima had taken care of him through his vulnerable years but he had dropped her like a hot potato when he took up with the fragrant, large-bosomed Katie.

Poor Jemima tried to pretend she wasn't sad. "Katie is such a sweet girl. So sensible. Although how long will she stick with Fionn? That's the question."

Nowadays, they only saw Fionn when he

called in to pick up his invitations to glamorous events. The first few times he'd pretended that it was a real visit, then Jemima had got wise. Now, she had taken to stacking the large, colored, exciting-looking envelopes in a neat pile on the escritoire, and when Fionn breezed in he'd make straight for it and start tearing things open.

He'd sicken you, him and his invitations. *Sicken* you. Three or four arrived every single day, sometimes not even by ordinary post, but by courier, and Fionn thought he was fucking fantastic. The more he got the more insufferable he became and Grudge would give all he owned to be able to point out that they only came because he was on some PR company's computer mailing list. No one really wanted him there. And to listen to him going on! Oh no, the album launch is the same night as the celebrity birthday party! Or: If we do the red carpet thing, but don't actually watch the movie, we can catch the end of the gallery opening.

Like anyone *cared.*

Admittedly, Fionn tried to cajole Jemima along to some of the shindigs — although Grudge suspected that Katie was almost certainly behind those kindnesses. But, pray tell, what use were those parties to Jemima? She was eighty-eight, an open-minded eighty-eight, for sure, but how much interest did Fionn expect her to have in test-driving the latest Ferrari? Eh? *Eh?*

Grudge blamed Fionn's new glamorous life on that horrible pushy Grainne Butcher. She'd given Fionn's details to every PR agency in the country and told him to get his face "out there" because the countdown to the first episode of *Your Own Private Eden* was underway. Only twelve days to go now and she wanted to build a "buzz."

Grudge couldn't bear the waiting. He just wanted the show to air and for it to get the slagging it so richly deserved. He'd seen the rough cut of the first episode and everyone — idiots! — had seemed to think it was good. It beggared belief! It was meant to be a gardening show, and instead there was some gobshite going round with a dirty jacket, producing weeds and stones from his pockets!

Your Own Private Eden would fail. It *must* fail.

DAY 9

"Maeve?"

"Mmm?"

Tell her, tell her, tell her. ". . . Ah . . ." *You useless plank, would you just tell her.* ". . . nothing."

Head of International Sales, that's what Matt was now. At least, that's what it said on the stiff new business cards he'd been presented with that afternoon in the Office of Fear, the day the Bank of British Columbia had said they were buying the Edios system. A storm of congratulations on his promotion had rained down on Matt from the Edios bigwigs. His hand had been shaken by the Finance Director, he'd been clapped on the back by the Chairman and he'd tried to keep his despair off his face as a stream of enthusiastic information flowed from Kevin Day, the MD. "Fighting fire with fire, that's the way to deal with this recession. You know what 'International' means, don't you, son? That's right — lots of travel! All those lovely new markets out there in the Far East, just waiting to be conquered, and who better to lead the raiding parties than our very own Matt Geary?"

No hike in pay, naturally. "A recession on, son, but you can't beat the prestige and, of course, *lots of travel.*"

Maeve would have a total freaker. When he told her.

But two weeks had passed and he still hadn't said anything. Time was barreling by, each twenty-four hours whipping around faster than the previous ones. Nat was working out her notice in Goliath; there were only ten more working days before she showed up to oust Matt from his desk.

Every night he went to bed weary with the weight of another day having elapsed without him telling Maeve, and every morning he knew with sick dread that he had to do it *right now.* Then a minute would pass, then another and another, and somehow all the minutes stacked up until, amazingly, it would be bedtime again and the words would still be locked inside him.

Turning down the new post had never been an option — it was a done deal, his old job was in the past, it had been taken from him and given to someone else — yet he couldn't possibly accept it either, and there was no way, absolutely no way, out of the bind.

Today stretched ahead of him and he knew

he wouldn't say anything and he'd go to bed tonight and he'd wake up tomorrow and he wouldn't tell Maeve and the day would pass and end and a new one would start and new days would keep on starting until Nat showed up in Edios and a plane would be waiting at Dublin airport ready to fly Matt to China, and what would happen then?

DAY 9 . . .

"Off out with Andrei tonight?"

Rosie attempted an enigmatic smile and busied herself in the syringe cupboard because, no, she was not off out with Andrei tonight, but she was hardly going to admit that to her colleague Evgenia. Never show weakness. Today was the eighth day since Andrei had last made himself available and Evgenia kept a tally.

Rosie didn't understand it. In the immediate aftermath of "Doorgate" she'd had Andrei exactly where she wanted him: on his knees. There had been red roses. There had been a heart-shaped charm that she'd had a jeweler take a look at; he'd valued it at 200 euro, not as high as she would have liked, but a respectable enough showing. There had been earnest promises that Andrei would ask his work if he could borrow the van so they could have a romantic weekend away in Kerry.

Then had come a sharp, inexplicable falling-off in his ardor. On their last two outings his face, when he gazed at her, had lost its customary melting expression, text messages had become patchy and there had been no further mention of Kerry.

"Make a fist, Mr. Dewy," she said to the old man in the high narrow bed. "Till we see about this blood."

"I'm Mr. Screed," he said, nervously watching the syringe in Rosie's hand.

Was he? So who was Mr. Dewy? Oh yes, the man who'd died in the next bed this morning, she remembered. Sure, they were all the fecking one.

"Mr. Screed." She tried to smile. "Sorry, pet. Long week." She tapped the crook of his elbow. "Have you any veins at all?"

The unexpected knock-back with that good-looking Fionn had rattled her confidence and it made her even more grateful for Andrei: *he'd* never leave her sitting in a pub on her own, he was a *gent*. Admittedly, she had been left waiting outside his flat but he genuinely hadn't heard her light-as-a-fairy knocking. She'd dressed the accident up as a great betrayal, because that was what you did, but she'd only been playing the game. It was what men like Andrei expected from girls like Rosie: wounded feelings, sensitivity, coaxing-requirements, et cetera.

Maybe — it was the obvious thing you'd

think of — Andrei's attentions had fallen off because he'd met someone else. She didn't think it was likely. Andrei wasn't like Fionn; he was steady and reliable.

But, funnily enough, she had the odd moment of anxiety about Lydia — even though she was so sharp and shouty and scratchy that Rosie couldn't imagine any man wanting her. But their flat was so small and men, even the good ones, were essentially animals . . .

DAY 9 . . .

Little clods of last night's mascara were dotted all over Katie's face, looking like dustings of soot. She gazed hard into her bathroom mirror, inspecting the damage. It was amazing really, she thought, that she didn't look more wrecked. She'd been getting by on no more than four hours sleep a night. Her skincare regime had gone to hell. She was eating crap at all the wrong times: chocolate cookies for breakfast, cheese on toast at four in the morning. And she wasn't lifting a finger in exercise. Apart from sex and, to be fair, she was doing an awful lot of that.

"Is there no milk?" Fionn called from the kitchen.

"Where would it come from?" She leaned on the door jamb and watched him foostering with a tea bag. "You've been with me since I finished work yesterday. Unless I went out in the middle of the night to buy it."

"I'll just nip down to Jemima and get some."

"Don't." It wasn't right to treat her like a shop.

"Why not? She won't mind."

She might, though. She just wouldn't let Fionn know. "Drink it black, it won't kill you."

"We'll have to get stuff." Vaguely, he waved a hand in the direction of the empty bread bin. "Food and that."

"How about tonight? Quiet night in?"

He frowned. Was she serious? Then they both burst out laughing. Every single night there was something. There was nothing — *nothing* — in Dublin that Fionn didn't get invited to: movie premieres, birthday parties, car launches, hotel openings. He kept all his invitations stuck in the frame of Katie's mirror and often he stood before it to admire them. "I spent all those years in the back-arse of nowhere," he'd say. "Look at what I was missing."

"In fairness, maybe we should go easy for a night," she said. Even Fionn looked a bit pale this morning and there were lines around his eyes that she hadn't seen before.

"Tomorrow night should be quiet," he said. "What's the plan?"

"My dad's birthday. Remember?"

"I know. What time?"

"Oh! Are you coming?"

After a pause, he said, ". . . Amn't I?"

Anguish stabbed at her. They were having so much fun, the two of them, surfing through their days and nights on adrenaline and excitement. It was like being on a permanent high from some delicious happy drug that didn't have side-effects or comedowns. Nothing would reintroduce her to the rough edges of real life faster than unleashing her family on Fionn.

"Well, you know, Fionn, it might be a bit soon." It would be like throwing him to the wolves. "My family, they're quite harsh."

Dark red crept up into his face. "A bit soon? We've been together for ages."

It was only three weeks — although, admittedly, it did feel a lot longer. "My family," she said awkwardly, "were horrible to Conall."

"I'm not Conall."

She had to laugh. "Tell me about it." To wipe away his look of dejection, she said, "How about if I set something up with them for maybe next weekend?"

"Okay."

"And I'm sorry about tomorrow night."

"No bother," he said, but he still sounded a bit huffy. "It'll probably be boring anyway."

Wistfully, she said, "If only."

"Will you come out afterward?"

"It might be a bit late."

"Ah Katie." Moodily, he banged the heel of

his boot against the fridge. "I hate not being with you."

DAY 9 . . .

Dementia. There it was, in black and white and shades of grey, a digital photo of Ellen Duffy's brain, showing clearly that she had Multiple Infarct Dementia.

"So she doesn't have Alzheimer's?" Murdy asked.

"No." Buddy Scutt latched on to the one piece of good news and rolled with it.

"Actually, she might." Lydia knew everything about it from the hours she'd spent trawling the net. "Sometimes multi-infarct can co-exist with Alzheimer's. It could even trigger it."

"If she doesn't have Alzheimer's, then we're grand," Murdy said heartily.

"We're not grand! She has another kind of dementia, just as bad. And she *might* have Alzheimer's."

"So what's this multiple-infarct thing when it's at home?" Ronnie asked Buddy Scutt.

"She's had a ton of mini-strokes," Lydia said.

"She did not have a stroke," Murdy said. "We'd know about it."

"Mini-strokes, mini-strokes! They're only small — the clue is in the name — but they've damaged the flow of blood to parts of her brain."

"Is that right?" Ronnie addressed Buddy Scutt, who was sitting on the far side of his desk, looking cowed and embarrassed. As well he might, Lydia thought darkly.

Buddy cleared his throat. "Multiple-infarct dementia results from a series of small strokes, which damage the flow of blood to parts of the brain."

"Sis just said that."

"You'd better fix that so." This from Ronnie. Just because he spoke softly didn't make him any less menacing.

"We can certainly ensure that it no longer happens. We'll start her immediately on medication to thin the blood and put an end to the seizures."

"And you'll fix the damage, doc?" Ronnie was quite insistent.

"Ah, you see," Buddy Scutt twisted miserably in his chair, "the damage already caused is irreversible."

"Irreversible?" Ronnie spoke even more quietly. "Dear me, no, that won't do at all."

"Believe me, Ronald, if I could fix your mother, I would."

"Sis here came to you nearly a year ago looking for a scan and you sent her packing. A whole year of Mum having them multiple things and her brain getting more and more damaged."

571

"We'll sue the arse off you!" Murdy declared. "We'll sue you for every miserable penny you have."

"That Beemer for starters." Out in the car park Murdy was already doing a review of Buddy Scutt's assets. "And he's got no wife, so he won't be able to move his property to her name. They do that a lot, his equals, so even when good people like us get the judgment in our favor, we end up getting nothing."

"Shut up, you gobshite," Lydia said wearily. "We're not going to sue him."

"He should be struck off."

"But he won't be. They stick together, doctors and whoever are meant to strike them off. The likes of us don't stand a chance."

"We might be able to arrange a little extrajudicial punishment all the same," Ronnie said, almost as if he was talking to himself.

"You shut up too. Forget about revenge."

The brothers were so on-side now, it was almost sickening. All in the gang together: Operation Madzer Mother. Only Raymond, cushioned from the worst of things in Stuttgart, was still keeping his distance.

"What are we going to do, to take care of Mum?"

"Aaaahhhh . . ."

"What does Hathaway have to say about all this?" Ronnie asked.

"He really should get down here for a parlay," Murdy said. "So we can put a plan together. When's he back from Vietnam?"

"He still has to go to Cambodia," Lydia said shortly. Love of God! *Hathaway?* He was nothing to Mum, no one, yet this pair were behaving like he was her savior.

"Cambodia?" Murdy grinned in appreciation. "He's a cool customer."

"Why don't we try putting a plan together ourselves?" Lydia suggested sweetly. "And we can run it by Hathaway when he gets back."

"Right so."

So there it was, Lydia thought, as she drove back to Dublin, finally alone to absorb the news. She'd known something terrible was wrong with Mum. She'd long passed the point of hoping she was imagining it, but to have it made official . . .

She'd been right. And everyone else had been wrong, and, although it wouldn't make Mum better, it was nice to be right.

But the waste, the awful, shameful waste. A whole extra year of Mum being eroded from within. Poor Mum.

And poor Lydia, she suddenly thought. Her mouth opened and she found herself howling, crying like a little girl, like her heart was breaking. She took one hand off the steering wheel and put it over her mouth, trying to stifle the shocking noise of her own grief.

Tears poured down her face and blurred her vision and she kept on driving, because what else could you do?

DAY 9 . . .

The taxi nosed aggressively across the ten-lane boulevard, navigating between vans, cars, bicycles and roaring motorbikes, and fetched up in the set-down area outside the glinty, glassy hotel doors. A liveried flunky stepped up, smartly opened the car door and Conall collapsed out into the soupy humid night. He handed the taxi driver a handful of crumpled notes and was making his way gratefully toward the cool, blandly international interior, when a shouted imprecation made him turn round again. It was the taxi driver, a tiny, skinny man sweating into a nylon shirt. His expression was mean and he'd got out — out! — of the car, something taxi drivers never did, especially if a large suitcase needed to be wrestled into the trunk. He was waving the handful of notes and addressing Conall in rapid, irate foreignness. The only words Conall understood were *Vietnam, Vietnam!*

His thoughts moved too slowly in the thick air. Had he underpaid him? But he was sure he'd added a hefty tip to the sum on the meter.

The flunky stepped in and explained. "He

574

says you have paid him in Vietnamese dong."

So?

"This is not Vietnam."

It wasn't? So where was it?

Conall's mind went entirely blank. Seeking clues, he gazed around him. Behind him, there was the glass and glitz hotel tower; across the hooting, teeming boulevard, a night market thronged with short brown men; beyond that, almost out of sight, was the beginning of some wretched shanties.

God, your man was right, it wasn't Vietnam. Vietnam had been yesterday. Today it was that other place. Another hot one. He'd think of it in a second. Indonesia!

"Cambodia, sir."

"That's right, Cambodia!" He produced his wallet. He should have some Cambodian currency here. There were notes in here all right, from many different places, but . . . "What does it look like?"

"May I, sir?" Politely, the flunky took Conall's wallet. Conall noticed the look of contempt that shot between the flunky and the taxi driver: this big rich white man with too much money.

"It's been a long day," Conall said. And it had been. It had started in another country, in another time zone.

The business was transacted with the driver and Conall's wallet returned to him. "Sorry about that."

"I gave him a tip," the doorman said.

"Thanks very much and, er, give yourself one too."

"Thank you, sir. Checking in?"

They put him in a suite, a massive place with a huge sitting room, a dressing room and two bathrooms. He'd be there for five hours. He was leaving to fly to Manila at 6 a.m. The decor was generic luxury hotel — velvet-flocked wallpaper, hefty armoires and suffocatingly deep carpets. Past the elaborately swagged windows, it was blazing hot out there.

He tried to pull off his tie, but it was already long gone. Somewhere during the course of today's challenges, he'd discarded it.

The work used to begin in the car from the airport but now people met him at the gate as he emerged from the plane and briefed him as they moved along the moving walkways and waited in the queue for passport control. Before he'd even left Phnom Penh airport this morning, he had absorbed huge chunks of information on the local infrastructure, the national corporate legislation and the pros and cons of the manpower.

As usual, a team of on-site lawyers, accountants, translators, transcribers and assistants had been put at his disposal. The Phnom Penh team were well on top of things and it had looked like this was going to be a fairly tidy shut-down — until Pheakdei

Thong had brought him a piece of local legislation: generous tax breaks had been given so that the Cambodian operation would stay open for ten years. It had been on the go for less than four. If Conall shut it down the directors would be subject to criminal charges.

Grappling with tricky treacherous local issues was exactly what Conall was paid for.

Hang the directors out to dry — that was the most cost-effective thing to do. But . . .

Pheakdei Thong had waited politely as Conall disappeared into his head, playing end games with myriad configurations, following the trail as every possible permutation branched, then split, then split again, until it came down to individual human beings dotted around the globe either losing their jobs or keeping them.

If I keep the warehouses in Hanoi, but shut the factories, do a deal with the suppliers in Laos, move the transport arm from Indonesia to . . . where? Possibly the Philippines, yeah okay, the Philippines. But in that case I need a port further north. Ho Chi Minh is a port. But the U.S. trade sanctions on Vietnam . . .

Right, let's try it another way.

Keep the suppliers in Laos and — how come no one has thought of this? — manufacture *in Laos, ship across the Mekong to Thailand, source warehouses there, eat the higher costs because of cheaper labor in Laos. But hold on, isn't there a cap on trade between Thailand and Laos . . . ?*

He had tried out several more versions, wishing he could split himself in two, three, even six and nip back to the Philippines or Vietnam or Laos to clarify the local situation. Eventually, it had become clear that the solution to moving past this sticky impasse lay in the Philippines. He'd have to go back to Manila. Bollocks.

He'd stood up. "We're done here."

Pheakdei Thong had looked surprised. "What's happening?"

"Nothing. You're staying as you are." It was a sickener: all that work wasted. "Could someone book me a flight to the Philippines?"

They had been openly delighted to get rid of him. At times, you know, he'd thought wearily, it could be a little depressing being hated and feared as much as he was. He'd left them celebrating his departure and caught a taxi to his hotel — where, due to exhaustion, he'd forgotten what country he was in.

He had to eat something; he couldn't remember when he'd last had a meal. He didn't have to look at the room-service menu to know what would be on it: Caesar salad, club sandwich, mushroom pizza.

But he was too depleted to face the chat when the food came. How was your day, Mr.

Hathaway? Will I pour your coffee now, Mr. Hathaway? Will I leave it here, Mr. Hathaway?

These places always had M&Ms in their minibars, a fixed point in an uncertain world. Sure enough, there they were, his little friends. Gingerly, as if his body was stiff and bruised, Conall lowered himself until he was lying on the floor, then he tipped the entire bag of sugar-coated pearls of delight into his mouth.

When the phone rang at 6 a.m., he was still stretched out on the floor beside the minibar, a clod of half-crunched M&Ms in his open mouth.

THREE YEARS AGO

Two days after Maeve returned from her honeymoon she met David in the corridor at work. Guiltily, she braced herself for him to hang his head woefully and sidle past her with dramatic sadness, as he had done every time their paths had crossed in the previous months, but this time, to her great surprise, he advanced toward her, presenting a pleasant smile.

"Welcome back, Maeve, or should I say Mrs. Geary?" he said, cordially. "Nice honeymoon?"

"Um . . . yes . . ."

"Sorry I didn't show on the big day . . ."

"No! Please! Don't worry, I get it. Did you mind being invited? It was like if we don't invite you, you'll be pissed off; if we do invite you, you'll be pissed off."

"Yeah, I know, I know."

"David, I'm really sorry," she said, quietly.

"It's okay."

"Thanks."

"For what?"

"Forgiving me."

"Hey, I never said that." But he smiled and boulders of guilt tumbled away from her and she felt light and free. A new day had dawned in Maeve–David relations.

"I didn't mean to hurt you, David." Fiercely, she said, "You meant a lot to me. You're a good man. It was the last thing I ever wanted to do."

"I know that." Almost shamefaced, he said, "I got you guys a wedding present."

"Oh David . . ."

"But I don't want to show up here with it. I'd feel a bit . . ."

"I know! Of course."

"You could pick it up from my place."

"Sure, like, whatever suits you."

"Tonight?"

"Sure, why not?"

Actually, tonight suited her perfectly. Matt was going out for dinner with potential clients; only back from his honeymoon and straight back into the schmoozing he did so well. Out of nowhere, a little voice in her head piped up that it might be best if she didn't tell Matt about this. Obviously, he'd know after the event, with a brand-new wedding present sitting in the middle of their flat, but was there any need to tell him in advance? He might tell her she shouldn't bother, that David was in the past. But this was her chance to mend fences with David, to lessen her load of guilt. It was okay for Matt, Natalie was so arrogant that nothing could knock her faith in herself for long, but Maeve had done lasting damage to David and it was doing her head in.

DAY 8

At first, Lydia thought the flat was empty. But Andrei was sitting very quietly in the living room.

"Hello," he said, his face a polite mask. "You have been in Boyne?"

"Yeah. I borrowed your bag."

"I notice."

She squinted. Was that a snarky remark or a statement of fact?

He gazed back at her — and it was as if they'd been launched from a catapult. Suddenly, they were clawing at each other's clothes, hair, skin. Moving as one, they backed across the landing, bumped into his bedroom door, then crashed on to his bed. He handled her with purpose and, in moments, he was sliding himself inside her. No foreplay or niceties, it was fast and furious, and she wanted it fast and furious. Whatever force overtook them, it could only be acted out in a frenzy. No talking, no technique, just straight down to business.

He was like an animal. And so was she, when she was with him. It was all about instinct and feeling.

But, as soon as it was over, sanity returned. She was . . . well, she was *surprised.*

She'd thought that Conall Hathaway had cured her of Andrei. But, now that she examined the facts, she realized that she had barely seen Andrei in the last two weeks, and on the couple of occasions she had seen him, Jan was in tow. It was easy to be cured of accidentally having frantic sex with someone when you didn't see him.

"That was the last time," Lydia said. "Last time ever. I've got a boyfriend."

"You want medal? I have girlfrie—" Andrei froze. Sounds were coming from beyond the bedroom. "Jan. He is home."

Andrei sprang from the bed and began pulling clothes on over his sweaty body. "Get dressed!"

"*You* get dressed!" It was mildly insulting how much Andrei wanted to hide things from Jan, but Lydia didn't want Jan finding out either. It's not like what they were doing was illegal or anything, but the fewer people who knew, the easier it was for her to believe that it hadn't taken place at all. Mind you, it was a miracle that Jan hadn't guessed yet even if you did factor in his monumental stupidity.

He was singing to himself out there. There was a clinky noise as he dumped stuff onto

584

the kitchen table, then he went into the bathroom. As soon as the lock clicked, Andrei said urgently, "Go."

She rang Poppy, but she didn't pick up. "Pops, ring me. I'm not cured."

Then she rang Sissy, but she didn't pick up either.

She had no option but to ring Shoane, although as a moral arbiter, Shoane wouldn't be her first choice. "I've had sex with Andrei again."

"Riiiggghhhtt." She heard Shoane light a cigarette, settling in for a chat.

"He's going on his holidays to Poland at the end of next week, but I'll have to live with him till then. What if it happens again? Like, Hathaway's sort of my boyfriend now. I don't like being a two-timer." Having a series of boyfriends, grand. Having a new one three days after she'd dumped the previous one, fine. But two-timing, no. It just didn't feel right to her.

"Ah, I wouldn't worry," Shoane said. "I'm sure Hathaway gets prostitutes when he's in those hotels."

"You think?"

"Well, maybe. Like, he could. He has enough money and he'd be in those business places and, look, I'm only saying, don't worry about it."

"Well, okay. Thanks for your words of

585

comfort. I suppose."

DAY 8 . . .

Maeve and Dr. Shrigley were sitting in silence. Neither had spoken for over seven minutes.

". . . I don't know." Wearily, Maeve rubbed her face.

"Are you still being bothered by Fionn?"

"Um . . . no . . . he has a girlfriend now. Katie. She lives in the same house as me."

But it made no difference. The damage had been done. Fionn's letters and blatant gawking had started some kind of unraveling, and even though he'd lost interest in her, it wasn't enough to reverse the momentum.

"That's good," Dr. Shrigley said. ". . . Isn't it? Maeve? Are you with me?"

"Sorry. Yes."

"Are you still doing your daily Act of Kindness?"

"Yeah." She hadn't done any in ages.

Once again they eddied back down into quiet.

"You were late today," Dr. Shrigley said suddenly. This surprised Maeve. Dr. Shrigley rarely instigated any exchange. "You've been late for the last three sessions."

Maeve shrugged.

"All behavior is communication," Dr. Shrigley said. "Your lateness communicates that

586

you may no longer be committed to this process."

Relief began to steal through Maeve. It sounded like Dr. Shrigley was working her way round to sacking her. She wouldn't have to come here any longer and pretend. It would be the last part of the act to go.

DAY 8 . . .

Something had happened. Before Katie had even got her key out of her bag, her mum had wrenched open the front door. Penny was quivering with rage. "Your photograph was in the *Herald*," she hissed. "With your new boyfriend. What a thing to do to your father on his birthday."

"Oh really?" Katie was quite excited. Over the course of her career, she'd been in the paper disappointingly few times. Considering the number of launches she went to and the high-caliber celebrity of people she worked with, you'd think it would happen more often. "Was it nice?"

"No, it was not nice. You looked boss-eyed. And you're late. We're already sitting down."

Katie swung into the dining room. They were all there: Naomi and Ralph and the kids, Dad at the head of the table. Even Charlie had turned up.

"God!" Katie recoiled dramatically. "Haven't seen you since — ?" Since her birthday. Ages ago.

"Happy birthday, Dad." She slung him his present. "Right! Show us this photo."

"There are only two times in her life when a lady should appear in the press," Penny said. "On her marriage and on her death."

"Is that a real rule?" Katie asked. "Or did you just make it up?" Yet another way to make them all feel shit? "So come on. Where is it?"

"We threw it out," Penny said.

"You didn't?" Suddenly, she was quite riled. She'd be able to get a copy of it at work, but she wanted to see it now. "What did you do that for?" Mean old cow.

Penny looked speculatively at Katie. "Are you feeling all right?"

"Never better," Katie said, breezily. It was Fionn, he was her painkiller. She was scooting through life, too fast to touch the sides, and nothing could burst her bubble, not work, not a bitterly angry mother, nothing.

"And why, seeing as the entire country now knows about this romance, haven't we met this man?"

"It's just a fun, temporary thing."

"Fun?" Penny's brows furrowed in alarm. "Temporary?" She couldn't decide which was worse. "Katie, please remember that a woman's good reputation is all she has."

"I don't mean to be picky but I also have a flat, a car, a television —"

"Too small to matter," Charlie interrupted.

"— thirty-eight pairs of shoes, a Lucy Doyle painting and two hundred euros in the bank." And credit card debts that ran to thousands but no need, no need *at all,* to get into that now.

"None of them count for anything if you've got a name for yourself. And he's a gardener? A manual worker? A lot younger than you?"

They must have given Fionn's age in the paper — some age, anyway, it could have been anything.

"Katie, you're a professional woman! How much does he earn?"

"Feck all," Robert said, thinking of how much he and Penny paid their own gardener. "At least Conall Hathaway had a proper job. Instead of being a young wastrel who's only with you for your money."

"Fionn's making a television show." Although he was getting paid buttons (Grainne Butcher was shameless).

"A media whore." Penny had obviously come across the phrase only recently. "And Naomi says he lives with that old woman in your building? But he's not her son? Her grandson?"

"No. He's her foster —"

"Well, there it is, then," Robert declared. Fionn clearly made a habit of attaching himself to wealthy older women.

"And he's living there rent-free?" Charlie asked.

"We don't actually know that —"

"Just pokes the oul' wan from time to time to keep her sweet," Charlie said.

"Careful that he doesn't get you to change your will in his favor," Ralph said, his first contribution to the conversation. "And watch out for any cups of tea that taste of bitter almonds." He winked. "Arsenic poisoning."

"This is no laughing matter," Penny said. "Katie could be taken advantage of."

"Basically, you all think that Fionn seduced me for my money and I'm so old and loveless and vulnerable that I think he really loves me?"

"Seduced?" Penny said anxiously.

"Seduced."

The word hung in the air and Ralph muttered, "Christ, you've done it now."

"Mum." Katie smiled. "I have sex. I have done for many, many years. And Naomi smokes twenty cigarettes a day. And . . ." This was it, the moment she'd been waiting for, to reveal the secret that had come to her courtesy of Conall some months ago, to drop the bomb that would blow the whole respectable, rancorous family setup wide open. Could she do it? ". . . and Charlie has a little boy that none of us are supposed to know about."

DAY 7

Lydia tumbled into her room and came to an abrupt stop. It was all different. Her short, stumpy bed was draped with the Polish flag, and on her wall was a Blu-tacked poster of that Polish pope, which normally lived on the wall beside Jan's bed. Unfamiliar clothes — men's jeans and T-shirts — were hanging on her clothes rail.

"Where's my stuff?" she called.

She dashed into the other bedroom. The two single beds had been shoved together, to make a double bed with mismatched duvets. A wilted, decomposing gerbera, left over from a bouquet Conall had sent, had been flung on to it. It looked like an accusation. *A place of filth.*

"What's going on?" she yelped.

Jan appeared.

"So you find my movings?" He sounded bitter, most unlike Jan.

"You did this?"

"I am not so stupid. You are making the sex

with Andrei."

"I am *not* making the sex with Andrei."

"I know it. Do not lie."

Thinking fast, fast, fast, Lydia started talking. "Look, Jan, you're upset." Because he hero-worshipped Andrei and thought Lydia was unworthy of him. She knew there was no way Jan wanted Lydia and Andrei sharing a room; he was just making some sort of point about his feelings — maybe he felt humiliated that he'd been kept in the dark — but never mind Jan's feelings, she hadn't time for them now.

"Jan, would you listen to me? This is important. I admit it's happened a couple of times, but they were accidents."

She couldn't share a room with Andrei. The thought filled her with a horror beyond description. Trapped. Trapped. Trapped. No, no, no.

"Rosie is nice girl. Good girl."

"Jan, help me move the things back." *Quick, before Andrei gets home and decides it might actually be a good idea.*

"No. I will let you two love boats be as one."

"No, you won't. And you mean love birds."

"Oh, do I?" He gave a little shrug of defiance. "You are love birds?"

"Up! Shut! Quickly! Fast, fast, fast! Get all my stuff outtttttt!"

She'd managed to scare Jan into obedience

592

and inside fifteen minutes she was back in her own room, with her own stuff, but not feeling so good. This had got way too messy. She'd have to move out.

But no, I have plans for her. She *can't* move out.

THREE YEARS AGO

"Where's everyone?" Maeve asked, stepping into David's flat and noting the silence.

"Not home yet, I suppose. Go on in." He gestured to the sitting room. "You know where it is."

Nothing had changed — the rough woven throw on the couch, the Tibetan tapestry hanging on the wall, the Moroccan rug on the old wooden floor, the beanbags, the peasant ceramics, the lava lamp, the guitar in the corner. Stuff and dust and loose tobacco everywhere.

"Have you still the same —"

"— flatmates? No. Marta went back to Chile and Holly went traveling. Two guys from Turkey now. You might meet them later."

She wasn't planning on staying longer than an hour; but why talk about leaving when she'd only just arrived. He was so bright-eyed and happy to see her.

"Drink?" he asked.

"Okay. Tea, thanks."

"No, no. No. A *drink* drink. Not every day my ex-girlfriend gets married. Beer."

He produced two Dos Equis and clambered beside her onto the couch. "To old friends." He clinked bottles.

"Old friends," she repeated.

They drank in silence. "Good honeymoon?" he asked.

"Amazing!" Immediately, she wished she hadn't been so enthused.

"Malaysia, I hear. Tell me."

"Well —"

"An obvious military police presence?" David prompted.

"I didn't see any sign of it," Maeve said truthfully.

"Didn't you?" He sounded surprised. Disappointed, actually. She realized he'd have loved a story about fascisty storm troopers beating the tar out of local Hindus for some small show of faith, like letting a cow cross the road. She was sorry she couldn't oblige.

He changed his tack. "So Islam's in the driving seat?"

"God, I dunno, David. I'm not sure. Some of the women were veiled, some weren't."

"Interesting." Thoughtfully, he drummed his fingers on his chin. "It'll come back to bite them, but for the moment Malaysia's doing a canny job of walking that line."

She knew what line he was talking about, the one between American cultural imperialism and fundamentalist Islam. She cared about world politics too, but suddenly she understood that David had no interest in positive interpretations; it was like he wanted everything to be as bad as it could possibly be.

"I've missed you, Maeve." He reached out his hand and began to twirl his fingers in the curls at her neck. She sat very still. This felt wrong, but she'd been so cruel she couldn't add to the hurt by asking him to stop.

"I hope that we can be friends, David."

"Like the old days?"

"Like the old days, exactly! And when you get to know Matt properly, you'll love him —"

With an unexpected move, David was right in front of her and, to her shock, she realized he was about to kiss her. Quickly, she turned her head so that his mouth landed on her ear. "David, sorry, you know we can't do this."

He nuzzled at her neck and she said, "Sorry, David — look, I think I'd better go."

"But you haven't seen your wedding present."

She stood up. "Don't worry about it. Give it to me some other time. Sorry, but I'm going to go."

"There's nothing to be scared of." He seemed surprised and wounded. "After what you did to me, I just want to give you a wedding present."

"I know, it's just —"

"Come on, come and see it."

"Why? Where is it?"

"In there." He pointed toward his bedroom.

"Oh . . . no, David," she said haltingly. "Just bring it out here."

"I can't, it's too big. Just come in."

"Sorry, David, I don't feel right . . ."

He sighed heavily. "Have you any idea how this is making me feel?" He looked at her with injured eyes. "I'm not going to hurt you. Come on, it's cool, you'll love it."

"Okay." This was David, *David*.

As he opened the bedroom door, he said, "Close your eyes."

She felt the weight and heat of his hands on her shoulders, guiding her forward.

"Such a big deal." She laughed. "This'd better be worth it."

DAY 6

Rosie had her eyes tightly shut. She heard the whizzy sound of jeans being taken off, then the rustle of cotton (that must be his shirt going). She lay, naked and rigid, wondering what would happen next, and when Andrei's cold hand landed on her stomach, she jumped.

"Is okay," he crooned. "All okay, beautiful Rosie."

He was kissing her, her face, her mouth, her throat. Somewhere out there was his . . . *thing.* Hard and swollen. She knew what an erection was like; she'd done six months on the geriatric ward, where dementia-riddled men playing with themselves were ten a penny.

Andrei was going to stick his thing into her and it would hurt and he'd grunt and shout and sweat and swear and then it would be over and she'd still have a boyfriend.

She had always feared her life would come to this, ever since the age of six, when she'd watched *Grease* and seen that Olivia Newton-John had to become a bad girl to keep her man.

You better shape up . . .

Being virtuous and ladylike didn't seem to be keeping a hold of Andrei, so she was gambling her virginity and going for broke.

Her eyes still closed, she could feel Andrei *at* himself. Probably putting on the condom.

It's six days too soon but could I jump the gun here? It's the best chance I've had so far. Never mind the condom, that could be dealt with, no bother. I could tear it or burst it or, even before it's properly on, a couple of brave little sperms could leak, all you need is one, after all. But, *entre nous* and forgive me for being picky, I don't really like Rosie. Andrei's grand, a bit intense, God love him, but a decent man at heart. I wouldn't mind him. But not her.

Rosie screwed her eyes up tighter. In a moment, Andrei would clamber on top of her and he'd plunge it right in. Her entire body tensed at the thought. It would be awful, but worth it and . . . What was taking him so long? She was starting to get chilly. "What's happening?"

"I don't know," Andrei said. Something was wrong. He sounded ashamed.

She opened her eyes. "What?"

"I don't know . . ."

She sat up, leaned on her elbows and looked down. Where was the big purple battering ram? What was that shy, floppy, pink-and-white marshmallow thing?

Andrei turned and buried his face in his pillow. "I'm sorry, my Rosie." His voice was muffled but there was no mistaking his anguish.

Rosie went cold with horror. She'd called this all wrong. This was the worst possible thing she could have done, showing up at Andrei's flat and undressing herself and lying on his bed like a haddock on a slab. He wasn't that sort of man.

"I understand," she said, trying to radiate calm and retrieve what she could. With men, you must never show fear. Not real fear. *Fake* fear, obviously, when it was called for, to make them feel like the big man. But at a time like this you must take control. "You have too much respect for me."

Pertly, she hopped off the bed and began to dress herself. Andrei's face was still plunged into his pillow.

"I'll pop the kettle on," she said brightly. "And see you out in the sitting room."

DAY 6 . . .

Conall tumbled on to the wide hotel bed and eased his shoes off. Better book an alarm call before he fell asleep. He could set his phone but he didn't know what time it was here in Manila. At least he knew where he was. Then he had such a terrible thought that he groaned out loud: he'd forgotten to buy a new shirt and underwear today. It was over two weeks since he'd started crisscrossing Southeast Asia and his carry-on case barely held the basics. He'd run out of clean clothes forever ago, but he wasn't in any place long enough to get his laundry done so since Jakarta he'd been buying and discarding as he went.

He'd have to ring the concierge. He'd have to make nice. Christ.

"Concierge desk. How may I help you, Mr. Hathaway?"

"I have a special request."

"Certainly, sir!"

Your man was thinking, *Girls!* Conall realized. He didn't want a girl. He had a lovely girlfriend at home. A vague impression of bosoms and feminine fragrance comforted him. Katie. No, not Katie. A new one now. Lydia, yes, his hard shiny little diamond.

"I need a couple of shirts and some underwear."

"Certainly, sir. Anything else, sir?"

"Well, actually . . ." Bronagh had sent an email reminding him of her birthday.

As you are my uncle, my godfather and the

only millionaire in the family, I'd like a good present.

"Could you get a birthday present for a little girl?"

"What age?"

"Seven." Or was it eight? One of those ones.

He woke with a terrible start. Where was he? A hotel room . . . could be any one of millions. Someone was knocking, that was what had woken him. Smacking his tongue against the roof of his mouth, trying to scare away the appalling dryness, he opened the door. It was a helpful young lad bearing Conall's new shirts and jocks and a pair of sapphire earrings for Bronagh. Conall pawed around in his pocket and found currency of some description, with which he despatched the youth.

He looked at the clock. Nearly 5 a.m. Might as well make phone calls now that he was awake and it was some sort of time in Ireland.

"Happy birthday, Bronagh!"

Bronagh sighed elaborately. "Conall. A day late and a dollar short. As usual. My birthday was yesterday."

"I'm in Asia. Today is tomorrow."

"Then you're two days late."

Christ, she was right.

"I'm eight years of age. You're my uncle and my godfather. I reminded you, I made it

602

easy for you, and still you disappoint me."

Holy Christ. This was way too reminiscent of too many other phone calls.

"Better go now, hon. See you when I'm back."

Quickly, he rang Lydia.

"Hathaway?" she said briskly. "Are you home?"

"In Manila."

"Again?"

"Yeah, I had to come back. A problem arose with the Cambodian —"

"Lalalalala. I can't hear you. Oooou-uuuuuh!" She ceased wailing and asked cautiously, "Is it safe? Have you stopped?"

"Yeah." She'd told him not to talk to her about his work, that it was too boring. He could describe his hotel room to her, though, any time he felt like. Or the breakfast buffets, especially the hot plates where they made the pancakes.

"When are you coming home?"

"Some time next week."

"You said it would be this weekend."

"Like I said, things changed. The situa—"

"Whateves."

DAY 6 . . .

Andrei was plunged into the long dark night of the soul. His manhood had failed him. It was the first time he'd been the victim of such

603

a humiliation. Normally, he was supremely sexually confident.

And there was more bad news in store.

When Jan came home from work, he announced that he had been made redundant and was returning to Poland. For good.

"There are no more jobs here. And I want to go home. So does Magdalena."

Andrei was deeply shocked. Jan was his buddy, practically his brother. They'd arrived in Ireland on the same flight, and they'd shared everything from a bedroom to confidences to beers over the past two years.

And if Jan went, he'd be left alone with the pixie, just the two of them.

"Wait until after our visit home," Andrei said, in some desperation. In less than a week they were both going to Gdansk for their summer holidays. "You're homesick — so am I! But time with your family and friends will give you strength to get a new job and endure this Ireland for another year."

Jan shook his head. "No new job. When we go on Friday, I'm not coming back."

Jan wasn't the brightest, but once his mind was made up, it stayed made. Nothing could talk him out of a decision. Uncomfortably, Andrei wondered if he had guessed about himself and the evil pixie. Jan had a keen sense of right and wrong, keener even than Andrei's, and those sorts of high jinks would distress him terribly.

The thought of living in Ireland without Jan made him very sad, almost frightened. And the way he had disgraced himself with Rosie . . . surely she wouldn't bother with him again?

Perhaps he'd just stay in Poland with Jan.

No, Andrei, no!

DAY 5 (EARLY HOURS OF)

Andrei turned his pillow over again. For a few blessed moments, the cool cotton gave relief to his fevered face, then it wore off. He'd never known a night so long. Something must have gone wrong with time; it felt like it had been Sunday night for about a week. Was daylight ever going to come? He shifted and thrashed, unable to find escape from his tormenting thoughts. This was the issue: he had no idea if his marshmallow-textured failure was an isolated incident or if he was doomed for it to recur. He was so frightened of discovering the situation was ongoing that he wasn't sure he could chance having sex ever again.

Not that Rosie was likely to insist on any such thing — even if he could win her back, she was evidently repulsed by the sexual act . . . What a virtuous little flower she was. Such modesty was rare, yet she had offered herself up to him like a sacrifice on an altar. All of a sudden he was so humbled by how a good woman had gone bad in the name of love, that he wept into his overheated pillow.

Oh! If only daylight would come.

But as the sun began to rise, Andrei's shame at failing to consummate the deed with Rosie began to soften and blossom into a new and unexpected emotion: gratitude. Of course he couldn't have committed such an abomination on his little petal! Not until they were married.

Or engaged, at any rate.

As pearly, early morning light began to slip under his curtains, hope, beautiful hope, lifted him, and a course of action revealed itself, a daring but clear imperative. There could be no more Lydia. He needed to put himself beyond her reach forever. As this vision became a convincing possibility, his load became light, almost airborne. Quietly, in order to not wake Jan, he extracted a roll of banknotes from a sock on the floor of the wardrobe. He showered, dressed and drank two cups of coffee, and he was actually in the hall, almost gone, almost safe, when the rattle of a key in the lock made his heart plunge. Lydia was home from work. The door pushed open and she landed into the hall. She looked at him, he looked at her and a whiplash of sex crackled around them.

"No," he called, in terrible anguish. He threw himself at the open doorway. He had to escape, before she lured him in and ruined all his plans. He plunged headlong down the stairs, down, down, down; then he was in the street, walking fast until he was well beyond her reach.

He moved with purpose. He knew exactly where he was going: a small jeweler's on South Anne Street. He and Rosie had looked in the window one night, pointing out rings they liked, like people in a 1960s soap opera.

He had a certain amount of time to kill — the shop didn't open until 9 a.m. and it was now only 6:35 — but he remained clear-headed and focused, and by the time the jeweler rolled up the metal door guard and permitted him ingress, he was more sure than ever of the rightness of his path.

Andrei knew precisely which ring Rosie wanted. But he couldn't afford that. So he bought another one, the second cheapest in the shop. It was a simple band with a single diamond: sweet and humble, like Rosie herself. Then he made his way to her house where he rang the bell and got down on one knee.

In answer to his prayers, it was Rosie and not one of her housemates who answered the door.

"Rosie," he said, blind to the relief that rolled behind her eyes as he proffered the small velvet box. "Will you marry me?"

DAY 5 . . .

"You're not going to believe it." Fionn stalked into Katie's flat and threw a fax on to the kitchen table. "Look at that."

Katie smoothed out the crumpled page and gleaned the salient facts. Curses! Network 8 had put Fionn's show back by four weeks. They'd just managed to buy the rights to *DOA,* a hot U.S. crime show, and had decided to run that in the slot they'd earmarked for *Your Own Private Eden.*

"They offered Grainne Monday night instead, but she said that Monday night gets the worst viewing figures of the week. So they came back with Sunday night at nine, but we've got to wait until *Around Ireland in a Roasting Tin* finishes up and they'll put me in there instead."

"Oh poor Fionn."

"There's heat around me," Fionn said, obviously quoting Grainne. "I'm on fire right now. But we've to wait another four weeks. And then it might be too late."

Katie couldn't think of a thing to say. The media did inexplicable things *all the time.* She'd been burned on occasions far too numerous to count. How many times had she given an exclusive interview to a paper to publicize an Irish concert, only for the piece to disappear, then reappear long after the concert had happened and the artist had departed? She was used to it, but Fionn was an innocent newbie. His disillusionment was going to be painful.

Once a network began messing with transmission dates, it was usually an indication of a lack of confidence and a reshuffling of their priorities. Even if they still had complete faith in the show, the trajectory of success was interfered with; something was lost that could never be retrieved.

"Put on your happy face," Katie coaxed. "We're due at the Merrion in forty-five minutes, to bask in Bob Geldof's gorgeousness."

"I don't want to go."

"Oh, Fionn . . ."

"I feel like everyone will be laughing at me. I'm the television gardener without a show."

"You do have one."

But until it started running, he didn't, actually.

"And what am I meant to do? We finish filming on Friday."

Katie understood exactly what he meant: until the show aired, Excellent Little Productions had no idea whether or not it would be recommissioned. Should Fionn hang around and see what happened? Or should he go back, even temporarily, to Pokey, to hold on to his customers? Katie's stomach lurched as she realized that uncertain times loomed. For Fionn's bank account. For Fionn's ego.

Perhaps for Fionn's romance?

DAY 5 . . .

Matt's mobile beeped. A text.

Ure a prik.

It was from Russ. Matt still hadn't sent the check reimbursing Russ for the flight to Vegas he'd booked for him. He'd sworn black was white that Russ would get it today, but Matt couldn't do it. Maeve would notice the money gone from their account and it would blow the whole thing sky-high because what it came down to was that Matt couldn't go to Vegas for his brother's stag party. It was out of the question. To be gone a whole week? Maeve couldn't stay in the flat on her own and there was no Plan B. All their friends were gone. The only people left were her mum and dad and they were in Galway, too far away.

Matt felt shit about Russ, shit about leaving him in the lurch financially, shit about all the times he'd let him down, shit about the one time he'd actually managed to meet him to discuss what they should set up in Vegas for Alex, because he'd suggested nothing.

In a month's time, the day that they were all supposed to be getting on the plane would roll around and Matt had absolutely no idea what he would do.

But before he had to face that, there was even worse: the work stuff. The day of his first appointment with a bank in Shanghai was hurtling toward him like a rock from outer space and he couldn't get out of its path.

He was trapped in the most terrible position, with no space to maneuver. It made him think about a prisoner of war in one of those *Boy's Own* books he used to read in the old days: the man's legs had been broken and he'd been put into a cage in which he could neither stand up nor sit down. Matt felt as though, no matter which way he went, he was screwed.

Life was getting dark around the edges. It was like he was moving through a tunnel that was becoming narrower and blacker and more choked and airless, and soon there would be nothing left for him to breathe and no room for him to move.

DAY 5 . . .

Lydia's phone rang. It was Conall.

"Hathaway? Where now?"

"Jakarta."

"Remind me again."

"Capital of Indonesia. Look, I don't know how to tell you this, Lids, I am so, so sorry —"

"You slept with a hooker?"

612

"No."

"You've given me chlamydia?"

"I'm not going to make it back in time for Poppy's wedding on Wednesday. I swear I'll make it up to you."

"Settle the head, Hathaway. You're the one who wanted to go."

DAY 4

"Dzien dobry, Andrei." Jemima liked to greet those poor Polish boys in their native tongue. A small pleasantry that cost her nothing and might put a gloss on their day.

"Dzien dobry, Jemima. *Dzien dobry,* dog." Andrei dropped to his knees and began wrestling happily with Grudge.

"My dear, you seem positively joyous." *For once.*

"I'm gettingk married."

"Congratulations! The lovely Rosemary?"

Andrei nodded and reddened with evident pride. "We are looking for own place."

Is that a fact?

Jemima said, with interest, "I may be able to help you there. Shortly, my flat will be coming free."

"You are movingk out? When?"

"In a week or so, I would imagine."

"Good timingk. We are all going to Gdansk

614

on Friday, Jan, Rosie and I. When we come back, Rosie and I, we could move in then."

"You're bringing Rosie to meet your family? How delightful. Now, you'll like the flat, but there is a condition attached."

Well, Andrei thought sadly, wasn't there always?

"You must take care of my dog."

"That's condition? That's all? You cannot take dog to new place?"

"Regrettably, no."

"And your Fionn man? He will be moving out also?"

Yes, he just hadn't realized it yet.

"Fionn and Grudge don't see eye to eye, I'm afraid. Fionn is a grown man. All things considered, it's clear that Fionn will also be moving on."

"I like this dog." Andrei beamed. "Rosie too will like. She likes everyone."

"Just one thing. You're quite sure you and Rosemary wouldn't like a fresh start in an entirely new location? Far away from Star Street?"

Jemima lifted her chin and maintained steady eye contact with Andrei. Oh yes, she had heard himself and Lydia "at it." Many's the time. She might be hard of hearing but not even the stone deaf could have missed their enthusiastic yelping and groaning.

Not that she was passing judgment. That was not the way of the good-living person. But she would like to be sure that Andrei knew exactly what he was doing. She watched as countless emotions flickered across his face, a cocktail of shame, self-examination, absolution, fortitude and, finally, something approaching happiness.

"Thank you for concern," Andrei said, also lifting his chin and matching Jemima's steady eye contact with some fairly impressive eye contact of his own. "But Star Street is good. Handy for Luas. When we have babies, we will need bigger place, but for moment is good. How long will lease be? Six months? A year?"

"For as long as you like, my dear."

DAY 4 . . .

The Poles were going! They were going — and *not coming back!*

They were off on their summer holidays on Friday, which was excellent enough in itself. But big changes were afoot. Jan was returning to live in Poland and — in a shock move — Andrei had got engaged to Rosie, the last virgin in Ireland, and they were moving in together.

Jan related all of this to Lydia with no small amount of smug triumph. "Good girl wins," he said.

"If Andrei's the prize, you can keep it."

"We will pay you two months' rent," Jan said, which even she couldn't find fault with. "Lease is yours if you want."

She might keep it on, she thought, the location wasn't bad. But she might move somewhere else. She didn't have to live in her cupboard any longer because everything had changed. The catastrophe with her mum was still real but, with Murdy and Ronnie on side, she was no longer carrying the burden alone. And now that she wasn't so afraid, she saw how laughable her money-saving efforts had been. She could never have afforded to pay for a home for Mum, not even if she'd lived under a bridge.

And here came Andrei.

"The groom-to-be," she said. "I hear congratulations are in order."

He looked a little shy but undeniably proud.

"You went down on one knee, I believe?" she said. "The last of the great romantics."

They eyed each other with mutual dislike and there was a pinprick of time when a lunge was possible. Everything froze, the universe hovered on a knife-edge, not a breath was taken . . . then they both turned away.

Now that it's all calmed down, their individual heartbeats have separated out, and mother of

God, what a disaster. They're so mismatched, it's like they're talking two different languages.

DAY 3

"Katie? Katie!" She barely recognized Fionn's voice, he sounded so distraught. "My identity has been stolen."

"Fionn, where are you?" This must be something to do with his credit card being declined, she'd already decided. He'd probably forgotten to pay the bill.

"I'm at work. There's another one of me."

"Spending your money?"

"No! Have you seen today's *Irish Times*?"

Katie looked around. They got all the papers in the office. "Danno. Bring us the *Times*."

"Page sixteen," Fionn said.

Katie leafed through the pages and . . . *Curses.*

The headline shouted, GARDENING? THE NEW ROCK'N'ROLL? It was accompanied by a quarter-page photo of a tousle-haired, unshaven sex god, smiling a big dirty smile and rubbing a courgette with his big dirty hands. *But that man was not Fionn.*

Instead, it was one Barry Ragdale, the star of *Diggin' It,* a new gardening program on RTE, which would commence its run in two weeks' time. The gimmick was that Barry had once been a bass-player in a band and would play out the closing credits every week.

At once, Katie saw the worst-case implications. For Fionn. And for her.

"Is that why Channel 8 moved me?" Fionn asked.

It could be. They'd probably got wind of RTE's show and either they hadn't had the nerve to go head-to-head with the state broadcaster, or they were watching to see how it played out. If it was a disaster, they wouldn't bother running their version; if it was a flyer, they could coattail on Barry Ragdale's success.

"I'll tell you something, Katie," Fionn's voice was trembling, "I'm sorry I ever got involved in this whole lousy caper. I was happy in Pokey. Now, I'm jealous and insecure and I hate everyone."

Katie forced steadiness into her voice. "Fionn, listen to me. There are always going to be other artistes, other people in competition with you. It's a fact of life and even more so in something as cutthroat as television. You've got to play the long game. Wait and see. This Barry Ragdale could crash and burn spectacularly and you'll be ready to step into his place."

"Really?"

"Oh yes." She was good at this. After all, it was her job, calming down artists. Not so good at calming herself down, sadly. "And Channel 8 haven't pulled *Your Own Private Eden.* It's still full steam ahead for Sunday three weeks, right?" *That's not to say they won't pull it, but why dwell on the negative?*

"But what if they do pull it? Then it's all over for me here and I'll have to go right back to Pokey."

"Fionn, you're jumping several guns. Look at it this way: it's actually a compliment, another good-looking gardener getting his own show. It shows you're tapping into the zeitgeist."

"Oh, right, I hadn't thought of that."

"It's all good." *Well, who knew whether it was or it wasn't?*

"You're right, Katie, it *is* all good, especially because if I hadn't come to Dublin I would never have met you."

DAY 2

At first, it seemed like Matt was simply looking for an alternative route home. After twenty-three and a half frustrating minutes, inching along in traffic that was a smidgen speedier than a total standstill, he abruptly pulled a U-ee and sped off in the opposite direction. Any minute now, he'd do a sharp right turn, then another one and once again he'd be heading toward home. But he didn't. He put further and further distance between himself and Star Street, and before long he was driving by the river, making for the docklands. He pulled in off the quay, zigzagging through streets that became narrower and narrower, and soon enough he was bumping over cobbles.

He threw the car into the first space he saw, unconcerned that he was on a double yellow — boot the car, do what you like, he didn't care — and took up his lookout post outside No Brainer Technology.

Thirty-seven minutes elapsed before the

lanky, unkempt, poetic-type bloke appeared, rushing down the steps, his jeans almost falling off him, his hair tumbling into his eyes, his brown tweedy jacket looking as if it had been recently excavated from a bog where it had slumbered undisturbed for the last 123 years. He was hurrying after a tall, slender girl with an attractive gap between her front teeth. "Wait!" he called, placing a hand on her shoulder, halting her progress. "Steffie, wait!"

Like a dam had been opened, rage roared through Matt.

But wait a minute, I recognize the poet-bloke from Maeve's memory pools! He's —

"David!"

Yes, David. Maeve's old boyfriend, from before Matt. It's only now that Maeve is letting me in fully and I can get to know all the details of her past.

"David!" The gap-toothed girl's voice floated over to Matt. "You scared the life out of me!"

David said something that Matt couldn't hear, then he flung his arm around the girl's waist, gathered her close and snogged her energetically.

So now he had a girlfriend, Matt thought. She looked like a lovely girl and they seemed

623

happy. And the gas thing was that he could go over there right now — seven or eight strides would do it — and in a few choice sentences screw it all up for them. He could tell the lovely girl a thing or two about David that would have her hightailing it in the opposite direction.

He braced himself to move, he clenched his feet and calves to propel himself like a grenade into their lives — *go now, go now* — and then it was happening. He was walking with purpose and David, with the instinct of an animal sensing danger, saw him. He flickered with something — fear, Matt hoped — but Matt ignored him and focused all his attention on the girl. "I need to talk to you."

She shrank away and he realized his intensity was frightening her. "Look, sorry — Steffi, is it?" She nodded fearfully and he swallowed hard, as if that would stem the despair. "My name is Matt Geary."

"Maeve's husband?" Steffi said.

This was the last thing Matt had been expecting. Incredulously, he asked, "You know about me?"

"David told me."

Matt turned to look at David, who was smirking smugly, then he looked back at Steffi. "But he didn't tell you the truth."

"I did tell her the truth."

Matt ignored him. "Listen, Steffi, please listen —"

"Hey," David said. "You can't simply rock up here and start — There are laws against that sort of thing."

Laws. *Laws.* That was what did it for Matt. Suddenly, it all left him, every bit of impetus just drained to nothing, leaving him emptier than he'd thought a human being could be.

He limped away, as if he'd been physically injured. At his departing back, David yelled, "Get a grip on yourself. Get yourself some self-respect, man — and get fucking *over* it."

DAY 2 . . .

Conall gazed out of the plane window, blind to the housing estates of Dublin circling below him. He'd finally identified the uncomfortable sensation that had been clawing at his gut for the past ten days.

He should have let the Cambodian arm go. It was wildly inefficient, riddled with corruption and cursed with atrocious local infrastructure.

That one mistake had pinballed off myriad other situations and each of them had unleashed a chain of events, fanning out like falling dominoes, and what Conall had ultimately achieved was a bodge job.

He was famed throughout his industry for his slick, surgical work. When he chopped up a company, then put it together again, the scars disappeared fast, and very quickly the taut new version began to seem like the only possible one. No one would have believed that the old, saggy, bloated configuration had ever existed, never mind functioned.

But this time was different. What kept rising to the surface of his mind was that this scaled-down company would never entirely convince. He felt like a plastic surgeon who'd done a breast reduction and forgotten to sew the nipples back on.

He'd let the personal get in the way of the practical. He hadn't wanted those Cambodian directors to get thrown in chokey, and that reservation had hobbled the fluid, blue-sky thinking that was his talent. He'd eventually come up with a solution but, now that the job was done and dusted and he was almost home, he was hit with a bout of painful perspective.

He'd . . . he tried out the word; it was a new one for him . . . well, he'd *failed.*

Failed. No one else had guessed, his paymasters in Milan seemed happy enough, but Conall himself knew. And word would get out eventually. Conall Hathaway's lost it. Too old. Burned out. No longer reliable.

His innards clenched. Failing felt as bad as he'd always feared it might, but he had lived his life with the knowledge that, sooner or later, his judgment would let him down. It was something he'd spent his career on the run from. He'd taken on job after job, needing to stack up triumphs so that when his luck finally ran out, his average success rate would still be stratospheric. Now that failure had happened once, he knew it would happen again. Like when a plane commences a descent, you know the pressure has changed even before the pilot tells you. His unbroken chain of successes had been interfered with, and he had an irrational, superstitious conviction that the direction of his life had been altered and that he had to go where the new path took him.

Adapt! Adapt, adapt! That's what he needed to do: adapt to survive. And another chunk of awareness floated to the surface. He needed — wanted — someone to help him at work. Only now that this job was over and he was almost home, was it was safe to admit just how hard he'd found it. All those flights, those time-zone changes, the lack of sleep, the information overload . . . Too many times in the last three weeks he'd been seized with the ice-cold conviction that he simply wasn't able for it. Admittedly, he found every take-over frightening, it's what had made him so good — that level of fear had produced lots of adrenaline — but this had been different. It was madness to have attempted it on his own. An operation as big as that needed several Conalls.

A deputy. There, he'd said the unsayable: he needed a deputy. Someone to share the workload, to bounce ideas off, to assume some of the responsibility. He realized he even had a few candidates in mind, people younger than him, possibly even more cutthroat than he'd been at his prime, and already he was wondering which one he'd choose. But who said he had to have just one deputy? He could have two, even a team, a whole group of outside-the-box thinkers. Together they'd be terrifying.

But the more effective they were, the more it meant that Conall Hathaway, lone troubleshooter, was no more. That person was gone. Whatever the future brought, and it could be all good, it still meant that he was a failure.

What was it going to be like, he wondered idly. Being a failure? To get his adrenaline fix, was he going to have to start mountainclimbing or doing extreme sports, like a Southern Hemisphere person? God, no. He had a vision of himself and Jesse having underwater breath-holding competitions in Float — then he remembered Lydia. Thank Christ. She was extreme enough for anyone.

Finally, the plane was on the ground. Conall unfastened his seat belt and switched on his phone before he was told he could — he might have forgotten to sew the nipples back on but he would never obey their petty rules.

He stood up and stretched elaborately, almost hoping that the steward would berate him, then hit Lydia's number.

"Hathaway?"

"I'm home. My bed, forty-five minutes."

"If you want me, come and get me. I've been driving all day."

Entre nous, I'm delighted he's back in the country especially if, as seems to be the case, Andrei is off. I have plans for Hathaway. Oh yes, big plans.

DAY 2 . . .

She could actually run in them. Four and a half inches — although she would admit they had a half-inch platform, which made the descent less steep, but four inches was still very high — and she wasn't just walking fast, she was actually running. Not every woman could do that, especially not every woman over forty, and it was a handy skill to have because right now she was very late. She'd managed to talk Fionn out of his gloom so she was on her way home to get changed into a cocktail dress, then she had to race across town to meet him for a knees-up at the U.S. embassy. They were still going to every party they were invited to because she was defiantly refusing to think about the future and was determined to keep enjoying herself, right up until the last minute, whenever that would be. But all this socializing was time-consuming, and she was already late when

629

she left work, then she'd stopped off to buy milk and other basics and she'd got lured into a drugstore. She'd actually needed iron supplements (she couldn't sustain this pace for much longer without *something*), but she'd got sidetracked in the nail-care aisle and went into a trance. God, they had good stuff there, *excellent* stuff: a new brand of topcoat and emery boards patterned with Marimekko designs . . . She'd lost a lot of time but at least she was finally home and —

"Conall!" Oh my God. It was Conall. Hathaway. Standing outside the front door of 66 Star Street, looking huge. She hadn't seen him in ages.

He seemed just as shocked to see her. "Katie?"

"Conall."

"You look fantastic."

"You look . . . wrecked." His suit was rumpled and his hair was all over the place.

"Just off a plane from the Philippines."

"Nothing changes." She pointed her key at the lock. "Can I . . . Do you want me to let you in?"

"I'm waiting for . . . Ah —"

"Lydia?"

"Yeah, she's on her way down."

She's your —" Katie proceeded with caution, like she was crossing a broken old bridge with rotten slats that could snap beneath her without warning. "She's your girlfriend?"

"Um, yeah."

There, Katie thought. The words were said and she was fine. She hadn't plunged into a terrible abyss; in fact, she'd felt nothing. Fionn, what a fabulous painkiller he was. Better than anything on the market. He should license himself; he'd make a fortune.

"And," Conall said, "I hear you and — Fionn, is it? — are an item?"

"We are. Anyway, gotta go. I'm late."

"And it's going well with him?"

God, Conall — so competitive, always. What did he expect her to say? No one could ever be as good as you, Conall? Because they could. Fionn was. She contented herself with an enigmatic shrug and went on her way.

DAY 2 . . .

Slippers, shower caps, soaps, night-time chocolates, pens — a cornucopia of beautiful things all lifted from Conall's hotel rooms.

"Hathaway, this is good gear."

"Any time." Deftly, he unclipped Lydia's bra. He'd done a fine job of almost entirely undressing her while her attention was focused on her goody box.

"Oh!" She gasped with delight: Molton Brown shower gels. Far better than the own-brand shite he'd included.

Conall laughed and gently bit first her right nipple, then her left. "You love it, don't you?

631

The pleasuring?"

"Mmmm." He'd thought her gasp was sexual, she realized. She'd better focus. She had a naked Conall Hathaway before her, with a frisky-looking erection keen for action. The free shower gels could wait.

"That's what Katie used to call it," he said, lowering her to the bed.

Lydia froze. "Katie called what what?"

"Pleasuring. It was her word."

Lydia rolled away and sat up. "Don't ever mention Katie again. You mope."

". . . Oh . . ."

"*I* don't care. But when I kick you into touch, you'll never keep another girl. Mind you, the saps you've had in the past, maybe they put up with it because you've a house in Wellington Road. But if you want me to stick around —"

"Right . . . sorry."

"Have you forgotten that I told you Katie and Goldilocks are an item?"

"No."

"They're mad about each other. At it nonstop. Having baths in the middle of the night and chasing each other round the house and screeching and keeping hardworking people like me from their night's sleep."

Day 1

"What time will you be home?" Maeve asked.

"Could be quite late," Matt said.

"Oh Matt."

"You know what it's like." He smiled apologetically. "Potential clients, private room, tasting menu, expensive wine. These things drag on."

"Friday night's a funny one for that sort of do."

"Only night we could all manage. But you'll be grand. You've got Shrigley, right?"

"Mmm. And there's a leaving do at work." She didn't know why she'd said that. It wasn't as if she'd go.

"You could go to it after Shrigley. Then you wouldn't be on your own here for so long."

Maeve paused, a spoonful of porridge halfway to her mouth. Matt didn't usually try to persuade her to go out with her work colleagues.

"Why not? Try it for an hour," Matt said. "Might be good for you. If it gets too much, you can always leave."

Maeve looked at him doubtfully.

"Half an hour, maybe," he said. "You never know, you might find you're enjoying yourself."

"But Matt . . . even normal people don't enjoy leaving parties."

"Maeve, look." She saw desperation in his expression. "We've got to keep trying."

She dropped her eyes. No, no more trying. He was on his own with that particular mission.

"Maeve?"

She had to say something. "What restaurant are you going to?"

". . . Ah . . . Magnolia."

"I thought that had closed down."

". . . Ah . . . no, it hasn't."

Matt snapped two antidepressants out of their foil package and rolled one across the table to Maeve. "Like I say, I'll be late, so take your time."

Maeve threw the pill into her mouth and chased it with a gulp of water. She passed the glass to Matt. "I'll just brush my teeth and we'll get going."

She left the room. Matt tensed and listened hard to the sound of a tap running in the bathroom. When the buzzing sound of an electric toothbrush reached him, he threw himself on her satchel, rummaged urgently through it, produced a bunch of keys, clattered them into the cupboard under the sink, dumped the satchel down on to the floor and shoved himself back in front of the breakfast counter.

I've just noticed that something's wrong, something's terribly wrong. Matt and Maeve, well, their shared heartbeat . . . I can't feel it any more. It's gone and I realize it's actually been dead for a while, for a long while. What I was feeling wasn't the real thing, but something like a recorded message, an echo from the past. Like the light that reaches us from a long-dead star.

DAY 1 . . .

Lydia threw herself onto the floor, flat on to her stomach, to check there was nothing left under either of the beds. She wanted every last microfiber of the lads out of here. A couple of dust balls were rolling around, but other than that, nothing. The packing had been thorough; the last few days had been a frenzy of activity.

"Jan, don't forget your poster of the pope." She hopped up to unpeel it from the wall.

"You can have," Jan said. "It might help you."

"Me?" She couldn't stop grinning. "I'm beyond redemption."

"That looks like it." Andrei did a last sweep

635

of their bedroom.

"If you've forgotten anything, you can pick it up when you come back."

She hadn't cared even when she'd discovered that Andrei's new billet was just one floor away. He was an engaged man now and that operated like a repellent force field for her. That messy business was all in the past, a baffling little dabble, over for good.

She was so cheerful about getting rid of them that she'd helped carry the last of their boxes down to the van.

"Goodbye. Goodbye." Now that they were leaving, she felt almost sentimental. "Safe journey, all that."

As she watched the van disappear up the street, her phone rang. "Hathaway?"

"Tonight?"

"Cleaning. I'm moving into my lovely new big room. Sissy's calling over when she's finished work to help me kick over the traces. You can come too, seeing as you were such a dab hand at the cleaning down in Mum's. Not."

"I'll come. I can help." He sounded a little huffy. "Then do you want to come to my brother Joe's? To give Bronagh her birthday present?"

"Who's Bronagh?"

"My niece. I told you about her."

"Oh yeah." No, no memory. "The answer would be no."

"No?"

"I hate kids and kids hate me."

"But she's a laugh!"

"Believe me, Hathaway, not to me she won't be."

"Ah . . . all right. I'll go there on my own and then come over to you."

Day 1 . . .

". . . so then I flew back to Manila again and —"

"Yeah?" Joe said, drinking his tea and staring sightlessly around his kitchen.

Suddenly, Conall realized that he sounded like he was boasting. His brother had never been to Southeast Asia, he never *would* go there; it was just a faraway foreign part of the world that might sometimes be mentioned on the news. Conall abruptly shut up.

Without speaking, they drank their tea, Conall slurping energetically to demonstrate that he hadn't lost touch with his roots. He considered cracking his knuckles but feared it might be misinterpreted as a hostile gesture.

"Where's my present?" Bronagh's appearance broke the tension.

Conall reached into his pocket and produced the little box.

"Wicked," Bronagh breathed, unknotting ribbons and unpeeling silver paper. "This is a *proper* present." Reverentially, she removed the lid and gazed at the winking sparkling jewels.

"What the hell?" Joe asked.

"Are they . . . what are they?" Bronagh asked.

"Sapphires."

"Ah, for jayzus —"

Bronagh was wide eyed. "Are they real?"

Conall nodded.

"She's eight, bud." Joe sounded angry. "Her ears aren't even pierced."

"Adopt me, Conall." Bronagh began flinging herself dramatically around the kitchen, holding the sapphires to her earlobes. "Take me into your house as your ward. Rescue me from these smelly peasants."

"Ah, hahahah." Conall flamed with embarrassment. God, he'd messed this right up. Sweating with the need to fix things, he grabbed Bronagh and said, right into her eyes, "My brother is the best da you could have."

"You could be a good da too, if you didn't work so hard," Bronagh said. "But then you mightn't have the money to buy sapphire earrings. Hmmmmm. Tricky choice."

"I'll tell you something, Conall," Joe said hotly. "You might be going to the Philippines and all them places but I never have to leave the house. Having kids, that's the greatest adventure of them all."

"You're right, bud. Bang on. I'm beginning

to think that way."

Joe's face softened. Then froze. "— Oh no, Conall, bud. Having kids, it's not like buying a motorbike. You can't give it back when you get bored."

All my ducks are in a row for tomorrow. I think I'm going for Hathaway and Lydia. I know she says she doesn't like kids, but when it's her own baby, it'll be different. And Hathaway, he's ready. Well, he's fast coming round to the idea. By the time I arrive, I'll be welcome. Just in case things go unexpectedly skew-whiff, I've got Katie and Fionn as backup. But as for Matt and Maeve, I'm afraid we'd need a miracle.

DAY 1 . . .

"Anyone mind if I shoot off early today?" Matt asked. "Got my packing to do."

Good-natured, office-wide jeering sparked up. "Only ten past five and he's out through the door already! That's International Sales for you."

"Nothing left for me to do in Homeland Sales." The new name that had been given to the department selling systems within Ireland. "No point me hanging around, twiddling my thumbs." He grinned, pale and sweaty. "So, see ya."

"What time?" Salvatore asked.

"Say seven o'clock? At the Aer Lingus

check-in?"

Salvatore and Matt were due to fly to Shanghai on Monday morning.

"Good stuff. So see you at the airport!" Salvatore whooped. The start of a new venture, an exciting business.

"Yip," Matt said cheerily. "See you Monday morning at the airport."

Does Maeve know anything about this?

DAY 1 . . .

"How are you, Maeve?" Dr. Shrigley asked.

"Okay."

But she was far away, inside her head. She couldn't shake an image of herself being tossed up in the air, light and limp as a rag doll. The pictures were becoming more and more elaborate. She kept seeing it, the moment of impact, as a car hit her bike and she was sent flying, blood gushing from her mouth, her skull shattering like an eggshell as she landed on the road, and the light suddenly vanished from her eyes. The thought of the pain didn't concern her; she was so numb that she couldn't imagine feeling any.

She'd had four panic attacks in the last few weeks and with each one she'd felt the presence of death. She'd been afraid at the time, but she wasn't any longer.

She was looking forward to it all being over.

This was her last visit to Dr. Shrigley. She didn't know how to tell her, so she wouldn't bother. Dr. Shrigley would figure it out when Maeve stopped showing up. It didn't matter. None of it mattered.

She cycled home, fast and carelessly. When she got to Star Street she hopped off the bike and wheeled it the last few yards to the front door. It was amazing to her that she was still alive. I mean, what do you have to do to get killed around here?

For once she was glad that Matt wouldn't be home for a few hours. That way he wouldn't know that she hadn't gone to the drinks yoke at work. Although he couldn't have thought there was any real chance she'd go. Poor Matt. He wanted evidence that she was getting better, when everything indicated that she was getting worse.

She flicked a quick look over each shoulder to check that no one was lurking behind her, ready to bum-rush her into the empty flat, then she reached into her satchel for her keys. But she couldn't find them. Her hand clawed and closed, clawed and closed, like those swizzy things at a funfair, but she came up with nothing. Carefully setting her back against the front door, so she could keep an eye on all passers-by, she emptied the bag on to the step. No keys. Definitely, no keys. Her wallet was there. Why would someone take her keys and not her wallet? Creepy. Unless no one took anything and maybe the keys just fell out. But wouldn't she have heard them jingling?

Of all the nights to lose her keys. She fired off a quick text to Matt. He'd have to put his keys in a taxi. But the thought of a big burly taxi driver showing up with access to her flat . . . Quickly, she fired off another text.

Come home.

There was no point calling on any of the neighbors. None of them had a spare key. She didn't trust anyone with her keys.

Four men passing along the street stared at her, sitting on the step, her knees pulled up to her chest. She couldn't stay here, advertising her vulnerability to all and sundry. She should at least get into the communal hallway.

She hesitated about ringing the old woman because Hungry Fionn was living with her. What if he answered? She couldn't chance Katie in the top flat either because she and Fionn were an item. The only option was to ring the flat on the second floor. She was nervous of the Polish guys who lived there, but then she remembered that they were moving out when she was on her way to work this morning.

She pressed the buzzer and someone, probably the impatient taxi-girl, said, "Hatha-way?"

"This is Maeve from —"

The door clicked open. "Thanks," Maeve said to dead air, wheeling in her bike and leaning it against her door.

She sat on the bottom stair, gazing at her phone. Why hadn't Matt texted her back? What was keeping him? After a while, she rang him and it went straight to voice mail. He never turned his phone off. Why, today of all days? Sod's law.

A jingling of keys at the front door had her sitting up hopefully, but it was Katie. She tumbled into the hall, followed by Hungry Fionn. They were both in convulsions at something.

"Oh, sorry!" Katie laughed. "Didn't mean to nearly stand on you there. Maeve, isn't it? Are you all right?"

Maeve didn't want to tell, not with Fionn standing there.

"Are you locked out?" Katie asked.

Why else would she be sitting on the feck-ing stairs?

"Come on up to our place," Fionn invited.

Maeve suppressed a shudder.

"Do," Katie said. "We're going out in about an hour but you can stay as long as you like."

"I'm okay. My husband will be home soon."

"Do you need to ring him?" Already, Katie was reaching in her bag.

"He's on his way." Maeve displayed the little phone in her hand. "Thanks. I'm grand."

Matt still hadn't texted her back. It was weird. It had been ages. She checked the time on her phone — nearly fifteen minutes —

A voice spoke behind her. "What's the story?" It was Fionn. "Still sitting here?"

She scrambled to her feet. Her heart was suddenly pounding like the clappers and every instinct was telling her she was in mortal danger. Fionn bounded down the last few steps. He seemed almost amused. She was remembering the way he used to look at her, like he wanted to eat her. Devour her. Kill her.

"Come on up and wait in Katie's," he said.

She shook her head, unable to speak. Blood was roaring in her ears and fear was building, building, building in her chest, filling up the cavity, stopping her from breathing.

"There's nothing to be scared of."

There's nothing to be scared of.

He stepped nearer and reached out. "I'm not going to hurt you."

I'm not going to hurt you.

"Come on." He closed his hand around her arm.

She hadn't screamed the last time — that was her biggest mistake and she wouldn't make it again. "Stop! Please!"

Something was happening at the front door.

Someone was out there. The buzzer sounded.

"Matt," she shrieked. "Matt!"

But it wasn't Matt, it was that big, dark man. Conall, she thought his name was. Katie's boyfriend. At least he used to be.

"What the hell?" Conall asked, looking from Maeve to Fionn, at Fionn clasping Maeve's arm, at Maeve pulling away, trying to get free.

Conall stepped forward and Maeve's struggling and shrieking intensified. "Don't! Oh please! I'm begging you."

Immediately, Conall stepped back.

Maeve became vaguely aware that other faces had appeared on the stairs, looming over the banisters — Katie, snappish Lydia, some other girl and the old woman.

"Leave her alone," Conall said to Fionn. "You're scaring her."

"Me? I'm helping her."

"She's terrified of you. And me. Right?" he asked Maeve.

Conall and Maeve locked eyes. She nodded.

"She can't breathe," Conall said. "Maeve — is it Maeve? — will you let one of the girls help you?"

No. They might be in on it too. Maeve began to pant with fear. They might all be in on it.

"Someone get her a paper bag." No one moved. Everyone was frozen as if the pause button had been pressed on a big action scene, so without taking his eyes off her, Conall reached into his pocket and produced a big bag of Licorice Allsorts. He tipped them on to the letter table, then handed the empty bag to Maeve. "Breathe into that." He looked up the stairs at Katie. "Does it matter if it's plastic?"

"I don't know. I don't think so."

"Can someone tell me what's going on?" Conall asked.

"She's locked out," Katie said. "Her husband isn't here and none of us have spare keys."

"Do you know where he is?" Conall asked Maeve. "Matt? Is that his name?"

"He's on his way home."

"From where?"

"Magnolia."

"Magnolia?" both Conall and Katie said.

"I thought that closed down," Conall said, looking at Katie for confirmation.

"It did. About a month ago."

"That's what I thought," Maeve whispered. An uncomfortable silence ensued.

"We could try to pick the lock for you," Conall offered.

"How?" Maeve looked out from dazed eyes.

As if by a powerful force, the collective gaze was drawn to one point: Lydia.

"Why's everyone looking at me?" she asked. ". . . Oh *all right.*"

She ran upstairs and returned with a metal coat hanger, straightened it out and slid it into the keyhole, maneuvering carefully. Suddenly, she froze. She whipped out the wire. She'd gone quite pale. "It's locked from the inside. Key is still in it."

"He's in there?" Sissy mouthed.

"Matt's in there?" Conall asked Lydia.

"What do you mean, he's in there?" Maeve struggled for breath.

Conall banged on the door. "Matt? Matt?" He turned to Maeve. "Did you try the buzzer?" Mutely, she shook her head, so he opened the front door and stepped out to press the bell for Flat 1, long and hard. When no voice came from the intercom and Matt didn't appear to open the door, Conall said to Maeve, "Ring him. The landline."

Maeve handed him her phone. "It's under 'Home.' "

Conall tapped a few buttons then through the door came the sound of a phone ringing. They were all holding their breath, and when they heard the answering-machine message start up there was an unspoken understanding that they had somehow found themselves in the middle of a tragedy.

"Just because the key is in the door it doesn't mean that he's in there," Fionn said.

"How so?" Conall asked.

"He could have locked the door and gone out the window."

"But what are the chances?" Conall was removing Maeve's bicycle from where it was leaning against her door. "Stand back." To general shock — how had things got so serious so quickly? — Conall threw himself, shoulder first, at the door and bounced violently off it. (Jemima saw Fionn fail to suppress a smirk.) Conall tried again and the rebound wasn't quite so intense second time round.

"What's going on?" Maeve whispered. "I don't understand."

The third assault was accompanied by the sound of wood splintering. Two more onslaughts from Conall's shoulder and the door was swinging free of the lock.

"Right," he gasped. He looked around at the sea of faces. No one wanted to go in. It would have to be him. He perched in the doorway, like a man about to dive into a crocodile-infested river, then he took the plunge. For some moments a terrible silence prevailed, then they heard him. "Katie! Katie!"

White-faced, Katie disappeared, following his voice, and almost immediately returned full of orders. "Lydia, ring an ambulance. Fionn, go in, he needs you to help lift him. Jemima, stay with Maeve." As she was speaking, Katie was pulling up her skirt and pulling down her tights. She stepped out of them and ripped them in two at the weakest point, the crotch. "Tourniquets," she said.

Jemima put her hands on Maeve's shoulders. "This is not the time for advice, but we may not get another chance. Listen to what I have to say, it is very, very important. Your body belongs to you. Not to that man, whoever he was. Take it back from him."

Maeve's eyes were black and stunned-looking. She was stupefied, almost drugged from shock. "How do you know?" Her voice was a mumble.

"I'm very old. I've seen a lot. Your fear of men, your unrevealing clothing, it seemed clear to me —"

"What the hell . . . !" It was Sissy speaking. She placed a hand on Jemima's arm. "Is it, are you . . . Mystic *Maureen?*"

Not now, my dear, now is really not the time. Reluctantly, Jemima turned round. "Sissy, my dear?"

"I can't believe it's you!" Sissy shoved her face forward into Maeve's space. "Listen. You've got to listen. I mean, this woman!" Sissy threw her hands around, desperate to be emphatic. "Believe *whatever she tells you.* She's super-psychic."

"No, really, I'm not mystic. Merely old. But I —"

"Ambulance is here!"

"That was fast," someone said.

649

■ ■ ■ ■

Lydia watched as Matt's lifeless body, dripping red water and trailing sheer black nylon from both arms was stretchered out of the flat and up into the ambulance. She cornered Conall. His dark suit was wet and his white shirt was splashed with what looked like blood. He was on the phone to Eilish Hessard, organizing a new door for Maeve's flat. As soon as he hung up, she asked quietly, "What happened?"

Conall flicked a look at Maeve, checking that she wasn't listening. "In the bath. Cut his wrists."

Christ! Matt had slit his wrists! Very shocking and sad and everything but Lydia couldn't help thinking it was quite a *girlie* way for a man to kill himself.

One of the ambulance guys, a short, stocky bloke, was back in the hall. "Which one of yous is coming? Be quick about it."

"This is Matt's wife," Conall said.

"She can come in the bus, but there's no room for the rest of yous."

Maeve shrank into herself. "I can't," she said. "They're men."

"You must go, dear heart," Jemima said. "You must be with Matthew. But we will follow."

Katie draped her arm around Maeve's

shoulder and Maeve allowed herself to be led to the ambulance.

"I knew death was here." Jemima gazed at the ambulance doors as they slammed shut. "I've felt it for weeks. I was so sure it had come for me. Far better me than this young man."

For crying out loud! I'm not death. I'm the very opposite.

"Is your man, Matt, is he — actually, like dead?" Sissy swallowed.

Conall looked pained. ". . . I don't know. He didn't look too alive."

The sound of a siren made them all jump and the ambulance pulled away.

"Someone needs to go to the hospital to be with Maeve," Jemima said.

Lydia looked at her feet. This wasn't her sort of thing. You have to play to your strengths and she was no TLC merchant.

"I'll go," Katie said.

"I'll go if you think it'll do any good," Conall said.

"I'll go," Sissy said. "Even though she doesn't know me from a hole in the ground."

"She doesn't know any of us," Fionn said.

"I would like to go," Jemima said. "If none of you object."

No chance, Lydia thought. She could feel the wild relief of all concerned.

"Perhaps you will escort me, Fionn?" Jemima said.

"She's afraid of me," Fionn said.

Indignation stirred in Lydia. Okay, none of them wanted to go, it was gruesome and, yes, Maeve was petrified by Fionn and Conall, but you couldn't leave the old woman to go on her own. She was *ancient.* "Hey, I'll drive you."

"It's okay," Katie said. "I'll take you. My car isn't far."

"I will go and Fionn will escort me," Jemima declared. Fionn opened his mouth, then seemed to crumble to the inevitable. Jemima might be ancient, Lydia acknowledged, but she had a will of iron. "We can hail a taxi from right outside."

A further short squabble ensued when Lydia again offered her chauffeur services and Jemima declined them.

"Whateves." Lydia wasn't feeling so hot, not so hot at all. It was a relief to not have to drive.

Fionn went upstairs to change out of his wet, bloodstained clothes, then he and Jemima left, leaving Lydia with Conall, Sissy and Katie.

"Maybe we should get a drink," Sissy said.

"Okay," Conall said, and raised his eyebrows at Katie. "Any suggestions?"

"Flying Bottle?" she said. "It's handy. And

they won't object to a man with blood on his shirt."

"Practically obligatory." He gave a weak smile.

"Flying Bottle?" Lydia asked, her mouth awash with something bitter.

"You know, the pub just down the road there, whatever it's called," Conall said.

"There was a fight one night when we were there," Katie said to Lydia. "Hence the nickname. But it's early now, we should be grand."

"Grand," Lydia said. *Grand.*

If it was anywhere else except the Flying Bottle their appearance might have caused a few comments. Lydia and Sissy in grimy sweats and trainers, Katie in a classic little black dress and high heels, and Conall in a dark-grey Brioni suit, accessorized by splashes of blood that were already turning black.

"I'll go to the bar," Conall said, as Sissy tried to find four stools that hadn't been knifed open and had their foamy stuffing hanging out. "What'll you have?"

"Vodka and Red Bull," Lydia said.

"Me too," Sissy said.

"Katie?"

"Oh? Sorry!" Katie looked waxen and dazed. "Brandy, I think. It's meant to be good for shock."

"Okay. Lydia? Sissy? Sure you don't want to change your order? To brandy?"

"Quite sure," Lydia snapped.

She waited until Conall was standing at the bar with his back to them. "So," she said to Katie. "You know all about first aid?" Something was telling her that the answer to this question was important.

Miserably, Katie shook her head. "I'm just a keen amateur. I like getting spray and ointment from the drugstore, all the new stuff, every time they bring out a new type of Savlon, I get it, but when it comes down to it, like it did with Matt, I knew nothing." Her hands were shaking and she looked on the verge of tears.

"You knew about tourniquets."

"That's only from watching cowboys films. And what if it was too late? What if he was already . . . ?"

Katie's phone beeped and she looked at the screen. "It's Fionn. Matt is still alive. He's getting a transfusion."

"So does that mean he's okay?" Sissy asked.

"I don't know. He doesn't say. Maybe no one knows yet," Katie said.

Conall threw back his brandy, then got to his feet and looked at Lydia. "Are we right?" He needed to have frenzied sex to cast out the presence of death.

THREE YEARS AGO

As he opened the bedroom door, he said, "Close your eyes."

She felt the weight and heat of his hands on her shoulders, guiding her forward.

"Such a big deal." She laughed. "This'd better be worth it."

"It will be."

She had crumpled and hit the floor before she knew what was happening. Her understanding was two or three seconds behind events. She felt a sharp pain in her hip bone and a ringing in her skull before she realized that he'd put all his weight into his arms and pushed her downwards, that her knees had buckled neatly and she'd banged against the wooden floor. While she was still piecing this together, David had climbed on top of her, his knees on her shoulders, the full weight of his body on her torso.

No breath was going in or out of her; she'd been so busy falling and banging that she'd forgotten to inhale, and as soon as she tried, her chest couldn't expand because David's weight was crushing her.

In the confusion, she'd thought it was an accident. But David was on top of her, his face was red and smiling. Obviously, he'd meant to do this. It was a badly-thought-out joke, one that hurt people. Taking small sippy gasps, she said, "David, get up, get off me." She was exasperated, almost angry. Not afraid. Not yet.

With a litheness she didn't know he had, he shifted quickly so that he was now kneeling sideways on her flattened body, his right shin pinning her upper body to the floor, his left shin paralyzing her hips.

Never before had she felt the strength of another human being being used against her. He was taller, heavier and much, much stronger. This was an entirely new experience and nothing had equipped her for it. Apart from harmless stuff in the school playground, she knew nothing about force.

"David, let me up. Get off me. I can't breathe."

Desperately, she pressed her palms against the floor and shifted and wriggled beneath him, hoping to topple him off her, but his weight pinned her so perfectly to the ground that her movements were tiny.

He looked weird, like a stranger. She couldn't read the expression on his face, she didn't know what he wanted, but alarm bells were ringing. She was alone with him. No one knew she was here. And he was bitter and angry — she knew now that she'd been way wrong to think he'd forgiven her.

"Let me up and we'll go back into the sitting room and we'll have a talk. C'mon, David, you're a solid guy." Even then, she thought she could talk her way out of it.

She couldn't even lift her head, so when she felt rather than saw him fiddling for the button on her jeans, genuine panic kicked in.

"David, what are you doing?" He was trying to scare her. And it was working.

"David, no! This is crazy. You're hurt, you're pissed off, but this has gone too far. Stop it now!"

But he'd done it, the button was open. She'd always thought you could do something to protect yourself, you could scratch, you could kick, you could bite. But there was so much weight on her shoulders and upper arms that the nerves in her hands weren't working, they'd turned to sand, her feet were too far away from him to do any harm and her head was pinned to the floor.

Now he was unzipping her jeans.

Was he planning to . . . rape . . . her? It looked a bit that way, but it couldn't be true, because . . . Why not? Because things like that didn't happen to people like her.

"Okay," she gasped. "I'm scared now, it's working, it's worked. Time to let me up."

He was shifting about on top of her, redistributing his weight as he pulled down her jeans. "Please, David, don't, David."

I should yell. There might be people in the other flats; maybe they'd hear her. Bizarrely, she was almost embarrassed at the melodrama of shrieking, "Help!" After all, this was *David.* But when she opened her mouth it was a shock to discover how weak the scream was — she was flat on her back, there was no power to it.

Awkwardly but methodically, he was managing to pull down her knickers, first one side, then the other, tug by tug.

"Please stop, David, oh please." Silent tears were flowing from her eyes. She hadn't noticed them start.

And there was his erection, purple and angry.

My God, he's really going to rape me.

She clamped her thighs together, tensed with all her strength. Think, she beseeched herself, *think.* Somewhere she'd read that you should tell rapists about yourself, appeal to their sympathy, let them know that you're a human being. But David knew this already.

"I'm sorry I hurt you, David, I'm really sorry. But don't do this to me, please." Tears spilled down her temples.

He moved, to position himself for entry, and for a moment his weight was off her shoulders. This was her opportunity. She struggled to sit up and she let forth a proper scream this time, shrill and ringing.

He shoved her back down on to the floor, banging her head smartly against the wood, then lay his forearm across her throat and pushed. Not even that hard. Immediately, she began to choke. He leaned a little harder. Terrified, struggling, desperate to breathe, she saw how easily he could kill her. It happened all the time. Women got raped and killed and it was happening to her. Her vision was going black at the edges and instantly she became silent and floppy. She had to live through this. That was the only thing that really mattered. Anything else . . . well, she'd deal with it afterward, but she couldn't die.

He began to shove and batter at her with his penis and, unexpectedly, she had a pin-prick of hope: maybe it wouldn't happen, maybe she was too tense for him to get in. But he kept stabbing until he found an entry point, then he ground his way up into her. He began to move back and forth and it felt raw and terribly wrong.

I am being raped. This is what it's like.

For the first time since he'd brought her to the bedroom, he spoke. "Is it good for you?"

Mutely, she gazed at him, then she had the strangest sensation, of leaving her body, of spiraling away through the crown of her head. She was gone; she was waiting outside herself until it was over. She could see herself, rigid on the floor, her eyes tightly shut, tears leaking from beneath her lids; she could see him lying on top of her, thrusting and shoving and, strangest of all, whispering words of love. "You're beautiful." "I love you." "You really hurt me."

It seemed to go on forever. He lost his erection twice and they had to wait until he was ready to recommence. A few times she returned to her body and it would still be happening and she would have to leave again.

After a long time, he climaxed, spurting into her. Pregnancy, she thought. Chlamydia, she thought. Evidence.

Cold metal. An internal examination. Swabs and photos. An STD test. An Aids test. Too soon, of course, to do a pregnancy test. Feet back up in the stirrups for another internal. Matt holding her hand. Checks for bruising, tearing, internal bleeding. A whole world that she'd known nothing about.

After David had finished with her, he'd rolled off and lay on the bedroom floor, staring at the ceiling. She had lain rigid, wondering what he was going to do to her next. But, as the seconds had ticked by and nothing happened, she'd scooted away from him, and in a sudden frenzy of activity, she'd been pulling up her knickers and jeans, still expecting him to stop her, to wrestle her back down on to the floor and start it all over again.

A different woman might have said to him: You raped me and I'm going to tell everyone. But she'd had no thoughts of vengeance. All that had mattered was that she got away while she was still alive.

Downstairs, she'd unchained her bike. She hadn't been able to ride it, she couldn't get on the saddle, but she couldn't leave it here. She had to take away every part of herself; she could leave nothing for him. So she'd set off half-running, wheeling her bike a distance of over two miles, and the next moment, so it seemed, she'd arrived at her own front door.

She hadn't rung Matt; she hadn't wanted to disturb his evening. Instead, she'd sat, small and cold, on her sofa, waiting for him to come home. And when he did, he was confused, at least initially, but he believed her.

Two police, a man and a woman, took her statement.

"You got the . . . stuff?" Maeve asked, trying not to shudder. "You can do DNA, prove it was him?" She hadn't had a bath, she hadn't washed away any evidence; she was proud of that. She'd gone home and waited for Matt, and though she'd felt like she was dreaming it all, she'd intuitively known that she shouldn't even change her clothes.

"We're getting a bit ahead of ourselves

here," the man guard said. Vincent, his name was. "We don't know yet that it was nonconsensual."

Maeve looked at him blankly. "But it was." She looked at Sandra, the woman guard. "But it was," she repeated. She looked at Matt. "But it was."

"I know," Matt said.

Calmly, Sandra eyeballed them. "Let's start at the beginning. What were you wearing?"

"Those clothes." Maeve indicated the polythene evidence bag containing her jeans and underwear. Once again, she'd done exactly the right thing: she'd known her clothes would be taken from her, she'd known to bring a spare set.

"Not very provocative, are they?" Matt said, with a flash of defiance.

"It would be better if Mrs. Geary just answered the questions," Sandra said. "Maeve, you weren't wearing a dress?"

"What does that mean?"

"It's no easy job to pull down someone's jeans while restraining them."

"Yes, but . . . he did." How could she explain David's dead weight, his strength?

"Here." Vincent handed her a wad of tissues and Maeve realized that silent tears were streaming down her face.

"How would you describe your relationship with Mr. Price?" Sandra asked.

"Who — Oh, David. He used to be my

662

boyfriend. Before I met Matt."

"You went to his flat earlier this evening." Sandra checked her watch. "Still today, just about. You went alone, just the two of you? Why didn't your husband go?"

"He had a work thing," Maeve said at the same time that Matt said, "She has a right to her own life."

"But your husband approved of this visit?"

"He didn't know," Maeve had to admit.

"But I wouldn't have minded," Matt said.

"You didn't tell him that you were going to visit Mr. Price? Why was it a secret?"

"It wasn't a secret. It was just something I didn't tell him."

"You and Mr. Price had a drink together? Would it be fair to say that your inhibitions were lowered due to alcohol intoxication?"

"I had one beer. I didn't even drink it. Look, I didn't even want to see him but he said he wanted to give me a wedding present."

"A wedding present?" Sandra raised her eyebrow and Maeve realized how sleazy the phrase sounded.

"I have to ask you this, Mrs. Geary, because, if this case gets to court, you will be asked the question again: when you were the girlfriend of Mr. Price, did you have sexual intercourse?"

She swallowed. "We did, but this was different."

"You've been examined thoroughly. You

display no bruising or internal injuries."

"There must be bruises. I banged my head on the floor and he put his arm across my throat and tried to choke me."

"Your clothing isn't torn, you're not cut, there's no evidence of a struggle."

"But I did struggle."

"Any meaningful bruising would be visible within minutes. It's over four hours since the alleged incident."

"I did struggle but he was much stronger than me."

"If I was being raped, I'd put up a mighty struggle."

"I was afraid he'd kill me."

Again that raised eyebrow. "Kill you?" she asked, writing something down. "Wow."

"Well," Matt said heartily, as the two guards left the interview room. "She was a right cunt."

An unexpected giggle escaped Maeve. "You can't say that word."

"I wouldn't normally, but I'm prepared to make an exception for her."

"What do you think is happening?"

"They'll be talking to . . . *him*."

"And what, they'll arrest him? He'll go to prison . . . like, tonight? Is that how it works?"

"I don't know. He might get bail. Like, until the trial."

Trial. Court.

"Matt? I feel like I'm dreaming."

"So do I."

"This time three days ago we were on our honeymoon."

"We'll get through this."

With sudden urgency, she said, "Matt, don't tell Mam and Dad. They couldn't take it. They're so . . . innocent."

"It's okay. We'll keep it to ourselves, just you and me." They'd wrestle this huge, horrible thing into a little box, then they'd bury it and hide it forever.

"Matt, can you see a bruise on my throat?"

"Step nearer to the light, till I have a proper look."

"The front bit," she said. "On my Adam's apple."

"I think I can see something," he said uncertainly.

"Maybe there isn't anything there," she admitted miserably. "He didn't have to press very hard." The lightest of pressure had been enough to start her choking and put her in fear of death. "What about my head? Is there a bruise on the back of my head? Is there a lump?"

With gentle fingers, Matt explored the back of her skull. "I can't really see anything because of your hair. Does it hurt?"

She wished it did. "Not any more but it hurt a lot at the time." The unthinkable occurred to her. "God, Matt. What if there's no evidence? What if they think I'm making it up?"

"No one would think that."

Hours passed. Propped up against each other's shoulders, they waited while everything was being fixed and they could go home and back to normality. "I wish someone would just tell us what was happening," Maeve said, trying to keep her voice steady.

"They will soon. It'll all be grand."

Eventually, they both nodded off, and just after four in the morning, a sound at the door made them jerk into dry-mouthed wakefulness. The man cop, Vincent, had come back. He pulled up a chair and said, "Right, this is the situation. We've interviewed Mr. Price. He admits you had sexual intercourse. He says it was consensual."

Fear, sour and sticky, flooded into Maeve's mouth. "But it wasn't."

"It's your word against his. Look." Vincent leaned closer to her. "Are you sure you didn't just, you know, get a bout of the guilts? One last go, for old times' sake, then got afraid that hubby there might get wind."

"I'm sure."

"Are you sure you want to go ahead with this? Taking it further?"

"I'm sure."

"Because it'll ruin his life, you know. Just so as you know."

■ ■ ■ ■

Eight days later, Officer Vincent called to their flat. "The DPP isn't going ahead with the prosecution."

"What does that mean?"

"It means the DPP thinks there isn't enough evidence to get a conviction."

"But I know there is." Maeve couldn't feel her lips as she spoke.

"But you don't bring the case. It's the DPP. Director of Public Prosecutions."

"So . . . does that mean, like, there won't be a court case?"

"That's right. No court case."

She'd been dreading it, she knew they'd probe her about her sex life and they'd try to make out that she was a slut; but now that it wasn't going to happen, she felt as if she'd gone into freefall. They needed to go to court. How else could things be put right?

"Why not?" Matt's jaw was clenched.

"The DPP doesn't have to give reasons."

"You mean, you think David is innocent?" Maeve felt so dizzy she wondered if she might faint. "You think I made it up?"

"I mean that the DPP doesn't think there's enough evidence to get a conviction."

"So . . . so, like, nothing will happen to him?" Matt's face was white and pinched.

"Innocent until proven, and all that."

"But how can it be proved if it doesn't go to court? Maeve and I, we work in the same place as him. You're saying he'll just carry on with his job and everything like nothing happened?"

"In the eyes of the law he's done nothing wrong." The officer heaved himself up to leave. "Why should the man lose his job?"

"Wait. No, wait." Maeve couldn't let him go, not until he changed his mind. Because if he left now, with things as they were, they were stuck with them forever. "Can we appeal?"

He thought that was funny. "No, no, you can't appeal. DPP's decision is final and binding." Then he seemed to relent a little. "Mind you, you might be as well off, leaving things as they are. Awful lot of dirty linen gets washed in a case like this."

No one believed her.

She confided in Yvonne, her best friend from school. "David raped me."

"How could he rape you? He used to be your boyfriend. You already had sex with him."

She confided in Natalie. "David raped me."

"David doesn't need to rape anyone. He's a nice guy."

She confided in Jasmine, her ex-flatmate. "David raped me."

"But that's a terrible thing to say. He could sue you for that."

668

She stopped confiding in people.

But she was going back to work. In two weeks' time. Three weeks. At the start of next month. When her two-month certificate ran out. After the summer.

The panic attacks started. The first time it happened, she didn't even know what it was. All she knew, with absolutely certainty, was that she was about to die. Her heart was spasming in her chest, no air could get in or out and she didn't think she could survive the intensity of her fear. The same fear she'd felt on the floor of David's bedroom, his forearm lying so easily across her throat. The expectation of imminent death.

She became terrified of men, of their height, their strength, even a casual look in her direction.

She overate, both she and Matt did, shoving down the feelings with butter and sugar and sweetness. She put on weight, but not as much as she would have liked. She wanted to disappear into a roly-poly body, to become invisible in it, so that no one would fancy her ever again.

She couldn't be naked, not even alone. The touch of another human being, even Matt, stopped her from breathing. The last time she and Matt had had sex was on their honeymoon.

Her periods stopped. Her hair fell out. Her hands flaked, the skin sore with eczema. She couldn't sleep without the light on. By the time she finished reading a sentence, she'd forgotten the beginning. She barely spoke.

Fear was the only thing she felt. Otherwise, nothing. It was as though, when she'd spiraled outside her body that evening on David's floor, she'd never come back in again. Everything that happened to her . . . she seemed to see it almost like a movie. It was happening to someone else, another Maeve, not the real one.

Suddenly, around the four-month mark, things took an upward turn and Maeve felt confident enough to tackle going back to work. But on the morning that Matt drove her into the parking lot and she saw the entrance, she was seized with so much terror that her legs wouldn't support her. She couldn't get out of the car and Matt had to drive her home again. She'd tried too soon, and it was best to defer it until the following Monday. Or maybe the one after that.

A new home, Matt decided: that was the answer! A fresh start in a place with no horrible associations. Positive and energized, he visited an estate agent's, but Maeve found fault with every place he suggested and all Matt's enthusiasm drained to nothing, leaving him once more miserable and full of dread. Maeve was right. Better the devil you know. Keep the ship steady for the moment, and all that. And he had to admit it would have been a painful wrench to abandon the flat they'd bought, with such high hopes, to launch their married life in.

There was another reason to stay where they were. Money had become an issue. After six months' absence, Maeve's pay had been cut by half; now, a year on, it had been stopped entirely.

Then there was the garden — the back garden at 66 Star Street came with their flat. It had been the deciding factor in them buying the place because Maeve had been full of animated plans to grow foxgloves and carrots and tomatoes. "It's so easy! You'll see, Matt. We'll be self-sufficient before we know it!"

They were self-sufficient now, all right, but self-sufficient in the wrong way. They had no one except each other. All of their friends — *all* of them — had fallen away because they thought that Maeve had gone so weird, with her strange rape accusations, her insistence that this man was looking at her and that man was looking at her, and her drama-queen antics, the gasping and rocking backward and forwards and clutching her chest. Like, in *public*.

The social life that Matt shared with his male friends came to a halt because Maeve couldn't spend an entire night at home without him. She could just about handle it when he went to work things because she knew they had little choice: Matt's job was all that stood between them and complete penury.

The only person who remained sympathetic was Alex, Matt's brother, but, in the end, even he'd become wearied by Matt's chronic unavailability. "She's got to learn to be on her own sometime," he told Matt. "You're making it worse by always giving in to her."

Painful though it was to be rejected by people they'd previously depended on, there was a strange relief in it. They'd nothing in common with those people any more; their concerns seemed so trivial. To Maeve's eternal relief, she'd managed to keep her parents from knowing any of what had happened. Matt's parents were also in the dark. But putting on a show of normality in front of them was so exhausting that it couldn't be done very often. Her visits down home lessened, and two times out of three she faked sickness so that she didn't have to go to a Geary family do.

Burning them both up was the thought that David was walking around a free man while they were in prison.

Matt wanted to kill him. Actually really kill him. He saw him most days at work and he fantasized about following him home, lifting him from the street and bundling him into the back of a van, taking him to their flat, gagging him, binding him and making him suffer, making it last.

"I think about it too," Maeve said. "Did you know that a hit man costs only two grand. I Googled it."

"So did I."

But they agreed they couldn't take a contract out on David.

"It would only reduce us to his level," Maeve said.

"I don't care about that," Matt said.

And neither did Maeve. She was destroyed anyway. "But we'd get caught. We're the obvious suspects. We'd end up in prison. We can't let him ruin our life more than he has."

"I don't know how more people don't crack up and take the law into their own hands and just kill the bloke." Matt had discovered things he'd never before thought about: that only one in ten reported rapes make it to court; that out of them, only six in a hundred result in a conviction. And what about all the rapes that are never reported, because the girl is too scared. Of her rapist? Of the police? All those rapes unacknowledged, unavenged. It was enough to drive him mad. How was the world as normal as it was? How was all that rage and injustice and grief and fear contained?

When Matt saw that Maeve would never return to Goliath, that he didn't have to stay to protect her, he left too.

He had been determined that he wouldn't

leave, that that *bastard* wouldn't drive him out, the way he'd got rid of Maeve, but he was tired of shaking with rage in meetings, of trembling so much that his fingers couldn't type if your man was in the vicinity. It was a point of pride that Matt never let David see any weakness, any reaction at all. In his head he tortured him lengthily and horribly but in real life he presented a bland nothingy expression. A show of imperturbability was all that remained to him, a paper-thin comfort, but something nonetheless.

As for David, there was no evidence of remorse or guilt. He never spoke directly to Matt but the smirk in his eyes said it all. *You took her from me and I fucked it up on you.*

Matt left Goliath and went on to bigger and better at Edios. Evidently, he could still do his job.

Both Matt and Maeve started taking antidepressants, then they began weekly appointments with Dr. Shrigley until Dr. Shrigley tried to get Matt to admit that sometimes he'd doubted Maeve's story, so Matt stopped going.

But he did doubt Maeve. Sometimes. How could he not? Everyone else doubted her and he was only human. At times he hated her. He'd feel irrational rage that she'd got raped, that she'd ruined everything.

It was almost two years before Maeve got a job, a tiny, tame little thing, gifted to her because she was the only applicant who would agree to the very low salary. A routine was the way to go, she realized. That would keep her safe. She kept things very small and very predictable, and sometimes she caught a glimpse of all that she had lost. Had she really been that person, that light-hearted innocent who'd loved everyone? Who had approached the world with a wide-open heart, as if life were a great, big, juicy red apple, just waiting for her to bite into it?

She'd had it all. Within the bounds of her ordinary life, she'd had nirvana. She'd been loved and she'd had friends, a job, ordinary decent happiness. And it was all gone.

They kept track of David. But Matt didn't know that Maeve did and Maeve didn't know that Matt did. Now and again, independently of each other, they showed up outside No Brainer, in the hope that David might be showing signs of remorse, but they always came away feeling worse.

Even at the most hopeless of times, Matt showed an occasional burst of his old optimism and came up with bright ideas to cure them: they'd take up horse-riding or hillwalking or badminton or — most frequent of all — they'd move house.

Nothing lasted and nothing worked.

"Time wounds all heels," Matt sometimes said to Maeve.

But somewhere along the way, three years had passed and they were still wounded and waiting.

DAY 1 . . .

Conall hustled Lydia up the stairs and into his bedroom. He was desperate for her.

"What did you think?" Lydia shimmied out from under his grasp. "When you saw Matt in the bath?"

Conall tightened his lips. He didn't want to talk about it. When he'd opened that bathroom door, he'd been rooted to the spot with horror. Every one of his muscles had seized up and the backs of his calves had started cramping.

From all the blood and guts on the telly he'd expected to be inured to carnage, but *CSI: Miami* could never convey the power of a real dead person.

He kept seeing it again: the bath filled with Matt's blood; crimson blossoms swirling through the water; the waxy, lifeless face lolling on the taut red waterline.

"I thought he was dead," he said.

As he'd hovered in the doorway of that bathroom, the world felt like it had stopped turning, and battling with his horror was grief, a mesmerizing sense of loss at the waste of the young man's life.

In his time, Conall had done a lot of living:

676

he'd driven expensive cars at shamefully reckless speeds; he'd taken risks in his career that could have cost millions; he had experienced a lot of beauty — magazine-style girlfriends, priceless art, the most scenic spots on the planet. But in that endless moment he understood that you only truly know the value of life when you're face to face with death. Life seemed so appallingly valuable he wanted to howl.

"You thought he was dead?" Lydia said. "Nasty."

"It's over now." At least he hoped it was, but his calves were spasming again. He reached for Lydia, but she backed across his enormous bedroom. He followed her.

"Why did you call for Katie?" Lydia asked. "To come and help you?"

"Because . . . she was the obvious person."

"What way obvious?"

"She knows about first aid."

"Owning seven different versions of Savlon doesn't make you a paramedic. I asked her in your so-called Flying Bottle — thanks for that, by the way. Really rub it in, your private joke, why don't you? Anyway, she knows zip about first aid."

Conall looked quizzical. "Your point?"

"You were scared, really, really scared and Katie was the one you wanted."

Elaborately, he rolled his eyes.

"Oh no," she said. "You don't do that to

677

me. I'm not one of your sappy girls."

"I know you're not one of my 'sappy girls.' "

"No. *I* know I'm not one of your sappy girls."

"Okay." He said with elaborate patience. "*You* know you're not one of my 'sappy girls.' "

"You're not getting it, are you?"

He gazed at her, then something changed behind his eyes. "You're . . . breaking up with me?"

"Love of God, took you long enough. I can't believe your nerve, bringing me back here to have sex, when it's Katie you want."

"I don't want her. I want you."

"Love of God." She shook her head. "You haven't a clue. You'd want to cop on to yourself or you'll never be happy."

She disappeared into the bathroom and re-appeared with a cluster of bottles — shampoo and things — and threw them into her bag.

"What are you doing?"

"Getting my stuff."

"Why?"

"Because I'm going, thick-arse. In case you have to explain to people what's after happening, here it is: I've broken it off with you. And no, we can't be friends. You don't really *do* friends, do you? Another thing you'd want to sort out. I'll be bad-mouthing you every chance I get. If there's a rumor going round town that you're a premature ejaculator, I'm the one who started it."

She opened the bedside cabinet, fished out a packet of condoms and slid them into her jeans pocket. "Mine," she said. Then she cast one last contemptuous look around the room, checking that she had everything, before swaggering from the room and thundering down the stairs.

The house shuddered when she slammed the front door behind her. Automatically, Conall reached for his BlackBerry. What was Lydia's problem? She was too much of an attack dog, that's what it was. How could you reason with someone like her? Katie had been the obvious person to call for. She was capable, she was an adult, she understood things, she was . . . well, simply obvious.

Four new emails had arrived, and he read them hungrily, clicking quickly from one to the next, but none of them did the trick. He didn't feel so good, everything seemed slightly surreal. Sort of nasty. He put on Bruce Springsteen's *Nebraska,* but there was so much loss in it that he changed to the Sex Pistols. All that frenzied guitar didn't feel good either. *Madame Butterfly* maybe, but two minutes of listening to that aching abandonment and suddenly he had tears in his eyes. He wasn't having that! In alarm, he shut it off. Silence was safer.

He lay on his giant bed, staring at the far

wall. Time passed and, after a period of nothingness, he wondered if he should ring Katie. Just to find out what was happening with Matt.

Then he realized that Lydia was the one he should be ringing — apologizing, explaining, all that. There were rules, Conall knew. You weren't supposed to prefer your ex-girlfriend to your current one. But he didn't *prefer* Katie. It had been an emergency, for crying out loud: someone was dying, things needed to be done and done quickly. Katie had been the right person.

Or maybe Lydia was right, he admitted reluctantly. Maybe she was the one he should have called for. But she was so hard and what he'd needed, in those moments when it had seemed like the horror was going to over- whelm him . . . what he'd needed right then, was soft.

DAY 1 . . .

"Into the pillow," the nurse said. "Do it into the pillow, or you'll have to leave."

Maeve looked up. Her face was hot and sore with salt and her eyes were so swollen she could barely see. Another surge of uncon- trollable feeling rushed up through her.

"Pillow!" the nurse said. "There's other people here. They're upset too."

Maeve doubled over and buried her face

into the pillow, which had appeared from somewhere, and shrieked, "How could you do this to me? How could you leave me here all alone? I will *never* forgive you."

When she'd finally understood what Matt had done, she'd landed with an almighty bump back in her body, back in Maeve. It was like that suddenly present, super-real sensation when your ears pop on a plane. She was alive and in agony and blind with fury.

A red-curtained screen-on-wheels had been wrapped around Matt's trolley, in an attempt to give them some privacy from the rest of the ER. Maeve sat beside him on a hard, hospital chair. His wrists had been stitched, taped and swaddled in pristine white bandages; he'd been given 4 liters of blood and 2 liters of electrolytes. Wires connected him to drips and green beepy monitors. He looked at death's door but he was going to live.

"You must really hate me to do that to me!"

His eyes were closed, he looked unconscious, but she thought he was faking it.

"As soon as they let you out of this place, you get yourself straight round to our flat and move your stuff out." She lifted her face from the pillow, she couldn't stop herself. "Go to a hotel, move in with your parents." She tasted blood at the back of her throat. "I don't care *where* you go."

"Pillow!"

■ ■ ■ ■

Fionn paced up and down in the hospital car park. The ER was like the waiting room in hell, with its clusters of injured people crying and wailing, trailing entourages. Someone had given Jemima their chair, but there was nowhere for him. Not that he was able to sit, he was too agitated. He was feeling bad. Angry, actually. First with Jemima for insisting that he escort her to the hospital, leaving Katie with that territorial Conall. And, secondly, with Maeve for treating him like the anti-Christ. Somewhere during this evening's dramatic events, he'd realized that the emotion which used to light up Maeve's face at the sight of him wasn't awe. It was fear. Terrible paralyzing fear. He felt foolish, really quite *sore,* that he'd thought she was mad about him. And why wasn't she? Everyone else loved him.

They'd been here for hours. He wasn't sure how long but it was properly night now, good and dark.

He'd had enough of this.

He stomped back in through the polythene doors. Someone was shrieking like a banshee. It was Maeve, still at it. She'd end up being sectioned if she didn't watch it.

"What did I miss?" he asked Jemima. "Did he die or something?"

"No, you'll be delighted to hear he's going to survive."

"So why's she still shouting and that?"

"She's distressed."

"Can't they give her something?"

"Why ask me? I'm afraid I don't have medical training."

Well, tetchy! "Jemima, let's go."

"Maeve needs someone with her."

"She doesn't even want you here." Earlier, Maeve had slapped Jemima away when she'd tried to comfort her.

"What Maeve wants and what Maeve needs are two very different things."

"Does she even know you're still here?"

"*I* know I'm here."

God, Jemima could be infuriating.

"When the storm passes, which it will, she may be glad of my company. But you go home, Fionn. I'll be perfectly fine. Thank you for escorting me."

"So, like, what? You're just going to wait until she stops the shouting? She's not showing signs of doing that any time soon. Could you not knock off the do-gooding, Jemima? Like, at this hour of your life?"

Jemima gave a little smile. "I may not have many more chances."

"You?" He snorted. "You'll outlive us all."

"I may not, dear heart." She paused. "Fionn, remember when I had that little brush with cancer?"

683

"That was years ago."

"Four —"

"And you're better now."

"Well, the thing is, I —"

"Look, if you're sure you're not coming, I'm going to head off."

Taking the stairs three at once, Fionn bounded up to Katie. There were already men at work fitting a new door to Matt and Maeve's flat. That Conall, Mr. Make-it-Happen, he'd make you puke.

Katie was waiting at her open door. "Well?" She had been crying.

"He'll live."

"Thank God, oh thank God for that. And how's Maeve?"

"Tell me something." His wounded emotions erupted. "What did I ever do to her? What's her problem?"

Katie was staring at him. "Something happened to her. Obviously. Something to do with a man or men. We think that maybe she was . . . raped. You can't take it personally."

"Yeah, I suppose."

"She was just as scared of Conall."

He had to close his eyes. "You're comparing me to him?"

Silent seconds elapsed, then Katie took him by the hand and led him into the living room. "Fionn, come on. It's been a bad few hours. We're all rattled."

"Yeah, okay," he muttered. "So what did I miss?"

"Very little. Had a quick drink in the Flying Bottle with the others."

"What others?"

"Conall, Lydia and Sissy."

"Hold on a minute. You went with Conall?"

"And Lydia and Sissy."

"Why?"

"Because we were upset. Because we wanted a drink."

"And you thought it was okay to go with him, even though he's your ex-boyfriend? And even though he did his best to make me look like a, a *woman-pesterer* in front of everyone?"

"Fionn . . ." She wrapped her arms around him. "It's been a weird, horrible evening. We're all freaked out. Come and sit down. Come on. Listen, is Jemima okay?"

"Je*mi*ma? Never better."

He let himself be guided to the sofa but, as soon as he was sitting, he felt trapped. "Let's go out."

"What? Tonight?"

"Yeah. Now. There's a thing on in the Residence. Some launch."

"I don't want to go out." Katie sounded shocked. "I couldn't."

"Why not?"

"Because someone almost died and we were there. I'm in the horrors. I wouldn't be

685

able to be happy and chatty. I need to be quiet."

"A few drinks?"

"Fionn . . . no."

"You were happy enough to go for a drink with Conall."

"Fionn."

"So you're really not going to come out tonight?"

Katie tilted her head to one side and gazed at him. He tried to read what she was thinking. She looked scared. She looked confused. She looked — unexpectedly — sad. Then she looked calm and he knew he'd got her. But when she spoke, her words didn't match her look. "No, Fionn," she said. "But you go. Have a good time."

Christ alive. Their heart currents have gone right to hell. They had become as one, a perfect smooth union, but this thing with Matt has sent them flying and they've bounced and broken apart, like a peanut tumbling from its shell. And whatever way they landed, it's altered their heart currents. It's all arseways. Fionn's has speeded right up, beating an anxious, urgent tattoo, leaving Katie's for dust.

I'm in the soup now, rightly in the soup. They've all split up, all three couples, and I've less than a day to go.

DAY ZERO (EARLY HOURS OF)

5 hours remaining

"Sorry," Matt croaked, startling Maeve into wakefulness.

"Oh, you're alive," she said. "Sorry about that. Saving your life, and all, but it wasn't up to me. I'd have let you die."

"Maeve, I'm really, really sorry." His tears were flowing freely and he was the very picture of a broken man. "But I wasn't able to help you. Nothing was going to help."

"Don't blame me."

"I was just a reminder to you of what had happened. And I wanted to kill him all the time. I was bursting with anger every minute of the day and I was knackered from it."

"And what? You think I enjoyed it?"

"I shouldn't have done it. I didn't see it that way when I was doing it. I was at the end of my rope. I didn't feel like I was any use to you."

"You're not. You're going to be allowed out of here at seven o'clock. Come to the flat. I'll have made a start on packing your stuff."

"Where will I go?"

"What do I care? You were all set to die on me so don't be asking me to find you somewhere to live."

"How will I get home?"

"Get the bus. Get a taxi."

"You won't wait for me?"

"No."

Lydia pulled over to the curb. "Outttttt," she ordered.

"But we're not there yet," the fare, a young man, said.

"I told you. I warned you. If you didn't stop singing Neil Diamond songs I'd make you get out. You didn't stop, so get out. *Tttteeee.*"

Muttering about mad bitches, he nonetheless obeyed her and she shot away in a squeal of rubber. Better switch the old light off for a while. Not the best time to chance another fare. Not feeling too full of sweetness and light.

The *neck* of Hathaway. Obviously, he was still mad about the governess. Good luck to him, and all that. They were the right age for each other, both totally ancient, and Lydia didn't care, she'd never really been into him; it had only been a bit of a laugh. It was just, like, the *neck* of him . . .

She was talking to herself. That wasn't so good. She peered out at her surrounds; where exactly was she? She'd lost track of things around "Sweet Caroline." Right, she was in Parkgate Street. Close enough to Eugene's. She'd stop in, get a sugar fix and rant about her customers to anyone who'd listen.

"Doughnuts?" she asked Eugene. "Any custard ones?"

" 'Deed I have."

"Start me off with two. And I might be back for more."

She looked around for a seat and —

Hold on a minute, all might not be lost because —

— there, across the steam-filled café, was none other than Poor Fucker, aka Gilbert.

He probably wouldn't be my first choice but, at this stage in the game, I'm not left with many options.

They locked eyes and he began threading his way between the people, making for her. And there he was. Those eyelashes. The cool clothes. That voice.

"Hey, Lydia."

"Hey, Gilbert."

"How have you been?" He looked a little sheepish.

"Keeping good. You?" She presumed she

was looking a little sheepish herself.

"Yes. Excellent."

"Haven't seen you for a while." *Since I cheated on you.*

"No." *And not since I fessed up to cheating on you.*

"How are all the guys?"

"Good."

"Still killing each other over the Little Trees?"

"What? Oh? Not so much lately."

"Really?" They'd argued so passionately about them. It had been such an important part of their lives. Well, she realized, everything moves on. "Tell them I said hello."

"Will do. Business good?"

"Grand. You?"

"Grand also." A little pause opened up. "So Lydia . . ." He opened his eyes wide and spread his arms, looking surprised that there seemed to be nothing more to say. "Take care of yourself."

"You too."

He backed gracefully away from her, but, before he disappeared for ever, she called, "C'mere, Gilbert, I want to ask you something."

He looked a little alarmed. "What?"

"Do you have a wife and six kids back in Lagos?"

He laughed hard, his teeth flashing superwhite. "Me? Wife? Kids? Noooo, Lydia."

"Poppy *will* be disappointed." Quickly, she threw at him. "Are you allergic to eggs?"

It was too fast. He didn't have time to prepare a smooth response. ". . . Ah . . . no."

"So why did you say you were, you mope?"

He went inside his head to have a think. He shrugged. "Sometimes life, by itself, is not enough. If the truth isn't interesting, I have to . . . you know?"

"Couldn't you have come up with something better than eggs? How about you're the son of a Nigerian chieftain, oil reserves on your land, government troops, houses torched, that sort of thing?" He was impressed with that, she could see. "You're going to use that line, aren't you?" *On your next girlfriend?*

"Maybe. Yeah. Thanks."

Suddenly, she spotted a table being vacated by four men. "That's mine! Bye." She shot across the café and threw her bag on one chair, her hoodie on another and herself on a third, in the hope of discouraging some random person from asking, "Is this seat free?"

"Eugene," she yelled in the direction of the counter. "I'm over here. Anytime you like with the doughnuts." And then all was good with the world: she was sitting down, sugar was on its way, no one was singing Neil Diamond songs. She didn't see the door opening and closing as Gilbert left. A good-looking man, in a mildly ridiculous jacket, who'd once been her boyfriend.

She'd already forgotten him.

"A moment, dear heart!" Jemima managed to apprehend Maeve as she stalked from behind the red curtain shielding Matt and headed for the exit. "Are you leaving?"

"Yip."

"Without Matthew?"

"*Matthew* tried to kill himself. *Matthew* has made it clear that he doesn't want to be with me."

Sarcasm didn't become her, Jemima reflected. She was too sweet to pull it off with true aplomb. Bluster and swagger, but no genuine conviction.

"It is imperative that we speak, Maeve. You are mired in anger and betrayal, but it's vital that you are apprised of some facts. To wit: with men, the most common method of suicide is hanging. In other words, it's almost certain that Matthew wanted to be found."

Maeve stared stonily into the middle distance. "I'll never forgive him."

"Really, dear heart, such melodrama. When one thinks about it, he had to do *something*. How many more years were you going to spend lying on your sofa, watching the wretched goggle-box and eating cake?"

Maeve's face became luminous with shock.

"Yes. The truth is painful, Maeve. But face facts. You were stuck. Something needed to happen. And don't tell me that the notion of ending it all didn't occur to you also."

"But! How do you . . . ?"

"You were in despair," Jemima said airily. "It's what happens to human beings in despair, when all doors are locked and escape seems impossible."

With curiosity, Maeve asked, "Have you felt suicidal?"

"Me? Oh no, dear. Sadly, I'm not built that way. Genetics, I can only surmise. And I've certainly had my sorrows in my time. Giles and I longed for babies of our own but they were gifts that we were never granted. Despair would have been an appropriate response, but no, I just soldiered on. Made soup for the deserving poor, that sort of thing." She fell into a short reverie, before snapping back to the present and clapping her hands together. "Now, you and Matthew! You must have a baby."

After a long, almost hostile stare, Maeve asked, "Why?"

"Any *number* of reasons. Relations between you would have to be rekindled. You would feel the power of your body instead of its lamentable vulnerability. You would have someone to love, apart from each other. A baby will reclaim the innocence that was stolen from you both."

Maeve took a while to answer. "And that'll, like . . . exorcize everything that happened?"

Young people? Wherever did they get the notion that life operated in such absolutes?

In a gentler tone, Jemima said, "What has happened has happened. It can't unhappen. You are different, Matthew is different, but you must simply get on with it."

Maeve had a think. "So, a baby? Is that what you see for me? *See* it, like Sissy said?"

Oh dear. These young girls and their faith in mystic this and psychic that and no faith at all in their own autonomy. Well, if that was what it took . . . "That's what I see for you. You have a choice here, Maeve. You can go under or you can come out fighting —" A sudden spasm of pain in the region of Jemima's liver sent her eyes rolling into the back of her head.

"Cripes!" Maeve exclaimed. "What's up? Are you okay?"

"Perfectly fine. A tummy ache. Probably all the excitement."

"D'you want to sit down?"

"No, thank you, you are kind. I must go home now. But I beseech you to wait for Matthew. It's four-thirty and he'll be permitted to leave in two and a half hours. Can't you wait that long?"

Maeve bit her lip. She didn't want to do anything for Matt ever again, but Jemima having that pain in her stomach had shifted

694

the moral high ground in Jemima's favor.

"I assure you," Jemima said, her breath emerging as a pant as another spasm of pain took a grip. "I assure you, Maeve, that one day you will be happy again. Your life will get better."

"Back to the way it used to be?"

Jemima sighed. "One can never go back. You know that."

"So what am I to do?"

And where did they get the idea that Jemima had the answer to everything? ". . . Perhaps you could . . . try going forward?"

4 hours

A river of blood and he was wading his way through it. It was swirling around his legs and he was trying to push his way against it, but the current was too strong and — Conall awoke with a gasp. He'd been in the middle of a terrible dream, all that blood and . . . He was awake now. His heart was pounding into his throat, but he was in his own bed, it was okay. His clock said it was 4:45 a.m., so he could go back to sleep for a few hours. And then he thought: *The bath.*

It was still full of Matt's blood. When he and that prick Fionn had gingerly hoisted Matt's slippery body out, neither of them had been enough of a hero to plunge his arm into the bloody water and pull the plug. Maeve couldn't come home to that. She might be home already but, just in case it wasn't too late, Conall had to go there. The thought of going back into that terrible little room made all his muscles clench, but it had to be done.

Wearily, almost miserably, he clapped his hands and the room lit up, and he made a sudden fierce promise to himself that he was going to sort out that bloody light and go back to an ordinary switch. Even when he was totally alone, doing the clapping made him feel ridiculous. He yanked open the wardrobe and pulled on the first pair of jeans he found, and then he had a quick scout around, looking for some sort of shirt or T-shirt that wouldn't matter if he got blood on it. But everything he owned was expensive, and what did it matter anyway?

Katie awoke with a terrible bump, her mind racing like a speeded-up film through the atrocities of the previous evening: the key still in the lock; the door splintering and breaking; Conall disappearing into the hall; him calling her name and — the most terrible part of all — her first sight of Matt floating lifelessly in the red water. Although it couldn't have been more than a few seconds, it felt as though she'd stood in the doorway for hours, trying to make sense of the macabre scene before her. Matt? *Matt?* Young, cheery, smiley Matt, *that* Matt? What was he doing, drained of all color and life, bobbing in a bathful of his own blood . . . *The bath,* she realized, with a bang to her heart. That's what had woken her.

Was the bath water still in it? If so, it had to be emptied and cleaned, and the bloodied towels that had been abandoned on the floor needed to be washed before Maeve got home. She swung her feet on to the floor — and then it hit her: Fionn wasn't here. He'd gone out and obviously he hadn't come back. After he'd stomped off, she'd been reluctant — almost scared — to get into bed. She had curled up on the couch, watching crap stuff on telly, waiting for him to come back. If he was home before she went to bed, then everything was fine. By 2 a.m., she'd been so cold and odd-feeling that she had crept between the covers, promising herself that she wouldn't go to sleep. She'd had a superstitious conviction that it would be a disaster if she slept. But she'd obviously dozed off and here it was, 5 a.m., and he still wasn't home. There was a chance that he might be downstairs in Jemima's but even that would be a bit of a death knell; he hadn't slept there for weeks.

Real life had finally caught up with them, that's what had happened. For weeks they'd led it an effervescent dance, skipping and laughing, gleefully outpacing it, having a blast. But, all along, she'd been preparing herself for something like this. She'd predicted that his show would be a success and it would go to his head, or his show wouldn't fly and he'd go back to Pokey. Things hadn't played out exactly as she'd said; the success hadn't occurred, but it had still gone to his head. And all it had taken was one unpleasant event to reveal how little comfort they were to each other.

She couldn't wipe away the memory of Fionn's disregard for Jemima or his lack of empathy for Maeve, but, still, she couldn't dislike him either — at least she didn't at this very moment, who knew how she'd feel in an hour or a day or a week? Too much had happened to him too quickly. You'd have to have a rock-solid sense of self to remain unaltered in the face of all the attention he'd recently been showered with.

And, to be honest, she was knackered. She was worn fecking well out from all the late-night shenanigans and drinking and sex. Her skin was in flitters, the laundry hadn't been done in weeks and her laziness at work had been nothing short of outrageous.

Speaking of work, she didn't like the insidious way she'd started treating Fionn like one of her artistes. Promising him everything would be okay, *patronizing* him.

She was hit with a strange thought — certainly strange for a woman with her relationship with food — that being with Fionn was like eating chocolate all the time:

glorious in theory, but now and again you'd like some proper food.

A hoodie was lying on her chair and she pulled it on over her pajamas and slipped into a pair of her mid-height heels — she was feeling a little too fragile for the full five-inchers. From the cupboard under the sink, she gathered bathroom cleaner, rubber gloves and a couple of sponges, then slipped downstairs to the ground floor. In the light cast by the street lamps, she saw that a temporary door of raw plywood had been fitted to Matt and Maeve's flat. A brand-new, super-shiny lock sat in a frame of splinters and there were two equally super-shiny keys on the hall table.

All she had to do was pick one up and let herself in, but suddenly she was reluctant. Then the oddest impulse came over her. She decided to open the front door, the one to the street, because Conall Hathaway would be waiting outside.

She turned the knob, she swung the door and standing on the step was . . . "Conall?"

"Katie?"

So many weird things are happening, she thought. I can't keep up with them all.

"It's five in the morning," she said.

"Quarter past." He checked his watch, then fixed his eyes on her in utter astonishment. "I was just going to buzz your flat to let me in. Look." He demonstrated his hand. "I was just about to touch the thing that says your name.

And you just . . . materialized."

"I must have heard your car or something," Katie said, faintly. "Are you looking for Lydia?"

"Out working." Well, she might be; her car was nowhere to be seen. He wasn't getting into the breakup stuff with Katie. "I woke up, like, half an hour ago, just bolt upright, and my first thought was, *the bath.*"

"Me too." Katie indicated her cleaning stuff. "I didn't want Maeve —"

"— coming home to that horror —"

"— so I thought I'd come down and —"

"— empty the bath and —"

"— clean up a bit."

They chanced a wobbly smile at each other. "I like your shoes," he said.

"Standards must be maintained. And what's that you're wearing?" She touched the tips of her fingers to his black sweater. "Cashmere? To clean up blood?"

"I haven't a clue what it is," he said. "I needed to wear something and who cares if blood gets splashed on it?"

She nodded somberly. "I know what you mean. Kind of puts things in perspective, all right. But he's going to be okay. Fionn says they've given him four liters of blood and he'll be getting out in the morning."

Conall nodded. "Did you know him? Matt?"

"Only to say hello to. Did you?"

"Only to see."

"All the same."

"Yeah . . . I thought Maeve might be home already," Conall said.

"Fionn said she was still at the ER at midnight —"

"— and the keys are out here —"

"— so I suppose it's safe to go in —"

They let themselves into the silent flat and made their way down the short hallway to the bathroom. Conall pushed the door with his fingertips and it swung open and there it was, the bathful of blood. Redder and even more shocking than he remembered.

Conall swallowed noisily. "Better pull the plug."

They exchanged a look.

"I'll do it," Katie said.

"No, I'll —"

Two steps from Katie, the plunge of an arm, an efficient hoist and immediate gurgly draining noises. "There." She tried to smile. "Done."

". . . Ah . . . thanks. Christ, you're magnificent." He handed her a towel to dry her arm.

She shrugged, half-embarrassed. "Nothing to it."

"*I* didn't want to do it."

"Don't suppose anyone would actually *want* to do it."

"I thought he was dead," Conall said, his voice husky. "When I first came in. It was horrible. I'll never forget it."

"The weird thing was that I didn't know what I was looking at," Katie said. "I couldn't make sense of it."

"I know what you mean."

"Like, why was the water so red?"

"Yeah, and why did he look so . . . you know? Nothing prepares you for something like that."

"Nothing." She was emphatic. "It was the worst thing I ever saw. God . . ." Noiseless tears began to slide down her face.

"Don't cry!" Tentatively, Conall put a hand on her shoulder and, when she continued to cry, he gathered her awkwardly to him. "He's going to be okay."

"But it's so sad." She allowed herself to fall against him, just for a moment, against the softness of his sweater. It was such a comfort to let go. "What must they have gone through? To get to that point?"

He rested his chin on her head and she cried into his sweater. When the worst of the tears had passed, she pulled herself away. "I'm all right now."

"Sure?"

"Grand. Thanks." But being held by him had felt good and right and she had the unexpected thought that maybe herself and Conall would be friends after this.

"Let's get cleaning."

"Okay." Conall began gathering up bloody

702

towels from the floor. "What'll I do with these?"

"Stick them in the machine and — Oh, you probably haven't a clue how to put on a wash."

"Course I have."

"So let's see you."

"Come on!" Carrying his bundle of towels, he strode down the hall until he found the utility room, chucked the lot into the machine and slammed the door shut.

"Got to switch it on," Katie said. "Got to find the right program."

"I *know.*" He twisted a couple of dials — how hard could it be? — and waited for stuff to start happening.

"Powder," Katie said, handing him a box of detergent.

"Oh yeah, nearly forgot." He yanked the door open again and was about to sling in half the box when Katie stopped him.

"No. No. Not in there." She was laughing. She'd gone quite giddy. It must be delayed shock. "You haven't a clue, have you?"

He looked at her. He never admitted to not knowing something.

"This machine, it must be different to the model I have."

Steadily, she held his gaze, her eyes dancing, until he dropped the look and admitted, "Okay, I haven't a clue."

"Lovely," Katie said, almost cheerily.

"That's all I wanted to hear."

She added the powder, found the right program and, when the swishing started, they went back to the bathroom and together they scrubbed the bath and the floor and washed away the red splashes that decorated the walls and tiles, erasing all evidence. They worked in silence until the task was completed. "That's it, I think. All done." With a final flourish of her sponge, Katie wiped away the last smear, then sank to the floor, leaning her back against the bath. "God, that was hard." She used the sleeve of her hoodie to wipe the sweat from her face.

"Satisfying, though." Conall joined her on the floor, propping himself against the opposite wall.

"That too."

Buoyed up by the strange, almost celebratory mood, Katie decided to take a chance. "Come here, Conall. Can I ask you a question? Something I've been dying to know."

"Work away."

"Can you speak Portuguese?"

"Ah, you know. Enough to get by."

"Really? Honest to God for real?"

"Yeah."

"How did Jason know about it?"

". . . Let's see." Conall drummed his fingers on his lips as he thought. "Oh yeah! I met him at some yoke for the Portuguese Trade Board. His fiancée, wife now, I suppose, is

Portuguese — sure you know that."

"Nice to know that you didn't lie about absolutely everything."

He turned, looking aghast at her.

"Oh come on! Don't give me that look!"

With great urgency, he said, "Katie, I'm different now."

"Lucky Lydia. Didn't I always tell you it would be the girl after me who reaped the benefits of my hard work?"

"Yes, but Katie —"

"I *thought* I heard voices."

Conall and Katie jerked their heads round. Jemima, looking every one of her eighty-eight years, was standing in the bathroom doorway.

"I was anxious that evidence of Matthew's foolhardiness be cleared away before Maeve brings him home. But I see you pair of ministering angels have beaten me to it."

2 hours

Jemima, having persuaded Maeve to wait at the hospital until 7 a.m. to accompany Matt home, had one last good deed to do and, really, this charming setup here, with Katie and Conall having toiled side by side, simply couldn't be better. Life was all about timing. As indeed was death.

She placed the back of her hand against her forehead and permitted herself a neat little collapse, folding herself up like an accordion.

"Christl!" Conall leaped to his feet and caught her before her knees hit the floor. "Are you all right?"

Well, hardly, *dear. I've just done a picture-perfect swoon.*

"I think you'd better lie down." He looked for confirmation to Katie, who nodded.

"Jemima, if Conall carries you, can you make it upstairs to your place?" Katie asked.

"I think so," Jemima said faintly. What a sensible creature Katie was. It would be a very unpleasant homecoming indeed for Matthew and Maeve to discover a sick old woman prone on their sofa. And Jemima had plans of her own, which she would prefer to carry to fruition without interruption.

Conall insisted on carrying Jemima in his arms up to her own flat, where he expertly negotiated all the heavy furniture crowded into the front room and gently arranged her on the divan. Grudge skittered around anxiously, like a fussy old woman.

"I do apologize," Jemima murmured. "So much drama."

"We're all a bit wobbly since last night," Katie said.

"What can we get you?" Conall asked. "A glass of water? Are there tablets?"

"Goodness me, no," Jemima said. "I don't need a single thing. Except . . ."

"Except?" Katie said. "You'd like Fionn?" Concern passed over her face, her expression saying, *But I don't know where he is.*

"No need for Fionn, wherever he is." Much as Jemima loved him, she had other fish to fry. "But could both you and Conall bear to sit a while with me? It won't be for long, I assure you."

"Of course we will," Katie said.

"Sure." Conall chimed in.

Katie was such a sweet girl, Jemima thought. She'd known that she would stay. And naturally Conall would do whatever would please Katie.

So it was definite: Fionn hadn't stayed the night in Jemima's, Katie thought. Which meant he had stayed *somewhere else* — which conjured up all kinds of possibilities, none of them nice. *He met a girl, he slept with her.* But no! She wouldn't think about it! Not now. Some other time, when she was able for it. Because the thing was, it was going to hurt, a lot. Not just the jealousy of whatever he'd got up to during his missing hours, not just the grief of the demise of herself and Fionn — because it was looking like it had run its course — but there was so much other pain that Fionn had killed for her. He'd numbed out all her sadness about Conall, polished up the humdrum into a sparkling gem and shown her that there was life, plenty of it, after forty. Gone now, she acknowledged. All used up.

What she was dreading most of all was re-feeling that awful loss when she'd discovered that Conall was seeing Lydia. That had been utter agony and she didn't think she had the strength to go through it again. Some masochistic impulse couldn't resist having a little probe now, just to see how excruciating it was . . . and maybe she wasn't poking hard enough, because she felt surprisingly okay.

Maybe she was better! Could that have been Fionn's purpose? To come along and heal her? And then do a legger when she was fixed?

After all, she'd had a drink with Conall and his girlfriend. And she and Conall had cleaned a bathroom in an atmosphere of friendliness and cooperation. And look at them now, taking care of an old lady.

Or maybe she had the Fionn situation completely wrong. Maybe all that had happened was that she and Fionn had just had their first serious row. Maybe he'd spent the night with Grainne and Mervyn and any minute now he'd burst through the door, wild with remorse and bursting with love, and they'd fall into each other's arms and cry and say how sorry they were and they'd be all the stronger for it? It could happen!

Jemima pulled some hairpins out of her bun. "Digging into my skull," she explained. "I've endured daily discomfort for at least eighty years and I find I've had enough."

"You're letting your hair down," Conall said.

"Precisely, dear!"

"It's never too late."

"Hold that thought, Conall, as they say in those American shows. Now . . ." Jemima settled herself back on the divan, looking small and wan, the effort of yanking out the hairpins having taken its toll.

Katie knelt by the divan, a heavy, carved mahogany table behind her and an elaborately floral armchair at her side. "Would you like me to hold your hand?" She felt that Jemima needed some sort of comfort, but you never knew with posh Protestants. They could be gravely offended at any offers of affection.

"Would you, dear heart? That would be *such* a consolation." Her face creased into a grateful smile and she extended a veiny, bony hand.

"I could hold your other one," Conall offered.

"Conall!" Jemima said. "That would be entirely delightful."

Surprised, Katie looked at him. Since when had he started going round being kind to old ladies? He gave a shrug that said, *Why the hell not?*

Why the hell not, indeed.

Grudge took up the middle spot, between Katie and Conall, his woolly head on Jemima's lap, and all Katie could think about was how very, very weird it all was. Her! And Conall Hathaway! In Jemima's apartment, holding her hand! How had they ended up in such a bizarre triangle?

None of them spoke, all tired out probably, Katie realized, after all the events of the past twelve hours. After a while, an anxious little voice in her head began to wonder how long Jemima was expecting them to stay. Was she well enough to be left on her own yet? But it seemed like bad manners to ask and, anyway, any minute now Conall was bound to have to run off to catch a plane or to take over the world, and in the meantime she couldn't deny that sitting on Jemima's carpet and holding her hand was unexpectedly peaceful. All she could hear was the sound of their breath, Conall's and Jemima's and her own. And the dog's, of course.

"Might I . . ." Jemima said tentatively, "might I . . . that is, would you think badly of me if I asked a small favor?"

"Anything," Conall said.

"Could you tell me, you see I've always wanted to know, an item *of gossip.*"

1 hour

Raw, bare plywood. Maeve was angered at the sight of their new door.

"Look," she said to Matt. "See what you did."

710

"God." He stared at the bare wood, working out what must have happened. He looked sick.

"I suppose these must be the keys." Maeve snatched a set from the hall table and Matt held out his hand, expecting she'd give them to him, but she was already slotting one into a lock.

She was furious again. Jemima's lecture had calmed her, she'd felt bizarrely hopeful for a short while, but now the rage was back and all her senses were lit up with it — her skin felt thick, her hands clumsy, her eyeballs hot, her tongue swollen. It was so long since she'd felt anything and everything had come rushing at her all at once; her body was struggling to contain it.

It took her trembling fingers a while to get the hang of the new lock. "Fucking thing," she muttered. She rarely swore so using that word felt very satisfying. When the lock finally clicked, she gave the door a good, hard, enjoyable shove. The first thing she noticed was the clean, fresh smell in the flat. One of the neighbors must have come in and disappeared away the evidence of Matt's . . . Matt's . . . she didn't know how to describe what he'd done.

It was decent of whoever had come in. Probably Katie, she decided. But her rage couldn't help leaking out, even at that act of neighborly goodness. It would have done

711

Matt no harm to see more evidence of what he'd done.

"Do you want tea or something?" she asked ungraciously.

"I'd love a cup."

She put the kettle on, then went into the bedroom and wrenched the big suitcase out from under their bed. The last time it had been used was on their honeymoon; a Malaysian Air baggage tag still fluttered from it. She took the case in her arms and hurled it with force on to the bed, where it bounced a few times, then she clunked the lock and, sweeping her arms wide, flung it open.

She'd start with his shoes. There they were, lined together neatly on the floor of their wardrobe, and she began picking them up and lobbing them one by one toward the bed. Sometimes they landed in the case and sometimes they didn't, bouncing on the bed, clanging off the radiator, clattering against the window.

It was almost like a game, actually quite enjoyable, and she was sorry when she ran out of shoes.

The kettle was probably boiled by now anyway, so she went into the kitchen and made tea. Matt was sitting on the sofa in the front room, looking small and ashamed. "Tea." She thrust the mug at him. "I've started packing your things."

His face spasmed.

"Oh?" she asked. "You didn't think I meant it. But I do. It's real. It's happening."

"How will you live on your own?"

"You weren't thinking of that when you ran yourself that bath yesterday, were you?"

He hung his head. "I shouldn't have done it." His voice choked. "I wish I could take it back."

"I'll manage on my own. It'll be better than living with you and waiting for you to try to top yourself again." While she'd been sitting beside his trolley in the ER, she'd thought it all through. Kicking Matt out of the flat was just for show, an attempt to hurt him for the way he'd hurt her, because she was going back to live with Mam and Dad. Her life was over anyway, it had ended three years ago, and living in the back of beyond couldn't make it any more over. And if the screaming despair down on the farm got too terrible, well, she could always hang herself in a barn or mess around on the edge of a slurry pit or get too close to a combine harvester. Spoiled for choice. When you thought about it, it was an absolute miracle that any farm worker managed to live long enough to see their twenty-first birthday.

She'd been thinking about being dead for so long, she was very comfortable with the notion. Admittedly, she hadn't quite got to where Matt had got to, but she didn't want to go on living. She hadn't been exactly sure how to die. But she'd have got there.

30 minutes

Lydia was so shattered she felt sick. The high jinks of last night had taken their toll and she was fit for nothing. Not even sleep. Was that possible, she wondered. To be too tired to be able to sleep? But she was too tired to think about it. Telly, that's what she needed. She flung herself full-length on the couch and pawed around for the remote. Thank God it was Saturday and she didn't have to endure the usual weekday, early morning shite: fatso makeovers and diets and cookery. First she found a program about Botswana, then she found one on Cuba. She luxuriated in her indolence, half awake, half asleep, dreaming of foreign lands. God, this was great. She could drift off right here without fear of disturbance from grumpy Poles. It was *fabulous* living on her own.

When the doorbell rang, rudely interrupting her paradise, she was outraged. No! Nohhhhh! I'm not bloody well going.

It rang again.

No, still not going.

It rang again.

You can ring a million times, she told it. I'm still not going.

It rang again.

Love of God! Stomach-first, she vaulted

from the couch, like a high-jumper clearing the bar, stomped noisily into the hall and pressed the buzzer. Ten seconds later someone knocked on her door and she wrenched it open. *"What?"*

Standing there was a man with dark eyes and longish hair, a touch of wildness to him. Selling mops, she assumed. But, to her horror, she saw that he had some sort of musical instrument in a case under his oxter. A door-to-door busker? When did that lark start? God Almighty, do they torment us even in our own homes?

She said, "I'll give you money if you promise *not* to sing."

He looked confused. "I em Oleksander. Oleksander Shevchenko."

"Who? Oh! The person who was here before me." Not a roving entertainer! Her face lit up with relief.

"And you?" he said. "You are new tenant? You live now in little room?"

"Yes, yes. You're here for your letters? I suppose you'd better come in."

". . . And no one in your family had any idea about Charlie's secret love-child?" Jemima was incredulous.

"Not a clue," Conall said, with some smugness, glad to be able to contribute such a juicy item of gossip to Jemima. "Only Katie. Only because I knew, and it was pure chance that I found out." Conall had come by the information when he'd been "rationalizing" a company and a young woman had thrown herself on his mercy and begged to keep her job because she had a child to support and wasn't receiving a penny from the dad — who'd transpired to be Charlie Richmond, younger brother of Katie.

"But why would your brother neglect to tell your parents?" Jemima was struggling to understand. "Surely they would be delighted to discover they had a grandchild?"

"Because Katie's mother is a —" Conall paused and looked at Katie.

"What?" Katie asked.

Choosing his words with evident care, Conall said, "She's a . . . an unfulfilled woman who, ah, undermines all her children."

Katie dropped her eyes and smiled to herself. "You never said."

Conall's eyes lit with indignation. "As if, Katie. I made a lot of mistakes with you, way too many, but I wasn't a total idiot."

"I must say," Jemima said happily. "That really is a choice morsel of gossip. Well worth waiting a lifetime for." She shifted herself beneath the weight of Grudge's head. "Not there, my darling hound. Too painful."

"Oh?" Katie asked, just as Jemima had intended she would.

"I had cancer four years ago." With an airy wave, Jemima dismissed it as being barely worse than a stubbed toe. "The wretched thing has returned."

Katie and Conall exchanged a look.

"How do you know?" Katie asked cautiously. "Have you had tests?"

"No need. I can feel them. Tumors. One on my liver. Quite large. I can no longer button my skirt. Most vexing." She smiled. "When one's skirt no longer fits, it's time to go."

". . . Ah . . . we can get you a new skirt," Conall said, trying to hide his mortification beneath a veneer of jolliness. "A whole new wardrobe."

"Most kind. But that wouldn't banish the cluster of bumps under my left arm. Or those behind my knees."

That wiped the fake smile off Conall's face good and proper. He gazed anxiously at Katie. Was Jemima serious? Katie returned Conall's beseeching look and gave a small shake of her head: she hadn't a clue what was going on.

"I see I have embarrassed you," Jemima said. "For that I apologize. And I see that you doubt me, but I assure you I am deadly in earnest."

In response to their stunned silence, she repeated, "Deadly in earnest."

"I see . . ." Conall sounded stumped. "So how can we help you?"

"You can't."

"No such word as can't." Conall began

rummaging for his phone. "I'll find a doctor."

"He really is quite the Mr. Fix-it." Jemima smiled at Katie, who wasn't finding this at all amusing. "He'll be ringing that long-suffering Eilish, I'll wager. Find a new door, Eilish! Find a cancer specialist, Eilish! Poor woman. Conall, put that confounded contraption away. I'm beyond the help of a doctor."

She reached out to touch Conall's Black-Berry and, as she did, her body twisted, lifting her skirt and revealing alien-like clusters of lumps and bumps, like mini mountain ranges, behind each knee.

Jesus Christ, Katie thought. Jemima certainly wasn't exaggerating.

She stared at Conall and the look on his face said that he had gone beyond shock. "Right! That's it!" Conall knew when he was in over his head. "I'm ringing an ambulance!"

"Absolutely not," Jemima said, in ringing tones. "Absolutely not! I forbid you."

To his great surprise, Conall found he was afraid to defy her.

"It's far too late," Jemima said.

"No." Conall was having a series of speedy visions, of Jemima being wheeled into surgery, of Jemima having infusions of magic drugs, of a hundred different ways the doctors could fix her. Agitatedly, he flipped his BlackBerry from hand to hand.

"Far too late, dear heart," Jemima repeated.

"We can't just *do nothing.*" He thought he would burst with frustration.

"Yes, we can," Jemima said. "A good lesson for you to learn, Conall. Sometimes nothing is the very best thing one can do."

"But why didn't you do anything before now?" Katie exclaimed. Why hadn't Fionn insisted she got help? And why hadn't Fionn told her that Jemima was sick?

Jemima looked ashamed. "Would you think me a coward if I admitted a reluctance to endure chemo again? It was deeply unpleasant. I'm eighty-eight, and it's been a good life, except, of course, for the dearth of gossip."

"But what about the pain? Aren't you in pain?" Conall asked.

"Oh, pain," Jemima said dismissively. "Everyone is so frightened of pain. But how else is one to know one is alive? Conall, please put away your phone and hold my hand again, I was so enjoying that."

Reluctantly, Conall settled down again on the floor and Jemima extended her hands to be held.

"Why are you telling us this if you won't let us help you?" Conall asked.

"Don't be frightened, Conall. To all things there is a season."

"That's not answering my question."

Jemima laughed.

"And neither is that."

"Is there someone, people, you'd like us to ring?" Katie chose her words carefully. Jemima was clearly very sick, far sicker than they'd known when she'd done her little swoon downstairs in Matt and Maeve's, and she wasn't showing signs of getting up off the divan any time soon: how appropriate was it that herself and Conall were the ones by her side? Jemima knew Katie fairly well, but Conall was practically a total stranger. "To be here with you?"

"You're the two I want."

Why? "Well —" and Katie had to force herself to be brave — "at the very least Fionn should be here." That meant Katie would have to try to find him, and she didn't want to because she might bump up against all kinds of painful stuff.

"I sought opportunities over these past few days to tell him, but we were always interrupted."

"You mean . . . ?" Jesus Christ. *Fionn didn't know.* "Conall, quick, give me your phone, mine's upstairs."

With fumbling hands, Conall passed it over and Katie left a quick, terse message for Fionn. "You need to come home right now. It's urgent."

"I wanted to kill myself too," Maeve said suddenly.

Matt looked aghast. "Why didn't you tell me?"

"Why didn't *you* tell *me?*"

Matt stared up at her, his shoulders bowed, his eyes dead. "Christ, what a shambles," he said, with terrible weariness. "You wanted to kill yourself. I actually tried to. I suppose the real miracle is how we managed to keep going for so long."

"It's been . . ." Maeve had to stop. "I can't think of the right word. A nightmare wouldn't describe it, it wouldn't come close."

"Nightmares end."

"And this just went on and on. Sometimes, when I was a kid, I used to think about my life and wonder what was going to happen, because they always said that bad stuff would happen to everyone at some stage. And I thought about things, you know? Trying to prepare myself. But I never thought about this. I never thought I could be raped. And I never thought I'd feel so . . . so . . . I had no idea that anyone could feel this bad for so long."

"Sweetheart . . ."

"And I'm sorry, Matt. It was very hard for you, I know that. You just got caught up in someone else's stuff. You didn't bargain on any of this when you married me."

"I loved you."

"It was too much for us, though. We're only

human. Both of us suicidal, that's not a good sign."

He gave a weak smile.

"How do you feel now?" Maeve asked. "Still not able to go on?"

"Not the way we were."

"Me either. Come on, you can help me pack your stuff."

In the bedroom, Matt slowly gathered his shoes from all the places they'd landed and lined them up on the floor.

"It's probably better if the clothes go in first," he said.

"Grand." She opened one of Matt's drawers, gathered an armload of clothes and dumped them in the case. And the memories hit her. It was the smell, she realized. A cloud of it had risen from the impact of the clothes. She could smell their honeymoon — sea salt and sandalwood and moist fecund air — as if they were there right now. Wasn't it unbelievable that the residue had survived so strongly for three long years? Dried rose petals were still strewn in the bottom of the case and she picked out a couple.

"Remember these?"

"Oh, I do." Matt's eyes sparked briefly at the memory. "It was every night after dinner, wasn't it?" They'd come back to their room and find that some mysterious person had used handfuls of rose petals to draw a big red heart on their duvet.

"And in the beginning we thought it was so romantic."

"Ah no, I always thought it was cheesy."

"No, you didn't, Matt, you loved it!"

"Wellll, I guess I thought it was nice that someone would go to the trouble."

"But then we started getting ungrateful, d'you remember? And we'd be saying that the hearts were getting smaller and more crooked."

"And the petals would get into the bed —"

"— and we used to be finding them in all kinds of places," she said.

"*All* kinds of places," he repeated.

"And do you remember the bath the butler bloke ran us?"

"No . . . Oh yes! That's right. More bloody petals!"

"And we were covered with them and we couldn't get them off us —"

"— and they'd gone black from the water so we looked like we had Kaposi's sarcoma."

And even that hadn't put them off drying each other with elaborate care and having sex for about the hundredth time. It was amazing, really, Maeve thought, just how much sex they'd had during those two weeks. Almost as if they'd known it was all going to come to a sudden stop and that they'd better make hay while they could.

"We were so happy then," Maeve said. "Like, we were, we really were, weren't we?

I'm not making it up?"

"I felt like the luckiest man on the planet. I'm not joking. You were everything I ever wanted . . . No, it's more like you were everything I hadn't even known I'd wanted and I was so scared that I'd never get you."

"And look at how it ended up. Three years later you try to kill yourself."

The shock of it hit her afresh and a storm of crying overtook her.

"Maeve, please, it was only because I thought you'd be better off without me. I thought I was no use to you."

"Yeah? Well, you were."

She snatched hold of him and held tightly on to his body, pressing herself against the solidity, the realness, the warmth, the life in it, feeling his heartbeat and her own.

"Don't ever do that to me again," she whispered. "It was worse than anything else that's happened in the last three years. Miles worse."

"Come on, come in, your letters are in the kitchen. I've no time for chat, I'm in the middle of watching —"

Softly, Oleksander Shevchenko asked, "And do you find my bed comfortable?"

Lydia had almost turned away, but at this impertinence she twisted back to him, a sharp put-down in her mouth. The *neck* of him. Nothing but men being necky recently.

724

"My bed . . . ?" he insisted, his expression full of sauciness. "To your likingk?"

"Actually," Lydia stared him right in the eye, "your bed *is* to my liking." She could more than hold her own with random sauce-merchants.

Wait a minute! Their heart currents are going berserk, right here on the doorstep, with flashing lights and the sound of applause, like a fruit machine when someone hits the jackpot.

But is it enough? Is there time? Can they fall in love and have sex in the next twenty-two minutes? Because that's all I have left.

Then — no, no, don't — Lydia remembered the girl who had come looking for Oleksander, she remembered the promise she had made that if Oleksander ever showed up she was to give him her phone number. As far as Lydia was concerned, a promise was a promise. "Someone came here looking for you."

Fear shot across Oleksander's face. "Big mens with guns?"

"No, a girl."

"I vos jokingk." He sighed with abrupt gloom. "Ukrainians are a joke-loving people. Like you Ireesh, we, as you say, love the craic, but the language barrier . . . I joke, joke, joke all the day long but Ireesh do not understand."

"Come on, do you want the letters or not?"

He followed her into the kitchen, where she hunted for the pile of post.

"The girl who came?" he asked. "It was Viktoriya?"

"No," Lydia said thoughtfully. "Not Viktoriya, nothing like Viktoriya. Siobhan, I think her name was, an Irish debt-collector, looking to give you a court order."

He looked terrified. "But I hev not . . . I did not . . ."

Lydia let three seconds pass. Four. Five. Then she said sweetly, "I vos jokingk."

"Ah! Having the craic with me!"

"Having the craic, just as you say. I heard you love it."

Oh, this pair are perfect for each other, simply perfect! Eyebrow-raising and defiant expressions and much sexy eye contact. If I could just steer them toward the bedroom . . . Lydia wouldn't give me any crap about not sleeping with a man less than ten minutes after they'd first met. For spontaneity, for catching life by the balls, she's my girl.

"Yes, it was Viktoriya who came."

Never mind Viktoriya! Forget her, forget her!

Oleksander's face lit up. And promptly fell. "I do not hev phone number."

"It's okay, she wrote it down. And she said to tell you something . . ." What the hell was it? "A man. *The* man —"

"From Department of Egriculture?"

"That's the one. She said to tell you he smelled of cows."

Oleksander laughed softly to himself. "Bed smell, huh?"

"Unless you like the smell of cows, I suppose. Here it is." Lydia had located Viktoriya's note. "And here's your mail."

20 minutes

The only sound in the room was the ticking of a big wooden clock. Jemima's eyes were closed in peaceful silence and Katie, Conall and Grudge lovingly watched over her. Katie had let go of any thoughts of making an escape and, from the calmness she could feel off Conall, she knew he'd obviously given up on his frantic notions of life-saving surgery and last-minute chemo. The room was so still and tranquil that Katie began to eddy down into a pre-sleep state and was brought back to the now when Jemima spoke.

"I've had a good and happy time on earth," she said.

"What more can you ask for, really?" Conall said.

"Death is only sad if one hasn't lived one's life."

Death? *Death?* Katie and Conall looked at

each other.

"I'm entirely ready to go."

Did she mean she was planning to die now?

"Yes, dears."

Right now? Right *here?*

"In the next few minutes. And I want to be here, in my own home, with both of you here with me." Katie and Conall shared another look.

I say we should let her have her way, Conall's eyes said.

So do I.

Will we forget about ambulances and all of that?

Let's just do what she's asking and . . .

. . . *Let's just go where this takes us.*

But how did it get so serious so quickly?

"This hasn't come upon me suddenly," Jemima said. "The presence of death has been in this house for weeks."

That's when I realize that, actually, she hasn't got the wrong end of the stick; there has been a presence here. Other than mine, I mean. Those times when I was so good I scared myself — that wasn't me at all. That was our friend, the Grim Reaper, the old buzz-wrecker himself.

It's often the policy: one in and one out.

In quiet harmony, Maeve and Matt filled the suitcase with Matt's clothes. Oddly, the longer they packed, the less likely it seemed that he was leaving.

"I'll be back in a second," he said to Maeve.

"Where are you going?"

"I'm a bit cold."

"If you will go cutting your wrists . . ."

"I'll never do it again."

"You'd better bloody well not."

"I know it's August but do you mind if I put on the heat?"

She thought about it. "Let's get into the bed for a while. It's probably warmer there."

They shoved the suitcase to the floor and most of the things they'd packed fell out, then they lay fully clothed on the bed and threw the duvet up in the air, letting it fall and wrap itself softly about them. Maeve twined her legs tightly around Matt and briskly rubbed his back, his shoulders, his arms. "Any warmer?"

"Yes."

"Good."

"Listen, I've an idea!" Matt said suddenly.

"What is it?"

"We could get a kitten. Or a puppy."

"A puppy?" Maeve said slowly. "No, it would be jealous."

Lydia handed Oleksander a small bundle of envelopes. "Tell me where you live now, give me your address."

He tilted his head and gazed at her with

quite naked sauce. "So you can visit and see my new sleeping place?"

Lydia wore an expression of polite irritation. *I'll see your naked sauce,* her look said. *And I'll raise you a provocative stare.*

"So I can send your stuff on," she said. "And stop you calling around, interrupting me watching Michael Palin."

Now, now! Do it now, get on with it now! Sex and plenty of it! My life depends on it!

15 minutes

"Be kind to each other," Jemima murmured, closing her eyes.

"Who?" Conall asked. He just wanted to be sure.

"You two. You and Katie."

"Okay."

Jemima's breathing became quieter and the fall and rise of her chest softer and weaker until it became invisible. Conall was — well, he didn't know exactly how he felt, except that he was no longer scared, the way he had been a while ago when Jemima had revealed how sick she was. He no longer needed to make phone calls or organize the unorganizable or run away. He was prepared to sit on this violently patterned rug, sit here for as long as it took, holding the hand of a dying woman.

How weirdly coincidental that, for the

second time in a day, he was right up against the thin membrane that divided life and death. But this time was different, this time felt strangely beautiful.

Oleksander leans closer to accept the letters. His face is so close to Lydia's that he'd barely have to move to kiss her.

I'm telling you, the air is hopping with sex! One kiss and they'd be overtaken by passion; there's so much of it fizzing and popping between them. One kiss, that's all I'm asking for and the rest will take care of itself.

But Oleksander laughs softly, then lounges out through the door and down the stairs.

He'll be back. But not in time for me. Bollocks.

"So your man Conall actually broke down the door?" Matt asked.

"And took complete charge. Shouting orders left, right and center and everyone hopping to it. Are you warm yet?"

"No. Keep rubbing."

"We'll have to do something to thank him."

"We will. Any ideas?"

"Yes."

". . . Ah, feel like sharing them with me?"

"We'll call our baby after him."

"What baby?"

"We're going to have a baby."

"Are we?" Matt pulled back from Maeve, in order to look properly into her face.

"The wise old woman upstairs says we are."

"But . . . how are we going to manage that?"

"Like this." Maeve wrenched her T-shirt over her head and wriggled out of her cords and knickers. "Will you . . . ?"

His eyes locked on to hers and, wearing an expression almost of panic, as if he was afraid she'd change her mind, Matt pulled off his clothes, then slid his arms around her and carefully gathered her fullness to him. For the first time in three years, he felt her soft naked body next to his, thigh against thigh, chest against chest, the bliss of his hand on the smoothness of her hip bone.

Tears spilled down her face and he kissed them away.

"Will I stop?" he asked.

"No, no, no."

"Is this okay?" Gently, he touched her.

She nodded.

"And this?"

"All of it, Matt, all of it's okay."

5 minutes

Conall slipped his spare hand into Katie's and she looked at him and smiled.

And would you credit it! Can you believe it! Their heart currents are in perfect harmony again.

It was now or never. Conall had to speak. He had something very important to say. "Katie, I —"

A noise at the door made them both look up.

"Fionn!" Katie exclaimed.

No! No, no, no!

Fionn was staring at Jemima on the divan, at Grudge whimpering quietly, at Conall's hand in Katie's.

Then, more gently, Katie spoke again and clambered to her feet. "Fionn . . ."

It was only when Grudge threw back his head and began to howl, that Conall realized what had happened.

Gently, slowly, patiently, his gaze never leaving her face, Matt let himself be guided by Maeve and, at the moment his body merged with hers, he paused and the look they shared was one of triumph.

"Cripes! We've done it," she said. She could barely believe it.

"You're right, we've done it." This was real. It was actually, really happening. With Maeve, his beautiful Maeve, who bewitched total strangers into collecting spilled coins from the floor of the Dart. "We've done it together, the two of us."

"Teamwork. More power to us."

"More power to our elbows."

"Matt, don't cry."

"Am I?" So he was. But why, when he was so happy? "Anyway, you're a fine one to talk."

Tears were spilling from the corners of Maeve's eyes. "I thought this would never happen again."

"Didn't you?"

"Didn't *you?*"

"Me? I never gave up hope!"

They were laughing, they were crying, with joy, with relief. They'd been lost to each other for such a long time, lost, they'd been so sure, for ever. But they'd found their way back to each other, they'd found their way home.

And just in the nick of time . . .

Here I go . . . I've had the tap to the head and it's happening, I'm dissolving, I'm already starting to forget. But . . . I'm in! I exist! Matt and Maeve's baby. I was always on my way to them but I must admit there were times when I wondered if I'd ever get here. Am I a boy or a girl? Not that it really matters because I'm finally in and . . . ooh, it's just like what happened to Killian in the story, everything's gone tingly and sparkly and, like the incoming tide washing away traces on the sand, I'm disappearing little by little, clearing the way for my soul to be rewritten by a brand-new —

And the man and woman, humble, good

734

people, kind and loving companions who shared the one soul, who had endured many sorrows in their lives, who had lived through times of fear and loneliness and despair, were full of heart and restored to happiness and love when they learned that their baby had finally been sent to them.

■ ■ ■ ■

EPILOGUE

■ ■ ■ ■

Four Months
Later . . .

It's a Saturday afternoon, at the end of November, and I'm flying over the streets of Dublin, looking for Star Street. Number 66, to be precise. My mission is to find my future parents. According to my information — which, by the way, isn't half as detailed as I'd like — at least one of them will be living there. Another pregnancy happened there four months ago, to a pair called Matt and Maeve, so it looks like a fertile sort of a spot.

But we're off to a bad start. It takes me ages to find the place and time is of the essence. There are — count 'em — not one, not two but *three* Star Streets in Dublin. The first Star Street showed up in jig time, but number 66 turned out to be a taxidermist's showroom. So I set off again, but the second 66 Star Street was an office block, all locked up because it's a Saturday.

Anyway, my traveling companion, who is killing time with me — he's always killing something, that same fellow — said he knew exactly how to get to the elusive third Star Street. He keeps going on about what an experienced traveler he is, always down here, he says, ending people's lives when they least expect it. So I put it up to him and said, all right so, show us this other Star Street, and he said, grand, I will, but I can't show you right now because I've got *my* mission to carry out, and it's very time-specific and you might as well come with me.

I was worried. Some in my situation get days, weeks, even months to identify their prospective parents, but I'd been given less than twenty-four hours — just the luck of the draw. Whatever was going to happen for me, it was going down today, and I wanted to get the lie of the land in 66 Star Street as soon as possible. On balance, though, I thought I'd be better off sticking with someone who actually knew how to get there. Waste some time to gain some time, as it were. So, swept along on my companion's self-important coattails, we arrive in the center of Dublin. I suppose you could say we're an odd couple, me about to give life and him about to take it away. But we aren't such an unlikely pair as we seem; life and death often work together, matching each other hit for hit.

We're in a wide street where some public rally is underway. I start reading the banners and listening to the chants and it appears to be a protest against the low conviction rate for Irish rapists and, as you might expect, the crowd is mostly women. Like, you wouldn't expect turkeys to be campaigning for extra Christmases.

Fast worker, my knowledgeable friend — in no time, he's spotted his mark: a lanky unkempt-looking yoke, name of David, one of the few men present. No surprises, David is with a girl; you wouldn't get too many lads going along to a rape protest on their own. And a lovely girl she is too: tall and slender, with a gap between her front teeth that doesn't look like she needs to go to the dentist for a brace, but just makes her all the better-looking, if you get me. Steffi is her name. And this David seems to be well aware of how lovely Steffi is, because his arm is clamped around her waist like a vice, like he's afraid she's going to do a legger.

Now, wait till I tell you something weird. David's vibrations are muted and harmless-seeming, but I'm picking up distress from Steffi. She doesn't want to be at the march. *She's only there because David was so insistent!* And she doesn't like the way he's holding on to her so tightly. All of a sudden she can't take it for one more second and she pops herself out from the rigid hold and he gives her this *look* and she says, sort of apologetically, "Too tight." And he gives her another look, very wounded-like, then he grabs her hand and squeezes it until it hurts.

My know-all companion is watching the sky, then eyeing the protesters, then watching the sky again. You wouldn't describe him as anxious, exactly, but attentive. His job, as he keeps telling me, calls for a lot of precision. Well, so does mine, as a matter of fact.

And then he's all smiles. "Ah, here it is."

Far above us, a plane has entered Irish airspace and its flight path is going to take it over the center of Dublin. I'm not liking this one bit. What has he lined up? A bomb? A crash? How many innocent people will be killed in order to take out this one individual?

"No." My companion laughs darkly (he does most things darkly; it's his way). "Nothing like that. It's quite ingenious, actually."

He points at the sky. "Up there, about a mile above us, a lump of ice is coming loose from the underside of the plane. Any second now it'll start to plummet to earth and it'll land right on top of me boyo here."

I'm impressed. I gaze upward, then back at the unkempt David, who hasn't a *clue* that he's living out his final seconds. I've a mad urge to alert him to do something really worthwhile with what remains of his life, but it's not like he'd listen. People never do. Anyway, a short way back in the march, he's just seen a couple of people he recognizes — a blondy-haired cheruby woman and a smiley man that you wouldn't exactly call plump, but you wouldn't exactly call not plump either, if you get me . . . Actually, hold on a minute, it's Matt and Maeve. From 66 Star Street. David has been hoping they'd be here and now that he's spotted them he lights up like a Christmas tree, but the kind they'd have in hell. Badness, blackness, that sort of thing. No stars or angels. Skulls, instead. Rotten teeth. Dead bats. And his vibrations start hopping with extra-strength venom. I'd had him all wrong.

Aha! David is thinking. *I'll go back there and taunt the pair of them. I'll introduce them to Steffi. I'll say that it's a crime that so many Irish rapists walk away free. It'll kill them!*

"Steffi! There's someone I want you to meet."

"Who?" Christ, you never saw anyone looking as miserable as her.

"My ex-girlfriend Maeve. Come and meet her."

Steffi's confused and afraid and, God, she *really* doesn't like him. "Why would I want to do that?"

"Just come on, would you?"

"No, David."

He tugs at her arm, pulling her with him, and she digs her heels in, so he gives her another hoick, much harder this time, and she wrenches herself backward, breaking free of him, and people are starting to look at him.

"Suit yourself," he says. Then he adds, "You bitch." And a cluster of banner-carrying girls

743

— strangers, like — gasp in shock. You can't be going round calling your girlfriend a bitch. But David doesn't care. He just steps forward, all business, and everyone around him scoots back and gives him space, because they know he's a bad hat.

Meanwhile, Matt and Maeve have spotted him and are presenting expressions of defiance. With a nasty little laugh, David walks one large pace, then another, deaf to the faint whistling sound that has suddenly started above his head, and oblivious of the breeze that's interfering with his already very messy hair.

"Now watch this," my companion murmurs to me.

And the very next thing, a smallish boulder of ice hurtles from the heavens and collides with David's head, sending him toppling to the ground. His head, shoulders and chest are covered with the jaggedy frozen ball and, from the way his blood is oozing out from under the ice, there's no doubt that he's dead.

There's a long silence and then everyone starts howling and yelping and running and tearing their hair and putting their arms protectively over their heads and gazing horror-struck at the sky and staring, their eyes bugging out of their heads, at the ball of ice, with the lower half of a body sticking out from under it.

However, and full credit to my companion

here, in spite of all the hoo-ha, no one else is hurt, not even a scratch from a stray ice chip.

"See," he says, swaggering around like the big man. "Talk about a precision strike."

"They'll be upset, though," I say. "Some of them will have nightmares and have to go on Valium. Look at poor Steffi there."

She's rooted to the spot and her mouth is wide open, trying to suck in oxygen. One of her hands is on her chest and the other is on her throat, and she's staring at her boyfriend's legs and at the blood that's oozing from beneath the boulder of ice. She's in profound shock. But, all the same, you can't miss the thick waves of relief that are coming off her.

"Steffi'll be grand," my companion says airily. "She's been trying to break it off with him for ages. They'll all be grand. Bit of counseling and Bob's your uncle."

"What about Matt and Maeve? She's pregnant. We don't want her going into shock and losing the baby."

My companion finds this highly amusing. "Take a look at them," he says.

Somehow, Matt and Maeve have fought their way to the front row of onlookers around David's body and their faces are luminous with some strange emotion — that isn't shock.

"Is he dead?" Maeve asks Matt.

"Sure looks like it. I fantasized about this. When I read about the balls of ice falling out of the sky, I wanted it to happen to him."

"Cripes, did you really?"

"And now look."

"It's enough to restore your faith."

"Right!" my companion says. "Job done. And a lovely neat one, if I may say so. Off we go to Star Street. We'll be there in five."

Five hours, more like. He was nothing like as familiar with the layout of Dublin as he'd given me to think and it took us *ages* to find the place. Flying back and forth over the city, time ticking away, me in a right panic. Anyway, I'm here now. Number 66, blue front door, knocker in the shape of a banana (no room for doubt), and in the ground-floor flat a throng of people — Salvatores and Fatimas and Cleos — are drinking beer and punch and eating sausage rolls. Matt and Maeve's leaving party, would you believe? They're departing Star Street and moving to a bigger place because of their forthcoming baby. So I start wafting myself around the crowded flat, finding out what's what. To my relief, neither Matt nor Maeve is showing any sign of delayed shock from the afternoon's icy events. On the contrary. They look wildly happy, chatting away good-oh to all their guests. Everyone asks about the baby. They already know it's a boy and they're calling him Conall, and although there *is* a Conall present at this party for whom the baby is being named, he is *not* the father.

In a quest for answers, I focus more on Conall, a fine, big, hunky specimen of a man, and suddenly I get a powerful tingling feeling: *he's the one.* He looks like a daddy; his dark hair has a neglected quality that bodes well, because daddies don't have time to be foostering around with hair gel and the like. And he wears the right kind of clothes — jeans and a dark-blue fleece — like he'd hoist you up on his shoulder and burp you and not care if you puked on him. His vibrations are decent, loving and humble (although I feel that the humility might be a fairly new addition to his bundle of characteristics). Most of all he's *ready.* In fairness, he'd want to be; he's forty-three.

Conall is watching the door, alert to each new arrival. Then there's this rush of energy, a spiky, barbed sort of a thing: Lydia has arrived. Apparently, she once had a short-lived fandango with Conall, but you'd never know. Through the multinational throng, they exchange a glance, but there's nothing left, not a zing, not a flash, sweet feck-all.

Lydia is trailed by a flashing-eyed, wild-haired musician, one Oleksander Shevchenko. He's a handsome devil, even if he is wearing an embarrassing scarf-meets-cravat type thing. Also, no jocks beneath his black jeans. Oleksander's eyes are sparking black angry fire because Lydia wouldn't let him bring his instrument, a special Ukrainian accordion, to the party. They've just had a fine, big, sexy shouting match in their flat two floors up.

You know what? This pair are worth considering. They *are* Very Much In Love . . . But, on second thoughts, I don't know . . . I'd be good-looking, no doubt about it, coming from that gene pool, and conception would be no bother (they do nothing except have sex), but Lydia has a lot of living in her yet. No way is she ready for me and I want to be wanted.

She seems to be making her way across the room to chew the fat with Conall, but, no, she's only getting herself a drink. But they're so close to each other that she realizes she can't ignore him.

"Howya, Hathaway. What is it? Dress-down Saturday?" Making some scornful reference to his jeans.

"Hello, Lydia," he says calmly. "You're looking well. How's Ellen?"

"Doing all right. Taking the tablets. She's not the full whack, obviously, never will be again, but she's not getting any worse."

"Murdy and Ronnie? Doing their duty?"

Lydia laughs. "Well, Murdy's *wife* does a lot. And Ronnie's produced a girlfriend from somewhere, some poor cow by the name of Shannon, and she's a dab hand at housework. But Mum's being taken care of and that's the main thing."

"And Raymond?"

"Still hiding out in Stuttgart. Ronnie wanted to send in a crack-squad to kidnap him, like the Secret Service does, and bring him back to face the music, but . . ." She shrugs. "You can't win every battle."

"Very wise. So, you still up and down to Boyne all the time?"

"I do Mondays and Tuesdays. We've a schedule; it's working okay."

"And Ellen's still living in her own house?"

"Still living in her own house. She asks about you sometimes. I'll tell her I saw you."

"Do. Do. And your brothers as well, tell them I said hey."

"They ask after you too. They took it very hard, me breaking it off with you. A lot harder than you did."

"Aaah, Lydia . . ."

Just one thing I've realized about Conall: he's not very happy. In fact, he's throbbing with a red-hot, long-last ache, like an ear infection, but of the heart . . . And something else: Conall doesn't *live* at 66 Star Street. So unless I can hook him up with a woman who resides here, it can't be him.

That starts a panic in me. I scoot to the top of the house, where a woman called Katie lives. She's sitting facing a handsome prince called Fionn. Their knees are touching, their heads are bent toward each other, there is a profound connection. Okay, she's no good for Conall but, if I'm stuck, she and Fionn would do.

The next floor down is where Lydia and Oleksander live. And the flat below that one houses a married couple, Andrei and Rosie. Mad-looking place. There's all this gloomy, heavy furniture but it looks like it's being edged out by a flood tide of bright, spriggy, yellow neatness.

The woman of the house, Rosie, is small, prim and pretty — *immensely* powerful. She's responsible for all the yellowness and she has plans for much more of it. She even made the yellow kitchen curtains herself. And Andrei? To be quite honest, I couldn't tell you the first thing about him because he has surrendered himself body and soul to this domestic dynamo.

In a basket in a corner, a great big donkey-like dog crouches, a leftover from the previous, dark-wood occupation and when Rosie is done with her decorating, he is all that will survive. Like Andrei, the dog adores Rosie. *Adores* her.

Andrei and Rosie are about to leave for the party and I follow them downstairs.

Just before Rosie knocks on Matt and Maeve's door, she taps her watch and says to Andrei, "An hour and fifteen minutes, we leave here at five past nine, not a second later. You can have two beers. Any more and there will be trouble."

Andrei nods. He's very happy. He likes to know what's what. Then Rosie smoothes her already smooth cotton shirtwaister — a great woman for the ironing — and summons up a sweet smile before rapping on the door.

And what I'm thinking is: no, not her. She's way too joyless. Andrei might be in the running if I could extricate him from Miss Prissy-knickers but I don't give much for my chances.

Maeve opens the door and Rosie hands over a little gingham-wrapped basket of home-made muffins and then they're in. Andrei's heartbeat steps up. He's on the alert, twisting his neck like a periscope, looking for Lydia — and then he sees her, poking her finger contemptuously through the sausage rolls. She must feel his eyes on her because she looks up sharply. Their gazes lock. Andrei is exhausted in so much panic that he thinks he might have a heart attack. As far as he's concerned, that lunacy with Lydia was the worst mistake he's ever made and he lives in terror of Rosie finding out. Automatically, he accepts a beer from Matt — one of his allotted two — and his panic starts to abate. And when all his fear has subsided, nothing else remains. As for Lydia, her eyes slide right over Andrei, like he's not even there.

Not them, so.

And now it transpires that it's two gay lads who are moving into Matt and Maeve's!

751

They're at the party, meeting their new neighbors. A likable pair, all smiles and banter and fashionable clobber, but neither of them is much use to me for conceiving a child with Conall.

Which means . . . there's no spare woman in this house for Conall.

What the hell. Make lemonade. It'll have to be Katie and Fionn.

Back up on the top floor there's no denying the bond between them. They're very close.

But something is off . . . They're close, but they're not together. They *were* together for a short time, but Fionn slept with someone called Alina the night Jemima, his foster-mother, died; and Katie found she didn't give a damn, so then the whole thing was wrecked. But they've stayed very fond of each other, all credit to them. You more often hear about the legs being cut off good suits, so it's nice to hear about a happy sundering for a change.

Fionn was knocked sideways by the death of his foster-mother. I suppose there'd be something wrong if he wasn't. He's saddled with a ton of guilt because he wasn't there for her, and Katie's been good to him.

Which means — all becomes clear — which means that Katie is available! Free to be with Conall! Katie's standing up. Because Fionn's leaving. He doesn't live here. He did for a spell, while he filmed a television show but it was never shown, and now he's gone back home, to some faraway rocky rural place called Pokey. He was only in Dublin today to pick up bits and pieces that used to belong to his foster-mother.

"Are you sure you won't pop in with me?" Katie asks, making for the door.

Fionn shakes his head. "Maeve doesn't like me."

Katie was trying to sympathize while simultaneously keeping them moving forward. "Don't be a baby."

Fionn stops in his tracks and gives a thousand-yard stare. "I'm not really a party person."

That makes Katie laugh good and hard.

"Okay," Fionn admits. "I was for a short while. But that wasn't who I really am. I'm a loner by nature."

"I know." Katie is patting him the way you would a small child. "Come on, out."

She locks her door and they go down a flight of stairs, and as they start going down the next one, Rosie and Andrei's dog tenses in his basket, then races out to his hall, barking and throwing himself with violence at the door. "Let me at him," he roars. "Let me at the yellow-haired prick. I'll have the shagging *leg* off him."

In response, Fionn gives the door a good hard kick and the lock rattles. "Fuck you too, you fucking psycho," he shouts. "You should be in a fucking *strait*jacket."

No love lost.

"He's a headcase," Fionn says to Katie.

"So you say, but it's Andrei's door now; you shouldn't really be kicking it."

"Can you believe Jemima actually left the flat to him? In her will?"

"I'm sure she had her reasons. What use is it to you? You hate Dublin."

Katie's anxious. Katie wants to keep things in motion because she wants to get to the party before —

Conall's leaving! Down on the ground floor he's said his goodbyes to Matt and Maeve, he's coming out of their door and now he's in the communal hall, and Fionn and Katie are still standing outside Andrei's flat, chin-wagging away about Jemima's will like they have all the time in the world. Like *I* have all the time in the world. Which I haven't.

"It was just a surprise, is all I'm saying," Fionn said.

"You can hardly complain. She left you all her money."

Come on. Come fecking ON! Downstairs, downstairs!

"And sure, what interest have I in property?" Fionn said.

"None at all. You're a man of the land."

"Speaking of which —" Fionn starts foostering in the pocket of his manky old jacket — "I've probably got something for you."

Oh sweet suffering Jesus! Would you COME

ON! One flight of stairs, that's all you have to do. Come down, come down! Fourteen steps. It's not going to kill you.

But Conall's opened the front door.

"Katie?"

Down in the hall, Conall's spotted Katie on the landing above him.

"Conall!" Katie's face blazes whiteness. She hasn't seen Conall since Jemima's funeral.

Followed by Fionn, who sticks close to her, she comes down the stairs. Walking slowly and oddly, because her legs are shaking.

"Fionn." Conall nods stiffly.

"Conall." Fionn nods back, just as stiffly.

No love lost there either. That Fionn, enemies everywhere. Peculiar vibration off him, actually. An unusual mix of self-sufficiency, neediness and root vegetables. Specifically, turnip.

But never mind Fionn. Conall's emotions have gone haywire. His terrible heartache is pulsing and pounding, each squeeze of his heart, each breath that he takes, more painful than the previous one. He's wild with relief at the sight of Katie, but seeing her with Fionn is like being wounded in the guts with a spear. Warmth, wound, joy, pain: a right old emotional stew. "Were you at Matt and Maeve's?" Katie asks him.

I love you. "I was just leaving."

"Back to work? At eight-thirty on a Saturday night? Some things never change."

I love you. "Katie, I'm not going to work." He's keen to splurge as much information as he can because he doesn't know how much time he has before Fionn sweeps her away. "That's all changed. I've taken on two partners and I'll be getting more. Things are different. I haven't left the country in . . ." he counts in his head, "nearly nine weeks."

"God. What are you doing with your time?"

Thinking about you. Non-stop. "Dunno. Over with Joe and Pat a lot. Bronagh asks about you."

"So if you're not going to work, why are you leaving the party?"

Conall opens his mouth, then closes it again. He's not sure what he should say, especially with Fionn standing at her shoulder, glowering possessively, but he came here today because he couldn't take the pain of not seeing her, so he might as well do what he set out to do. After all, he's a fighter, isn't he? Or is he? He's no longer sure. "I thought you weren't coming. I gave up waiting for you."

Katie screws up her face in a question. ". . . You were waiting for *me?*"

He nods, his eyes dark, all his intensity on her face.

"Why?"

". . . I wanted to see you."

This is too much for Fionn, who has been

feeling progressively edged out.

"Excuse me interrupting," Fionn says, with savage sarcasm. "But I have something for Katie."

"Sorry, Fionn." Katie looks a little stunned. "What is it?"

"I don't know yet, do I? I was just about to find out when your man here started shouting up to us." Fionn rummages around in his pocket and emerges with a dark-green sprig. He bites his lip, he doesn't seem happy.

"What is it?" Katie asks.

". . . Ah . . . bridewort. It's, er, the herb of love. Historically, the most popular strewing herb at weddings."

"Who's getting married?" Katie asks.

"You, according to the magic pocket. It must be a mistake. Hold on, I'm sure I can find you something better." A quick rootle produces another sprig. Fionn stares at it. "Ivy." He crumples it into nothing.

"But what does it mean?"

"Fidelity. There must be something better in here." He delves again, deeper this time, and finds a tiny seed. He swallows hard. "Licorice."

"And?"

"Fidelity and passion to a sexual union. I'll try another pocket. Ah!" Suddenly, Fionn's all smiles. "Vervain sinuata. For syphilis." He hands it to Conall. "Probably meant for you." Then the smile falls off Fionn's face. "It's not vervain, it's myrtle."

"Which means?"

Fionn doesn't want to say. But they're looking at him. He mutters, "Love and passion, the herb of Venus, the love goddess." Once again, his hand dives to the depths. "Let me try one more."

"This one?" Katie looks at the wilted leaf that emerges.

"Elderflower."

"And?"

"Brings blessing to a married couple."

Well, there's a silence, of a type you can't even start to describe. Conall looks confused and Katie looks perplexed, while Fionn glares from one to the other, then back again.

"I'm going home!" he announces. He steps out into the street, and over his departing shoulder, he throws back, "I hope the two of you will be very happy together."

"Fionn!" Katie hurries after him.

"Hey, look," Conall says, embarrassed. "I'll leave you —"

"No!" Katie places her hand on Conall's chest and hisses, "No, you stay right there. This won't take long."

"Fionn!" Katie catches up with him. "What is it?"

"You always loved him. That gobshite Conall Hathaway."

What can she say? Yes, she has always loved

him. She still loves him. The closeness she and Conall shared the morning that Jemima died felt intensely meaningful, like it was the beginning of a different sort of love, a solid, steady one. But, in the days afterward, Conall didn't contact her and more days passed and then they were into weeks, and around the two-month mark, she made herself admit that she must have imagined the intimate trust they'd shared. The pain was atomic, quite a surprise really. She thought she knew all the different kinds of heartbreak but this was a new one, a crushing sadness, an appalling knowledge of lost chances, of the life she and Conall could have had together if both of them had been just a little bit different, if he'd been less work-obsessed, if she'd been more willing to compromise.

She could have contacted him, a breezy text, a casual email — he was no longer with Lydia, no one could miss Lydia's antics with Oleksander — but she didn't, because . . . ? Because she wasn't starting that old thing again, begging for scraps of his time.

And then he turns up in her hallway, saying he only came to the party so he can see her. She was barely able to walk down the stairs, the way he was watching her. What was going on . . . ?

Fionn is still waiting for an answer. Quickly she says, "I loved you too, Fionn."

"I was just a bit of fun to you."

"Nothing wrong with fun. And we'll always be friends."

"Yeah." He looks a little contrite. "Sorry. Look, go back in to him. You're meant to be together."

"Ah, come on, Fionn —"

"No, *you* come on, Katie! Look at what my magic pockets were saying. Fidelity, love, union. The magic pocket never lies."

The magic pocket is far more of a hit-and-miss phenomenon, in Katie's opinion, but it is sort of weird that everything Fionn produced had to do with love.

"They mightn't have broadcast *Your Own Private Eden*, but there's no denying I've still got that old razzle-dazzle." Considerably cheered up by his own brilliance, Fionn strikes out in the direction of the Luas. "I'll ring you," he calls back to her.

"Grand." She watches him go, then she steps back into her hall.

Conall is sitting obediently on the stairs, just as she left him. There's something wrong, a certain bareness to the picture. She finally identifies it. "Your BlackBerry?" she says. "Where is it?"

"Oh . . ." He pats his jeans pockets. "Here. Do you need it?"

"No. It's just that I think this is the first time I've seen you doing nothing. Just sitting staring into space."

"I'm telling you, Katie, I'm different."

"So what goes on in your head now that you're not thinking of work all the time? Like what were you thinking while you've been sitting here?"

"I've been saying prayers."

"Prayers?" She knew this was too good to be true. He'd swapped workaholism for religion.

"Praying that you'll come back to me."

"Oh!" Well, maybe those sorts of prayers are okay.

"Look." She is suddenly somber. "What's going on, Conall? I don't hear a word from you for four months and now you show up, talking about prayers."

He puts his face in his hands, breathes deeply, seems to make a decision and sits upright. "All right, here's how it is. I've nothing to lose at this stage. I love you, Katie. I can't stop thinking about you. I never have, not since I first met you. But that morning, with Jemima, you and I being there when she died, I felt so much love for you, such a . . . an attachment. But you have a boyfriend, so I didn't know what to do."

"That doesn't sound like you."

"Because I'm not me, not any more. I'm different, Katie. All of that stuff happening at the same time, Matt trying to kill himself and Jemima dying and work going weird, it was no longer doing it for me, then when I heard about Maeve getting pregnant . . . I felt, I don't know, like a miracle had happened, and . . . you know?" He shrugs. "I thought you wouldn't meet me if I asked you to, but I was hoping to bump into you at the party."

Katie says nothing. She's been hoping that she'd bump into him too. She thought Fionn would never leave.

"I haven't," she says.

"Haven't what?"

"A boyfriend."

"But Fionn?"

"That's all over. It's been over since the night of Jemima."

"You're not serious." Conall slumps into himself. "All that time . . . I don't *believe* it. I thought I was going to have to fight him for you today."

"You're making a lot of assumptions, Conall. Does my opinion count for nothing?"

"It counts for everything, as it happens. I've a question for you." Conall gets to his feet and clears his throat as if he's about to make a speech. "Katie Richmond, I love you with all my heart and I will do my best to make you happy for the rest of your life. Will you marry me?"

"Conall, for God's sake! Can't you do anything like a normal person? If you're that keen, we could go for dinner or something."

"No. No dinners, no dates. I'm in agony

762

and I need to know. Are you in or are you out?"

"In or out? That's not a proper proposal."

"Katie Richmond, love of my life, owner of my heart, will you marry me?"

". . . Well, I don't know, now that you've given up your job . . . Will we be poor?"

"Not at all. Haven't you a job? We'll be grand." More seriously, he says. "No, we won't be poor."

"Have you a ring?"

"Yes, I have a ring."

"No!"

"What? You think I was going to make the same mistake twice?"

"Show me."

He produces a little box and flips it open and white light blazes at them. "Diamonds," Katie remarks.

"Unless you'd prefer emeralds?" Another box appears, containing a deep-green stone in an antique setting.

"You're not serious."

"Or sapphires?" And out comes another box.

"Stop, please. Conall, you haven't changed that much!"

"I just wanted to get it right."

"God." Katie presses her hands over her eyes. This is all too much. "Stop asking me things."

"For how long?"

"A while."

Five seconds passes. "That's a while," Conall says. "So what's it to be?"

". . . Ah . . . the diamonds."

"Christ! Is that a yes?"

"Yes."

"Yes?"

"Yes. It's a yes."

It's Lydia who discovers them. Us, I suppose you could say. She's highly indignant. All she's trying to do is get up her own stairs, but her way is *impeded* by Hathaway and the governess going at it hammer and tongs, snogging the face off each other. Disgusting. And *selfish!* Blocking public thoroughfares.

"Take it somewhere else!" she commands, curling her lip at their evident happiness.

They break apart to let her pass, and as she moves between them, Lydia is hit by a wave of emotion so potent it nearly gives her a nosebleed.

She stomps on up the steps and when they hear the door of her flat slam behind her, Katie murmurs, "She has a point."

"You mean — ?" Conall says.

"I do."

And the next thing, they've grasped each other's hands and they're running upstairs and I'm all swept up and enmeshed in their magical energy. And when we arrive at the top floor, the three of us tumble into Katie's

764

apartment and we fall on to the bed and, and, and . . .

. . . I'm waiting for my moment, and . . . and . . .

. . . any minute now . . .

. . . and . . . aaaannnndddd . . . here we go! Hold on to your hats. I'm going in.

WITH SPECIAL THANKS TO THE DUBLIN RAPE CRISIS CENTER

Thank you to my visionary editors, Louise Moore and Clare Ferraro, to Kate Burke and to Clare Parkinson for enabling me to transform raw material into an actual book. I'm very grateful. Thank you to everyone at Michael Joseph, for showing me the love and working with such enthusiasm and commitment on all of my books. I'm well aware of how lucky I am.

Thank you to the best agent in the world, Jonathan Lloyd, and everyone at Curtis Brown, for shepherding and minding this book (and all my others, too).

Countless people generously helped with my research: Gwen Hollingsworth; Tom and Debra Mauro; Magdalena Rawinis, Michal Szarecki, Lukasz Wozniak, Hubert Czubaj and Piotr Taborowski; Suzanne Benson, Kevin Day and Darryll Lewis of HPD Software; Sandra Hanlon and Margaret Nugent from the National Taxi Drivers Union; Karen Fitzpatrick and Gisela Boehnisch. I think that's the full list, but if I've forgotten anyone, I humbly apologize. My thanks to everyone above and I take entire responsibility for any mistakes.

For reading the manuscript as it was being written and for their constant advice and encouragement, I'd like to thank Shirley Baines, Jenny Boland, Ailish Connolly, Siobhan Coogan, Susan Dillon, Caron Freeborn, Gai Griffin, Cathy Kelly, Caitriona Keyes, Ljiljana Keyes, Mammy Keyes, Rita-Anne Keyes, Eileen Prendergast, AnneMarie Scanlan and Kate Thompson.

Just a quick note — I took a liberty with the rugby fixtures; there's a mention of an international match being played in the summer. I'm told this wouldn't happen *at all* in real life and I hope this wild departure from reality doesn't interfere with your reading enjoyment.

Thank you to James "Woolfman" Woolf and his wife, Karoline, and their daughters, Siena and Maya, who very generously bid in the ACT charity auction to have their names included in the book.

As always, thanks to my beloved Tony. None of it would be possible without him.

ABOUT THE AUTHOR

Marian Keyes is the internationally bestselling author of ten novels, most recently *This Charming Man* and *Anybody Out There?,* as well as two autobiographical works. Several of her novels have been adapted for television and film. Born in Limerick, Ireland, she now lives in Dún Laoghaire, Ireland, with her husband.